PRAISE FOR *ALICE B. TOKLAS IS MISSING*

"Robert Archambeau's clever and witty love letter to Jazz-age Paris sparkles with cameos of the writers, artists, and quirky personalities who defined the era. 1920s Philosophy and Art frame a romp of a literary missing-person case that sends Ida Caine on a scavenger hunt through the landmarks and catacombs of Paris. Searching for Alice B. Toklas, Ida discovers her true self and becomes an unlikely hero."

—Liza Nash Taylor, author of *Etiquette for Runaways* and *In All Good Faith*

"*Alice B. Toklas is Missing* is a delightful romp through the Paris of Gertrude Stein and Hemingway, Pound and Eliot and Joyce, where the only thing more potent than artistic ambition is artistic envy. Come for the intriguing plot but stay for the impressive cast of literary characters—including a touching and unlikely romance featuring T.S. Eliot himself. Robert Archambeau's debut novel is a don't-miss book. Absolutely delightful!

—Rebecca Johns author of *The Countess* and *Icebergs*

"Paris in the 1920s—artists, poets, writers, musicians, the whole modernist mélange, Cubists, Surrealists, Futurists, Hemingway, Eliot, Pound—caught here in a wonderful innocents-abroad, comic thriller. Ida Caine is at the center of it all, finding Alice, saving Paris—a perfect, wide-eyed and dauntless heroine, with T.S. Eliot as her companion. Not since Paula McLain's *The Paris Wife* has a novel taken us so thoroughly into the Paris of the lost generation."

—Michael Anania, author of *Nightsongs & Clamors*

ALICE B. TOKLAS IS MISSING

Robert Archambeau

Regal House Publishing

Published by
Regal House Publishing, LLC
Raleigh, NC 27605
All rights reserved

ISBN -13 (paperback): 9781646033850
ISBN -13 (epub): 9781646033867
Library of Congress Control Number: 2022920628

Cover images and design by © C. B. Royal

Regal House Publishing, LLC
https://regalhousepublishing.com

Printed in the United States of America

For Ida—I mean Lila

1

Her attention had been strained and her eyes dazzled after so many hours in the Louvre, so she allowed herself to collapse onto the green metal bench by the steps leading up to the Richelieu wing. She sat in the afternoon sunlight nursing an aesthetic headache. The Louvre had overwhelmed—no, swamped her. Endless waves of beauty had washed over her even before she'd navigated corridor after grand, airy corridor, and hauled her wooden panel up countless stairways to the tiny, stuffy room that justified the voyage from America, and where (as she learned on the eve of departure) she'd be working in front of an old painting to pay for her stay in Paris. Hers and Teddy's. He ought to be coming along soon.

Earlier that morning, at half past nine, Ida had lined up with a dozen other young women and a tiny old man in a musty suit, all of them silent before the little oval desk where a lumbering Frenchman, too large for the furniture, issued each applicant an easel, stool, and drop cloth; made them sign a thick ledger; and warned them not to be late returning the materials in the afternoon if they hoped to be admitted again tomorrow. Just one look at the painting she'd been commissioned to copy for Mrs. Rawling convinced Ida she'd need to come back for many, many tomorrows.

Jan van Eyck's *Madonna of Chancellor Rolin* wasn't large—just over two feet square—but the detail was astonishing, far more so than in the monochrome bookplate reproduction she'd consulted for her sketch in the attic of her father's house. And the colors were not what she'd expected. You could never tell from bookplates, but she'd always assumed the Madonna's robes would be blue, as they were in the windows at St. Mary's back in Lake Forest, and in every other church where she'd sat in a pew with her four sisters for weddings or first communions;

or for her mother's funeral when, as a small child, she'd cried in utter despondency at the loss. But here in the Louvre she saw van Eyck's robes were painted a scorching red that made their bright drapery crackle through five centuries of yellowed varnish.

She set up her easel and perched on the little stool, smoothing her simple blue cotton dress and smock, and setting her wooden panel in place. Van Eyck had worked some five hundred years ago, when artists painted more wood than canvas, and she meant to be as meticulous as she could about all the details of reproduction. Despite her eminently French, round-brimmed Breton hat, her shoes and the cut of her dress marked her as an American, though you couldn't say from where, exactly, unless you heard her speak. Her vowels, though not unpleasant, all aspired to the condition of the short "a": Midwestern.

You wouldn't know to look at her, in her painting clothes, whether she was rich or poor. There were few poor Americans in Paris these days, when the stock market seemed only to go up and up. Many left large blue and yellow French banknotes on café tables and didn't wait for change, but some wealthy Americans liked to pose as starving artists. Where did Teddy fit in? She wondered, sometimes. He was rich enough, or his family was. When he asked her to marry him and go off to Paris, she assumed his family would pay their way. They weren't having it, though: they didn't approve. Not of his plan to be a writer. Nor, as she'd always suspected, of her: a gardener's daughter and, worse, Irish Catholic. What stung most was how they assumed she was pregnant—a fortune hunter, little better than a prostitute, really. No, they weren't paying a nickel for Teddy's misadventure.

That's why Teddy made the arrangement for her with Mrs. Rawling. Painting was what she loved anyway, he said—she was always copying the masters in charcoal sketches at the Art Institute, or painting from images in books up in her father's attic. And Teddy was right: she was never really confident without a brush in her hand. Maybe he was right about his writing plans too—adventure first, and the words will follow. Adventure sounded good when Ida considered the lives that were waiting for her sisters back home. Maybe he was the real thing after all. Who was she to doubt it?

A layer of buff undercoating in oils went down first, then Ida selected a small brush and prepared a brownish-black for the underpainting. She traced van Eyck's main figures—the plump, robed chancellor on the left, the Virgin Mary to the right, with an angel above her and the infant Jesus in her lap—and as she did, Ida vanished from the world around her. This always happened when she painted: she lost herself in the careful copying of the original's lines, masses, and shading. Now she sketched the shadows in quickly with crosshatching. When she was in this state her lines were strong, confident, authoritative—such lines would have surprised the girls from the clapboard houses in the little neighborhood north of the train station. But they had never seen Ida paint: theirs was the world—gossipy, small, stunted—from which she willed herself to disappear when she stepped into someone else's art.

Of course, she hadn't vanished so much as made the world vanish to her. Ida didn't even notice the man in the gray English suit who walked past her while she worked, an umbrella tucked under his arm, casting his practiced, assessing gaze over her painting and her face as he asked himself, "Is she pretty, with that long nose, wide mouth, and broad but furrowed brow?" In a moment he decided, thinking, "Yes. Yes, I suppose she is, in a curious dark-haired way," and then moved on to other rooms, his eyes darting from painted to living beauty as he went. Ida's eyes ticked regularly back and forth between her sketch and van Eyck's red-robed Madonna. The color puzzled her, but the artist must have had his reasons. People usually did.

Like Teddy, who was late. Maybe, thought Ida, leaning back on the bench, he was busy fetching the surprise he'd promised to bring her when they set out under a pewter sky that cool, drizzling morning. "It'll be grand," he declared, "something that will make you," he paused for effect, "a *real Parisian*." And here he was now, suddenly in front of her, smiling in his trilby hat, his corduroys, and his baggy overcoat, green eyes mischievous as he pulled Ida up from the bench, twirled her like a dancer, and drew her toward him for an embrace. "Careful," she said, "still wet!" as he stepped back and picked up her painted panel, slightly smaller than the original, per the museum's regulations to deter forgers.

"I'm always careful with a lady's essentials, chipmunk," he said, taking the painting by the wire stretched across its back.

"And where's my surprise?" Ida asked while she playfully frisked Teddy's overcoat. He carried no bags or packages, though her pats revealed some intriguing lumps in the deep side pockets.

"All in good time," he beamed, "all in the full fullness of it. Now—do you know what I learned from Lewis today?" Lewis. Lewis mattered: Lewis was the first writer Teddy had met in Paris—three days ago, the morning after their arrival in Paris, at an inexpensive restaurant near their rather spartan rooms. Lewis was an Englishman but had been in France on and off since the war, writing, painting, and talking forcefully about the way forward for all the arts. Teddy had passed his days with Lewis while Ida sat in museum offices waiting for a copyist's permit. "My French, it turns out, isn't all it could be—but Lewis set me straight. Do you know, for example, what a pig says?"

Ida looked up at Teddy, a half-smile on her lips. "'Oink,' isn't it?"

"Ah, I see you are *Americaine*! Yes, correct. Correct as far as American pigs are concerned, and their stout British allies. But not a French pig. French pigs wouldn't disgrace themselves with such a trivial sound. The French pig is a pig of dignity and substance. A French pig says *gron gron gron.*"

"*Gron gron,*" Ida repeated, allowing herself to brush up against Teddy and trying again to reach into his coat pockets after the mysterious surprise.

"And just as indecipherable to their American cousins are the French geese, or ducks, or anyway some sort of foreign bird." Teddy leaned toward her for a kiss as he brushed her hand away from his pocket. She dodged playfully, noting the familiar licorice smell of Pernod on his breath. "*Glou glou* goes your French bird. Complete nonsense to the uninitiated."

"But very informative to those in the know, I'm sure," noted Ida, allowing herself to enter Teddy's relaxed mood as they walked on. She laughed when he did his tolerably good impersonation of Martin, the Alsatian man who collected the rent and ran the little cheese shop on the ground floor of the building where they'd set up house—if two rooms with cold water and a gas ring for cooking count as a house. Mrs. Rawling's allowance was not as generous as one might have hoped. As they turned—home at last—onto rue Victor Cousin, Teddy spread his arms in imitation of the Alsatian shopkeeper's habitual Gallic shrug, inadvertently striking a passing old woman with the back of Ida's painted panel. The woman's hands leapt to her face, her bag of onions spilling to the pavement. As onions bounced and rolled, and apologies flowed in English and French, Teddy and Ida scooped the woman's onions up from the paving stones. Unhurt, and charmed by the happy young couple, the woman smiled as Teddy held up a particularly impressive onion: massive, pale, and glossy.

"A grand specimen! From where?" he asked, in confident, accented French. "From *Les Halles*?" She replied in the affirmative as he began to juggle three of the onions. "But where in *Les Halles*? What stall?"

The lady readily described a vendor in the northeast corner of that great and sprawling market, adding, "And at the best price!" Teddy laughed, tossing the onions one by one into Ida's paint-stained hands. Ida passed them on to the old lady who grinned, glanced quickly at Teddy, and seemed to enjoy a bright moment in an otherwise routine day.

Then it was three flights up, and into their rooms—where the sickly green wallpaper, the ancient gaslight, the tiny window, and narrow bed did their best to conjure *la vie bohème*. "And my surprise?" Ida asked, taking her painted panel from

Teddy, and placing it carefully between a rickety wardrobe and the wall.

"Behold!" Teddy declared, in the voice of a sideshow conjurer, as he pulled a wedge of cheese from one pocket, and a string of small, grubby onions from the other. "We'll dine on French onion soup in our garret tonight—true Parisians at last!"

Ida stared at Teddy blankly for a moment. Was all this charming? For a moment Ida didn't know. It wasn't as though she'd expected a tiara. Then she imagined how the evening might still unfold: how they'd impersonate the Alsatian, cook over the gas ring, and make French animal noises together before Teddy chased her into the bed, which, though narrow, was more than sufficiently soft. She pulled out her best smile—broad, bright, sunnily Midwestern—and poured a thick French accent onto the syllables "*Fan-tas-tique!*"

"Fantastique indeed, my pink little *porcelet*," Teddy continued, while Ida looked quizzical, her French classes having been more concerned with grammar and the pronunciation of vowels than with the inhabitants of barnyards. "My *porcelet*," he repeated, smiling and slow, "my *petit cochon*." He slid behind her, reached round and squeezed her thigh. "My piglet, just plump enough where we like it, eh? Now, while you cook up *la soupe*, I'll nip out for a quick Pernod. Back in half an hour!" He flipped his hat back over his sandy hair and dashed out the door with a boyish grin.

Teddy was gone for more than half an hour—considerably more, as he often was lately. These periods alone would often stretch out long and empty, so Ida filled them with charcoal sketching, this time drawing Teddy as he juggled three large onions. But before she finished, she smudged her work out with the ball of her thumb. She hadn't captured him correctly, or so she told herself.

2

Lugging her easel down the corridors of the Louvre the next morning, Ida wasn't sure if she was excited or brimming with dread. This would be the day, Teddy announced when he came back last night, that they'd arrive at the heart, the very bullseye center of the modern movement in the arts: twenty-seven rue de Fleurus, the salon of Gertrude Stein. "No need for dinner," Teddy said, "we can eat there while we gab with the scribblers and paint-slingers. Free food is half the reason these starved French artists go. Lewis says everyone shows up at the door on Saturdays—and some are even allowed in."

That last bit unnerved her. What if they were turned away? Or worse—what if they were let in? Teddy, she imagined, would be all right in any crowd: he could talk his way through anything, just like his father; Ted senior had talked his way from a rickety house in Rockford to a partnership in a law firm on LaSalle Street. Her own family was full of talkers—at least the women, who surrounded her silent father at the dinner table with a choppy surf of words. But they were shopgirl words, thought Ida. She'd been a shopgirl for two years herself, serving little German cakes to the rich ladies who came to Market Square. The people at the salon will look at me, part of her believed, and ask me to serve the torte. *Tout le beau monde des arts moderne* will ask me for cake.

She hadn't mentioned her misgivings to Teddy as they'd strolled toward the museum earlier that morning on the path beside the Seine, he carrying her painted panel, she with her paint box, an apple, and hunk of bread for lunch. He was too dizzy with the prospect of finally arriving where he felt he ought to be. They paused at a bookstall where Teddy had it on good authority that stereopticon cards with nude photographs were sold to those who knew how to ask. The identical side-by-side images just popped right out at you, in all their fleshy glory, when you slipped them into the viewer, he said. She punched him playfully on the arm. He rolled his eyes and grinned.

Now, on her own and puffing for breath in the Louvre's endlessly long Grande Galerie, Ida set down her easel and rested on a wide, low bench in the center of the gallery. On the wall before her sprawled an enormous painting—a good five feet high and twice as wide. She knew it, too: Tintoretto's *Coronation of the Virgin*: her guidebook confirmed it. A whirlpool of cloud layers, circling up and up, groaning under the weight of the massing apostles, saints, patriarchs, angels, and prophets—not to mention popes and martyrs, with Adam and Eve holding down the lower corners. Ida remembered it from the art lectures at the town library. One benefit of living in the poor part of a rich town was having access to a library with more money than it knew how to get rid of. There was always a roster of bespectacled young men nervously lecturing on everything up to, but most certainly not including, socialism.

But, no, it wasn't Lake Forest where she first heard about the painting, but at the Art Institute in Chicago, when the dapper little man from Harvard with the trim beard and white linen suit came to talk about Renaissance painting. The figures depicted at the top of Tintoretto's painting, he said, were the most holy. By arranging things that way an artist could show deference while maintaining the modern idea of perspective. In earlier times, he said, the more important figures were simply painted larger than everyone else—the Egyptians made their pharaohs into giants, and it was the same for kings and saints in the Middle Ages. "Hierarchical perspective," he called it. But the Renaissance saw things otherwise. Everything was painted to look as it would if you stood before the scene. And it was you, the viewer, who became important, even when you were looking at an image of a king or a saint. You were at the center: "The viewer," he said, "was a little king of all he surveyed." From here he went on to talk—perhaps too long for his audience in the sweltering auditorium—about the rise of individualism. Ida preferred what he said about the way good paintings subordinated every part to the whole, concentrating on creating a single effect. She saw that now: everything in the Tintoretto swirled up to a single focal point, the holy Virgin Mary crowned in a rosy heaven. It was all served up for the viewer like a wedding cake, layer after layer, and the little bride up top. See, she wasn't the cake shopgirl today, thought Ida: she was being served. She knew art, all right. She knew she knew, and the crowd at twenty-seven rue de Fleurus would welcome what she had to say.

Later, as she worked on the underpainting for her copy of the *Madonna of Chancellor Rolin*, Ida thought about van Eyck's perspective. Definitely not hierarchical: if anything, the bulky, almost jowly chancellor was bigger than the slender Mary. But the perspective was not quite right as far as depth went: the row of columns in the background couldn't be more than five or six feet behind the two figures, and even Mary would have had a hard time squeezing between them out to the terrace beyond. A shallow pictorial space. Why? she wondered, sitting outside with her modest lunch. Van Eyck had his reasons. Sketch it in and worry later. Sketch in the chancellor's bowl cut and his heavy book. And tomorrow add the color, that puzzling red, still bright over the centuries. It shone; the paint was probably mixed with ground glass. It would be hard to replicate. Did Mrs. Rawling, plump among her throw pillows, merit the effort? Such an unlikely choice of painting, too—so many tiny details, so hard to copy, and with that shrewd-eyed, unsightly man in it. "They say he was in the family," said Mrs. Rawling from the wicker throne on her veranda, "'Rolin' became 'Rawling' when it crossed to England." Did family vanity deserve Ida's best efforts? Well, van Eyck deserved them. Ida saw his red and knew what it was. She'd do it right: she owed that to herself.

Hauling her borrowed easel down the stairs at the end of the afternoon's work, Ida felt tired but strong. Yes, she knew art. She knew what an artist did, and she often had an inkling as to why. She'd seen the gloss in van Eyck's red and known about the glass. She knew enough and had nothing to fear in the evening ahead. And she needn't fear Teddy's habitual lateness, not today—here he was, miraculously early and eager to go. They walked quickly to their rooms to drop off the panel. While there, Ida poked nervously through the modest selection of clothes in the wardrobe, but nothing presented any improvement over her simple blue dress. She wished she had a colorful scarf to dress it up but would have to make do without. They left, decided against a quick, cheap café meal, and arrived at their destination in short order, a white stone building with a wrought-iron gate leading to a courtyard beyond. "She's rich, then?" Ida asked.

"Rich and strange, they say."

"Strange how?"

"We're about to find out, if luck holds."

They walked through the gate and into the courtyard, to a smaller structure divided in two by a foyer. Ida took Teddy's hand and, looking down, noticed the pattern on the foyer tiles: repeating octagons, like little stop signs. Teddy knocked, and the door opened a few inches, revealing a small, birdlike woman with a long nose and a black sack of a dress. Her bobbed black hair shone glossily under the electric lights, and thick, chunky bracelets clanked on her thin wrists and forearms. The woman quickly looked them up and down, then gave a sharp bark in American English: "Who sent you?"

"Lewis," said Teddy. "Wyndham Lewis."

"Well," said the woman, cracking the thinnest of smiles, "come in anyway." The door swung wide and in they stepped. Just like that.

It was a large room, more than thirty feet long and just as wide, and packed with little trios and quartets of people, half of them chattering, half eyeballing the paintings that filled every possible space on every whitewashed wall, up from the heavy credenzas to the high ceiling itself. The people were extraordinary, if only because there was no discernable pattern to them. American and British voices rang out, familiar in a congress of accents. A formally dressed French couple snickered quietly at a painting their bodies concealed from Ida's view. They were as bad as Ida's sisters, when she'd foolishly taken them to see Monet's work at the Art Institute: all four sisters, who agreed on nothing, concurred that one painting looked like nothing more than a purple smudge. Behind the formal couple an intense little man in a striped suit spoke grave, terse Spanish to some younger men in shirtsleeves gathered around him. Ida recognized a distinguished man in a checked sport coat as Claude McKay, the leading light of the Harlem Renaissance—his picture had appeared in the *Chicago Tribune*. You never see people of different races mixing socially in Lake Forest, thought Ida, as a slim blond man in a striped shirt danced his way to McKay through the crowd, took him by the hand, and kissed him on the mouth. You didn't see that in Lake Forest either.

Greek-accented English vied with what might have been Russian-accented French; a Hungarian argued passionately in broken English with a broad-shouldered Italian wearing a magnificent moustache. A somber, dark-suited German stood before a painted nude in an attitude of reverence, as if he were about to genuflect or light a votive candle. Some wore the latest fashions; some looked as though they'd slept in their clothes; one slender man wore a sailor's hat and shining golden waistcoat, from which he pulled a folded sheet with a poem written in an elegant hand. A woman with long loops of pearls and a cloche hat held a similar woman's hand, leaning in to whisper in her ear. And across this expanse of mismatched humanity, perched with her legs tucked under her in a squat, square chair by the fireplace was a Buddha, a sphynx, a corpulent barefoot empress in a brown corduroy dress, laughing a big-bellied guffaw and beckoning a guest to her chair with a pudgy hand. This was Gertrude Stein herself, smiling the smile of an indulgent mother as the gold-vested man in the sailor hat approached, bowed low, and offered her his poem. Gertrude Stein, at the center of her own whirlwind, as surely as was Tintoretto's Madonna.

But even this scene from the royal court of some lost Bohemian empire couldn't hold Ida's darting gaze for long. Not with the riot of paintings on the walls. They rose up, three, sometimes four tiers of them, like the saints in the Tintoretto. But that was the end of any resemblance to the art in the Louvre. She may know art, she told herself, but she didn't know these. Some couldn't possibly be finished—figures outlined with crude black, childish lines; colors daubed here and there and parts of a canvas left blank, unpainted, indecently nude; the shadows on a man's face in a monstrous green. But more than that, it was the painting closest to where Ida stood that shook her. Three feet square and showing, at the center, what must be a jagged-edged guitar or cello in outline, it dizzied. Lines and planes, lines and planes and blocks of color; she couldn't understand where it put her. Tintoretto put her at the center of a world, which opened before her in holy glory. This painting put her first to the left of that cello, then to the right, above, behind. This painting didn't put her anywhere, or put her everywhere at once, and when she settled somewhere it poked her off balance and she landed somewhere else. So did the one that hung above it.

This was awful. She knew nothing about art. This was loony. This was great. She knew nothing. This was insolent, it was spitting on the graves of the masters. No. This was. . . this was a hoard of art she did not understand. She wouldn't snicker. She was not like her sisters; she was not like the well-dressed French couple now turning to laugh on their way out the door. But she was certainly not who she thought she was this afternoon in the Louvre. What did she know now of what an artist did, or why?

The birdlike woman was at her side, had taken her elbow and Teddy's too. "Alice," she said. "I'm Alice. I entertain the wives of these geniuses in the room on the other side of the foyer, with the lemon cake. And what do you do?"

"Teddy's a detective and a Chicago bootlegger," boomed an English voice from behind them, "but I haven't been able to get him to share a single tale of gruesome murder—at least not yet."

"Lewis!" Teddy cried, pivoting to smile at his friend, who had materialized, long hair flopping out from under the broad-brimmed hat that he wore, even indoors. "And he writes too," added Lewis, addressing Alice.

Teddy wasn't a detective, wasn't a bootlegger either, thought Ida, but it was the sort of thing he liked to tell people in bar-rooms, especially far from home. He liked to take advantage of his Lake Forest connection and pretend he was a friend of Scott Fitzgerald, though they'd never met when Fitzgerald had come to town to court one of the local debutantes. It was when she heard Teddy hold forth over a glass that Ida most believed in him as a storyteller who might, someday, actually write.

"How thrilling," said Alice, in the voice of someone who had seen it all. "And you," she asked, dark eyes pinning Ida to the wall, "what about you?"

She copied old paintings. That was what she did. She copied old paintings for an old lady with old money. Was that considered painting? she wondered—was it *artist's* painting? If what she saw around her on the walls of the Stein studio was paint-ing, what she did was not—was it? What to say? How to answer Alice? She wanted to reach for a glass of the plum brandy that seemed to be the house pour at twenty-seven rue de Fleurus, but none was within reach, so there was no way she could take a sip and play for time. She copied pictures and would be sent across the foyer to a different room, one without strange little paintings of guitars or cellos. She would be exiled to the room with the wives. "I paint," said Ida, suddenly and with surprising urgency. She said it a second time to make it feel more real.

"Grand, grand," said Alice, nodding absently, jangling her bracelets and adding, "I'll let Lewis show you around," before slipping away. But Lewis was already steering Teddy to a corner, an arm draped over his shoulder.

"You must tell Jay about your bootlegging days," Lewis was saying to Teddy. "Jay's American too. Our Little Lindbergh! Just hopped the channel in his biplane." And just like that, Ida stood alone, a forlorn island in a sea of loud voices and turned backs.

Teddy gave her a helpless look but did not resist as Lewis led him to a small group in the corner, where two men in suits stood on either side of a wiry little fellow with a grubby waistcoat, an unevenly buttoned shirt, and the most extraordinarily vertical red hair blasting up from his head.

Abandoned, Ida looked after the retreating Teddy until she saw the red-haired man's eyes flick to a space beside her and a smile break across his twitchy face. Following the vector of the redheaded man's gaze, Ida's eyes lit on the only man in the room who did not appear to be arguing, opining, or gesticulating. He was tallish, trim, and in his mid-thirties, she guessed, dark hair carefully parted and smoothed. He wore a gray suit of English cut, and for some reason still held his cane-handled umbrella. Ida did not recognize him as the man who had passed her while she worked in the Louvre yesterday, but she did recognize the kind of smile that broke on his face when he caught her gaze. She'd seen that same smile at the Louvre, in the long gallery through which she hauled her easel, panel, and drop cloth: *la Gioconda. The Mona Lisa.* The smile of someone with a secret, someone who knew something you did not.

She'd been looking at him a bit too long, she realized. Perhaps he felt much the same: he stepped forward, extending a hand with surprising formality, given the behavior of this decidedly artistic crowd. "Tom," he said, his voice not quite American, but not exactly English either. "Tom Eliot. And you are Miss—?"

"Caine," she replied, letting him take her hand. "Ida Caine." Ida heard her own voice as if from afar, noticing that she hadn't corrected him with an added "Mrs." She knew she should have said something. Teddy had spent their ring money on the tickets for their passage, so her finger was bare, and Mr. Eliot had made an honest mistake.

"And you paint?"

"If I don't, will Alice really send me to the wives?" Something about Tom's smile made Ida feel as if they were in league with one another.

"Miss Stein has few rules," Tom replied (American, Ida decided, listening to his slightly plummy voice, definitely American, though perhaps he was trying to hide it). "However, our hostess insists on the distinction between *les femmes décorative*, those who primarily please the eye, and *les femmes d'intérieur*, whose charms are found in the creative mind. Perhaps, in your case," he added, looking at Ida for a moment with that strange, knowing smile ever more in evidence, "she was understandably confused."

Not sure how to respond to this unexpected, but not unwelcome, gallantry, Ida looked down, glanced back up, and blurted out the first thing that popped into her head. "You've kept your umbrella inside—no one else has."

He was unfazed. "Many of these people," he made a small circling gesture at the crowd with the handle of his umbrella, "are bohemians." He paused, as if unsure of how to explain what this meant to him. "They make art, they love ideas. But," he lowered his voice and moved slightly closer to Ida, increasing the sense of a conspiracy of two in a room bustling with bodies, "bohemians steal."

"Do they?"

"The man who painted that?" Here Tom raised the tip of his umbrella in the direction of the guitar or cello painting that had so unnerved her. "He once stole my dinner roll—and in this very room. But that was years ago, before Pablo was rich. He painted that one too," he added, indicating a nearby painting of a large woman in a brown robe. It might, Ida thought, be a portrait of Miss Stein herself—if Miss Stein's face were an imposing, half-human, half-skew-eyed mask. "Yes," Tom answered Ida's unasked question, "that's Miss Stein—and it's not the only portrait of her in the room."

Sensing a challenge, Ida swiveled her head, quickly catching sight of another portrait, a more realistic representation of the woman who sat enthroned across the room. "That one's a better likeness," she said.

"Valloton's?" Tom seemed interested in Ida's response.

"Yes, certainly. And a worse painting, don't you think? She's regal, there, almost a monument. But Valloton doesn't get Miss Stein's. . . aura, I suppose we'd call it. The Picasso is like a totemic mask, and doesn't that catch something about her? I don't want to blaspheme, but doesn't she have something of the character of a goddess? I mean, a genius loci, like a Greek divinity tied to a specific place?" He seemed a little embarrassed by his own statement, as if a particularly pious aunt had caught him hiding an adventure story in a hymnal. Ida wanted to rescue him.

"Is that why he painted her that way?"

A reedy cackle prevented Tom from answering. It was the man with the astonishing mass of red hair, now stepping past her and jabbing Tom in the ribs. It was far from clear that Tom appreciated the gesture. "Ole Possum!" cried the redheaded man, twitching his head. "Don't fill her dainty cranium with rot. Pee-cass-ow painted it that way"—the man spoke in a parody of an old Colorado prospector's voice—"to be noticed. Back in them days all of Paree came here to gawp at what Matisse had daubed up. 'Ooh-la-la, a *fauvre*, they'd say, a *beast*, a beast with his beastly bright colors! Shadows in purple and green!' And ole Pablo with his sad, sad blues and grays couldn't win in that fight. No, the only way to box with a champion boxer is to rassle him instead. So, it was out with the color and in with the mask—the mask and the money too."

His eye has a tic, thought Ida, not liking the man. And he's stuffed his necktie into his waistcoat pocket and forgotten it's there.

"This is Mr. Ezra Pound," Tom said carefully, as if presenting a scientific specimen. "An old. . .friend. Ezra, meet Miss Ida Caine."

"Mrs.," added Ida, quietly. Teddy, Lewis, and the two suited gentlemen had drifted over while Pound was speaking.

"Yours, eh?" said Pound to Teddy, with a leer that implied several unsavory ideas and no regard for Ida's presence.

Before Teddy could respond, the shorter of the two suited men cut in. "Miss Stein says Matisse's paintings were the children of Cézanne." This man spoke in precise English but with a heavy French accent, the severity of his dark, swept-back hair reinforcing the air of intensity in his eyes. Ida noticed he wore an emerald ring. "And she says Picasso had no father," the man continued, "that he emerged fully formed, as if from an enormous egg. But I say he has a father! Many fathers. That face, that mask? You see it. His father is Africa, the ancient life of Africa, still with us today, a miracle! I buy such masks at *les puces*—the flea market—and I dream better dreams with one by my bedside."

Tom, having surrendered any hope of manners from this crew of pirates, whispered in Ida's ear, "André Breton, the Surrealist—I don't know the other fellow."

Quite a crowd was now gathering around them. A heroically mustachioed Italian of middle age had joined the discussion, his hair graying, his well-cut suit a tad threadbare. He placed a hand on Breton's shoulders, and boomed, "No talk of fathers! Breton here sniffs the fumes of Dr. Freud's elixirs, and they make him weak and queasy. And sometimes he sniffs the rotten corpse of Marx, which makes him mad, a state he mistakes for strength." Ida couldn't see Breton's reaction because the Italian had pushed his bulk between her and the Surrealist. "Real art," the Italian boomed again, to no one and to everyone at once. "Real art is for the future, and this"—his arms swept about in a semicircle, indicating the walls full of paintings—"is already a…a mausoleum! Paintings? Corpses! Bah!" Tom attempted to speak, but the Italian shot a hand forward, like a policeman stopping traffic. "No, to your introductions! No, to manners; no, to forms!"

"Marinetti," the defeated Tom said softly into Ida's ear, "a remnant of the Futurist movement."

"But even ideas such as these are archaic!" said Marinetti, shaking his large head, a sheen of sweat on his brow. "As old as my manifesto, at least." His looked to the others for their reaction.

Lewis, who had been leaning forward, waiting impatiently to

speak, took a deep breath and opened his mouth, but it was not his voice the room heard next.

"The future, you say?"

It was Alice's voice, her speech slurred as she returned from the other side of the foyer with a fresh bottle of plum brandy in one hand and a thin black cigarette in the other. "You want George Antheil." Everyone paused. For habitués of the Stein salon, it was as if one of the paintings had spoken out loud and offered an opinion. Alice was only supposed to work the door and divide the geniuses from the wives of geniuses. Gertrude was always the one who spoke. "You want George, but you can't have him now, no you can't," said Alice, her voice a little sloppy and lilting. Ida decided Alice must be drunk. She was singing her words, happy and loose, like Teddy after a glass too many. "Too bad for all of you—you'll have to wait. Dear Antheil is away in Africa until the great premiere in two weeks' time."

Alice then pushed her little body between Ida and Marinetti and stood at the center of the circle, arms stretched wide. She began to turn slowly, a sorceress, a sibyl, an oracle from Greece, clutching a potion bottle and a smoking wand in her hands. "Before he left, Antheil was quite fas-cin-ating about his *Ballet Mécanique*. Sixteen player pianos! And three xylophones. Kettle drums, sirens, electric bells. And you, Jay," Alice pointed her strange-smelling cigarette at a trim man who stood with Breton, "even you will like this—there's an airplane engine! Everything plays at once, com-plete-ly synchronized, and not, I say not, a single musician in the room!" She had them, thought Ida—Alice had them all in her spell, as the room fell into a hush.

For several more minutes, the room belonged to Alice alone. Breton closed his eyes, soaking up her words dreamily. Pound bounced on his heels and grinned. Marinetti leaned in close, devouring each sentence hungrily. Alice spoke of pneumatics, the treachery of piano rolls that won't keep in time with one another on their own, of the mysteries of the pallet valve and the electrical pulse. "Sixteen pianos, playing perfectly together, connected only by wires to George's little box. He said that if the wires were long enough, he could put the pianos all over the *Jardin du Luxembourg*. All over Paris. The world! And the mechanical timpani will go *boom* together, all on their own."

Here at last Alice came to a halt, like an antic wind-up toy whose coiled spring had finally unwound. Lewis, who stood glowering the whole while, broke the silence, his voice flat, icy, the veil of civility draped over a contempt so thin you could see through it. "Sounds like little Antheil wants attention." He stepped forward with a sneer on his face, placed a hand on Alice's shoulder and turned to the crowd. "And little Alice wants to be noticed, too, eh?" Alice wilted at this assault.

Ida had not spoken since she'd quietly owned up to being Teddy's wife. She'd passed so many days in silence, intent over her easel, and here she stood among so many ideas, so many geniuses, so many forcefully spoken words. Picasso and African mask dreams and the art of the future, and now, from Alice, something she barely understood but thirsted to know. And Lewis had smashed it. Lewis, with his flopping hair and his hat indoors. Lewis, who practiced drooping his cigarette just to seem nonchalant. Lewis, that ass who drinks his nights away with Teddy.

"They're clearly not the only ones who want attention." The words Ida spoke were louder than she intended, and the room stood quiet, everyone looking at her—even Gertrude, inscrutable in distant majesty. Lewis glared at Ida as if she knew nothing, was nothing. No, worse. It was something worse she caught in his eyes.

"To whom," said Lewis slowly, turning on Ida, rage simmering in his voice, "to whom do you refer?"

Ida looked around the room: at the man in the sailor hat and gold vest, his poem still in his hand; at fiery little Pound with his tie in his pocket; at Marinetti, who had bellowed and swept his arms around like a magician—any of them. It could be any of them she'd meant. But she didn't say that. In the stillness of the room she uttered, "You, Lewis. I mean you."

The longest two seconds in the world ended with a screeching cackle from Ezra Pound, followed by a general peal of laughter. Lewis burned, shifted, and the room quieted quickly. Ida felt Lewis might strike her. She knew Lewis felt it too and wanted to do it. Was it the aura of the Stein salon, a kind of temple, that kept him from violence? Was it Teddy, standing there, blushing at what she'd said? Ida didn't know. But what Lewis finally did was even lower, worse.

"Alice, you've met Ida?" Lewis asked, his gaze still riveted on Ida, his words flat and quiet. "Ida paints copies, in the Louvre. She paints copies for money." Lewis took the bottle of brandy from Alice's hand. "I believe the ladies across the hall need more brandy. Perhaps Ida can help when you take her with you."

Everything of the sorceress had fled Alice, who now touched Ida's arm and motioned with her head toward the door. Numb, Ida let herself be led across the foyer to the room of the wives of the geniuses. "To hell with Lewis and his brandy," Alice said, collecting herself. "We'll have something just for ourselves," she added, opening the door to a smallish parlor with stuffed chairs, where a dozen world-weary women sat talking idly.

What would it be? Ida wondered. Talk of perfume, hats, and babies, as with the rich Lake Forest ladies in their drawing rooms and at the marble-topped tables in the pastry shop? Or thin-eyed gossip, like her sisters when they clustered in the kitchen? Ida stood at the door, silent yet enflamed, as Alice stepped to a sideboard, picked up a knife, and sliced into a flat yellow cake. "Ida dear," she said, her speech slurring, "be a darling and help. I'll cut; you'll serve."

3

Oh, she was happy here, she was. Alice lay curled around the gentle curves of Gertrude's body where she'd collapsed at the end of a long Saturday night. The big Morris chair in the salon room held them both comfortingly close, the sleeping Gertrude's feet splayed out on the ottoman. No one, mused Alice, would ever call Gertrude maternal—nothing like it—but when Alice let her arms fall around Gertrude's large, soft belly, she felt safer than she had since her childhood, knew a comfort and peace she hadn't known since her mother had died, younger than Alice was now. Maybe she should ask Breton about maternal attraction—he'd met that Viennese Dr. Freud whom everyone was mad about. But Alice didn't need to understand anything. She just needed the sustaining warmth, the deep breathing comfort, the body close and radiant with solace.

Alice let one eye slide open to gaze on Picasso's portrait of Gertrude, hanging in front of them on the wall: the African mask Gertrude; the goddess Gertrude, an image both benevolent and fierce. This was the Gertrude the world knew—if, that is, the world was Left Bank Paris. As indeed it was, for them and for all the other refugees fleeing from respectability and convention. In this room, the short-statured Gertrude towered: an icon, an idol, a totem or star. Only Alice knew the self-consciousness that used to so pain Gertrude. Who else would Gertrude have told about what they used to say at Radcliffe, when Gertrude and her classmates would ramble in the country and joke that they had nothing to fear from any strange man— they'd just have Gertrude jump on him, squash him flat, and sit atop the luckless fool until the police arrived. They didn't know how it hurt her, and nobody else knew about it at all. Nobody but Alice.

How different Gertrude must have been then! How different she'd been when they first met, in this very room, some
two decades ago. Leo Stein had ushered Alice in—a breathless
American naïf freshly arrived in the City of Lights, hoping to
play concert piano. Leo, ever the talker, with his sharp beard
jutting and wagging. Leo, taking off his wide-brimmed hat and
his tartan cloak, folding his body into a chair only to unfold it,
rise, and choose another seat for a better view of his Cézannes
on the wall. One had been hanging right where Picasso's portrait
of Gertrude hung today. Leo went on and on about Cézanne
who, to be fair, he'd all but discovered. And Gertrude? Hardly
a word. Hands folded in front of her, she stood in the corner,
shy and watching, watching, watching, still learning from Leo
how to see. She seemed shorter then, very much the little sister
who followed Leo like a puppy, from Oakland to Boston, from
Boston to Baltimore where he looked at old paintings and she
failed her medical school exams. Then Gertrude followed him
from Baltimore onto a ship bound for Europe, where, alone in
her cabin, she pined for a handsome New York girl and told no
one about her yearning, no one except the lone reader of her
unpublished novel about the affair—or, rather, about the sad
lack of one. And she'd sworn that reader, Alice, to silence and
secrecy.

For the longest time Gertrude hadn't had a readership, or
even a reader, save for Alice. Not long after Leo moved out
under the spell of a coal-eyed beauty, Alice moved in. On the
first day, Gertrude asked her if she could type and she'd said no,
but that she played the piano and supposed that amounted to
much the same thing. So, Alice sat down in front of a clattery
Underwood and God knows how many thousands of handwritten pages and typed out Gertrude's goliath of a novel—if
that's what you'd call it—*The Making of Americans*. One sentence
tugged at something inside Alice, made her feel for Gertrude
more than ever. "Bear it in your mind my reader," Gertrude
had written in her whorled scrawl, "but truly I can never feel
it that there ever can be such a creature; no, it is this scribbled

and dirty and lined paper that is really to be to me always my receiver." Well, she has me, thought Alice, and we're enough for each other. When she hit the return lever at the end of a typed row, a little bell rang, just as a one had rung brightly inside her the moment she'd first talked to Gertrude alone. It signaled attraction, that bell, but more than that—it went off when Alice met true genius. She'd heard it, too, when Picasso stormed into the salon, angry with hunger and a Spaniard's abhorrence of the blue-gray Parisian winter. It was around that time when Alice had left off with the piano; you can only pound keys so many hours in a day. And she preferred to play for Gertrude than for any audience in the world.

Gertrude had learned to see paintings by the time Alice moved in, as had Alice, so together they collected the best of the best on the cheap. They bought the art no one else wanted to buy—or, if others did, they were as poor as the painters themselves. But Gertrude had learned more than just how to see; she'd learned how to be seen. She learned that covering her walls with Matisse and Picasso brought all the painters and writers to her salon—and that dancers and playwrights and composers came with them. She learned they were curious about her, the strange American woman who was said to write like James Joyce—as wild as him and every bit as good (just don't let her hear you say his name). Gertrude learned that being a curiosity meant something different in Paris than in Boston or Baltimore—at least in her Paris, the only one that mattered.

Word got out she was a genius, and she'd grown. Not taller, though it felt that way. She'd grown into a legend that could sit silent as a sphinx or talk and talk like Leo used to do. No, she was better. He explained, exemplified, expounded. She looped and twirled and when she drew the sword of wit, it flashed and dazzled in blazing light. She had needed just the one reader to believe, one solitary shaft of light in the gloom, to bask in and rise as someone new. When Picasso had unveiled his portrait of her, some fool in a dinner jacket opined that Gertrude didn't look like that. "No," said Picasso, his voice both ice and fire, "but she will." And she did, she did, thought Alice—to everyone but her. Alice nuzzled happily up against her Gertrude and listened until she heard Gertrude's soft, familiar, reassuring snore.

But Alice found she couldn't sleep quite yet. Breton always claimed that he slept best with an African mask by his bedside, but that mask-like face in Picasso's painting of Gertrude, something about it disconcerted Alice tonight. Did the look seem cold, or distant? Alice brooded a while, almost admitting to herself what she'd been feeling, more and more—that lately Gertrude drew less sustenance from Alice than from the endless procession of artists and poets who clustered at her feet at her Saturday salons. Perhaps that's why Alice had stormed into the room and raved about Antheil. Dear George Antheil—American naïf, piano player, young. About to find his fame. Was it something about him that got at her? Or something about Gertrude blandly accepting that gold-vested popinjay Cocteau's poem like a tribute to a goddess, while Alice had stormed and raved... What had she been thinking, making such a scene? Oh, she hoped she hadn't offended Gertrude with her display. Had she? She was sure she must have; Gertrude relied on her to keep things running smoothly. Wasn't that Alice's job, her role? But she'd apologize tomorrow. She'd apologize first thing, promise to be good, and everything would be fine. It surely would, wouldn't it? It would. Alice yawned. Sleep would see to her at last.

Alice woke the next morning when Gertrude stroked her hair and smiled down at her. "Lazy thing, aren't you, for a change," said Gertrude, stretching in her dressing gown. "Not one of our best gatherings, last night, was it? Two new Americans, and Lewis bent out of shape about something or other, as usual. Did anything notable happen? Anything at all? How I wish *something* had."

I should feel relieved she thinks nothing of my outburst, thought Alice—so why don't I?

Gertrude stepped into the foyer, calling, "Hélène! Un café noir!"

4

The lithe, angular man stared into his hand mirror, adjusted the angle of his sailor's hat, and puffed out his cheeks with an exhalation that was something between a despairing sigh and a dismissive snort. After all his efforts she simply hadn't cared, had she? No, she'd hardly even noticed when he had literally bowed down in obeisance and, stretching his arm in an elegant, courtly gesture—almost a serpentine curve, offered a poem in tribute to her. And a good one at that! If this kind of humility couldn't garner attention, what would?

Well, yes, he granted it was hard to be noticed in that room of art and *artistes*. Half the people present just gawked at the paintings, and the other half? They watched each other watching each other, or they scanned the horizon for some shiny novelty among the familiar faces of the demimonde. Every week a raft of foreigners washed up on the shores of Miss Stein's salon, each one seeming as exotic and appetizing to the salon habitués as a pineapple in a Parisian winter. Some were just as prickly too. How to compete with that? A real Parisian seemed drab in comparison. Of course, he himself was not a real Parisian, not quite, not by some half-dozen miles—he knew that, but he'd escaped his horse-breeding hometown, with its sleepy château and sleepier bourgeoisie. It could lie in its stately stupor forever as far as he was concerned, as dead to him as the father who hadn't had the courtesy to live to see how his son could shine.

But had he really been shining lately? It hadn't felt that way at the salon, where there were always young ones, Parisian or otherwise, shooting up like fireworks to dazzle. Or fizzle...we can hope a few will fizzle, eh *mon vieux*? André Breton, beaming like a child, had introduced him to one of these youths—a handsome writer from Chicago who was also a detective and a rum-running bootlegger. That one would certainly get noticed—one could just imagine him posing for press photos, his dark-haired wife smiling with quiet pride behind him. Oh, it was all too possible—but entirely *insupportable*—and utterly unfair.

Jean Cocteau plonked down his hand mirror, then tore the sailor's cap from his head, and flung it across the long room that served as his bedroom, studio, sitting room, and, as the rack of jackets, suits, robes, and well-pressed trousers attested, his closet. Had the hat been a mistake?

He'd worn it to a cabaret the night before he'd gone to Miss Stein's, and the little Dutch waiter had liked it well enough, lifting it from Cocteau's head to try it on his own, playing the sailor on shore leave looking for a night of fun. *Le Bœuf sur le toit*—the Ox on the Roof. Cocteau had given the place its name, and it was a good Surreal one. And he's the one who made the reputation of the place when, a few years back, old Moyses came to him, in tears and clutching his apron. Soft-hearted as ever, Moyses worried that he'd have to fire the jazz pianist in order to keep his more conservative customers, the old-timers who plugged their ears, grimacing at American ragtime and scoffing at improvisation. "Fire the pianist?" Cocteau had quipped. "No, no, dear Moyses. Keep the pianist and fire the audience." Cocteau was always surprised when one of his *bon mots* was taken seriously—they were made for display, not for use—but the scheme had worked. But perhaps it had worked too well. The new, more open-minded crowd was less literary and more musical. Like fat Milhaud and Poulenc with his barn-door ears, they just came for the music, and shushed him—him, *Jean Cocteau*—if he talked over the solos. Bah to Milhaud, tucking into his pommes frites and fried mussels like the Marseilles hick he was! No visual sense at all in that bumpkin—what did he care about how hard Cocteau had worked to stay as svelte as he was when he posed for the portrait Modigliani had painted of him? Oh, how it had stung to crane his neck to look at the picture in a corner of the *Bœuf en toit*, only to find it obscured by the coat rack and low-hanging Chinese lanterns.

A pale light slanted in through the narrow windows of Cocteau's narrow room as he bent his lean frame over an elegant escritoire littered with diagrams. He liked to look at these when he was feeling neglected—the theater sets he'd designed for his own play, *Orphée*. A thin smile crept across his lips as he recalled Breton's applause at the end of the scene where Eurydice complained that Orpheus paid more attention to his horse than to her. The horse, Orpheus had said, taps out messages from the unknown with his hooves, each one more astonishing than the words of any poet in the world. Oh, Breton had liked that, and when Breton clapped everyone clapped. Everyone, of course, except the witless majority whose silence is true applause to the avant-garde.

There, on the shelf above the escritoire, sat a flat silver rectangle, no bigger than a deck of cards, engraved with Chinese characters, some rubbed almost entirely away from frequent handling. A long tube and mouthpiece extended from the top of this metal box, Cocteau's opium pipe. This, at least, could comfort him in the aftermath of the salon, where Alice, mousy little Alice, had somehow contrived to upstage him, just at the exact moment he was hoping Miss Stein would declaim his poem. He sighed deeply, let his eyelids flutter down, and remembered his last dream under the influence of the pipe: the sky had shimmered like a pool of water struck by a thousand drops of rain, and then every little circle in the water became an eye staring directly at him, at him, at him. He basked, he wriggled in delicate delight at such admiration until, all at once, the eyes blinked and shut, leaving him nothing but a vacant darkness where he lay immobile, invisible, impotent against the nothingness.

No, not now. He opened his eyes. Not the pipe, which he'd started to suspect he took up too often. And not these old drawings from *Orphée*. No. He twisted to fetch a new, different set of diagrams, something he'd been dreaming up for days. Now these—these would make for something hard to ignore, eh *mon vieux*?

5

Before the dim light of Monday morning could shake itself free from the blanketing clouds and settle on the blue-gray rooftops of the sixth arrondissement, a man in a trilby hat had already positioned himself in a recessed doorway across from the entrance to the courtyard, a folded copy of *Le Monde* in one hand, ready to be raised should he need to hide his face. He placed a Woodbine between his lips—so much better than French tobacco, which always stank of tar—then stuck the paper under his arm, struck a match and, cupping his hands against the wind, lit the cigarette. If he couldn't have coffee when he needed it most, he could at least have this. He should have remembered from yesterday's vigil that he'd want coffee by now, not just for the kick of it but for the warmth inside, but surveillance was a new art to him, quite different from his usual métier. He looked at his watch. If anyone observed him from the sleeping windows above, they would have assumed he was waiting impatiently for a rendezvous of some kind, for he checked his watch every minute or so and kept looking furtively up and down the street.

A sputtering noise startled the man into alertness, but he slouched back into the doorway as a rattling farm truck drove past, its engine insisting that it would never finish the long morning's trek to the markets of Les Halles. Nothing to do but wait. Patience, patience, and perhaps another Woodbine. Yes.

No. Not now—that's her. The man shrank farther into the shadows and raised his newspaper to his face. Peeking from behind it, he watched the object of his interest walk past on the other side of the street, toward the Luxembourg gardens, with her dog in tow as always. The poodle she walked might prove a challenge, though not an insurmountable one. The concern, he thought, was more a matter of noise than of biting. He would be wearing heavy leather gloves anyway, and an overcoat on top of a thick tweed jacket: try biting through that! Good armor if the beast turned nasty. Ridiculous things anyway, poodles. Ought to be put down, all of them.

One more quick check of his watch, and he stepped out from the recess and followed the dog walker. Same time as yesterday, almost to the minute. Same direction. And now she turns—same corner. A creature of habit, this one. That's good. And the only early riser on the block. That's better still.

He rounded the corner, watched his prey for a while, then turned back and looked down the street for a long time. Yes, he knew the very spot, just there. It would do nicely. Until tomorrow, then.

Had the sun even risen yet? Tuesdays started slowly, like Mondays or Sundays, and the sun always seemed to wake late in Paris on autumn days like these. In this thick, pale fog it was hard to tell what time it was, and the mist rolling through the streets in soft gusts wasn't the only fog this morning: Alice, standing in the foyer deciding whether or not to pluck an umbrella from the stand by the coat rack, was lost in her misty thoughts. She still wasn't sure what had gotten into her the other night, holding forth about George Antheil like that. Surely some of it was the plum brandy, and much of the rest was likely the hashish she'd smoked, wasn't it? The hashish had been a hostess gift from a pale, almond-eyed Austrian heiress, a woman with mischief in her eyes and tales to tell from a recent visit to Lebanon. But fog or no fog, Basket needed to be walked. The poodle was particular about relieving herself, with preferred trees in the Luxembourg Gardens a short walk to the east. So, it was with a little sigh that Alice left her umbrella behind, clicked the leash onto Basket's collar, and made her way out through the courtyard to the rue de Fleurus, her heels echoing on the cobblestones.

The new American girl wasn't half bad, Alice thought. Perhaps she'll come again this Saturday, though she had clearly been upset about something. Well, many of the provincial ones found the kind of manners in the salon, or the lack of them, a bit of a shock at first. Alice would never forget the expression on the American painter Mary Cassatt's face when—a veteran of Paris but not of Gertrude's Paris—Cassatt had visited the salon years ago. It was impossible to say what appalled the poor thing more: the paintings or the painters. It was probably the painters, Alice supposed. They'd played a kind of table tennis using slim books of poetry as paddles and pastries as balls, and one overzealous lob had very nearly resulted in a stained Matisse. Anyway, the new woman, Ada or Ida, would likely get used to it in time—provided she and that tall, grinning husband of hers didn't run out of money or illusions first. Alice hoped they'd stay a while. She wanted to see the girl's broad mouth smile, and she suspected there was more in that head than she'd seen on Saturday, when the girl—what was she, twenty years old? —plonked down on a sofa with a plate of cake on her knee and a dark cloud swirling invisibly around her. She wouldn't even let Carlotta ply her with that marvelous hashish.

As Basket towed her past rue d'Assas, Alice dwelt upon the loveliness of the hashish, and of the American girl's pale throat. She did not notice the figure stepping out of the dark doorway of the still unopened pharmacy, following along behind her, taking care to walk quietly, and quickening his pace to close the distance between them as they neared the entrance to the gardens. Large, with his hat pulled low and—unusual in this weather—a scarf wrapped around his face, the man strode with purpose. They passed beneath an awning where the sidewalk narrowed and where a long, low-slung automobile, its cloth top up and its engine throbbing quietly, was lying in wait.

Alice wished Ada or Ida had given the women in the parlor more of a chance: they were a good lot, when you got to know them, full of ironic humor about the French; about their husbands and girlfriends; about the time Pablo Neruda had caught the Surrealist Breton revising his "automatic writing" because, as he said, "it wasn't automatic enough." And hadn't Alice rescued the girl from that dreadful stiff, Tom Eliot? Why was he over here anyway? Probably something to do with the *Criterion*, that magazine of his that Lady Rothermere funded as an act of penance for that dreadful *Daily Mirror* her husband inflicted on the public.

Further meditations on British periodicals ended abruptly when a strong arm encircled Alice's waist and a gloved hand pushed something with a cloying, sweet smell over her mouth and nose. Stunned, Alice writhed against the assailant's body, which twisted in turn to kick at the snarling Basket, who emitted a series of sharp yips. A dispassionate observer would have to admit that, as awkward as her assailant was, he had chosen the spot well. Between the locked storefront and the parked car, and under the awning, only someone nearby on this side of the street could have noticed them in the fog.

The door of the waiting car was flung open from inside, ricocheted shut from the violence of the hand that pushed it open, then shot open again. Alice struggled, spitting the cloth from her face, and attempting a scream before the gloved hand silenced her and the bulk of man who held her clumsily pushed her down and into the car.

"The bottle!" a raspy voice barked in English from behind the man's scarf as he thrust Alice into the back of the car and tumbled in after her. "I need more!" The driver passed something to him, and he fumbled with it with one free hand, his other grinding Alice's face into the floorboards. His knee crushed her torso. She tried to kick at him, but to no avail. And now the car rumbled off down the street, loyal Basket in pursuit, the leash dragging behind, until the car turned onto the broad rue Guynemer and roared away.

The man managed to soak one end of his scarf with the fluid, then he pressed it against Alice's nose and mouth. Alice bit at it, turned her head, and pulled the scarf down from the man's face. Those dark eyes—she knew them, she thought as a hazy vagueness gripped her. And now, as her body went slack, and her mind fell numb, she whispered, or thought she whispered into the rising darkness: "You won't be invited back."

6

The sun first peeked above the rooftops almost two hours ago, and now the last of the fog was burning off. As she brushed her hair, Ida looked out the narrow window as people walked by in the street below. Paris on a Tuesday was all business, she thought—the men slight, dapper, and hurried; the women shepherding little flocks of children off to school. Nothing much had happened since Saturday—lolling in bed with Teddy on Sunday, toiling away in the Louvre on Monday while Teddy went off to the cafés. But Saturday had been something.

Teddy had positively reveled in the events at the salon, thought Ida—she'd heard sudden explosions of laughter and excited shouts from the salon room—but for Ida the night had been lemon cake and…and she didn't quite know what. It wasn't humiliation, or anyway not only that. She had to admit that the wives of geniuses were good company: Alice kind, Carlotta solicitous. And they hadn't talked about hats and perfume. Everyone but Ida had smoked Carlotta's hashish and made ironic comments about the geniuses across the foyer—how they wanted to change the arts, and the world, but hardly any of them could even change their own bed linen. They talked, too, about all sorts of things she never heard discussed in Lake Forest: Dr. Freud's theories of sex (it needed a theory?); the death of Lenin; and that great American disgrace, Prohibition. Talk of the famine in Russia somehow led to Carlotta's theory of the abominable snowman, which led in turn to a comparative anthropology of national traditions in men's whiskers. Carlotta talked of how Virginia Woolf, an acquaintance of hers, sometimes dressed as a man; another guest casually mentioned the Danish prime minister—so fond of turtle soup, don't you know—as a dear friend, though a trifle pompous in front of a crowd. The women Ida met weren't Miss Stein's designated geniuses, but they weren't like the smiling women herding children in the street below, either. What were they? Ida wondered, sipping tea by the window. And was she one of them?

Ida turned, standing over the bed where Teddy still sprawled in sleep, his feet protruding from under the coverlet, one sock on and one off. Grinning a little, Ida grabbed the sock by the toe and yanked it off. Teddy heaved himself awake. "Eessh," he wheezed. "Oosh." He sat up slowly and swung his feet to the floor. "Drinking Pernod—never again, dear Ida. I swear it by all your popish saints, never!" His head in his hands, he looked like he meant it.

Teddy had been reveling in his triumph at the salon since they left Miss Stein's late Saturday night, telling and retelling tales of his encounters with the luminaries. He told them again now. The geniuses, he said, had lapped up his stories of Chicago gangsters and prize fighters and laughed at his jokes. It turned out, Teddy told Ida, that one of Jay's Princeton friends knew one of Teddy's pals from Northwestern—small world! And Lewis! Here Teddy shot Ida a sympathetic look as she watched a pair of eggs boil in a small pot on the gas ring. Lewis, he said, was just being Lewis. He couldn't help it, and she'd got his number, too, got him good, hadn't she? Ida supposed she had. "We've arrived, my goose," Teddy had said the morning after, "arrived in the heart of what's modern and best. But our work has just begun! There's a lot to know if I'm to write and keep up with the big boys in the avant-garde." That, Ida supposed, was what Teddy had been doing at the cafés since Saturday: keeping up with the big boys. She glared at the eggs, which seemed to stare back at her with unearthly patience.

Now Teddy stood at last, pulled on the undershirt he'd left hanging on the bedpost, stretched, and gently pulled Ida to him by her waist. "Enough delay. Today we'll split up, chipmunk. I'm to meet that pilot, Jay, at his hotel—the Ritz. You'll do some research and hunt down the necessary documents. Like my old times at college, I'll need to do some cramming. Not the old and dead this time, though; the real stuff." Teddy released Ida and began to count off on his fingers. "A book by Pound, and one of Stein's—mustn't neglect Her Majesty. Something from that Antheil fellow Alice went on about. André Breton says he edits his own magazine—one of those, then. And Marinetti mentioned some kind of manifesto." Alice noticed that he didn't mention money—rich boys never do. "We'll read together tonight," Teddy continued, crossing the room in a single broad step, and embracing Ida from behind. "Scheherazade and the sultan on our plush divan."

"Did you really tell them you were a bootlegger?" Ida asked.

"Sure. They like that. A bootlegger, a detective, a gentleman hobo. Should I have added lion tamer? Or," he nuzzled into her neck and pulled her close, "a tamer of geese?"

"*Glou glou*," Ida replied, nuzzling back and twisting into his kiss. So why not hunt down some books? Well, perhaps not just now, not while Teddy's lips moved softly down, down to her throat, then down some more. No, not now at all.

It was early afternoon by the time Ida pulled herself from Teddy's embraces and pushed through the door to the American bookshop, Shakespeare and Company. Shelves of books both new and old lined the walls, but the center of the bright little shop was set up like a parlor—low, comfortable chairs and rickety occasional tables ringed a large, faded carpet. It was used like a parlor, too—at least by one thin man with thick glasses and a grubby black suit, who crossed and re-crossed his thin legs, sipping a cup of tea in one hand, and holding a small, squarish magazine inches from his squinting eyes with the other. People—mostly Americans, by the look of them—came and went as Ida browsed. Some bought books or newspapers in English, others seemed to be dropping books off at the desk or asking if any mail had come in for them. The proprietress, a woman in her mid-thirties, and the perfect cross between a prim schoolteacher and a habitué of Stein's salon, seemed both terribly efficient and completely at ease in a brown velvet jacket, high-collared shirt, and man's bow tie.

Under a handwritten sign reading "Poetry" Ida soon found a slim book by Pound—*Hugh Selwyn Mauberley* by name—and scanned the shelves for other writers on her list. An American voice from behind her asked, "Is there something in particular?" Ida turned: it was the woman in brown velvet.

"Antheil, the musician," said Ida. "André Breton's magazine, the Futurist manifesto, and something, anything really, by Gertrude Stein."

"George doesn't write," said the woman, introducing herself as Sylvia Beach. "Not a word, though his wife, Boski, tells me he keeps threatening to type up some memoirs. They live upstairs. I'd introduce you, but I think they've run off somewhere—someone was just in asking after them. No matter. Have you met Miss Stein?"

"My husband and I were at her place Saturday night, but I didn't meet her... I've met Alice."

"Ah." Ida wasn't sure if this response meant she'd just been filed away on an index card labeled "wives of geniuses" or not. "You haven't seen Alice today, have you? Gertrude was in not an hour ago asking after her. It seems," Sylvia arched a penciled eyebrow, "she's vanished."

"She could vanish, and the city would gleam a tad brighter," echoed a voice, high and clear and liltingly Irish. It was the man with the glasses, his teacup empty and the open magazine on his lap. "You're a friend of Miss Stein?"

"Not exactly," replied Ida, sensing from the man's tone that this topic might be a minefield to pick through carefully.

"Nor am I." He stood, proffering his bony hand. "Germ's Choice, but you can call me Shame's Voice."

"Mr. James Joyce," said Sylvia, by way of clarification. "Forgive him. We all do."

He grinned as Ida took his hand and introduced herself.

"Don't tell Miss Stein you shook my hand," said Joyce. "She thinks I picked her pocket."

"And did you?" asked Ida.

"The greatest poverty is to be bereft of a style of one's own," declared Joyce. "When Miss Stein heard of my *Ulysses*"—Ida had heard of that book herself, if only as a scandal, and looked on Joyce with a new interest—"she felt she already held title to the territory. A signature style is the very currency of genius, and she thought I'd forged hers. She denies my genius, but what is hers, really?" Anger swelled inside his words. "Her true genius is to spend a different kind of currency on the current crop of geniuses. A crop, a-cropper, mostly. A commodity. You've seen the paintings on her walls?"

"I've seen her Picassos."

"Then you've seen the dark oval one, *The Architect's Table*?"

"No, only her portrait," said Ida adding, less certainly, "and a guitar."

"There are two signatures on the Picasso I have in mind—Pablo's, certainly. But should you ever deign to be in that den again, do look at the one I mean. Clearest thing in it is an image of Miss Stein's calling card, at the bottom of Pablo's pile of angles. He knew the way to divert the current of her currency. A patron loves to appear in a painting, and he made sure she did."

Ida nodded. She wasn't going to take sides in a war of geniuses in the realm of Bohemia, but this was interesting—no, not so much interesting as comfortable, familiar. Many of the old masters worked patrons into corners of their paintings, standing with the Magi at the manger or kneeling discreetly in a corner, eyes heavenward. Van Eyck had painted his patron as large as the Virgin Mary, and no one thought ill of him for it. In this, at least, the new art wasn't so very different from the old. They all painted for patrons. Like she did, for Mrs. Rawling.

"So I blame Miss Stein for my exile," Joyce continued, "not from old Ireland, but from her salon, land of bounteous brandy." He smiled as if he found it funny, but not convincingly. There was bad blood between Joyce and Stein. Ida could tell.

"This is one of Gertrude's." It was Sylvia, back from the shelves and pressing a book into Ida's hands. "For the Breton, you'll have to go to the Bureau of Surrealist Research—I've written the address on my card and put it in the book. For Marinetti, I'm no help. The manifesto was published in *Le Figaro*, the newspaper, years ago."

"Any idea where one might be found?" asked Ida.

"Pound's got it, if anyone has," chimed Joyce from his chair. "Man's a pack rat. If you want him this afternoon, he'll be at the American gym." He squinted at Ida myopically before adding, "Bit of a rough place. Two blocks north from the Surrealists, and down some stairs."

Ida nodded her thanks, not sure if she was being advised against going. Before she could reply, Sylvia asked her if she would be buying or borrowing the books.

"Borrowing," said Ida, remembering the diminishing roll of banknotes at the bottom of her handbag.

"I'll sign you up, then. Three books at once, return when ready, there's a library membership to pay and a deposit." Sylvia pulled a short pencil and yellowed notebook from her pocket to take down details. "Are these for you or your husband?"

"These are for him, for Teddy Caine," said Ida. "And I'd like something by Tom Eliot. That's for me."

7

A quarter of an hour's brisk walk westward took Ida to the narrow rue de Grenelle, cool in the shade of the tall buildings that stood on either side. Ida stopped and consulted the card Sylvia had given her: number fifteen. And here it was, a storefront like any other, though with heavy curtains covering the lower half of the windows, obscuring the interior from sight. A frosted glass door read *"Centrale Surréaliste"* in large letters, with a smaller *"bureau de recherches surréalistes"* beneath. She hesitated. Everything about Shakespeare & Company had felt familiar, welcoming: American voices, American books, the feel and furniture of an American front parlor, and expats like herself—she was an expat, not a tourist, wasn't she?—greeting one another with smiles while checking their mail. Whatever lay beyond the frosted door promised to be otherwise. Did you simply walk in, as into a shop? Did you need an appointment? A password? A secret handshake? All she knew of Surrealism was that André Breton seemed to be the ringleader, and the whole group cultivated the bizarre. But she was on a quest, she told herself, and entering new worlds was simply what people on quests did. She tried to think of a painting of an Arthurian knight braving all danger, but the only thing that came to mind was a John William Waterhouse picture she'd seen in a book—the Lady of Shalott, alone in a rowboat, drawing in her breath. Ida was sure the artist wanted her to look alluring, but those open lips, as Ida remembered them, just made her look distressed. Ida drew in a breath of her own and pushed through the door.

She didn't know what she'd expected inside—dragons, maybe, but not this. The Bureau of Surrealist Research resembled nothing so much as the outer office of a minor Chicago ward politician, or perhaps a settlement house, where immigrants were given brochures for English lessons and a map to the public baths. The room was sparse, with a single long table stacked with pamphlets and books, a couple of framed photographs on the wall, and two doors toward the back. At a large desk in the center of the room two men in shirtsleeves sat opposite one another, shuffling papers. No one spoke to Ida, so she stood and watched. The first man—round-faced, with a bulbous nose and a bristly salt-and-pepper beard the same length as his bristly white hair—was blotting paper with ink, then methodically folding the sheets in two to make symmetrical smudges. The second man, squat and solid like his peer, was writing a word or phrase on a small index card, then using those funny triangular French paper clips to attach the cards to the blotted sheets. Although the second man was bald and beardless, the two looked much alike. Could they be brothers? Ida wondered.

The two took no interest in Ida, so she spoke in her best French. "I am looking for a journal of Surrealist literature." Both heads swiveled toward her at once, like synchronized automatons. Then the bearded one looked at his companion. "Marcel," he said, "she wants Surrealist literature."

"There is no Surrealist literature," said Marcel flatly, his eyes boring into Ida as if he wanted to see through her, or inside, like an X-ray. "Surrealism is not literature. Surrealism," he gestured to the table of ink blots and index cards, as if this were sufficient explanation, "is research."

Ida chose to be unfazed. "I am searching for Mr. Breton's magazine," she said.

"Breton?" Marcel looked incredulous. "Did he say it was… literature?" The last word seemed to be held with tongs, as if it were somehow infectious. He snapped his head to look at his companion. "Did you put him up to this, Gabriel? You wouldn't!"

Gabriel began to spread his arms in a Gallic shrug, but Ida intervened. "Mr. Breton said nothing of the kind. The error is mine. *Désolé, messieurs.* But you do have a copy?"

"We may have one for you," said Marcel, in the tone of an

impatient bureaucrat of the pedigreed variety bred exclusively in France, "but all visitors must participate in research."

Gabriel stood and, with a slight bow and a kindly tone, asked, "Won't you take part?"

Ida peered at the table. One ink blot's index card read *The mother*, another, simply, *fear*.

"What is it," Ida asked, "that you research?"

"The unconscious," said Gabriel, at the same time as his companion blurted out, "Liberation!"

They looked at each other. "Liberation," said Gabriel, carefully, looking to the other for confirmation, "of the unconscious—for the freeing of desire." His companion bristled slightly at this assertion.

Marcel kept his gaze on Gabriel, suspicion in his eyes, but he nodded, adding, "for the freeing of desire and therefore for the revolution—the total renovation of dead, bourgeois society and all its forms, laws, institutions—even its poor and failing arts." Gabriel gestured to Marcel with an open palm, as if accepting a tenuous truce. Marcel attached an index card reading *machine gun* to a sheet of paper with a large, roundish blot of ink, then rose from his chair. "Chance brought you here!" he declared, as if reciting lines from a sermon he had given many times. "Sacred chance! Chance, unlikely juxtaposition, coincidence, dreams—these are the tools of our research, unlocking what we keep from our conscious minds."

It was, thought Ida, Sylvia's directions and her own curiosity—now piqued—that brought her here. That, and Teddy's fear of appearing to be behind the times. But Marcel continued, "And now, we must ask—what impulse moves you?" He rose and took a step toward Ida. "What coincidence haunts you? And what did you dream? Last night, mademoiselle, what did you dream?" The last words were enunciated with great precision and emphasis: a prosecutor skewering a witness pitilessly. While Marcel spoke, Gabriel took a large ledger from the desk.

Coincidence? With what? Ida wondered. And what dreams? She looked around the room, as if that would jog her memory.

She saw the stacks of dusty pamphlets, the plain furniture, and then the photographs on the walls. The first depicted a group of well-dressed people in an ordinary parlor, staring intently at a bare mantelpiece as if it held the most fascinating oddity. The other photo showed a woman—one from the other photo, Ida noticed—sitting in a chair in an attitude of exaggerated horror, her arms thrown up, her eyes protruding, her mouth opening as if to scream at the sight of the object on a table before her: an ordinary hen's egg. Marcel cleared his throat, impatient at Ida's long pause.

"The egg!" blurted Ida. "The egg!" Both men looked at her in excitement, Gabriel pausing over the ledger he had opened on the desk. "Last night," she continued, "I dreamed of an egg." It was true, and the two men reacted in great urgency, leaping away from the desk, pulling a chair back for her, thrusting a pen into her hand and placing the great yellowed ledger before her, open to a ruled page.

"Write!" said Marcel, hot breath in her ear.

"Don't think!" added Gabriel. "It's better not to let the pen pause, even for a moment!"

Ida wrote. She wrote quickly, brow furrowed, biting her tongue a little as she did when taking exams in school. "Faster!" cried Gabriel, as she wrote.

"More automatic!" added Marcel, urgently.

A dream of a giant egg. Chancellor Rolin and the Virgin Mary on either side of it. The angel from van Eyck's painting no longer holds a crown over Mary's head, but over the egg, which trembles as if it is about to crack open, hatching…what? What? And two other figures in the background, looking out over a city—not any city, but Paris. They have turned away from us… Who are they? When the egg hatches, they will turn, and I am afraid their faces will be terrifying… The egg is cracking wider, and something—no someone—is curled inside, a bare foot and shin kick through the shell—

She could remember no more. The pen dropped from Ida's hand. How long had that taken? Seconds, maybe, but it had exhausted her.

"Merci, mademoiselle," said the Marcel, his voice clipped, cold, and clinical as he lifted the ledger from the desktop, snapped it shut without so much as a glance at what she'd written, and returned it to its drawer. "You have contributed to the grand project. Gabriel," he looked to his companion, "please bring her the new issue of *Le Surréalisme au Service de la Revolution*."

"That's not what it is called," said Gabriel over his shoulder as he stepped over to the table to fish among a sea of cluttered books and brochures.

"Not yet," said Marcel firmly. "You know what I mean."

Gabriel selected an item from a stack on the table and passed it to Marcel—a thin, large format journal with a flimsy card cover.

"Come," said Marcel to Ida. "You'll see what it is." With that he crossed to the door on the left and flung it open, revealing a coat closet empty except for a pair of rubber boots. Stepping inside, he gestured for Ida to follow. His sudden, thin-lipped smile was not reassuring.

Quests and new worlds. Even strange ones, even with strange men. Through the gate of dragons: Go! With a slight shake of her head, Ida followed. Marcel, the journal clutched to his chest, pulled the door shut with a click, and they stood in darkness. His body was close, his breath hot on her neck, and she felt him move. Ida wondered if the door opened from the inside.

"*Voila!*" cried Marcel. And in front of Ida in the darkness glowed the phosphorescent words on paper: *LE RÉVOLU-TION SURRÉALISTE*. "It glows," Marcel said with pride, as if that weren't already evident. "That was my idea." He opened the door and Ida saw his sheepish grin as he placed the journal into her hands.

The men wouldn't take her money and sent her on her way like a convert to the cause. Gabriel, standing at the door, called out after her, "Return soon, comrade, return!"

8

A short walk down a series of cobblestone streets brought Ida to the American gym where she'd been assured that she would find Ezra Pound. Broad stairs led down to a sunken courtyard where tall double doors stood flanked by large, arched windows on either side. Ida pushed through the doors and stood in a vast, high-ceilinged room, the floor concrete, the air flooded with light and the distinct tang of sweating men, leather, and chalk. In the back were two doors, both labeled in English: one read *Boxing*, the other *Showers*.

Pommel horses, placed at regular intervals, dominated the center of the room. Two men hung from gymnast's rings in one corner, mats on the floor beneath them. The rest was less familiar—near the door, one man sat on a metal perch above bicycle pedals, his feet pumping furiously, his eyes intent on a big round meter, like a grocery scale, a foot or so in front of his face, the dial indicating either distance or speed. Another man held what appeared to be ski poles fastened to a clanking conveyor belt, which moved like the treads of tanks from the end of the last war. He walked slowly in place, face grim in concentration, balance unsteady. Some distance to his left a large man in a snug striped singlet leaned forward into a broad cloth band that extended behind him, its ends disappearing into a machine that agitated it, causing the man's belly to jiggle like Saint Nick's. Toward the back a scrawny older man, all knees and elbows, stood in an attitude of crucifixion in a metal frame that swung from side to side like a pendulum, beneath a metal plate bearing the manufacturer's name: *Gymno-Frame*. It was unclear how this provided any form of exercise.

No women were in evidence. Was she even allowed?

A compact young man with a compact mustache approached her, his newsboy's cap pushed back on his head, a sleeveless jersey revealing the lean musculature of his arms and shoulders. "No ladies on the premises," he said. "Club rule." Well, that answered that.

Should she turn back? Pound owned a copy of Marinetti's manifesto—James Joyce had seemed sure of it. Ida had no idea where else to find one, and to give up on Pound now would mean waiting for next weekend to find him again at Miss Stein's salon. Ida felt every eye upon her as she stood, as alone and exposed as Waterhouse's *Lady of Shalott*. The painter had gotten so much right in that image: the sense of menace, of a dangerous element all around the lone woman. But that open mouth of hers, all pulchritude and peril…no. No. Let's repaint that. Set her chin, give her a brazen determination. Yes. And why not? What harm in this small change? And what harm in giving the lady an oar or a paddle. Let her push on under her own power. Let her steer.

"No ladies, lady. You gotta go." It was the compact man again.

"I'm—I'm conducting research," said Ida, surprising herself at how readily the lie came. Her voice sounded more confident than she felt.

"What kind of research?"

Ida looked around the room, where the poor man in the Gymno-Frame had gone green and looked ready to vomit, and St. Nicholas of the weight-reducing strap had set his machine to a higher, bowl-full-of-jelly setting.

"Surrealist research," she said, pulling *Le Révolution Surréaliste* from her bag and presenting it as if it were a set of press credentials.

"Good place for it," said the man, with what might have been a smile. "Well, I shouldn't be in the American gym myself. I'm Canadian," he admitted, his voice lowered, as if he was revealing a compromising secret. "Morley Callaghan."

"Ida Caine."

"Teddy's wife? Well, he said you were a looker."

Ida chose to paddle on, past this comment. "I'm looking for Mr. Pound."

"Ez?" said Morley, picking a towel from a stack on a bench and draping it over his shoulder. "Flailing around in back. Follow me." He led Ida through the door marked *Boxing*.

In the raised boxing ring that dominated the cool, bare room, Ezra Pound lunged forward and leapt back, shirtless in baggy striped trousers and tennis shoes. Spry for a man of forty, he danced around a larger man, throwing punch after ineffective punch. The big man, half a head taller than Pound and powerfully built, kept his head tucked down, right fist near his chin, left arm extended full-length, keeping the antic Pound at bay.

"Pound's all offense, no defense," said Callaghan. "Hem there would knock him flat if he didn't want to spare his feelings. But Hemingway's all offense too—that's why he won't box me." Ida looked at Callaghan, who answered her look by saying, "Yeah, I'm small, but..." He tilted his head and gave Ida a cocksure grin.

Pound leapt forward one last time, limbs flailing when Hemingway at last struck a blow. It landed with a hollow thud on Pound's chest, knocking him back into the ropes. "Attaboy! Attaboy!" shrieked Pound, waving his opponent off. "Thus," he panted, "endeth the lesson, my boy. Same time next week?" Hemingway nodded and ducked out of the ring silently, striding to a far corner to douse his head with a ladle of water from a steel bucket.

"Lady to see you, Ez," said Callaghan. "She seems all right."

Pound entangled and disentangled himself as he writhed through the ropes and down to the floor. He retrieved a thin, greasy towel from a bentwood chair draped with clothing and rubbed it through his hair.

"Mrs. Caine, isn't it?" His eyes looked her up and down. "Come for a boxing lesson?"

"I came for a manifesto. Mr. Joyce said you might have it."

"He's got a million of those," said Callaghan.

Pound ignored him. "Pol'tics or Poe-ee-tree?" he asked Ida. There was that prospector's voice of his again.

"Futurist," said Ida. "Mr. Marinetti's, in *Le Figaro*."

"Figaro, Figaro, Figaro!" sung Pound, more bravado than music in his voice, as he slipped into an open-necked peasant shirt and a short velvet jacket. "So, it's pol'tics via poe-ee-tree. Or t'other way 'round." He shook out his greasy towel, tying it round his neck like a filthy ascot. "Come, Mrs. Caine, to the Ez-u-versity, and we'll issue you your textbook while you sit at the knee of the sage." He slapped his thigh, wheezed out a laugh, and motioned for Ida to follow him through the front room and out to the street. He didn't so much as glance at the door to the showers.

Pound's rooms proved to be just around the corner, at the top of a flight of stairs up which he flew—although the image he presented, thought Ida, was more that of a gawkily sprinting bird, an emu or ostrich in brown velvet. At the top of the stairs Pound jammed first one key, then another, then yet another, into the lock on a narrow door. At last, they entered a long, narrow room, the furniture a homespun version of someone's idea of what a medieval farmhouse might hold. Broad birch boards formed makeshift shelves and tables. Squat, square chairs had been nailed together with more enthusiasm than finesse. The sole ornament was a Chinese scroll curling away from the wall, bold characters proclaiming Ida knew not what.

"Is it you or Teddy who's come around to the Duke?" asked Pound, flapping his arm out in what may or may not have been an invitation to sit.

Ida stood. "The what?"

"The Duke…the boss—Il Duce! Advanced news for Chicago, but Teddy the detective must have snooped it out. Musso, I mean!" Ida looked at him without comprehension, so he continued. "Benito Mussolini! He's doing great things in Italy, and Marinetti's on board." He reached under a table for a largish pine box, as casually nailed together as everything else in the room, and rummaged inside. Ida noticed a hammer on one of the shelves, as well as a saw and a cardboard box of bandages that had, evidently, been torn open with haste.

"The Italian prime minister?"

Pound pointed to the Chinese banner as if it were sufficient explanation. "Master Kung knew it all! The unwavering pivot! All that is old is new again in Italy. For all his blather about breaking the statues, Marinetti gets it. He got it back in '09 in the manifesto. Advanced, advanced…"

Pound pulled a carefully folded old newspaper from the box and passed it into Ida's waiting hand. Realizing with new urgency just how seriously Mr. Pound should have considered that shower, Ida discovered she must be elsewhere at once and, with thanks and apologies, showed herself out. Pound, at the top of the stairs, lifted an arm, sniffed, and wheezed out a cackling laugh.

ॐ

Teddy came home hours late for dinner again, this time smelling of gin rather than Pernod. He'd kept a box of matches from the Ritz and used one to light an American cigarette he'd bummed from Jay. "Oh," he sighed wistfully, "the taste of home." He'd never smoked in Chicago. "You awake?" He nudged Ida, who lay on the bed, not quite sure what an accurate answer to that question might be. She'd been reading Tom Eliot's poems before her eyes closed. "We had oysters," Teddy continued, "oysters and"—he yawned, his speech a little slurred—"oysters and lobster. Skinny little fellows, French lobsters, but with garlic and butter. You eat?"

She hadn't eaten except for the last heel of bread and suddenly felt hungry. Rising, she took the book of matches from him, struck one, and lit the gas ring. There were still onions left for soup. She gestured with her head to the modest stack of books on the floor by the bed.

"The haul! The intelligence!" said Teddy, faux enthusiasm battling with gin and drowsiness in his voice.

"You can sleep," said Ida, chopping an onion with their one dull knife. "You won't need to impress the geniuses until the salon next Saturday."

"Not so," said Teddy, raising an index finger. "We're to see

Gertrude the Great tomorrow morning." He yawned as he spoke, distorting his words. Ida looked at him inquisitively. "Seems Alice has walked out on her, without a reason and without a trace," Teddy continued. "And everyone's to come 'round to comfort the jilted widow Stein."

"Well, you're in no shape to read now." Ida looked at Teddy sitting on the bed, struggling drunkenly to remove a shoe. He'd somehow already managed to kick the other one across the room.

"True, but that's why I need you, my Scheherazade." He flung himself back on the bed, outside the covers. "Tell me a tale, Ancient Mariner."

Ida waited until the soup began simmering, then scooped up the stack of books and sat cross-legged on the floor by the bed. Pound? She wrinkled her nose. Stein? She thought of her exile from the room of geniuses. The Surrealists? Teddy was too fuzzy for them just now. Not Eliot. She held Pound's old copy of *Le Figaro* in her hands. Marinetti. Why not start here?

"We want to sing the love of danger, the habit of energy and rashness," she read in the clear voice of a Sunday school teacher, translating the French as she went for her drowsy husband. "The essential elements of our poetry will be courage, audacity, and revolt." She looked up at Teddy, who nodded, eyes fluttering shut. "The Futurist Manifesto," she added, before continuing. "Literature has up to now magnified pensive immobility, ecstasy, and slumber. We want to exalt movements of aggression, feverish sleeplessness, the double march, the perilous leap, the slap and the blow with the fist." She read on, Marinetti's words extolling the beauty of automobiles, condemning Greek statues, and proclaiming the death of time and space in a new age of speed. "We want to glorify war—the only cure for the world—militarism, patriotism, the destructive gesture of the anarchists, the beautiful ideas which kill, and contempt for woman. We want to demolish museums and libraries, fight morality, feminism, and all opportunist and utilitarian cowardice." Did they now? Ida continued to read aloud, a bit of scorn in her voice, although she had to admit—there was something in it when Marinetti compared museums to mausoleums. She'd often felt entombed in that small room with van Eyck's chancellor and Virgin Mary.

"It gives me a headache," groaned Teddy from behind closed eyes. "Read something short, my goose—poems, read me some poems."

Happy to comply, Ida pulled Stein's *Tender Buttons* from the stack. "A Carafe," she said, reading the title of the first poem, or perhaps it was a bit of prose. "That is a Blind Glass." She read on, slowly, page after page, not quite knowing what waters she was wading into. These words weren't there to tell her things, she felt, and it came as a bit of a relief after the relentless harangue of the Futurist's manifesto. These words weren't clear, they were a clutter standing between her and clarity. They started you thinking they'd go one way and mean one thing, and suddenly, with a twist of sound, they went another way. They were about things—ordinary household things, Ida thought, a glass on a shelf, a cushion, a copper pot. But they hid those things—which were no clearer than the cello or guitar in the Picasso painting she'd noticed in Stein's salon. Just as Picasso's lines and angles were lines and angles first, representations only sometimes and only later; these words were sounds first, or syllables. But there was something there, there was. With growing wonderment Ida saw, or thought she saw, what Stein was after. Not a genius born from an egg, this Gertrude; Pablo, surely, was her father. Oh, Stein wouldn't like that, but there it was: she did with words what Picasso did first with paint on canvas. But in doing that, Stein had done something, something no one else had done. Was that genius? Was that signature style? She was about to ask Teddy what he thought when she heard his familiar sharp snort and long, trailing snore.

She rose, turned off the gas ring, poured her soup into a bowl, and settled down to eat and read silently into the night.

9

Paris, old and splendid, is nevertheless just as much a city of hurried business as any modern metropolis. But there has always been another, darker Paris, a city just as real. This Paris knows no church bell Sundays, knows no daylight at all. Paris was a city of tunnels and caverns long before it learned its modern name. It had, of course, the usual modern tunnels for drainage, sewage, and the maintenance of gas and electric lines, as well as points of access to *la pneumatique*, the system of tubes delivering mail from one postal station to another. These were the tunnels accessed by workers in blue coveralls climbing down iron rung ladders beneath manhole covers. The figure carefully making his way through rubble-strewn corridors might well be mistaken for such a worker if he were to come to the surface. The coil of copper wire slung over his shoulder and the electrical box lantern in his left hand would only add to his credibility as a member of that useful tribe of plumbers, gas fitters, and electricians who kept modern Paris functional. But it was not in the service tunnels that he walked, his rubber boots splashing through the murky fluid beneath his feet.

Paris has long had need of other sorts of tunnels and underground chambers. Centuries of wars, plagues, and clever tax collectors have, on occasion, driven Parisians underground. Secret doors connected cellar to cellar; wines cooled in hidden chambers, fortunes in gold and ancient coins sat in buried vaults, many long forgotten. Cramped tunnels and broad corridors still survived from when the Romans dug them for the limestone quarries that provided them with their bathhouses, and later gave much of Paris its building stones. The oldest and densest subway system in the world, *le Metro*, rumbled day and night through narrow tubes and brightly lit, white-tiled stations. Canals, swollen with rainwater or parched to summer trickles, wound for miles beneath the city's streets, water dripping from the roof above and echoing endlessly in the inky dark. Sometimes a canal bubbled inexplicably. Sometimes a patch of water glowed bright green where light poured blindingly down from an iron grate above. Here and there a narrow, dirt-walled tunnel or a broad stone corridor had collapsed, sealing off a passage or chamber, along with any unfortunate explorer caught behind the rubble.

Eerier than any of these were another species of tunnel, sometimes wide, sometimes narrow, sometimes opening into grand and cavernous chambers: the catacombs, into which an expanding city poured the dead unearthed from its ancient cemeteries. Walls of skulls grinned in the brave visitor's lamplight; femurs and tibia lay stacked in piles like cordwood. A bleached white cross stood grimly here and there amid the piled bones. The dead far outnumbered the inhabitants of the city above, the city of the living—a briefly blooming blossom above the graves.

The man with the coil of wire held his lantern high and stooped as he turned into an oval-shaped tunnel, taller than it was wide, a thin stream of water running along its center. He counted his steps, passing side-tunnels until he came upon the opening he sought. He turned, and a few steps farther on paused where a pipe ran up the wall. He turned a spigot, let the bucket below fill with icy water, picked it up and continued on until he came to a flat-floored room with a skull set in the wall and a roughly made plank wood door. His lantern revealed a rusty padlock, and the word *interdit*—prohibited—painted on the door in red. The key he wore on a chain around his neck unlocked the door and he passed inside.

With a little fumbling, he lit the oil lantern that sat on the large crate serving as a table. The light revealed a surprisingly dry room, with a camp bed, a homemade chair, and a work bench. Lengths of electrical wire hung from hooks on the wall, an elaborate chart lay open on the crate, with several others rolled up beside it. Mechanical parts littered the floor, along with grimy screwdrivers, wrenches, and a rubber mallet. A second door stood ahead, as casually rigged as the first but painted a dull yellow. The man set down his lantern and bucket of water, pulled the coil of wire off his shoulders, and gazed at the chart on the table. He was silent for several minutes, then picked up a pencil and made a mark.

A scratching came from beyond the yellow door, and a woman's voice asked quietly, "Is anybody there?"

10

Oh, but he didn't!" gasped Rosemary in mock astonishment from beneath her daringly stylish bangs.

"Oh, but he did—Opal, tell her!"

"He did. He did, he did! Twice, out by the lilacs." Opal covered her mouth as she said this, then giggled. "And he will again if Dahlia has anything to do with it!"

Ida, in her white cap and apron, kept her head down, hoping not to be seen. To be seen was to be called upon to do something—to pick a dropped napkin off the floor, say, or bring a hotter cup of tea. She stole a glance at the trio of young ladies in their new drop-waist cotton frocks over at their usual table in Richter's Cake Shop. It didn't matter which of the society boys Dahlia Garnett and her sister were nattering about with Rosemary Cowler. He'd either be a classmate of Opal's at Northwestern or a Lake Forest Academy boy Dahlia had met at a Ferry Hall-LFA mixer. At this time of year, the other local boys were still either in prep school or college out east. Or, like Ida, they were the offspring of the plumbers, gardeners, chauffeurs, maids, and cooks who trekked south to the public school they attended with the tough Italians from Highwood and the children of the Jewish accountants and lawyers from Highland Park. These public school boys were as invisible to Rosemary Cowler and the Garnett sisters as Ida tried to be now, pressing back against the tiled wall behind the bakery counter. She leaned a little to one side, which relieved the pinching from her hand-me-down shoes. She noticed her sketchbook, carelessly left open on the far corner of the counter during a quiet spell when the shop was empty. Should she stow it in the cabinet? The young women at the table were lost in their talk of boys, field hockey, and Rosemary's new hairstyle (the Garnett sisters still wore swirling blond mounds on their heads—like cinnamon buns, Ida always thought). Ida wanted to retrieve her sketchbook, but if she moved it'd be just like them to find something more for her to do. Still, she didn't want anyone seeing the open page with its unfinished sketch of a lonely waif selling flowers at the bottom of the steps of the Art Institute. Ida made her move.

"D'you know what?" It was Dahlia's voice, suddenly a little louder and higher pitched. "I don't want this lemon slice—I want the sesame cake after all." Rosemary was eating sesame cake, which must have seemed to Dahlia like the more modern thing to do. "Take this away and bring me a piece of what she's having." The order could only be addressed to Ida, who let her sketchbook lie on the counter and hastened to obey. But before she returned to the counter Ida was summoned again, this time by Opal. She'd have the sesame too. Ida returned with another piece of sesame cake and turned again toward the counter.

"Not this one." It was Opal's voice, now even louder. "I always get a corner piece. You people should know that by now!" There was no one working but Ida, and it was clear she'd been subsumed into a general group, those who brought cake to the table at Richter's, served dessert in the gracious dining rooms of the wealthy, or in some other capacity wore a white cap, fetched things, and kept quiet.

"Do I hear a lady in distress?" It was a man's voice. Ida turned and saw a tall sandy-haired young fellow stride through the entrance and, with a snap of the wrist, toss his straw boater onto the hat rack. She'd seen him around Market Square now and then. He was one of the old LFA boys, but now, to judge by the oversized letter on his purple cardigan, he attended Northwestern like Opal. He caught Ida's eye and, with a broad smile, reached down to scoop up the offending slice of sesame cake in one large hand and shove it into his mouth. His cheeks bulged and his eyes bugged, but with a shake of his head he swallowed hard. The offending cake was gone. "Now, a corner slice! Quickly!" He looked at Ida, his eyes softening. "Help me, won't you? Point the way!"

Ida extended an arm to indicate the glass case filled with assorted cakes. In an instant the young man was behind the counter, shoveling a slice onto a plate with a silver pastry server in exaggerated haste, as if he were putting out a fire or saving a dying man's life. "One side, my lady!" He guided Ida out of his path with a gentle hand in the center of her back and dropped the plate down in front of an astonished Opal. "Miss Garnett," he said dryly with a slight bow, quickly pivoting away before she could respond. He took Ida by the hand and guided her back behind the counter with an exaggerated, courtly gesture and an almost successful sidestep reminiscent of the Charleston. "Water," he whispered into Ida's ear, as they both stood behind the counter. "For the love of God, water… That cake is strangling me!" Suppressing a smile, Ida rushed into the back room to oblige.

When she returned, Teddy was looking at her open sketchbook, the sun catching his profile and flecking his hair with honey-colored highlights. "Yours?" he asked, as she passed him a glass of water. She nodded while he drank. "Very interesting," he said, passing her both the emptied glass and the sketchbook. "You got the shadows just right." He looked away from her to the table where Dahlia, Opal, and Rosemary gaped back at them. "I'm always impressed by a young lady with talent." He'd said it a little more loudly than was necessary, as if he wanted to be sure the women at the table heard him. Looking back at Ida, he leaned in toward her and said, more quietly, "If you like the Art Institute, why not meet me there come Friday? Noon, say, on the steps?"

Do what? When? With—me? Ida didn't know what to say. The young man smiled. "I'm Teddy Caine," he said, "and though I can wolf down a piece of cake at unsafe speed, I don't bite. Also, I'll be with my father—his law office isn't far away and he's going spend the morning trying to convince me to work there as a clerk this summer so he can rope me in for real when the time's right." A smile broke across Teddy's face, boyish but also just a little devil-may-care. "Come see my old man try not to look disappointed in me while we all have lunch at the University Club. Then you and I can cross the street and a have quick gander at whatever they keep behind the bronze lions at the top of those steps you've drawn."

Ida was floored. This boy ran at a different speed than the rest of her world. But there was something disarming in his smile, and she felt…what was the word? *Seen*, maybe. She'd worked hard on the shadows in her sketch: they were the best things in it. As it happened, she was free Friday—and his father would be there, at least at the beginning, and the Art Institute was familiar ground. And she still felt a little tingle where he'd touched her back during their Charleston by the Garnett sisters' table. She gave a little nod and Teddy's smile gained a watt or two. "I'm Ida," she said, quietly. "Ida Byrne."

"It's a date, then, Miss Ida Byrne," Teddy called out as he stepped away and retrieved his boater from the hat rack. "For some reason I'm no longer hungry," he added, glancing at the young ladies frowning down at their slices of cake. "Ladies," he said, tipping the hat he'd just settled on his tousled hair. And he was gone.

A moment later Ida wondered: was he supposed to have paid for that sesame cake?

࿇

"Oh no, you won't!"

"I will, though, whether you like it or not."

"Would mother have liked it? Would she?"

Waves of argument crashed like an angry sea around the kitchen table. It was Theresa vs. Agnes this time, though Ida knew the feuds and alliances of her sisters could change completely in the time it took to eat a plate of corned beef and cabbage. Agnes vs. Bea, Bea vs. Bridgette, Bridgette and Bea vs. Theresa and back again. Ida tried her best not to be noticed, lest the riptide of hostility catch her and drag her down to where she'd drown. This time it was all about a boy named Johnny, whose real name was Gianni—a son of the bent little man who cut hair at the train station barber shop. The lad, said Theresa, had taken a shine to her, and she didn't mind at all. Agnes, the eldest and the self-appointed guardian of standards since the passing of their mother, wasn't having it. "His mother can't even speak English!" she cried. "What would *our* mother say if she could see that!" Agnes looked to the head of the table for confirmation from their father. She should have known none would be forthcoming.

It was rare for anyone to look at the ever-silent Mr. Byrne, who sat, as always, looking as worn out as his faded plaid shirt, as wilted as the cabbage that now lay, half-eaten, on his chipped china plate. Ida sometimes thought she'd learned her strategy of silence from her father, though it had gone far beyond a strategy with him. Following the death of his wife all those years ago, silence had grown heavier and heavier upon him, until finally it was less a form of camouflage than his very identity. Silence and invisibility—these made up most of who he was: a man adrift in a sea of sniping, unseen in the maelstrom. And if the world didn't see him, he responded in kind, his watery eyes focusing nowhere, seeing nothing. Agnes waited a moment for her father to respond, then rejoined the battle with Theresa, where Bea now took up Theresa's side.

"At least Theresa's got a fella interested," Bea declared, around a mouthful of boiled potato, her fork pointing accusingly at Ida. "Not like Ida, the madwoman in the attic with her box of paints!" They'd all been forced to read *Jane Eyre* in high school, except for Agnes, who'd left school after ninth grade. One of the few things the sisters could agree on was which character Ida reminded them of.

"I'm seeing a boy on Friday," said Ida, quietly staring into her lap, unsure of whether she was proud or ashamed. No matter. No one heard her, as the sisters thundered at each other with volleys of ire. The battlefield moved on from Johnny or Gianni to someone using up all the hot water, and whose turn it was to clean the coal dust from the grate. Ida held her tongue and looked to her father. If his eyes were focused on anything, it was on the picture calendar tacked to the far wall of the kitchen. His "Injun Princess," he called it, this faded image of a maiden in a buckskin dress, a single feather in her hair, seated on a cliff overlooking a waterfall, her hand cupped to her ear as if listening to the distant water's roar. Today for the first time Ida imagined something other than the crashing waterfall's din: something like a voice calling out to the woman, saying, "Do I hear a lady in distress?" Ida cast her eyes down and hid a quiet smile.

Teddy swirled a little brush in his silver cup, working up some lather for a shave. Friday morning—must look sharp when I let father down about working at the firm this summer. Must look responsible enough to get away with it. Ought to look good for the cake girl too. He was not entirely sure she would show up—perhaps it didn't matter, though her presence might tamp down any outward display of his father's inevitable irritation. Teddy had pranced into Richter's to let Opal Garnett see how little he cared for her, or for the fact that she never said more than a quick hello to him. Oh, he'd shown her, hadn't he—throwing her over for a shopgirl. And the bit with the sketchbook had been brilliant, hadn't it? He's artistic, that's what they'll say about me now. Unconventional. A maverick, even! He looked in the mirror and lathered half his face. "How eccentric!" they'd whisper about him, for taking up with a girl like that, who was…well, she was actually good looking in her own way, wasn't she? Not soft and bland like the Garnett sisters, but something different. Quiet. Intense. A poor girl who made charcoal drawings. He's gone bohemian, that's what they'd say about old Teddy Caine, especially when they heard he'd walked away from his father's law firm. Bohemian—he liked that. The brush stilled in his hand. Maybe he wouldn't shave after all.

11

Teddy and Ida stood before Gertrude Stein's front door, where the morning light had not yet reached the courtyard's paving stones. Teddy had been slow to rise that morning, complaining of a headache from too much drink the night before, but once on his feet he'd been very keen to get out the door and over to the rue de Fleurus. "We show up, look concerned, and participate in the rites of sympathy," he said, pulling yesterday's shirt clumsily over his head, "and then we'll be initiates—intimates! Members of the club!"

Was that really what he yearned for? wondered Ida as they stood in the shadowy courtyard, her sober gray dress not quite warm enough in the chilly air. Teddy needed to be special, Ida had always known that, and she understood why. New money in a town of old money suffered in a special way, though not one her sisters could sympathize with. If Teddy played at the same game as other young men in Lake Forest, he would always play at a disadvantage. He'd probably be allowed to join their clubs—well, most of their clubs—if he acted the part, made light of his humble origins, and didn't get ahead of himself. But the hometown hierarchy was every bit as clear as the order of saints and angels that Tintoretto painted in his *Coronation of the Virgin*. If Teddy remained pious and humble, then he could surely have a place somewhere near the bottom. He could appear among the privileged celestials, sure, but no amount of money would ever make his mother the childhood playmate of his friends' mothers; and no distinction in a law firm on LaSalle Street could make his father so much as a distant cousin of the higher orders of angels, the Swifts and Armours and McCormicks, perched on their summer verandas in all their haloed glory. Teddy could never win as one of them, so he became...

well, what had he become? He'd imagined a thousand lives for himself and settled on "writer in Paris." And Ida had decided to believe in him, hadn't she?

"I'll knock again," said Teddy. Ida shook herself from her reverie long enough to realize they had been standing outside the door for some time, and her legs were cold. Teddy always liked her legs, but perhaps what he really liked, she thought, was how wrong she was for him. She didn't appear anywhere in the cloudy tiers of what she now imagined as Tintoretto's *Virgin of Lake Forest*. It certainly wasn't her at the top and center of the canvas, receiving a crown—that would be a debutante, not her. Teddy could have settled for an arriviste or the daughter of a ruined fortune—but why do that, when he could surprise everyone by picking a strange, quiet girl, someone poor but pretty in her way. For Teddy, marrying Ida was a declaration of independence. As much a sign of personal distinction as Pound's shabby shirts or the sailor hat Cocteau had worn at Stein's salon. Was that all she was to Teddy? Ida wondered. And what was he to her?

"Still no answer." Teddy shook his head.

"Answering the door was Alice's job," replied Ida. "Let's push on in." A vision of Waterhouse's *Lady of Shalott*, repainted with an oar in hand and chin set in determination, flashed in Ida's mind. Wherever Alice may have gotten to, she wasn't here now and couldn't keep Ida out of the room of the geniuses.

Teddy and Ida entered and passed through into the large room where Stein held her salon. Gertrude herself was there, enthroned by the fireplace as before. Surrounding her in ragged circles were the supportive, the concerned, and the sycophantic. Cocteau knelt at Gertrude's side, this time without a sailor hat—he was dressed entirely in mournful black except for a silk scarf in brilliant blue blazoned with golden stars. It wound round his neck and draped artfully over a shoulder. Opposite the poet sat the dog Basket, mournful and silent. Breton was here, with Marcel from the Bureau of Surrealist Research: each wore a raven's feather in his buttonhole. Marinetti stood to the side with a group of men, worry in his dark eyes, his hands twisting a handkerchief—could this be the same man who'd penned such a blustering manifesto? Pound sat in a chair, impatient but quiet. Carlotta stood behind a small sofa, draping her arms over the shoulders of its occupant, a Valkyrie of a woman dressed as if on her way to a round of golf. Behind a cluster of slim young men, Tom Eliot stood quietly in a corner, hair slicked down, his part so straight and authoritative it looked like something an Abrahamic God would cut through the Red Sea. Ida noticed he'd kept his umbrella with him.

Enthroned Gertrude may have been, but exultant she was not. She sat in the attitude of Rodin's *Thinker*, and may have even shed a tear before looking up and declaiming, in a quavering voice, "Alone...alone is alone is a..." She trailed off, drooped forward, shaking. The kneeling Cocteau rested his head on her knee, only to be pushed aside.

Just then a stout woman in a striped apron and striped dress rushed into the room. "Madame! Madame!" she cried. "The police have come at last." No sooner had the words been spoken than a short, sharp-nosed man of middle age strode into the room, followed by another man, younger and taller. The short man had a trim mustache and wore a policeman's kepi—the round, short-billed hat of the Parisian police. His hip-length cape was adorned with his badge of office, and at his neck gleamed the blue and gold fleur-de-lis of the ultra-conservative *Action Française*. He wore this last ornament with a defiant pride, though it had no place on a policeman's uniform. The younger man wore a blue police uniform, one brass button dangling by a thread. He held his kepi in his hand and stood a step behind his superior.

"I am Inspector LaMarck. No one speak, no one move," said the senior officer, his hands on his hips as his head swiveled slowly, like a gun turret on the deck of a battleship. His eyes declared his contempt for the people—for the very type of people—before him. "Your cook has told me the details," he glanced at the woman in the apron, "and she may leave us now." The younger officer smiled awkwardly and gestured for the woman to leave. She stood fast.

"You may go, Hélène," said Gertrude, radiating a regal authority. As she spoke her gaze stayed fixed on the senior officer.

Inspector LaMarck smirked at this co-opting of an authority he saw as his alone and shook his head slightly: Charlemagne's warhorse ridding itself of a fly. "Your cook has informed me, Miss Stein, of the disappearance, yesterday morning, of your..." He paused, then spat out the next word as if it were an accusation, "*companion*, Miss Alice Toklas. People sometimes disappear and then return. Though lovers, you know, often run off for good." Gertrude took a sharp breath as if to speak, but LaMarck extended his hand forward, halting her. "Yes, it happens sometimes—especially in cases of unnatural affection." Carlotta's Valkyrie emitted a hiss, leaned forward from her seat, but did not speak. LaMarck gave her a stony stare. His junior companion blushed and did not know where to look.

The inspector continued. "Perhaps"—there was that smirk again—"perhaps Miss Toklas has found herself a man." He looked over his shoulder at the blushing officer. "Eh, Clement? A man! Now that would be an improvement, eh?" He chuckled a little, looked to Gertrude, and added, "No, no, not likely—her condition is incurable, so you have nothing to worry about, Miss Stein. Except when it comes to your own soul. Some Jews do have them, do they not?" A yawning silence gaped open.

"Out!" The word seemed to echo down from the heavens and shake the very earth. Gertrude had risen, her brown robes somehow imperial, her right arm extended, her finger pointing to the door. Ida saw, now, the African mask face Picasso had painted in his portrait of Gertrude. She saw its primal force, its power. "Out!" The word rang again.

"Your failure to cooperate has been noted," said Inspector LaMarck, his gaze meeting the gaze of Gertrude, a woman who was now quite clearly his opponent. "Clement," he continued, without looking back, "make a note of Miss Stein's failure to cooperate." Clement fumbled for a notebook in one pocket, then for a stubby pencil in another. He dropped the pencil, bent to pick it up, but found it had rolled beneath a table. LaMarck looked back, shaking his head in disgust. He mumbled an insult and, taking Clement by the arm, dragged him through the door. The room sat silent, except for the gradually fading sound of the inspector berating Clement as they strode through the courtyard and out the gate.

Gertrude collapsed into her chair, but not in defeat. She surveyed the gathered artists and writers like a general assessing the survivors of a battle. Her eyes lit on Teddy. "The police," she announced, "will not help us."

"Death to the pigs," said Marcel the Surrealist, but the comment sounded rote, a refrain uttered ritualistically at any mention of the police.

"They will not help," continued Gertrude, ignoring the interruption. "Mr. Caine, they say you work as a detective in Chicago. You must do what the police will not. You must find Alice."

This was terrible, impossible, thought Ida. Teddy was no detective, no more than he was a bootlegger, a riverboat gambler, or whatever other character he played in the fantasies he spun out to impress himself and others. And now he'd have to tell them he was a fraud. How could he admit this, after bragging about God knows how many imaginary exploits? How? And these were the people he yearned to impress. He would be devastated, humiliated. He would be consumed with shame.

"I'll take the case," said Teddy. "You can count on me."

12

Wearing a dark, double-breasted chalk-stripe suit, with his slicked-back hair, and a carefully knotted tie, André Breton would have looked dapper had he not chosen a shirt as dark as his tie and jacket. As it was, he looked as though his natural habitat was less the lobby of the Ritz than the sort of speakeasy seen in American gangster films. He thought as much as he caught sight of his reflection in the window of the Café de la Place Blanche, but it didn't bother him at all. Thirtyish, with a high forehead and full lower lip, Breton was just starting to fill out his frame with a bit of excess flesh. He took one last, almost prim drag on his hand-rolled cigarette and flicked it away. The sunlight caught the emerald on his pinky ring as he reached both hands to his temples and adjusted his round, green-tinted glasses until they sat just so. Yes, that's the look he wanted: anyone he stared down would feel like a woodland creature caught in the headlamps of an oncoming cargo truck. Or maybe a sports coupe. No, the truck. That would hit harder, no? He tugged his jacket so it fit snug and sleek around the shoulders. A sports coupe, certainly.

"Your Holiness." Red Georges, headwaiter of the café, smiled as he pushed the door open and gestured for Breton to come inside. Suppressing a smile, Breton complied. He chuckled when people referred to him as the Pope of Surrealism, but he secretly enjoyed it. He kept a list in his pocket of those he might expel—or excommunicate—if they made a fuss about signing his next declaration. One of the people on the list would play an important part in this afternoon's proceedings. Blinking his eyes to adjust to the dim interior, Breton saw that everything was in place: the floor was empty except for a single table, all the others having been removed, so the only seating that remained consisted of the banquettes lining the walls.

Murmuring figures crowded there, and among the shadows he made out a smiling Man Ray, the wild hair of Giacometti, and the fierce eyes of Nora Mitrani in her Peter Pan collar and schoolgirl cardigan. Comrade Gabriel from the Bureau stood impassively by the table in the center of the room. Dressed in a black turtleneck and rumpled suit, he held, tucked under his arm, an archaic, elaborately carved wooden box with a pointed top like a dollhouse. Breton looked to his left, where a quick shuffling of bodies on the banquettes soon made room for him to sit. Settling in next to Man Ray, he called out to Gabriel, "Comrade Marcel running late?"

"He has other entanglements," replied Gabriel, "and may arrive later. But someone has volunteered to take his part. Let me introduce Toyen, our comrade from Prague. She assures me she is passionate about the matter at hand." At this a small woman in her mid-twenties stepped from the shadows at the back of the café. Hair cut short as a boy's lay plastered against her head, a clean part on one side, a single sculpted black curl drooping down over her forehead like an upside-down question mark. She wore oversized denim coveralls cinched with a wide band of leather at the hips, a belt covered with—what were they? Little loops. It was an ammunition belt, the kind they issued to machine gunners in the war. But the most striking feature of all was the slash of bright red cloth draped over her shoulder and tied at the hip like a sash. Well, that and her eyes, so intense they took Breton by surprise. He froze a moment in her gaze, a rabbit on the railroad tracks.

"Toyen," said Breton, recovering his composure. "Is that a Czech name? I've never heard it—"

"Citoyen," said the woman, her voice accented, flat and cold. "It's short for citoyen—citizen. I am Comrade Citoyen. My friends may call me 'Toyen.'" She shot an icy, thin-lipped smile at Gabriel, while Breton resolved to find ways to avoid addressing her at all. He didn't want to find out whether she considered him an ally or an enemy, and he suspected that she divided the world quite firmly into those two camps.

"Our visitor," Gabriel said, apparently as unsure of the proper address as Breton, "will take the case for the prosecution, provided there is no objection."

Pas moyen! No chance, thought Breton. You don't object to a woman whose glare lowers a room's temperature the way hers does. All eyes turned to Breton, who managed a curt little nod before giving the order to proceed. Gabriel set his carved box on the table, where the amethysts and pearls set in the lid caught the light. "Where," asked Breton, after a pause threatened to grow awkward, "is the defendant?"

"Everywhere," Gabriel said, gesturing broadly, "and nowhere at all. But for our purposes…here." He indicated the box with a sweep of his arm. "Let this reliquary stand in for today's defendant—the past itself!"

The crowd whispered, and Man Ray leaned back with a broad smile. Breton nodded in vigorous approval. This would certainly be better than last week, when some silk-scarfed wag from Barcelona wanted to put a parrot on trial. Superficial, these Spaniards were—would they ever be a credit to the movement? Must remember that one's name, he thought, and add it to the list in his pocket.

"*J'accuse!*" the shout echoed across the bare floor of the café. Toyen stood taller than her short stature, pointing at the jeweled box. "I accuse the past of stifling the imagination. It is a gaudy box in which to imprison us with habit! With submission! With hierarchy!" She turned to Breton and caught his eye. Something inside him demanded he flee at once, while something else forbade any movement at all. "I accuse the past of senility. It is a cracked wall built to stand in the path of all creative effort. It. Must. Fall." She stamped her foot like a flamenco dancer and spun round to stare down the gentle-eyed Gabriel.

"Leonardo da Vinci spoke of cracked walls," said Gabriel with quiet equanimity. "'Stare at a decrepit wall's decaying plaster,' said Leonardo to his students, 'stare long and with an empty mind, and you will see in those cracks forms and scenes and landscapes more wonderful than any in the fallen world—draw what you see, and you will draw a world more marvelous than what we are pleased to call the real."

Toyen smiled again, not thinly but broadly, a wide smile that showed her teeth. Battle was joined, and battle was where she lived. Not believing in anything so bourgeois as the soul, she would never admit that battle was where her bright soul sang. Gabriel, like a lighthouse among crashing ocean waves, also seemed very much in his element: over the next half hour he met every barrage, every fusillade, with a gentle smile and a firm refutation.

"This very trial is a nightmare!" declaimed Toyen at one point, frustrated by Gabriel's unflappability.

"Then you grant it the greatest authority," countered Gabriel, "the authority of dreams!" The crowd muttered assent. He'd won that skirmish.

"You stole your ideas from Breton's manifesto!" Toyen shot back, to scattered applause.

"He stole his manifesto from my subconscious!" countered Gabriel with a shrug. The crowd howled in approval.

Toyen felt the room slipping away from her. She paced like a panther around the table in the center of the room. "What is this box where you have housed the past? And what festers inside its jeweled facade?"

"Ah." Gabriel raised his eyebrows. "We come to it at last—it is the reliquary of a saint!"

The crowd gasped. Someone called out "*écrasez l'infâme,*" but only after a short pause—that was usually Marcel's line, but he was absent.

Toyen swiveled her head from the reliquary to stare back at Gabriel—a battleship's gun turret taking aim at a fat and helpless merchant vessel. "This is the past you wish to defend? The past, then, is truly dead. Surrealism has no need to convict it."

"This box," Gabriel ignored Toyen's remark and gently patted the reliquary, "this box contains the better part of the left shin bone of St. Chillian the Itinerant." Gabriel turned and raised his eyes to the dull light of the chandelier above.

"Comrades, this bone has, for some twelve hundred years, preserved the memory of the venerable Irishman who converted Prince Gozbert of Würzburg. And how did he sway the pagan princeling? By allowing the devil to steal his enemy's horses and ride them into hell. Know well that water taken from the saint's tomb and used to moisten the navel will restore virginity! Turnips planted on St. Chillian's day will grow to unusual size. Moreover, comrades, if these turnips are ground to a paste and smeared on the abdomen, they will protect against all seductions by witches, except for those born with a third nipple. And if one sees a glowing fern on St. Chillian's night and eats of it, one will walk invisible among one's kinsmen. The bone in this reliquary cured one prince of syphilis and another of congenital stupidity. This little box," Gabriel turned, picking up the reliquary and cradling it against his chest, "is the past, yes—and the past is Surreal. We cannot condemn our own."

The crowd whooped with delight. Breton stood, stepped toward Gabriel, and extended his hand, as if it were to be shaken or perhaps kissed on the emerald ring. But before Gabriel could respond, the crowd was on its feet and a shout rose up—"*Vive le passé! Vive le passé!* Long live the past!" Just then the door to the café swung open, revealing Marcel's silhouette outlined against the light. Man Ray stood, leaned over to Breton, nodded in Marcel's direction, and said, in his strong Philadelphian vowels, "He's not going to like the verdict."

13

Alice didn't know where she was or how long she'd been there when she blinked herself awake. Cold. It was cold, dim, and smelled of mold. She lay curled on her left side on a rough stone floor, hurting in the shoulders and back. Thirst burned. Hunger gnawed. She must have been here a long time. She recalled waking in the back of her captor's car, being forced to the floor. Later, she'd been dragged out of the car and indoors by two men, to a room where voices—how many?—had spoken quickly and harshly before a fat-barreled syringe had been plunged into her left arm. After that she'd felt only a growing darkness.

Trying hesitantly to move, she found that her hands were tied behind her, her ankles bound together with tight cords that bit into her skin. Fear came, sharp and hard in her stomach. Fear beat in her pulses. She could hear her heartbeat quicken. Breathe, breathe. Breathe and dare to open one eye, then the other. The gloom was alleviated only by a weak light coming from high above—four glass bricks forming a grimy window to whatever lay beyond. Squinting, she surveyed what she could. The room was large and bare, brick-walled and damp.

Alice struggled to sit, finally managed it, then rested her back on the wall. The rope binding her hands forced her shoulders into an unnatural posture. But sitting, she decided, hurt no less than lying down, and had more dignity, whatever that was worth. Silence reigned: perhaps a good sign. No scurrying rodents, and no one to torment her, at least not yet. From her new vantage point, she saw vague shapes in the dark, shapes that resolved into a broken chair, a small stack of boards, and something else. Was it—yes. A wine rack, empty except for two dusty old bottles. And nearby, to her right side—her stiff neck ached when she turned—a big white bowl, filled with what looked like water, and a chipped plate with some sort of porridge slopped on it. Well, whoever put her here hadn't put her here to die of starvation. Alice shifted, lowering her head to sniff at the substance on the plate. No odor. She touched it with her tongue, once, lightly, then again. Not oatmeal. Polenta? Though hungry, she would not eat like a dog, face to the dish. But her thirst commanded her, and she leaned over, hoped for the best, put her face in the bowl, and drank. The water was fresh and clean, and very soon it was gone. It had not been enough.

It occurred to Alice that her captors, who knew so well when and where to find her, who had taken such pains to bind her and leave her provisions, hadn't gagged her. That was either a lapse—unlikely—or a sign that screams would not avail. Neither, she guessed, would pushing against the heavy door she now saw on the wall just to her right, but she felt she should try. She inched over and pushed to no effect. Then she stood—painfully, unsteadily, breathing heavily from the effort, and leaned awkwardly on the wall for support. She turned her back to the door and tried the latch with her bound hands. It did not move. A scream, then? Who knew what it would bring? Think first, Alice. You're good at it. Think.

The bottles. She must get to the wine bottles. Leaning against the door, Alice slowly lowered her unsteady body, flames of pain devouring her shoulders and spine. On the floor now, she slowly worked her way to the rickety wine rack, rose to a kneeling position, and used her bound hands to pull the higher of the two bottles forward from its place, letting it drop to the floor. Good luck: it shattered. Careful, then, careful. Alice shakily lowered herself to the floor, wincing at the pain of the effort, and groped behind her for a shard of glass. There. No, a sharper one, and not so large. Yes. Slowly, slowly, she worked its sharper edge against the ropes that bound her wrists. A nick in the palm is nothing, she told herself as the glass bit her skin. Another cut—she drew in a hissing breath. But that is nothing too. She worked away in the silence, her awkward hands bleeding. The shard dropped from her hands, and she could not find it. Taking another, she began again. Time passed. She didn't know how much.

Finally, success: one cord was severed. She twisted, discovered she must cut another. A deep breath and she began again. This cord took longer than the first, but it too parted; her hands were now free. She rested a moment in quiet triumph, then stretched her arms, not sure if this was relief or just a new flavor of pain. If she bent forward, then she could untie her ankles. Drop the glass shard and try. Yes, she could bend if she could endure the pain radiating down her spine. Too much. Try again, slowly, slowly. She brought her knees up, reached for the ropes that bound her legs, and stopped short. That was a sound. Outside the door, yes. Sitting on the floor with her legs in front of her, she returned her arms to their bound position, reached for her shard of glass and found it. Yes, there was the sound again. She rasped out an indistinct word as the door flew open, flooding the room with light.

"You didn't eat your breakfast." The voice was low, and English. "But you lapped up your water like a good dog." Blinking in the light, Alice saw a silhouette: a man, large, in a trench coat. She blinked again and saw that it was Lewis. "Scream if you like," he said, a smile on his lips. "I won't mind at all."

Alice tried, but what came out was more of a wheeze or a whimper. Pain, again, in her back and shoulders. Pain in her wounded sense of dignity. Lewis's ghastly smile grew, and the eyes—the eyes said something she'd rather not understand, because part of what they communicated was glee.

Lewis strode across the room, picked up the broken chair, placed it in front of Alice and sat, leaning forward on its mangled back. "Tell me about George Antheil," he said. "Tell me everything he told you about *Ballet Mécanique*."

This was absurd. She had been kidnapped, bound, and thrown in this dungeon, and Lewis—Wyndham Lewis!—wanted to talk about an avant-garde composer. Alice tried to speak, finally succeeding. "Music lover," she choked out, the words abrading her throat, "are you?"

"Better not be flippant," said Lewis, rising from the chair. "Talk."

"*Ballet Mécanique*," said Alice, swallowing hard, "premieres when and where the posters say it will. Sixteen player pianos and xylophones, sirens, electric bells. An airplane engine as well. Modern music, with no musicians. At the end they all play one great note in triumph."

"And how will that work?" Lewis drew a flask from his pocket, unscrewed the top, forced it into Alice's mouth. She drank—a fiery liquor. Her throat burned. She choked, spat, and tried to speak more clearly.

"You heard at the salon." Was that really what he wanted to know?

"I heard how the instruments will synchronize. I heard how they are wired and linked to go off on cue. What I didn't hear was how the control box functions."

Alice, still incredulous, slowly described everything she knew, as she had that night at the salon. She stopped where she had stopped then. George Antheil had not told her everything that day he and Boski had stopped in. George and Boski—such a fine couple, young, innocent, and full of joy—had been so pleased to tell her what they were up to. George seemed to bubble over like a kettle on high flame, having kept his great plan too secret for too long. Boski gave him one of her looks, as if he shouldn't tell secrets. But they both knew her, quiet little Alice. She swore she wouldn't tell a soul, and hadn't, until that night in the salon. Curse Carlotta's hashish. Curse plum brandy. Curse Lewis and his gleaming sadist's eyes.

"If you know more and aren't telling me," said Lewis, slowly, "I'll make you pay." He loomed over her, shoved her chest with his foot and knocked her flat, her hands still clasped behind her back. He rubbed the edge of his shoe on her face. "Don't make me be unkind." He walked toward the door, then turned and looked Alice in the eye. "Don't think I won't hurt you. Part of why you're here is to punish you, you know. I had to convince my partners that we needed to take you and threatened to scuttle the whole project if we didn't.'" What madness was this? Alice wondered. She didn't have to wonder long.

"It's because of you they laughed at me," Lewis continued. "You and that shrewish little American. No one laughs at me. You can't just kick Wyndham Lewis to the ground and trample all over him. Not without paying, and you'll pay."

I will not cry, thought Alice, her back a storm of small spasms. He can do what he will and I will not cry. And I will not lie still. She struggled to sit upright, felt the piece of broken bottle cupped in her palm. "That's all I know. It's all George said."

Lewis looked at her long and hard. "And where is Antheil?"

"In Africa. He went to Algeria. Perhaps he wants to be able to say his concert took place without any musicians, no conductor either, and with the mastermind on another continent."

"If you're lying…" Lewis bent down and loomed closer. Alice was lying. Maybe it was because she thought he may sense this that something inside her told her *now*, and she swung her arm, aiming her glass shard at his filthy, gleaming eyes. She made contact just before he caught her wrist. Then the shard of glass flew from her hand and skittered to a corner.

"Bitch!" cried Lewis, jumping back and pulling Alice up from the floor. "Bitch!" She tried to writhe away, but to no avail. He thrust her against the wall, and she crumpled and lay still. Lewis, breathing hard, backed away, a hand clutching his bleeding cheek. He retreated and slammed the door.

As he stood in the outer room holding a bloody handkerchief to his face, Lewis heard a door open above, and footsteps come down the narrow stairs.

"It did not go well?" a voice asked from behind him.

"It did not go well," Lewis replied.

"I told you kidnapping was inadvisable. And now the situation is even worse. That detective friend of yours?"

"Teddy, yes."

"He has to go away."

14

Ida hunched over her easel, staring at van Eyck's *Madonna of Chancellor Rolin* and seeing nothing. She'd been at the Louvre for at least an hour, and Teddy? Still asleep, as far as she knew.

After yesterday's gathering at the Stein place, they had strolled around the Luxembourg Gardens, Ida quiet, Teddy elated. "We're in!" he'd said, picking up a small flat stone and skipping it across the pond by the palace. "They know me now—all of them." Ida watched as a man with military bearing offered his small son an ice cream from a vendor. Teddy seemed more like the child than the father at the moment, she thought. At least he was happy, but for how long? It was warmer today, the child's ice cream already melting a little.

"But you're not a detective," Ida had insisted.

"No? Well, I've read *The Moonstone* and half of Conan Doyle," Teddy replied. "Have faith, Dr. Watson, have faith."

Ida had nodded silently, trying hard not to worry. Perhaps Alice would come home on her own after all. Perhaps that awful little policeman LaMarck would come through in the end.

After the gardens, they had walked to a little café in St. Germain, to meet an American writer who did not write, Robert McAlmon. McAlmon listened to Teddy talk, bought them drinks, and toasted Teddy's new investigation. Teddy was delighted, though perhaps he wouldn't be if he'd known that McAlmon always bought everyone's drinks. A slight man with a lean, craggy face, bulging eyes, and a tuft of brown hair, he was known on the boulevards as McAlimony, having married an heiress who wanted nothing to do with him and paid him to stay away. Drinking and pretending to write occupied all his time. He and Teddy got on famously. An hour into the evening Ida had excused herself and gone home—was it really home?—to sketch. But she reread Tom Eliot's poems instead. They were better the second time through, in fact very good. She was asleep when Teddy finally stumbled in, bumping against the wardrobe and cursing in the dark.

Ida shook her head, squinted, looked again at van Eyck's painting on the wall of the gallery in front of her. She could do it—she could make a decent copy, a good one, even. She had no doubt of that. But why? For Mrs. Rawling—or, more to the point, for Mrs. Rawling's money, a portion of which was expected at the Western Union office, and none too soon. But why had Ida always painted only copies, or sketched them in the Art Institute? Yesterday, during her second visit to the rue de Fleurus, while the poets and choreographers offered condolences to Gertrude and speculated wildly on the fate of Alice, Ida had focused on the paintings—and though she didn't always understand the wild invention of the artists, Ida knew her technique was as good as any of them. Well, maybe not any of them. But some of them, certainly. She might not know modern painting, but she did know paint.

Escaping to the Art Institute had always been an adventure, thought Ida, an adventure into the city—flying off, often on her own. Was solitude the real reason for the sketching trips, when she'd bow down in homage before the old masters? Maybe. But most of the copies she made had been painted from library books up in her father's attic, where she had hidden herself away morning after undisturbed morning. Adventures into the city; hiding in the attic—weren't these incompatible instincts? Perhaps she had always copied art simply to be alone, to be free of a world of hierarchy and social order. Tintoretto's echelons of angels glittered for a moment in Ida's head. No, that wasn't what she had tried to escape, that was the world Teddy had left behind. She was never in that Tintoretto painting at all, never had any purchase on the cloud-tiers of the celestials. Her place in Lake Forest was clear—most afternoons she wore an apron and white cap in the cake shop and served up fat slices of torte to the sainted heiresses and to the rich boys with gilded halos.

The rest of the time she lived in an unruly, cramped house of carping sisters, piled laundry, and ever-changing arrays of foul odors and nagging worries. A squalid house always a dollar short of making the rent, a crowded house of half-finished repairs, lines for the unreliable toilet, and hand-me-down shoes. Tintoretto never painted a world like hers at all.

Tintoretto's painting wasn't for her, and neither was van Eyck's, Ida reflected, working her brush carefully into the red on her palette and brightening the cheeks of the angel who held a crown over van Eyck's Virgin Mary. No, she knew now which painting she'd grown up in: *The Raft of the Medusa*, Géricault's enormous canvas, hanging in the grand gallery below. Ida passed it every time she came to the Louvre, sometimes pausing to gaze on it; something about it always tugged at her, and now she thought she understood why. It showed a raft carrying the survivors of a shipwreck. Piled on top of one another, they were all ribcages and tangled limbs. Everything was jerry-rigged, crammed with twisting bodies in ragged clothes jostling each other for space. An improvised, inadequate sail hung from a spar like a dingy, yellowed sheet on the clothesline behind her family's house on a humid summer day. That painting was her world, the house she had grown up in. And where was she in the picture? Oh, she was there. She was the figure that had pulled away from the others, frantically waving a rag at the ocean's horizon, signaling for help from a distant ship that may or may not see her.

Maybe that ship's captain had been Teddy. Surely, he'd seen her signal because here she was, an ocean away from home, the floorboards of the Louvre beneath her—the deck of her rescue vessel. The good ship Paris; the good ship *La Vie Bohème*. Oh, Captain Teddy, so merry with your mateys, so merry with your grog. Do you know what port your ship is bound for? Do you ever think of storms? And if Teddy was the vessel's captain, what was she going to be when she climbed aboard? A passenger, Waterhouse's *Lady of Shalott*, with no oars in evidence? No, she was not even that woman, who was at least a lady, leisured.

Ida dragged her paintbrush across the wooden panel before her, swabbing the deck. One vessel lay on the distant horizon: a galleon laden with Mrs. Rawling's gold.

"Coming along?" It was Teddy, standing behind her in the gallery. "Time for my breakfast, and time for your lunch." He made no comment on her painting but motioned for her to follow him. She secured the small "*ne pas déranger*" sign that the Louvre clerk had issued her to her easel, followed Teddy down the stairs, through the corridors, and into the soft light of the crisp autumn day.

They bought a thin baguette and a soft cheese to share and ate on a bench by the river. Teddy fished in his pockets for two small apples, cut slices for Ida with his penknife, and smiled. Ida took a proffered slice, smiled back. "What are you going to do about Alice?" she asked.

"Investigation's on hiatus for today," Teddy announced, chewing his apple. "Jay wants to fly off somewhere in that biplane of his, so it's time to toast his safe journey. Lewis came by and told me not long after you left me at the café last night. He and I are joining Jay at the Ritz this afternoon."

The bar at the Ritz? This wasn't the worst place that Teddy could be, thought Ida, nodding and forcing a smile. At least he couldn't get into any great mischief, bother the police inspector, or somehow get himself hurt playing at being a real detective. She tried to remember if anything really bad had ever happened to Sherlock Holmes.

Half an hour later Ida was back in her little gallery tucked away in the Louvre, taking the sign off her easel and choosing a brush. Copying, again. She thought she understood something now about why she painted, but she still wondered about herself as a painter. All those years following someone else's brushstrokes, someone else's dream of beauty. Maybe that was simply another way of hiding in the attic—dissolving into someone else's vision, ceasing to be anything but a brush in someone else's hand. She was eggshell thin, she felt it. The original artists were reborn from her when she painted. They kicked and thrashed and broke through the shell that was Ida, emerging somewhere new—van Eyck suddenly rising up from the floor of a Lake Forest drawing room, where Mrs. Rawling would have a maid serve him lemonade and a cucumber sandwich in the heavy air of a Midwestern summer. Mrs. Rawling would talk of her ancestor, the canny old Chancellor Rolin. Jan van Eyck, Jan from Eyck. But who was she? asked Ida. She was shell shards on the floor. Ida daubed Mary's robes in angry red.

When she returned, alone, to the rented rooms, she made soup, knowing Teddy would be late again. She sketched the view from the window in charcoal—an empty street. Unsatisfactory. She tore it up and tried again. Darker now, better. Well, less bad. She waited, adrift, took herself to bed, and nodded off.

15

The dream came to him again last night, so unlike most of the dreams that haunted him these last few years. The new dream had no looming clock tower booming the passing hours as he ran through the streets, aware only that the time to complete some unknown, urgent task had come and gone. Nor did the new dream see him at the center of a circle of shady figures, each with its back turned to him as he tried to find a voice to speak. No, this dream was different. And last night it was as beautiful as it had been the first time, after Alice had conjured Antheil's vision from the air. The image had been beautiful, yes, but not with the soft beauty of a woman—weakness—nor even of a goddess, grave in her drapery. His dream was permeated with the beauty of a firm young god, skin gleaming beneath a hard, bright sky—his body strong and lean, his movements graceful and confident. A god shaking his full dark mane of hair, flexing his golden limbs in the vast glow of the admiring sun. It was a dream of youth, but also a dream of fire and stone towers tumbling, broken, to the ground.

The dream always began with an aircraft, its engine sleek and greased, popping and sputtering as it sparked to life. The howling of the machine grew, enveloped the world, and the aircraft rose, borne upward by the hand of the blank-faced, hard-eyed god. The receding world sprawled beneath, a docile land, the people mired in a blind and passive stupor. There were farms where peasants bent their shoulders to the plough; towns where sly merchants put their thumbs on their scales; cities where old professors squabbled, and fat bankers grew fatter still. Here and there lazed an ancient, slumbering chateau, its inhabitants sated, drunk on the crushed grapes of history. The airplane engine bellowed like a beast, bore him on toward a great metropolis, site of the only beauty the apathetic earth offered: smoke belching from factory chimneys, and Eiffel's triumphant tower, lean, iron, true.

Circling lower now—the aircraft agile, responsive to his will—he saw the city's bright river curl around its islands, islands cancerous with cathedrals. North of the river the Louvre sprawled like a corpse. The nearby domes of the Bibliothèque Richelieu protruded like the sickening teats of a dying beast. And that stench from the south? The Sorbonne, rotting and festering in the light of a justly angered sun.

This was not the dream's beauty. That beauty was to yet come.

The aircraft's thrumming engine reached a crescendo, was joined by tympani, by many pianolas and xylophones hidden somewhere in the sky. Everything pulsed in rhythm. Mighty cymbals crashed. The young god straddled the landscape, a colossus, a giant stopwatch in his enormous hand. He raised the hand like the conductor of an orchestra, and the engine and the music fell silent. The only sound was the wind rushing past the aircraft's wings.

A city of the weak and foolish lay bound by the past, by convention, cast down by the festering of commerce. The dead-eyed dreamless sleepwalking city must awaken, rise, and be reborn as a city without priests or fathers, without bankers, without fools.

The young god looked to his stopwatch and nodded. It was time.

A sudden, mighty note echoed, with all instruments together, one machine, one thunderous roar—and all the museums, all the churches, every cathedral and university, all the archives and libraries, all at once erupted in fire. Towering flames, red roiled with pitchy smoke. Fire thrusting up, a writhing and a living thing in this city of death-in-life. Rejuvenation, purgation! The dream was a dream of rebirth: a fearsome, cleansing beauty.

Now at last the multitude would understand. The god had spoken, chosen him for his long service, and found him allies. Hatched from an iron egg, half man, half engine, the dreamer would awaken, unfurl his iron wings beneath the gaze of his approving god. His belly an engine, the dreamer would rise, young again, and strong. He would fly.

Lewis was there in the dream, somewhere—too small to matter, too weak to lead. A wretched boy pulling wings from flies, but he too would serve the god. He and the others, soft-headed makers of a palsied art, but allies all the same.

Enough with dreams. Alice had proved disappointing, so other plans must be set in motion. And there was still the question: what to do with her? They couldn't let her go, and they couldn't simply kill her, not the way Lewis wanted to. They were artists, not murderers. But if her death became a part of the performance…yes. That would do. That sort of blood had beauty to it, didn't it? That sort of blood was clean.

16

Ida squirmed sleepily in the early light, reached out an arm to embrace Teddy beside her in their narrow bed, and found he wasn't there. Prying her eyes open, she could see he wasn't anywhere in their rooms. Gone to pick up croissants, perhaps? No, she thought, as an hour ticked by. But where had he ended up? She hoped he hadn't drunkenly asked for a room at the Ritz—their money wouldn't stretch that far. He must have ended up on a sofa in Jay's suite. Or had he and Lewis drifted off to sleep on a bench by the river, an empty wine bottle on the seat between them, the two of them snoring there still like a pair of ragged *clochards*?

Ida dressed without hurry, brushed the tangles from her hair, scavenged up a bit of stale bread and some glorious soft cheese from the tiny cupboard for her breakfast, biding her time until Teddy's return. She decided she wouldn't scold him, even though she wanted to. She knew him well enough to know he'd bring her something—a little gift, a story—to make her forgive everything and smile. She'd fall for it because she wanted to, at least partly, and because she always had.

Ida told herself she wouldn't go to the Louvre until Teddy showed up and toyed with her charcoal but didn't sketch. Gazing out the small window, she watched an old woman—the one for whom Teddy had juggled onions—pass on the street below, accompanied by a small silver-haired man. They looked like they'd been married forever and held hands as they strolled to the end of the road. Ida watched until they turned the corner, then rose, opened the door, and strode out, not quite sure where she would go.

Martin looked up when Ida stepped into his little shop on the ground floor of her building. In addition to selling cheese, he functioned as a kind of concierge. "Madame Caine," he said by way of greeting, offering what passed for a polite smile among Parisian shopkeepers.

"Have you seen Teddy?" The words came out quickly and weren't what Ida had planned on saying.

"Yesterday morning. He bought Camembert."

"No, Martin, it was a wedge of Langres!" called a woman's voice from the back room.

"Camembert. I am certain," said Martin, not looking back. The cheese from the cupboard this morning had been creamy, thought Ida, but was not Camembert.

"Have you seen Teddy since then?"

"No. Just Monsieur McAlmon, who came in this morning, also for Camembert. He said he'd been out with the two of you the other night."

"Absolutely incorrect," cried the voice from the back. "Morbier, not Camembert! Same as Monsieur McAlmon always buys."

Martin lowered his voice, leaned over the counter, and whispered to Ida, "It was Camembert. I swear to you on the soul of my sainted mother, it was Camembert."

"Teddy and I weren't with McAlmon yesterday." Ida thought for a moment, then added, "Teddy said he was going with Monsieur Lewis to see an American pilot named Jay at the Ritz."

"Ah," said Martin, speaking once again in a conspiratorial whisper. He liked Ida; he liked how she walked past the shop in the morning with her paint box and panel, looking as if she were delving so deep into her own thoughts that she might someday strike a vein of gold. He sometimes saw Teddy reel drunkenly home at night, alone or with others, and he didn't like that at all. "Perhaps that is what your Teddy has told you. But, of course, you are also aware that Monsieur McAlmon can be very generous to his fellow writers, yes?"

"I have observed the phenomenon," replied Ida, lowering her voice to match the Martin's.

"You have seen this generosity at a drinking establishment?"

"Is Monsieur McAlmon ever elsewhere in the evenings?"

"Often, yes. And his largesse extends to his friends when they visit…" The man glanced quickly over his shoulder toward the back room, turned back to look at Ida, and continued in an even lower whisper, "another sort of establishment."

Ida tried to think if she'd ever seen McAlmon anywhere that didn't sell a drink. The dog track? He talked about betting on the greyhounds. Surely French dogs didn't race in the evenings?

"But I have bewildered you," said Martin, apologetically. He motioned for Ida to lean in closer, cupped his hand by her head and whispered into her ear, "Monsieur McAlmon enjoys the company of those who must be paid for their intimate hospitality, you understand. And he is very generous when drunk."

Ida's spine stiffened. "That isn't Teddy," she said. "That isn't Teddy at all. Teddy was with Lewis at the Ritz."

Wincing a little, and holding his palms up in surrender, the shopkeeper replied, "Of course, of course." He'd said too much and knew it. A tense silence fell. "Did you perhaps want a nice Camembert?" He looked over his shoulder again, adding, "Or maybe some Langres?"

Ida, lips pressed firmly together, shook her head, and left. A few minutes' walk took Ida to Shakespeare and Company. Perhaps one of the Americans who congregated there had seen Teddy. Sylvia smiled warmly as Ida came in and adjusted her hair. "Ida my dear!" she cried. "Finished with Miss Stein's book already? We've plenty more if that's your taste."

"Finished with the blemished, ready to be replenished?" came a lilting voice from behind a newspaper held close to thick spectacles. Joyce. "Miss Stein finished is a reader famished."

Sylvia looked at Ida the way a mother looks when an adored infant has spat up on a visiting neighbor: *He does that*, her eyes and eyebrows seemed to say. *I'm sure you understand.* Neither Sylvia nor Joyce had seen Teddy, and Ida demurred when Sylvia tried to slip a slim volume by Djuna Barnes into her hands. Asking for a piece of note paper, Ida wrote the time and date, then added, *Missed you this morning. Please wait for me at our rooms, love Ida* and left the note with instructions to pass it to Teddy if he stopped in.Sylvia nodded, and gave Ida a look that was as sympathetic as it was enigmatic. For a moment—she wasn't sure why—Ida wondered if Martin may have had a point about McAlmon's dubious generosity.

Increasingly vexed, Ida crossed the river on the Pont des Arts, passed the Louvre, and made her way to the arched doorways of the Ritz. Standing outside the hotel's imposing oak doors, she thought of the neoclassical façade of Marshall Fields, the department store that dominated Market Square in Lake Forest. One of her sisters worked there for a year and would sometimes let Ida in the back entrance after hours to walk reverently among the racks of goods neither of them could afford. She'd never gone in by the front door, and never imagined she would. Now, taking a deep breath, Ida determined she would be her own version of Waterhouse's *Lady of Shalott*—chin set, rowing forward in determination. Squaring her shoulders, she mounted the steps and thrust herself into the lobby of the Ritz, a great, high-ceilinged volume of marble-clad space that gleamed with polished brass. Ida's shoes—her humble shoes, she suddenly thought—clacked across the marble floor. A desk clerk with the weary face of Father Time looked up from his ledger. Though the tall, ancient clerk stood right in front of her, Ida used all her strength to smack her palm down and ring the silver bell that sat by his elbow. The sound rang hard and bright against the room's marble, and the clerk assessed her instantly and not uncritically. He spoke in almost-unaccented English. "How may I assist you, miss?"

"Mrs.," said Ida, firmly. "Mrs. Caine. I am here for a guest, an American like myself. His name is Jay."

"We have no Mr. Jay," replied the clerk impassively. His suit was crisp and funeral-director black.

"Jay is his given name," said Ida. She hesitated, then added, "I don't know his surname."

The clerk's expression sank one degree down the thermometer of emotion. "In that case, I regret that I cannot assist you, madame."

"My husband, Mr. Theodore Caine of Lake Forest, Illinois, was here with a Mr. Lewis last night. They met Mr....they met Jay. I need to know if they are here, and, if not, where they have gone."

The clerk let the mercury drop even more precipitously in the thermometer before replying in clipped tones, "I regret I cannot assist." His omission of "madame" felt significant.

"My husband did not come home last night. If you do not help me, I will speak to the American Embassy. I will speak to the police!"

The clerk said nothing. He reached for an elegantly embossed sheet of stationery and, in beautiful script, wrote with an authoritative flourish. "The addresses of the Embassy and the nearest police station," he said, passing her the sheet and adding a positively arctic "madame." The clerk's attention returned to his ledger. Thus dismissed, Ida fled, snow flurries buffeting her retreating back.

The police, then. Once outside, Ida consulted the paper. She knew the street. It wasn't far.

17

Except for a sober little sign reading *Préfecture de Police*, the exterior of the police station was indistinguishable from any other building that Baron Hausmann had imposed on Paris during the great renovations of the nineteenth century. Walls of cream-colored limestone rose to meet the blue-gray mansard roof five stories above, declaring a sedate, bourgeois respectability in firm yet understated formality. The interior, Ida soon discovered, offered something rather different. She entered a large square room, at the center of which stood an imposing oak kiosk. A clerk's head appeared several feet above her own, as if peeking out from the ramparts of a castle. A uniformed officer stood just to the right of the kiosk, a truncheon hanging from his belt, while his charge, a squat, bearded man in a dark woolen suit, stood before the clerk, his back to Ida, his cap in his hands. Benches ringed the outer walls, propping up an assortment of what could only be called rabble—two old drunks in broken shoes that reeked of urine; a ragged, angry-looking woman with a black eye clutching a shrieking infant; a thin, pale-faced man holding his knees and rocking gently back and forth, his hair lank, his face without expression. From somewhere beyond came indistinct shouts in a language Ida did not recognize, outbursts that stopped short after a sudden crash.

Just then the squat man turned from the clerk, saw Ida, and with a start, called out, "Comrade!" He stole a quick look at the bored, truncheon-bearing guard, then addressed Ida again, in a low voice. "Comrade! What brings you to this den of oppression?" It was Gabriel, the bearded man from the Bureau of Surrealist Research.

"I've come to find my husband," said Ida.

"You wish to marry one of *les flics?*" Gabriel smiled and cast a furtive, disapproving gaze at a passing gendarme.

"My husband has gone missing—but…are you in some sort of trouble?"

"It is those who are not in trouble with the police who have real trouble," Gabriel replied, not without a bit of the orator's flourish—a difficult feat for someone not wishing to be over-heard by the nearby police. He waved the thought away. "But, no, it's not for my own sake that I'm here. It's Marcel."

"He's not missing as well? First Alice Toklas, then my husband, and now—"

"No, no, not at all," said Gabriel, rushing to reassure her. "Marcel was arrested for painting *'écrasez l'infâme'* on the church of Saint-Joseph-des-Carmes." Seeing Ida's bewilderment, he explained, "It is a venerable, indeed perhaps too respectable, phrase of condemnation for the church. But I have paid Marcel's fine—and here he is!"

A door opened at the back of the room, and a bedraggled Marcel staggered out, blinking as if emerging into the light after some time underground. He held an official yellow form in one hand, a torn black cardigan in the other. He quickened at the sight of Gabriel and Ida, crossed the room with a stiff gait, and joined them. Ida was once again struck by the resemblance between the two Surrealists; had it not been for Gabriel's beard, she might mistake one for the other.

"Death to the pigs," Marcel whispered hoarsely. "My thanks to you, Comrade Gabriel—and to you for coming as well, Comrade…Comrade mademoiselle."

"Ida Caine," said Ida, extending her hand. She realized she had not introduced herself, nor been asked to do so, during her visit to the Bureau of Surrealist Research. "Mrs., not Miss." Marcel bent his head and took her hand as if to kiss it.

Gabriel nodded. "Gabriel," he said, "and my colleague Marcel. We don't use last names." Turning to Marcel, he added, "Comrade Ida has misplaced her husband."

"Then she must come back to the Bureau," said Marcel.

"Our kind of research is most effective, especially when it comes to that which is forgotten, misplaced, or ignored. When the pigs here fail to help you, you will come back to us, yes?" While he spoke, Gabriel fished in his pockets, retrieved what looked like a business card, and placed it in Ida's hand.

"I—well, thank you," said Ida, accepting the card. The two men nodded in eerie unison, then turned and strode out the doors to the street without another word.

"Next!" rang a harsh voice from above. It was the clerk in the kiosk, glaring down at Ida while his round-lensed eyeglasses caught a flash of light. The effect was like the firing of cannon on a distant hillside battery.

Ida stepped forward to speak, realized she was too close to look at him without straining her neck, took a step back and peered up. The man was bald, and what she could see of his uniform was immaculate. "I am here to report a missing person, my husband, Mr. Theodore Caine of Lake Forest, Illinois. He's just over six feet tall, with—" But the clerk cut her off with the raised hand and brusque efficiency of a traffic cop.

"When did you last see Monsieur Caine?"

"Last evening. I left him at the Café DuPont with—"

Again, the clerk's high, clear voice snapped out, cutting her sentence off, like shears severing a tree branch. "You are too soon. We need a full twenty-four hours before a man is termed missing. Your husband is merely absent, not missing."

Ida decided to try a new strategy, one she loathed, but knew was sometimes effective. She adopted the helpless expression of so many damsels waiting to be rescued in so many paintings from the previous century. Waterhouse's *Lady of Shalott* wasn't far from the mark, but a bit too exquisite and helplessly alluring. It hadn't come to that, and Ida wouldn't let it. "But, monsieur!" she called out, looking up at the clerk's gleaming pate with pleading eyes. "What shall I do?"

"Return," he said, expressionless behind his spectacles, "at the appropriate time."

"I was with him last evening at the Dupont," said Ida, as if she hadn't heard. "I left him with his friends, having an evening drink, and he…he never came home." Ida had intended the pause as mere drama, but her emotion had been real. The lump in her throat confirmed it.

The police clerk's brow darkened with irritation. "So, he was drinking?"

"Yes, with Robert McAl—"

Once again, the clerk's voice severed her sentence. "He continued drinking after you went home?"

Ida nodded.

"Then it is perhaps for the best," said the clerk, impatiently. He gestured with his pen to the woman with the black eye. "Sometimes it is better when men do their drinking away from women."

Ida swallowed her anger. "And what will you do when I come back—at the appropriate time?"

"I will allow you to fill out this form," said the clerk, holding up a pale blue sheet in his left hand. Ida glared, but the clerk continued, "and I will endorse it with this." He raised a rubber stamp in his right hand.

"That's all?" Ida was incredulous, no longer affecting a helpless demeanor. The clerk did not reply. Instead, he shuffled some papers and slammed his stamp onto one, then another, then another.

Thus dismissed, Ida walked slowly toward the door, but the policeman with the truncheon followed and touched her arm. She turned and looked at him. He was middle-aged, his face weathered but not unkind. He stood close, smelling of tobacco and garlic. "You are *Americaine*, no?" he asked. Ida nodded. "The Dupont is a place where American bohemians and artists gather," the policeman continued, as if speaking to a child. "Bohemians live irregular lives." He lowered his voice. "Police prefer regularity, routine. His kind"—he jerked his head toward the clerk in the kiosk—"will not help you. Better just to wait. If your man wants to return, he'll return." Still holding Ida's arm, the policeman gave her a leering look and added, "I know

I would." Ida tore her arm away and rushed out of the station.

෨

Tom Eliot had been on the go since early morning, when he enjoyed the credible approximation of an English breakfast offered by the kitchen at his hotel for visitors from across the channel. This was his last full day before returning to London, and he still had several errands ahead of him. For the most part, he'd been meeting with writers and receiving manuscripts or promises of manuscripts for his magazine, *The Criterion*. He wanted the best stories and poems, and so many of the people who wrote such things lived here now, full time or otherwise. But Tom was never comfortable in bohemian circles—the informality left him feeling exposed, as if every interaction was a scene improvised in a music hall melodrama or bawdy comedy. It's what he also disliked about America: all of the much-vaunted back-slapping informality. It felt forced, some-how. At least in England they knew who was to sit where at the table, a viscount above a baron above a baronet. An American poet, editor, and onetime banker sat below the salt at such a table, but there was no dishonor in that. Everyone knew their spot. Everyone fit in the order of things, arrayed correctly like the silverware. Bohemians, in contrast, ate with their hands and laughed open-mouthed while chewing, spraying innocent by-standers with spittle and food. Putting on that sort of display? Well, it was simply not the way to treat people, though it did get one noticed. Wasn't that what the girl from Chicago had said Lewis wanted, attention? Oh, she'd seen through Lewis, that girl had. She was a clever one—you could tell just by looking at her.

Tom sat in a cane-backed chair at a little marble table in Le Balzar, having just fortified himself for the day's remaining tasks with a plate of sauerkraut and a small glass of lager. Ezra Pound had urged him to go to Gertrude's salon that Saturday night, he recalled, and for once he didn't regret letting Pound take him somewhere. Pound was always supportive of him,

and, indeed, of anyone making contributions to the art of poetry. He could be showy about it, though—dramatically pulling
his sweater off over his head, say, and offering it to a poet who
lacked warm clothes for the damp English winter. But in his
braying, showboating way, Pound was sincere about his love
of art. Well, Pound was sometimes too sincere, thought Eliot,
especially about politics. Pound had once dragged him to one
of those fascist meetings, and demanded they stand in silent
admiration while an Italian had droned on about the glories of
Mussolini. Tom certainly disliked some of the same things the
fascists hated—the world as a gigantic cash register, say—but
he was a monarchist, damn it all, and an Anglo-Catholic as well.
He loved church windows and evensong, not uniforms and
ridiculous continental salutes.

Leaving money on the table for the waiter, Tom rose, taking
with him his valise, heavy with manuscripts. Cheese was what
was needed. England did itself proud with Stilton, Cheshire,
and Cornish Larg, but there was no beating France for cheese.
If he must come to the continent and consort with bohemians to secure good manuscripts, he would at least make all the
bother worthwhile by hunting down the best cheeses the world
could offer.

The afternoon passed, and not unpleasantly; Tom wended
his way from cheese shop to cheese shop, guided by a small,
well-worn, and deeply creased map he had drawn by hand for
this very purpose on a previous journey to France. They understood him, the French cheese sellers. Never looked twice when
he demanded to see an uncut wheel of Reblochon, lowered his
ear to the center of the circle, and listened intently as he rapped
the edges with his knuckles. No, this wheel would not do. Could
they bring him another? Yes…a few knocks made it plain to
anyone with ears to hear—this one was ready. Wrap the whole
wheel—carefully, please. It has a long voyage ahead of it.

Tom sighed a bit as he stepped out to the street, thinking of
the voyage back to London. It was, alas, a voyage that would
take him back to his wife. Vivienne—pale, high-strung, broad-

faced Vivienne, with her fevers, her headaches, her endless insomnia, and her shattered nerves. Vivienne, banging angrily at the piano; Vivienne of the mood swings and the many doctors. She'd retreated more and more frequently to her dubious physicians and their nerve-cures, so much now that he felt he barely knew her; hadn't known her as a husband knows a wife for years. Divorce was out of the question—the church was clear on that, and if the church was firm, so too was Tom. But Vivienne drained him, until his nerves were as ruined as hers. He could hate her for the things she screamed, but only in the moment. Poor Viv, poor Tom, poor Viv.

He'd traveled quite a distance, with just one more cheese shop left on his map. Pausing for a moment, he set down his bags. How many pounds of cheese? How many manuscripts, heavy with genius? Tom leaned on an iron railing outside a nearby police station, letting his head droop. What an extraordinary visit it had turned out to be, with poor Alice wandering off, or worse.

Someone was standing before him, blocking the light. He looked up. "Miss Caine," he said, noting the light play around her figure. "What a pleasant surprise."

18

At first, she saw only a pair of immaculately shined Oxford shoes, gray flannel trousers, a leather valise, and a small pile of packages on the sidewalk, each carefully wrapped in butcher paper and tied with twine. When Ida looked up, she saw a smiling man in a blue blazer, the part in his slicked-back hair as straight as the Greenwich meridian. It was Tom Eliot, his sudden bright smile so deeply at odds with the sea of emotions churning inside her—anger, disgust, frustration, fear. He was saying something but she didn't hear. Ida flung her arms out, clutching him to her as if he were a life preserver thrown onto a storm-tossed ocean. She sobbed.

Tom hadn't felt a woman's embrace since the last time Vivienne threw her arms around him and wailed, wailed, wailed with the voices of all her demons, and that had been...well, Tom didn't care to recollect how long ago that had been. But this embrace wasn't like that at all. And it was already over. Ida had pushed herself away, wiping her eyes quickly on the sleeve of her blouse. She took a step back.

"I'm so sorry," Ida said. "I mean...hello, Tom. That is... forgive me. It's been a terrible day." By the end of the sentence she had regained much of her equanimity.

"Quite all right, quite all right," replied Tom, who found it better than all right. "We all have our moments." His right hand offered Ida a handkerchief, while his left reached to smooth his still-immaculate hair.

"Have you seen Teddy? Today, or last night?" Ida's voice was not as calm as she labored to make it sound. She dabbed her eyes with Tom's handkerchief, then added, "He's gone missing."

Tom motioned for Ida to lean on the railing next to him, and felt her warm presence when she joined him. "Better tell me about it," he said, soothingly.

Ida recounted the events of the previous evening, and to-day's increasingly frustrating ordeal, omitting only the leering policeman. As she spoke, she passed Tom's handkerchief back to him and, noticing she still held Gabriel's card, slipped it into the small green handbag she carried by a strap over her shoulder.

"No note, no message—just vanished?" asked Tom. Ida nodded and Tom continued, "But a private detective—a *Chicago* detective—certainly knows how to take care of himself. You can be sure of it."

Ida drew a deep breath. Teddy would never forgive her for what she was about to confess. "But that's just it. He's not a detective, he's nothing of the kind—he's…" She trailed off, thinking of Teddy's boyish smile, his tousled sandy hair, his face flushed with drink and bonhomie. What was he? *Young*, she thought. Teddy was young. Tom stood close beside her, a decade Teddy's senior, maybe more. "Teddy just likes to pretend. Please don't tell him I told you."

Tom nodded once. The two remained in silent proximity for a moment, then he spoke. "And you fear he's gotten in over his head, chasing after Alice?"

"I do."

"I imagine you have already discovered how unhelpful the gendarmes can be. They don't much care for all the foreigners who come here to drink and…behave like bohemians. People think of Paris as a city in love with art, but in truth there's just a small archipelago of neighborhoods in Paris where that's true. The police are conservative, at best. They will see you"—Tom's eyes cut quickly to Ida's hands, which she now noticed were stained with paint— "and they will assume you are the kind of foreigner who does things in Paris the locals would prefer not be done."

"I don't even know what to do," she sighed. "I don't know where to go. I don't want to return to our rooms." She paused, then continued, "I think I should go talk to Miss Stein. If Teddy has mixed himself up with Alice's disappearance, I should know whether Alice has come home." Strangely, she felt better—lighter—despite the circumstances. Confessing her worries, and allowing another to share them, did much to ease her troubled mind.

Tom looked quietly thoughtful for a moment, then spoke. "But isn't it precisely to your rooms that you should go? You've been out all day—perhaps Teddy has come home in the interim? Perhaps he's there right now."

Tom was right, of course. But Ida couldn't face the possibility of empty rooms, a day gone by and Teddy still not there. No, she would, she must. Paddle on, she thought. Paddle on even if it is toward a waterfall. Better to paddle than drift.

"It's getting late, and I leave for London tomorrow afternoon," said Tom. "I have errands to run tonight, but I'm meant to meet Miss Stein tomorrow morning to pick up a manuscript for *The Criterion*. Allow me to collect you tomorrow morning. You can join us, and if Teddy hasn't materialized, we'll find out anything Miss Stein knows that might be useful. But I'm quite sure Teddy will be home tonight. Quite sure." Tom didn't feel confident, but he gave it a solid effort for Ida's sake.

Tom looked skyward, toward the ethereal gallery where he kept the portraits of his ancestors—thin-lipped, wan, throttled with respectability—to see if the plan forming in his mind met with their oft-withheld approval. They leaned out from their frames, whispered in one another's ears, heads tilted in consultation. Yes, it would be proper. It would be gentlemanly. "May I," Tom said, clearing his throat, "may I walk you home? That is, if I...may..." When Ida nodded her assent, they started off. Despite Ida's protestations, Tom wouldn't let her carry a single wedge of cheese.

As they walked, Tom asked Ida about herself. She was reticent, so he talked about his own past. Despite his Bostonian family, he'd grown up in the Midwest, and knew Lake Forest. Did she know the Smiths? The Palmers? The Rawlings? She knew the Rawlings, all right, but didn't want to think about the higher and lower cloud banks of social celestials. He took the cue and talked about St. Louis, how he'd learned to dance there, and how the St. Louis ballroom dip, so much deeper than what the English were used to, had alarmed more than one lady in London. When they arrived at her address, Ida thanked Tom and left him at the entrance to her building—she didn't want him to see her reaction if Teddy wasn't there. Tom had looked as if he wanted to say something, but the look on her face stopped him short. He said a polite goodbye and waited for her to pass inside, promising to come in the morning. Alone, Ida climbed the stairs and stood outside the door to the rooms where she and Teddy stayed, not wanting to open it. When she did, it was as she feared—he wasn't there, and everything was precisely as she'd left it. She sat on the bed. She would wait, she told herself. She would wait and Teddy would return, smiling and full of stories and she wouldn't even be angry at all if he just came back. She would forgive anything if he came home. She would wait.

Unable to endure the silence, Ida decided to disappear. Her oldest and best vanishing trick had always been to lose herself in painting, in meticulous copying. She took out the wooden panel with the half-finished copy of van Eyck's *Madonna of Chancellor Rolin*, leaned it against the wall, and prepared her paints and brushes. The light was bad, but she had often painted in dimness. She angled her easel to catch the fading light. Yes, she knew the painting well enough to complete some of the background, even in this light, and even without the original in front of her. The Virgin Mary on the right side was flanked by an angel—a figure of pure grace. Too complex to approach now. But on the left, just behind the chancellor, were the carved capitals of architectural columns, each depicting a scene from the Bible. She would finish those now, the scenes from Genesis already sketched in with grisaille: the expulsion of Adam and Eve from the Garden of Eden; the murder of Abel by the treacherous Cain; the drunkenness of Noah. Even as she painted, though, she still couldn't get Teddy out of her mind.

Work on the face, then. The chancellor's broad-chinned

face. The Virgin Mary looked down to the infant Jesus on her lap, but the chancellor looked straight across the center of the picture plane, with the hard, shrewd eyes of a man who sees right through you, assessing, judging. Maybe she'd taken that aspect too far. Maybe it needed softening, maybe we needed to see how the chancellor was capable of private laughter, even quiet charm. Yes, mix the flesh tone, set to work with a fine brush. A man of principle, the chancellor. Perhaps more mature than judgmental. The nose could be a little longer. The chin still broad but less so. She was sure she'd done the hair right, but it felt wrong, now. That monkish bowl cut couldn't be right. Leave it, though, and work instead on the nose, the lips, the eyes. She painted faster now, with confidence and vigor, losing herself in the task. Yes, work some more. A tiny hint of buried mischief ought to be there, held in check but present nonetheless.

Ida closed her eyes. She feared that if she opened them, she'd discover how much careful work she had just undone. She feared that instead of Chancellor Rolin she'd been painting Teddy. She opened her eyes and saw that the situation was more troubling still: she'd been painting Tom.

19

Hélène huffed as she hustled back and forth in the narrow kitchen that jutted out behind 27 rue de Fleurus, tarpaper-roofed, ramshackle, and low. She worried about Miss Toklas, worried almost as much as Miss Stein, whom she hadn't seen so quiet and despondent since...well, ever, really. Not even when she was Mr. Leo's mousy little sister. Her mind ran through a thousand scenarios for Miss Toklas's fate, imagined through the lurid covers of pulp novels of crime and adventure—*Fantômas, The Phantom of the Opera*, Jules Verne, or any of the others she read in her room at the end of a long day's work. No, no, she shook her head as she stoked the potbelly stove—Miss Alice is not with Captain Nemo. You are not an imbecile, and you know better than that. She will be home. And this bread will be burnt if you leave it on the cast-iron grill much longer. Butter it up and get some jam. The last of the strawberry stuff, thick with seeds and far too sweet, sent from Miss Stein's aunt in Baltimore. If anything will cheer her that will, eh? Hélène arranged a tray with the grilled, crusty bread, jam, and a large cup of coffee. No milk, no sugar—she couldn't convince Miss Stein to take it properly and had long since given up. There, she thought, folding a napkin into a clever looping flower. That will make her happy (no, no, nothing will make her happy, and you're a fool to try with a childish trick). Hélène bit her lower lip, as she always did to stop herself from crying. You are not prone to hysteria like Miss Stein's friends, shouting and laughing and crying whenever they wanted to. Think of the nuns at school and what they would say if you let yourself blubber every time something vexed you. Steady on. Hold fast. Steady. She balanced the tray on one hand, held high, while she stoked the stove with another bit of kindling, turned, and opened the door to the foyer. Up the stairs carefully, round the corner, tray held high, face without expression. She stopped in front of the bedroom door and knocked twice softly. Nothing. Another knock was answered by a muffled groan from inside. Hélène gave an instinctive bob of the head and left the tray on a small table outside the door.

The coffee cooled. The shadows slowly grew shorter, and enterprising black ants discovered the sweetness of Maryland strawberry jam before the bedroom door opened and a pair of feet in sturdy sheepskin slippers made their slow way up the corridor and down the stairs. Gertrude crossed the landing and stood in the doorway to the salon, which spread before her, as quiet as a fairground when the last laughing children have gone for the night, the season, the year. She folded and unfolded her arms, her purple silk dressing gown rustling softly. To the great oak library table that served as her desk, then. She will write and writing will absorb her and if she is absorbed she won't really be here or anywhere at all and if she isn't anywhere she isn't anybody and if she isn't anybody she isn't anybody who hurts. She sat and took a sheet of her square writing paper from a wooden box, then reached for a pencil and let the words flow down onto the page. They came that way, down the arm from some part of the brain she never paid much attention to. If she tried too hard to see where they came from, then they wouldn't come at all, and even if she did, it would ruin the surprise of seeing them manifest on the page, her pencil a magician's wand conjuring she knew not what.

Alone, her pencil wrote. *Alone is…* Her hand paused. Gertrude set down her pencil, crumpled the paper in one hand, and left it on the table as she paced up and down the room. If that's what the wand conjured, she wanted no part of it. She wanted no part of anything or anyone but Alice. Gertrude paused in front of a typewriter on its low Italian sideboard, where Alice so often sat on a piano bench commandeered from the spinet across the room. A stack of Gertrude's square paper, scrawled over with her handwriting, lay to one side of the typewriter, propped up on a Chinese lacquer box so Alice could see it better when she typed. She'd just started on this one, Gertrude noted, looking at the sheet in the typewriter: *Four Saints in Three Acts*, read the title. The libretto Gertrude wrote for sweet little Virgil Thomson, with his Kansas City drawl. Poulenc first brought him here one Saturday and the young man had practically swooned when Satie played his *Gymnopedies* on the spinet, so softly no one in the room dared to so much as breathe. He and Alice—swooning both. Alice loved when someone played that well, shutting her eyes and swaying, sometimes hugging herself in quiet ecstasy—though she never touched the spinet anymore herself.

Perhaps typing would absorb her, thought Gertrude, sitting at the piano bench. She looked at the sheet, where Alice had dutifully typed:

> Steps and portal of the cathedral, the latter closed off by a small curtain.
>
> CHORUS: To know to know to love her so.

That wouldn't do at all, not at all. Besides, she couldn't type. She stared at the keyboard, surprised to find the letters were not in alphabetical order. Was that a French thing? Gertrude looked up, let her eyes wander over the paintings crowding the walls. There, Picasso's portrait of her, with the face of stone, the penetrating eyes—look at that one a while. Her old courage-giver. Look at that and then look like it, just as Pablo said you would. Gertrude rose and paced the room again, eyes wandering from canvas to canvas, searching for…for what? For Alice, of course. Strange to think she'd never noticed that among all those paintings not one showed Alice's face. Two of the best showed Gertrude, but for Alice? Nothing. It felt wrong. It never had before.

20

It came as an immense relief to Ida when the tin clock she'd been staring at indicated it was 8:30 in the morning, finally close enough to the time she had agreed to meet Tom to get up and ready herself to go to the café across the street. She had slept only in snatches, tossing and sweating on the narrow bed alone. What could have happened to Teddy? What would happen to her without him? And—she shot a look at her van Eyck panel, now turned to the wall—what had she done to Mrs. Rawling's painting? Rising with dread, she tilted the panel back and looked more carefully. Oh, it was bad, what she'd done. The figures from Genesis were good, she was sure of it, but the man in the picture wasn't Chancellor Rolin at all, not anymore. But she couldn't think of that now, had to pull herself together and go meet Tom. Ida combed her hair, put on a dove gray dress with an embroidered waistband—she needed to look her best to plead with Miss Stein—then carefully donned her Breton hat and slightly dingy gloves, and headed out.

Down the stairs and out the door—motion helped, it gave the illusion of some sort of progress, some sort of agency. The worries of the night had been terrible, and the worries of the day were troubling in different ways—how would she confess to Miss Stein that Teddy had lied about being a detective, and then beg for help?

Tom was already sitting at a little table outside the café, dressed in a light gray suit, trilby hat, and yellow vest, somewhat pessimistically carrying an umbrella on a day that promised more sun than cloud. He'd already ordered a small pot of coffee, which sat on the table along with three cups and saucers. Tom saw Ida, stood, and followed her gaze to the cups on the table. "Oh dear," he said. "I was sure Teddy… He's not upstairs?"

"He didn't come home yesterday, or last night." She tried to sound brave.

In return, Tom tried to sound reassuring, remarking on how artistic men often have irregular habits, especially in Paris, especially Americans, who often feel as if they've suddenly been set free. And he'd once been a student here himself, you know. Ida was sure Tom didn't want to sound as disapproving as he did. His left eye was squinting a bit; she noticed he did that when he wasn't comfortable with the conversation.

The waiter arrived with three croissants. Ida couldn't eat, so Tom didn't either. They drank their coffee in silence, until she noticed Tom looking across the street toward the Alsatian's shop. "Would you like to go there?" she asked. "We have a little time before we call on Miss Stein."

Tom looked abashed. Surely cheese should be of no concern at a time like this, but he was leaving for London today, and that Camembert in the window looked very promising indeed. "If it isn't too selfish of me to delay us..." For just a flickering moment, Ida saw something of Teddy's readiness for adventure in Tom's expression. He left payment on the table; then Ida took him by the elbow, insisting that they cross the street and go into the shop.

Their visit to Martin's shop was a mixed success: Tom left without Camembert—something about it not having "the right knock"—but he seemed very pleased with his purchase of an Alsatian specialty, Tomme des Vosges: a foot-wide wheel so hard Martin the shopkeeper joked that they could use it to sharpen knives. "No need to wrap it," Tom said, hefting it with satisfaction. Ida left with nothing but a civil, though firm, reminder that the rent was due for the rooms upstairs. She would have to find time to stop in at the Western Union office and hope that Mrs. Rawling hadn't forgotten to wire the promised allowance. Tom made no mention of Ida's embarrassment about the rent on the walk over to twenty-seven rue de Fleurus and followed Ida's lead in not talking about the missing Teddy. He filled the silence with tales of his own student days in Paris, hoping to imply that Teddy's absence was likely just the result of youthful high spirits and poor judgment.

As Ida and Tom entered one end of the passage to Stein's courtyard, a figure walking toward them stopped short at the other end, hesitated, turned back, then turned again and waved hello. It was Marinetti, in a dark suit, fedora, and overcoat, as magnificently mustachioed as ever.

"Good morning, Mr. Marinetti!" called Ida. "Are you coming or going?"

"Ah…just coming to see if Alice has returned, and, if not, to offer comfort. But just now I thought perhaps I should not come empty handed but bring flowers. I see"—he looked at the great white wheel of cheese tucked under Tom's arm with the word *Alsace* stamped on it in bold red—"that you have brought your own gift for Miss Stein. So, I must rush off and find one to bring myself."

"Not at all," said Tom. "This is my own cheese, a personal indulgence. But won't you come in with us?"

Marinetti looked uncertain until Tom rang the bell. The cook, Hélène, answered the door and escorted them to the salon, taking the men's hats, Marinetti's overcoat, and Tom's cheese and umbrella, then saying Miss Stein would be down shortly. When Hélène disappeared to fetch coffee, the three sat in awkward silence. Ida was positioned across from that Picasso painting with the cello—or was it a guitar? She understood it better now, or at least imagined she did. All those maddening, disoriented angles didn't let you know where you stood in relation to things. And that was certainly how she felt now, with Teddy gone, Alice a missing enigma, rent due, and the prospect of confessing to Gertrude that Teddy had lied to her about matters of great importance—perhaps matters of life and death. The point of Picasso's painting was that it wouldn't let you settle. She understood that now, and looked away, feeling a little unwell.

Marinetti, Ida noticed, seemed nervous too. And Tom kept glancing into the foyer at the heavy oak hall stand where Hélène had stowed his umbrella and cheese. They were saved from having to make conversation when Gertrude shimmered into being in the doorway in sandals and a purple caftan. She seemed weary, distracted. Apparently, Ida wasn't the only one losing sleep. "Three bodies in three chairs at nine. Simple multiplication, illustrated," said Gertrude, her voice flat, emotionless, as though she felt the obligation to offer wordplay and witticisms, but hadn't the heart for it. She nodded to Marinetti and Tom, then looked at Ida. "Has your husband anything to report?" she asked with something like hope in her expression. "The police have been impossible."

The anticipation in Gertrude's pallid face made what Ida had to say that much harder. "No," said Ida, "but there is something I must tell you."

Gertrude hurried from the doorway to sit on an ottoman near Ida's chair. She'd never seemed so small before. "Yes? And?"

"Teddy…doesn't have as much experience as he may have led you to believe. In fact, he…is not really a detective. He likes to make things up. He should never have got mixed up in this. And now he's gone missing as well."

All vestiges of hope vanished from Gertrude's eyes. She didn't just seem small, now; for the first time she seemed old, and when she spoke her voice was old and small too. "You let him lie to me—"

"Yes." There it was. "I was wrong. And now I need your help."

Gertrude stood, collected herself. No longer old, no longer small, she glared at Ida with the same mask-like face Picasso had depicted in his portrait of her. "And how? And why? And what could you want from me?" Gertrude's voice rose as she spoke. Hélène appeared in the doorway, watching.

Tom looked at Ida, ready to respond if she could not. But Ida managed to speak. "I fear Teddy and Alice are missing for the same reason, and I wonder if there's anything unusual you may have noticed—anything Alice did or said." Gertrude glowered, and Ida hastened to add, "I mean no disrespect. We both have a problem, and the police have been no more useful to me than they've been to you. We must rely on ourselves."

"But Alice did nothing unusual, not since… Well, Cocteau tells me she put on something of a display at the salon." Gertrude paused. "And I suppose she did, when she went on and on about George Antheil. I thought nothing of it at the time."

"Maybe that's it. Maybe he's involved somehow. But Alice said Antheil's in Africa until…when?" asked Ida.

"Antheil"—Gertrude waved a hand dismissively—"is not in Africa." Marinetti looked up in interest, as did Tom. "I didn't listen to all his talk of pianolas and tubes and wires and aircraft engines, but I do remember he planned a little publicity stunt. He would tell everyone he'd gone to Africa, and the music was going to play itself, no musicians, no conductor—then he was going to show up at the concert and surprise us all. Knowing George, he wanted to see the crowd looking appalled and confused at the modern racket."

"So where is he, then?" asked Marinetti, leaning forward in his chair.

"Oh, the catacombs," said Gertrude. "He mentioned he'd hole up underground somewhere in Montmartre—near that restaurant the impoverished Hungarian count owns, the place Boski likes. You really think Antheil can help us?"

"I have no idea," said Ida, "but I'd like to find out. How do people even enter the catacombs?"

"Haven't a clue." Gertrude shook her head. "Ask André Breton—his Surrealists love to poke around underground, among the bones. I'm sure they know all sorts of ways in and out."

Ida felt a chill. She had heard of the catacombs, and the prospect of wandering alone in a labyrinth of skulls and bones was not a welcome one. Could she do it? Was she a fool to imagine she might?

"I will accompany you!" It was Marinetti who came to Ida's rescue, rising to his feet as he did, moving an arm as if tossing a cavalier's cloak over his shoulder.

It took Tom only the briefest moment to envision the gallery of his ancestors, all of whom expressed misgivings. No, such an expedition would not be prudent: he had a train to catch, then a boat, and another train. He had business in London. He had a wife, holed up with her nerve doctors in the country. St. Louis notwithstanding, Tom was an Eliot of the Boston Eliots, and as such had no business whatsoever poking around in a French catacomb with another man's wife. He looked at Ida, who was twisting the strap of her handbag, summoning her courage. He looked at Marinetti—for some reason wondering if he too were a married man. Tom stared down his ancestors with an awful daring and sprang to his feet. "I will go too," he declared. "London can wait."

In that ethereal hall of portraits, a monocle fell from an ancient Eliot's eye and pinged as it bounced off the floor.

21

K*uchisabishii,*" said Sam, shaking his head at Sandy's suggestion they stop at a patisserie on their way back to the apartment for a couple of *croquembouches* or a cheap *mille-feuille.* "You've got it again." *Kuchisabishii* was one of the words his Japanese father used in the letters he'd send to Sam at that horrible boarding school in Indiana. It referred to the feeling you had when you were no longer hungry, but (as his father, ever the poet, explained in a bold, calligraphic hand) your mouth felt lonely. Sam had the opportunity to use the word frequently ever since he and Sandy arrived in Paris a few months ago. Short, mop-haired, mustached Sandy was already thickening in the middle from the glories of French baking, and his faded denim shirt pulled apart a bit at the lowest button.

"Okay, then." Sandy smiled as he leaned against the railing above the small park at the tip of the Île de la Cité, his back to the breeze coming from the river. "But we've got to move on—I'm tired of looking at this hunk of pig iron." He nodded at the statue of Henri IV on horseback looming above them. They'd spent the last few minutes debating whether it was the work of Giambologna or Francavilla. In the end, they decided it didn't matter, concluding that it was just the sort of statue Sandy's grandfather made back in Philadelphia—"something heroic," Sandy had said, "for pigeons to shit on."

The two men headed south across the Pont Neuf toward the Left Bank, pausing in front of a milliner's shop to admire the sculptural shapes of the hat blocks. "It's a shame they'll be covered with those bulbous, feathered hats," said Sandy, shaking his head. Sam agreed: the best shapes in Paris, the most truly artistic, were always the ones you were meant to overlook—a rack for drying wine bottles, say, or the clever iron latches on those boxy green bookstalls along the Seine. The pigeons knew better than to shit on anything as beautiful as those.

They followed the rue Dauphine south to the rue André Mazet, a narrow lane that sprouted off the broader street at an angle like a slim twig growing from the trunk of a mighty oak. Their boots nimbly dodged the gutter's stream of foul-smelling liquid, stepping lightly to avoid the odd clump of horse dung and the reeking refuse flung out the front door of the butcher's shop. This was a workingman's street, and on a good day it smelled of sawdust from the carpenter's shop—but today was not a good day. Five flights up to their shared garret took the wind out of them at first, but also gave them some distance from the foul odors of the street below.

Sam turned the old iron key, then shouldered open the sticky door with a hard shove. They probably didn't need to lock the place, he thought—only the most stubborn of thieves could get this sticky door open, lock or no lock. But still—he and Sandy valued what was inside, even if it looked like nothing more than a pile of rubbish to the ordinary eye. Two cots stood at either end of the low-ceilinged room, one neatly made up with a scruffy old blanket, the other a jumbled mess. A chamber pot stood guard in one corner, and a small square window let in a sallow shaft of sunlight. The landlord had informed them they could dump the chamber pot into the street below if they did it at night. Indeed, by doing so, said the landlord, they would be participating in a proud tradition of the *Rive Gauche* dating back to the Middle Ages, when students slept beneath garret roofs. When the landlord left, Sandy had declared this tradition a good reason not to swoon too much over the past.

But neither cot nor pot concerned them now. Their attention turned immediately to the stacked materials that filled almost every inch of the tiny room. Coils of ropes, collections of wire in various lengths, tin cans scavenged from the trash, loops of rubber hoses, and coffee cans filled with nails and unidentifiable bits of hardware—all had been carefully assembled around two huge suitcases, which lay on the floor with their wide sides up beside the strewn inner workings of a disassembled Victrola. Sam took off his boots and sat cross-legged on the floor. Sandy produced a pair of metal shears from somewhere in his pockets and set to work cutting an oblong from a foot-long piece of corrugated tin.

Sam mused for a moment over a length of floppy rubber tubing. "Do you think we can pull it off when the day comes?" he asked Sandy, who was almost too lost in his work to answer.

"Dunno," Sandy replied after a moment. "Depends if we can get all the performers coordinated."

"Well," said Sam with a thin grin, "you're the puppet master. So all that is up to you."

Sandy hummed as he worked—the song "Ramona," by Dolores del Rio. At the chorus Sam joined in. They worked on quietly for hours as the daylight from the window faded.

"Patisserie?" asked Sandy, looking up at last. "This time of day it'll be half price."

22

A crisp breeze at their backs, Tom, Ida, and Marinetti made their way north from the rue de Fleurus toward the Bureau of Surrealist Research. If Breton wasn't there, perhaps one of the other Surrealists could point them toward an entrance to the catacombs. As they walked down the broad, tree-lined boulevard Raspail, Ida spied the Western Union office just across the street. It seemed strange to have to stop in at a time like this, when she was on a desperate mission to find Alice and her missing husband, but Ida still needed to see if Mrs. Rawling had wired the money that she'd need to pay the rent. There was no avoiding the shopkeeper who collected it for the landlord: he stood like a sentinel at his counter all day and could see anyone going in or out. She asked Tom and Marinetti if they'd mind waiting while she went in. Tom agreed politely; Marinetti nodded and reached for his silver cigarette case. The two men settled on a narrow green bench as Ida disappeared inside the Western Union building.

The Western Union office functioned as an outpost of America and presented itself as such. A cheap print of *Washington Crossing the Delaware* hung on the wall next to a National League baseball schedule. Somewhere in back a typewriter clattered, while its operator whistled a ragtime tune to the machine's jagged rhythm. A ceiling fan spun lazily overhead, suspended on a long brass pipe from the impossibly high pressed-tin ceiling; clerks in shirtsleeves and bow ties drank large cups of watery American coffee and chatted behind a broad wooden counter with frosted glass dividers while the stars and stripes hung in furled glory from a flagpole in the corner. Ida approached the counter, gave Teddy's name to the clerk, showed her passport to indicate that she was his wife, and asked after Mrs. Rawling's wire transfer. Yes, it had come through, she was told in a broad

Brooklyn accent—just that morning. Could she have it in cash? For small sums like this it wasn't a problem. The owlish clerk, his round-lensed eyeglasses balanced on his forehead, wet a finger and began counting out a small stack of francs. He paused mid-way through. "Theodore Caine, you said—your husband?"

"Yes. Theodore Caine—Teddy."

"Mel!" the clerk shouted without looking up. "D'we get a telegram for a Theodore Caine? Goes by Teddy?"

"Nope. But hold on…there's this." Mel, portly in a tan sport coat, picked up a small slip of paper from a wire basket on his desk, stepped up to the counter, and placed it in front of his colleague. The owlish clerk slid his glasses down onto his nose and squinted.

"This ain't for no Mr. Caine," said the clerk, shaking his head. "This is *from* Mr. Caine. For an Ida Caine." He looked up at Ida over his glasses. "That you?"

The floor dropped out from under Ida. She recovered her footing. The floor moved again, like the deck of a storm-tossed ship, but she recovered, fumbled in her handbag for the passport she had just put away, and held it up, open to a blank page. "I'm Ida!" she gasped.

"I guess I shoulda known." The clerk smiled sheepishly. "Telegram for you." He slid the paper across the counter. Ida stood rigid and silent. "No charge," he added.

Ida picked up the slip and read:

ARRIVED WITH JAY STOP NO ANTHEIL STOP NO LIONS EITHER BUT SUNSHINE AND ROAST LAMB STOP NEXT TO TUNISIA STOP CAN FIND A DRINK HERE IF YOU CAN FIND A FRENCHMAN STOP YOUR TEDDY

Ida read the words again. And again. None of it made sense. Well, one thing did—Teddy was alive. She hadn't known until now how strong her fear had been that he wasn't. She exhaled, then nodded, and, holding the telegram in both hands, turned to leave, walking as if in a dream. The clerk had to call her back to collect her money, still sitting on the counter.

"Is there any way to tell where this was sent from?" Ida asked. The clerk pointed to a line typed above the main text, next to a series of numbers. *Western Union/Algiers, Algérie Française* it read, along with a street address that meant nothing to her. She shook her head slightly and read the words once again. George Antheil might not be in Africa—but Teddy certainly was, with Jay. Why hadn't he said something before he left? How could it have seemed right to him, to run off with no notice—without packing a thing? Why go there anyway? To find Antheil—the same quest she was on now? And how had he managed to get there so quickly? That last one she could answer: they must have flown in Jay's airplane, the two of them buffeted by winds in an open cockpit all the way across the Mediterranean.

"Help you with something, miss? I mean, Mrs. Caine?" asked the clerk. Ida had been standing in front of him for some time, telegram in one hand, slim stack of banknotes in the other.

"Could I send a telegram?" she asked.

"Next station," said the clerk, motioning down the counter with a jerk of his chin. Ida sidled over.

"Mel!" barked the clerk, again without looking back. "Customer!"

Mel heaved himself from his chair and up to where Ida stood. "Telegram. Right." He took a form from a box beneath the counter and a stubby pencil from behind a shiny ear. "Who to?"

"To my husband—but I don't know where he is."

"That'll be a problem," said Mel. "Want to try the office that sent this one?" He pointed to the original telegram, still clutched in Ida's hand.

Ida skimmed Teddy's telegram again, then looked over at her other hand, the one holding Mrs. Rawling's money. "Yes. No... to Tunis. And Algiers. Both. How much does it cost?"

Mel tapped the counter where a piece of glass covered a sheet of paper listing the schedule of fees. Western Union charged by the word. As Ida scanned the sheet she ran a quick calculation in her head, then ran it again. Never before had concision seemed such a remarkable virtue. She left Mel with a simple message to cable to Teddy, care of the Western Union offices in Tunis and Algiers:

EXPLAIN STOP IDA

She thought for a moment of adding the word "love" before her name to indicate that Teddy's disappearance had changed nothing between them but decided against it. She told herself she needed to be careful with money.

Outside, Marinetti was preoccupied with trying to light a new cigarette from the dying embers of an old one, while Tom gazed intently at the wheel of cheese that he'd purchased at the shop that morning. He looked up and rose as Ida approached, and after a slight, confused hesitation, Marinetti stood as well, half leaping, half bowing in the process.

"For the life of me," said Marinetti as Ida approached, "I cannot decipher your expression. I don't know whether to congratulate or console you, or perhaps both."

Ida silently passed Teddy's telegram into Marinetti's hand. He read the message, looked to Ida for confirmation, and passed it to Tom. "So, Teddy is—well?"

Ida nodded. "And in Algeria. He must have flown in Jay's aircraft. They were together the night before. It's a relief, but also terribly puzzling. I sent a telegram to him in Algiers and in Tunis." Ida frowned, adding, "But why wouldn't he tell me before he left?"

"Perhaps he tried?" said Tom.

Marinetti stood silent for a moment with his unlit cigarette forgotten in his hand. Then he stroked his mustache and spoke. "What is the expression in English? 'High spirits?'—two young Americans and an airplane... I would think nothing of it. He will return. Let us continue on our way, happy to know the man is safe, and on his own adventure."

Ida was by no means prepared to think nothing of it. "Teddy said he was going to see Lewis at the Ritz with Jay. We—I—I think we should talk to Lewis."

"God knows where Lewis is," said Marinetti. "He's probably

gone back to London." He motioned for them to continue down the boulevard Raspail toward the Bureau of Surrealist Research on rue de Grenelle. "Shall we?"

"We must press on, for Alice's sake. Lewis and the Bureau are both important priorities," said Tom, "but neither should come before something to eat. You could eat now, couldn't you?" He addressed his question to Ida, who was suddenly ravenous. A few steps brought them to a small bistro with black-and-white checked tablecloths, connected to an equally tiny hotel. In a few moments Tom and Ida tucked hungrily into mushroom omelets, delicious on chipped plates. Marinetti ordered the same, but only toyed with his food until they resumed their journey. Once again, Tom paid *l'addition*.

As they approached the unassuming exterior of the Bureau of Surrealist Research, Marinetti grew visibly uncomfortable. Tom dropped back, motioning for Ida to do the same. He leaned his head next to hers, whispering as they continued toward the Bureau, "He's a Futurist—doesn't get on with the Surrealists. The radical right versus the radical left."

"And you?"

"A monarchist from St. Louis. Implicitly Surreal, some would say. Just cast an eye on any king's regalia and you'll see at once that they have a point." Ida smiled, thinking of Hyacinthe Rigaud's portrait of Louis XIV, now hanging in the Louvre. Here indeed was a Surrealist king, laden with white lace, white ermine, and golden fleur-de-lis—a man of great gravitas in Flemish hosiery, high heels, with a luxuriously curled wig that rose like a forested mountain from the top of his head.

"We go in, then?" said Marinetti, gesturing to the door. Tom nodded, and Ida strode forward to lead the way.

23

The Bureau of Surrealist Research appeared unchanged since Ida's last visit except for one detail. The same long table held the same books and pamphlets, the same uncanny photographs—the family group fascinated by the empty mantelpiece, the woman horrified by an egg—hung on the wall, and the same desk sat in the center of the room, once again with Gabriel and Marcel in their shirtsleeves, this time seated shoulder-to-shoulder. Opposite them, though, with her profile to Ida, sat a striking young woman—no older than her, perhaps younger—in a black sweater and skirt, her eyes dark and her bobbed hair darker, her nose long, her chin strong, and her mouth, which seemed to be suppressing a smile, almost as wide as Ida's. The woman was playing chess on two boards, beating Marcel soundly on one of them. It was hard to say who was winning on the other board, Gabriel or the young woman—there were no squares, and all of the pieces were red. All three chess players turned to face Ida and her companions at once, swiveling in unison.

"Comrade Ida!" belted Gabriel, rising from his chair, while at the same moment Marcel's eyes riveted on Marinetti and two astonished words escaped his lips—"You! Here?"

Marinetti raised his right hand in something between a Roman salute and a sign of surrender. "I am not! That is, I am…here. But this is not as it appears." Marinetti struggled for words. "I do not condone Surrealism! The unconscious is the soft dream of…ah, of soft dreamers. I am here strictly to increase the efficiency of a mission."

Marcel was unappeased, rising slowly and looking with suspicious eyes from Marinetti to Tom and Ida. But Gabriel seemed pleased. "You admit that things are not as they appear!" he said, rubbing his hands together. "This is a tremendous progression toward the mysteries of the unconscious and away from the—forgive me—infantile obsessions of your Futurism. Marcel! Quickly—the ledger!"

Marinetti, who had not lowered his right hand, now raised the left in an identical gesture, appearing as if he were someone pushing against the air. "No ledger," he said. "We want Breton."

"Do not move!" It was the dark-haired young woman who spoke, now standing with something in her hands. "Monsieur Marinetti—do not move!" Marinetti immediately raised his hands higher, into a more definite gesture of surrender, and the woman snapped his photograph with a collapsible camera. "You may resume and thank you very much." She sat down, still wearing the same curiously amused expression as before.

Marinetti slowly lowered his hands, looking slightly sheepish.

"Comrade André is not here," said Gabriel, "just Marcel, me, and Comrade Dora. Comrade Dora, meet Comrade Ida. You know Marinetti, of course."

"And this is Tom," Ida said, "known to the public as Mr. T. S. Eliot, the American poet." A brief scramble ensued, as various bodies navigated around the table and hands were shaken, much to the relief of Tom, who had feared Marinetti's hand gestures and the use of the term "comrade" presaged a series of politically radical Franco-Italian salutes, for which Tom simply did not know the etiquette. Handshakes were quite enough for him while keeping his grip on both an umbrella and a wheel of hard Alsatian cheese.

Marcel, who appeared a bit distressed by the bourgeois formalities of these greetings, spoke when the shuffling scrum of introductions subsided. "But why do you want Comrade André?"

"It's not him in particular we need," explained Ida. "We have to find a way into the catacombs, and Miss Stein told us Breton or his comrades here at the Bureau might know the way."

"Of course, we can help," said Gabriel, quieting Marcel with a sharp glance. "We help all of those who participate in our research." He took a step toward the visitors. "Best if we divide into pairs. Comrade Dora, perhaps you will accompany Comrade Ida to the back room. Marinetti, you will come—"

"With me!" blurted Marcel, cutting off Gabriel. "And you may assist Comrade Tom." Tom winced at the appellation but felt great relief that no one else one seemed to notice.

Dora gestured toward the door that led to the back room, and Ida followed—an old hand now at the ways of the Surrealists, or so she thought. Except for the fact that its dimensions were similar, the room that greeted Ida beyond the door could not have presented a starker contrast to the bureau's outer room. Overflowing bookshelves covered two walls, rising to the ceiling and groaning under the weight of countless ancient tomes. Another wall seemed like a shrine from an unknown religion founded by a deranged explorer or archeologist—wooden statues from Africa crowded brass Buddhas and plaster saints; a tribal shield and two whaling harpoons formed a kind of coat of arms; a huge painting depicted kidney bean shapes in what Ida thought of as cow-barn red; Chinese embroidered cloths hung like banners from the moldings; and a small shelf held a menagerie of tin toys—elephants and tigers as well as a complex mechanical bird and a monkey with a drum. In the middle of the room a heavy, ornately carved table held two metal boxes and a pair of enormous brass candlesticks, arrayed as if on a strange altar. Two surprisingly simple chairs completed the tableau. Dora sat in one and gestured to the other, but when Ida pulled the chair back from the table, she found the seat was already occupied by a shockingly white human skull.

"Oh, don't mind him," said Dora, as Ida's eyes widened in alarm. "It's just the Comte de Villiers de l'Isle-Adam. He was one of us before we existed. Just put him anywhere."

Ida hesitated. But if she was going into the catacombs, she couldn't let a single skull put her off. She picked up the skull, sat down, and, deciding she'd rather not look at the thing, held it in her lap. No, she thought, this is worse. But she'd made a choice, and something about Dora made Ida want to seem decisive. The skull stayed.

"My comrades knew you when you came in," said Dora, still wearing her mysterious half-smile. "You have been here before?"

"I wrote a dream in their ledger," said Ida. "They put it away without looking."

"You wanted someone to look?"

"I thought that was the point."

"Surrealist research is for the one who does the research," Dora explained. "Not for Gabriel or Marcel, nor even for Breton. For you." She gave Ida a sympathetic look, adding, "but you can tell me your dream. Do you want to?"

Ida did indeed. It seemed somehow important to tell someone. "It was...about an egg. A very large one, sitting on the floor between Chancellor Rolin and the Virgin Mary in a van Eyck painting. The egg was about to hatch." She recounted the rest of the dream.

Dora nodded when Ida finished. "I dreamed about a seashell," she said, "and wrote about it in the ledger. Like your egg, the shell was very large. A woman's hand came out of it, as if reaching for something...I don't know what." Dora looked directly into Ida's eyes. "You see, then—we are much the same."

Ida wasn't sure what Dora meant—if anything, she and Dora seemed entirely different. She couldn't even place Dora's accent, which was not native French. "May I—may I ask where you're from?" asked Ida. "Your French is so good, but you're not from here, are you?"

"No. I am Czech by birth. We lived here in Paris when I was small, but I grew up in Buenos Aires. My father, alas, was the only architect not to grow rich in that city, so we came back to Paris. Like you, then—I'm from the new world."

Buenos Aires didn't seem much like the American Midwest. But something about Dora tugged at Ida. "And then you became a Surrealist?" Ida was sure Dora was younger than she was.

"I study at the Académie Julian, which has one great advantage—they teach women the same things they teach the men. But for them art is merely decoration. When I met Breton at the Café de la Place Blanche, he showed me that art is not different from knowledge."

"And you just…became a Surrealist?"

"Surrealism is a conversation. I take part."

Ida stopped herself from asking the question that seemed to force itself upon her, a question that could not quite find its way into words. It had something to do with permission. It had something to do with what Ezra Pound said in the salon about how Picasso had painted Gertrude with a masklike face because the Fauves were interested in color and he wanted to be noticed. It had something to do with…a hatching egg, or a woman's hand reaching out from a shell.

"You like van Eyck?" Dora asked the question idly. She was opening one of the table's two boxes with a small brass key.

"I'm painting a copy of one of his works," Ida replied. She felt slightly ashamed to say so.

Dora brightened. "Then you must go to Ghent, in Belgium," she said. "Van Eyck painted the most extraordinary altarpiece there. The heavens above, the world below. Gabriel says it is Surrealism *avant-la-lettre*, but what I like most are the birds. High in a corner of one of the panels. I saw them when the panel was taken down for cleaning. No one can see them when the panel is hanging properly. So who do you suppose he painted them for?"

Not for Mrs. Rawling, thought Ida. Before she could form a better answer, though, Dora continued. "Now," she said, closing the box and laying two decks of cards on the table, "how much time do you have for research?" One stack of cards was twice as tall as the other.

"We must get to the catacombs," said Ida, suddenly conscious of the skull in her lap.

Dora tapped the shorter stack. "The major arcana, then. Shuffle the deck as long as you wish, then please turn the top card."

Tarot cards? That two-bit trick of carnival women who dressed up as gypsies and told greedy men they would grow rich and lonely women they would marry? Ida always thought the practice was absurd, but somehow a room like this one and a skull in one's lap made a concern with absurdity seem irrelevant. She shuffled the cards quickly, turned the top card and placed it before her. Small, grubby, well used, and certainly antique, the card's faded colors showed a woman standing over some sort of large dog. From Ida's perspective, the image was upside down, so she picked the card up for a closer look. No, not a dog, it was a lion—the woman holding it gently by its head. The woman on the card seemed serene, and smiled ever so slightly, the way Dora did. The symbol of infinity floated over her head like a halo. Ida squinted to read the text, written in strange letters. *Forteza*, perhaps? She put the card down so that it faced up from her perspective. Dora shot an expressive eyebrow upward.

"That card," said Dora, "is you. Inverted, it means one thing, but you picked it up and turned it, now it means another."

"What is it?" asked Ida.

"Weakness, discord. Disgrace. Until you turned it. Now it's courage, or fortitude. Turn another."

Ida turned another card. A woman in blue robes, a curtain of some sort behind her, a pillar on each side. "What is it?" she asked.

"As the second card, it shows what you most desire. This is a very ancient card, *La Papesse*. The female pope, Pope Joan. She dressed as a man and sat on the throne in Rome. Turn another. This one will reveal what you fear."

Was this how the carnival fortune-tellers did it? Ida turned another card: *La Lune*, two dogs baying at the moon.

"Conspirators who move in the dark," said Dora. "Now turn three more."

Ida turned, in succession, a card with Adam and Eve in a garden beneath a benevolently smiling God; a card depicting a man in robes standing before a table of unidentifiable objects; and, finally, a card showing a great stone tower shattered and in flames.

"The lovers," said Dora. "That is your strength—you have a husband, yes? Or a man who has taken an interest?" Ida did not reply. She was trying to see Teddy as her strength, but nothing quite came into focus. "And this man," Dora continued, pointing to the man in front of the table, "he is *Le Bateleur*, your nemesis—he has many tricks, and knows how to deceive."

"And what is the tower?" asked Ida.

"The outcome. The result."

Ida stared at the card for a moment. Lightning rent the structure at the top, and a figure in blue—a man or woman?—plummeted from the crumbling tower. It was not a reassuring image.

"What does it all mean?" Ida spoke in wonder, all her skepticism about carnival trickery evaporating under the intensity of Dora's gaze.

"That is what you must now write in the ledger," said Dora, rising and taking Ida firmly by the hand.

24

Ida rose from her chair and followed her companion to the door. *She* must interpret the tarot cards? This wasn't how it went with sideshow fortune-tellers, that much Ida knew; that sort told you whatever made you feel your money was well spent. Dora said that Surrealist research was designed to benefit those who availed themselves of it. Maybe that was why Marcel had snapped the ledger shut so quickly after Ida had written her egg dream in its pages—what was it to him, but a note in an archive? And what would she write now, after seeing the tarot cards? So lost was Ida in this maze of thought that she walked to the door with the skull of the Comte de Villiers de l'Isle-Adam in her right hand, her fingers in the eye sockets as if she held a bowling ball.

Dora cracked the door open, peeked into the room beyond and, looking back over her shoulder at Ida, whispered, "I think they're almost done now." From her vantage point behind Dora, Ida could just make out Tom at the table, hunched over intently with a hand outstretched to touch something she couldn't quite see. Dora closed the door quietly, cutting off the view before Ida could make it out properly.

The two women stood facing each other, eye to eye. They were of a similar height, though only because Dora wore Cuban heels and Ida's walking shoes were prudently flat. "How..." began Ida, trailing off when she realized she couldn't quite give form to what she wanted to ask. "You said you are a Surrealist? I mean, you yourself?" she said, feeling slightly foolish.

Dora smiled and tipped her hand to the side in a gesture that, though unfamiliar to Ida, seemed to say that she allowed that she was.

"And was there a..." Again Ida paused. She had wanted to

say "course of study," thought better of it, considered "application process," but again it felt wrong.

"There's no initiation ritual, if that's what you mean." Dora sounded amused. "It's not one of your American sororities."

Did Dora really think of her as a college girl? Ida both wanted her to, and didn't. She thought of books and art and the bespectacled lecturer from Harvard who talked about the Renaissance at the Art Institute. Then again, there were also the Lake Forest debutantes chatting at summer's end in the cake shop before packing off to Northwestern or Lawrence or Oberlin. Ida had always looked down on that particular sort of rich girl, the kind intent on studying nothing so much as how to put themselves in front of the right young men.

Dora studied Ida for a moment, then added, "They are very welcoming, the Surrealists. If they like you, they'll claim you before you volunteer, won't they...Comrade Ida? And then all you have to do is assume they were right." There was that smile again. "Sometimes you don't need to do anything at all—they claimed your friend the comte, and he'd been dead for years." Dora tapped twice on the forehead of the skull. Ida blushed and put the skull back on the chair where she'd found it.

Suddenly Géricault's *Raft of the Medusa* tossed on the seas of Ida's imagination, the figure waving for help dropping his cloth, diving into the sea, and swimming toward the ship he'd seen in the distance. No need to wait for rescue. On to salvation under one's own power, through the waves. Just go. Dora would swim for it, wouldn't she? Indeed, isn't that what Dora had already done?

Dora, who'd put her ear to the door, looked up. "I think they're done." The two women entered the front room, where Tom was writing intently in the ledger with a sharp pencil, his tongue between his teeth like a concentrating child. Gabriel sat across from him, beaming as if watching a favorite student. The determined part in Tom's slicked-back hair reinforced the impression of a schoolboy, thought Ida. She was certain Tom had gotten straight As, probably at Harvard.

Tom laid down his pencil, and both men looked up at the women. "But where is Marinetti?" asked Ida.

"They must be almost done by now," said Gabriel, looking toward the closet where Marcel had shown Ida the phosphorescent cover of the Surrealist's journal. Tom, Ida, and Dora looked too. In the quiet, they heard a moment of indistinct but agitated whispering, then the door flew open, and Marinetti and Marcel spilled out in a tangle of limbs, Marinetti's face red with fury.

"Please write in the ledger," said Gabriel, rising to offer the pencil and his chair to the Futurist.

"I will take no further part in your absurd games!" bellowed Marinetti, his hand cutting a line in the air in front of his chest as if drawing a border that must not be crossed. "*Una follia ridicola!*" he added, drawing the same line in the opposite direction. A bead of sweat glistened on his forehead. He strode toward the door that led to the street.

Marcel glared at the retreating Marinetti and spoke firmly. "But I must insist."

Marinetti halted, pivoted on the heel of his gleaming black shoe, and fired off a glare with the force of an artillery barrage. "*Che cosa?* What do you say?"

"I must insist," repeated Marcel, icily. "The ledger!"

Gabriel handed the open ledger to Marcel, who in turn passed it to Marinetti. Marinetti did not sit, but instead drew a gleaming black fountain pen from his jacket pocket, scrawled a quick word or two into the open ledger, then slammed it shut and flung it onto the desk. He looked toward Tom and Ida, saying, "I'll wait for you outside," before marching to the door, struggling with the suddenly uncooperative doorknob, and storming out to the street with a slam.

"Your turn now," said Dora, nudging Ida and giving her a friendly push toward the table. It felt as if she were a friend encouraging Ida to climb on a diving board and leap into icy water. Tom stood and offered his chair to Ida, who sat, then opened the ledger to a fresh page, and reached for Gabriel's pencil. Through the thin paper Ida could see the reverse image of the words Marinetti had scrawled in luxurious ink: *annulla cronologia!* He had underlined it twice, shaking a fat drop of ink loose from his pen in the process. It had soaked through and stained the page where Ida now must write.

And what would she put down? Was it supposed to be a story, like a fairy tale, with a moral at the end? The woman with the lion, sent on a quest by *La Papesse* to save the lovers from *Le Bateleur*, so they could live happily ever after in the tower? Or was that too childish? Was she supposed to write about the ancient symbolism the cards had accreted over centuries? What did she know except what Dora had told her?

"Don't worry—no one will read it." It was Dora, placing a hand on Ida's shoulder and whispering in her ear. When Dora stepped back, Ida drew a breath and began to write.

Conspirators stalk the lovers, she wrote. *The lovers seek Pope Joan, who's gone away. The burning tower...*

Here Ida stopped. The pressure to interpret had traveled down her arm to her hand. She pressed too hard, snapping the pencil's lead. Holding the pencil up and indicating helplessness with her eyebrows, Ida looked to Gabriel, who made a silent "oh" with his mouth, extended his index finger, and made for the back room. Before he could return, the door to the street burst open, and Marinetti stormed back in.

"We," he said, clutching his fist to his chest, "must go!" He cast his arms forward, as if to release imaginary birds from his hands. Not doves, thought Ida. Eagles, maybe, or ravens. But certainly not doves.

"But we haven't been told a way to the catacombs," said Tom.

"You already have a map. We gave it to you," Marcel said, in a steely voice.

"*Bene!*" Marinetti recaptured his birds. "*Andiamo!*" He released them again, pulling Ida from her chair and lurching out the door with her. Tom, who had kept his umbrella at his side, scooped up his cheese from the table, tucked it in the crook of his elbow, and followed, looking concerned. As their visitors departed, Gabriel looked bemused, but Marcel simply shrugged and snapped the ledger shut.

"See here!" said Tom, firmly, racing to catch up with Marinetti, who was all but dragging Ida down the street. Marinetti turned with a blank look, then seemed to deflate a little.

"*Scusa, scusa*—I apologize," he said, more to Tom than to Ida. "It's these horrible Surrealists. I cannot abide them. I will never return to that…that charnel house." He turned to Ida, releasing his grip. "Forgive me, *bellisima*. But—you have a map already? And you didn't say?"

"But I have nothing!" gasped Ida, at a complete loss.

"Nor I," said Tom. "What could Marcel possibly mean?"

"His tone tells me he's not interested in explaining," said Ida.

"And I will listen to no explanation," said Marinetti, crossing his arms like an angry toddler. "None."

"So, they gave neither of you anything, either," said Tom. The three began to walk more slowly down the street.

"Unless," said Ida, thoughtfully, "the research we did was a clue, or in fact the map itself. What did they have you do, Tom? If I may ask?"

"Ouija board," said Tom, shaking his head. "I put a hand on a little wooden triangle, and Gabriel did too. I sensed he may have tugged it where he wanted it—it spelled two words."

Ida couldn't imagine Tom with a Ouija board, but he had apparently indulged Gabriel. "What was the message?" she asked.

Tom looked at her with raised eyebrows. "Sea change," he said. "Maybe part of me—an unconscious part—guided my hand without my knowledge," he admitted uneasily. Noticing Marinetti's visible disgust, Tom explained. "The words had some importance to me when I was writing one of my poems a few years back."

"And you endured this—this chicanery?" blustered Marinetti. "Talking to the putrid spirits of the dead?"

"Oh," said Tom, with a hint of a smile. "Ouija is more Billy Yeats's thing, but I talk to my own ancestors more than

I'd care to admit. It's never anything quite like what happened with that board just now—that's an experience which I won't be repeating." Somewhere in the gallery of Tom's ancestors, a thin-faced woman glanced up from brooding, her pursed lips relaxing so slightly that only her most intimate associates would recognize it for the thaw it was—her disapproval of the occult melting ever so slightly away at Tom's expression of reluctance to commit future indiscretions.

"Sea change?" said Marinetti, shaking his head. With his arms still crossed, the impression of a frustrated child only increased. "What is the meaning?"

"A sea change is a transformation, slowly wrought by the ocean on things lost there," said Tom. "'Those are pearls that were his eyes.'"

Lines from *The Tempest*. Ida knew that. Marinetti either didn't or didn't care. He shook his head with increased energy.

"They showed me tarot cards," said Ida. "Nothing like a map among them."

Tom turned to look at her with interest, but it was Marinetti who spoke. "We have nothing," he said. "Nothing. And I will not go back."

"What did they have you do?" asked Ida, looking at Marinetti.

"Eh? Ah. The same." Marinetti waved a hand, as if brushing the question away.

"Which the same? Tarot? Ouija?" asked Ida.

"The. . .ah. What do you say in English? Same as the French. *Séance*. It was nothing. Parlor tricks for the morbid. And in a closet! Buffoons!"

The closet! A memory tugged at Ida—they had, in fact, given her something. "I was in that closet before," she said. "They gave me a copy of their journal, a special one whose cover glowed in the dark."

"That may well be it!" said Tom.

Marinetti agreed, adding a few grumbling remarks about gimmicks and mountebanks. Ida patted his arm soothingly.

"The journal they gave me is back at my rooms," said Ida, glad of her flat-soled shoes. "Gentlemen, we have some walking to do."

25

Walk? Walk? *Stai scherzando!* I will not walk a single step," declared Marinetti, "until I have a drink to wash the foul taste of Surrealism out of my mouth." Ida thought better of pointing out the irony when Marinetti immediately followed his refusal to walk with a full-speed march down the street, looking left and right for the nearest drinking establishment. Tom and Ida trailed behind the accelerating Futurist, who was surprisingly fast for a man of his years. When Marinetti came to the end of the street, he looked to his left, then pointed, as if about to shout "Land Ho!" from the crow's nest of a galleon. He disappeared around the corner, with Tom and Ida struggling to keep up. Soon, Marinetti was waving them through a doorway like an irate crossing guard, and the group found itself ensconced in a tiny establishment named, simply enough, Bar Americain. The dim room couldn't have been six feet wide and was dominated by a zinc stand-up bar behind which loomed shelves of bottles arrayed in tiers to the ceiling. Marinetti barked for red wine, and the expressionless bartender set out three glasses and poured. He then fished behind the counter and produced a small dish of unshelled peanuts—a gesture designed, Ida assumed, as a show of American authenticity. The crushed shells on floor indicated that this was a very popular snack, or perhaps that the staff took a cavalier attitude toward cleaning.

"Are you quite certain," said Tom slowly, "that the map in question is in, or is part of, this journal you have?" He was seated between Ida and Marinetti, and while he addressed his words to Ida, he watched the agitated Marinetti out of the corner of his eye.

"No," said Ida. "I'm not at all certain."

"But was there anything in it, anything at all, that looked promising?" Tom asked. Marinetti had finished his wine and was signaling the barman for more.

Ida squinted, tried to envision the journal the Surrealists had given her when she'd first visited the bureau, while picking up items from Teddy's reading list. It seemed like such a long time ago. *La Révolution Surrealiste*—that was the title, she remembered. But what else? She pictured the journal with its cardstock cover—maybe fifty pages, and about the size of a sheet of typing paper—between her hands. "The cover was phosphorescent," she began.

"Legerdemain—the work of frauds!" said Marinetti, his voice simmering with contempt but not quite rising to the level of a shout. His hands crushed the lapels of his jacket as he spoke.

"And inside," asked Tom, "any images?"

"Several," Ida recalled, looking at Tom. "There was a picture of a Navajo doll from New Mexico."

"So that's it," grumbled Marinetti. "We enter the catacombs from D. H. Lawrence's ranch in Taos. Book us passage on an ocean liner, dear Ida, if you will."

"Surely," said Tom, giving Ida a sympathetic look, "there were more…"

Ida closed her eyes and tried to recall. "A line drawing of a cluster of fellows in workingmen's clothing," Ida remembered. "Some smoked cigarettes, one had a gun…there was a child, too, I think…and a distressed-looking gendarme. The scene had a title…*L'armé du Crime.*" She opened her eyes, adding, "But I don't recall any monument or building in the background. Also, there was a picture of a painting by Giorgio de Chirico…quiet streets…" Ida could see the image clearly now in her mind. "With a clock and a cannon. But it wasn't a real place, I'm sure of it—everything about it felt like something from a dream."

"Typical," spat Marinetti, shaking his head, then emptying his glass. "Surrealist Freudian decadence. And to think de Chirico could have been one of us! He had his chance." He wiped his luxuriant, curving mustache with the back of his hand. This brought another image from the journal to Ida's mind, a drawing of circus ringmaster's whiskers, but she didn't bother to mention it. No mustache, no matter how distinguished, would help lead them to the catacombs.

"Was there text?" asked Tom. "Perhaps that would provide a clue."

Ida, who had merely leafed through the journal, could remember only a few striking phrases, mostly titles: *Les Dragons de Vertu; Le Point Cardinal* (could that be it?); *Philosophie des Paratonnerres.* She had to look up that last word in Teddy's French-English dictionary. It meant lightning rods—but they were to be found on rooftops, and an entrance to the catacombs would take you down, not up. "I'm sorry," she said, "but nothing stands out. I'm afraid we'll have to go look." She thought of the little stack of books by her bed with Marinetti's manifesto at the bottom of it, as if imagining it could somehow help.

"Unless the map wasn't in the journal, but was something else the Surrealists gave us," said Tom. "The words 'sea change' won't do us much good, unless the catacombs are in the ocean. Was there anything the dark-haired girl showed you that could help?"

La Tour, La Lune, La Papesse... "No," said Ida. "If there was anything, I didn't understand it."

"And my séance with Marcel was simply blather," said Marinetti. "So let's settle up and go." He stood, then started for the door as Tom signaled the barman. Ida was torn for a moment—she didn't have money to spare, but Tom had been taking care of all expenses without a peep of complaint, and his continued generosity seemed to invite an interpretation of their relationship that Ida couldn't quite name, and couldn't fully condone—could she? To convince herself the answer was 'no' she reached into her green handbag to draw some francs from the sheaf of banknotes she'd received at the Western Union office. Her hand found something else as well, though, and she drew it out. It was the small card Gabriel had given her at the police station. She'd forgotten all about it and looked at it now for the first time: a most curious object.

"Wait!" Ida called out after Marinetti's retreating back. "Here's something else the Surrealists gave me." Marinetti stopped, grunted in assent, and turned. Ida, now standing between the two men, laid the card on the bar. It was slightly larger than a business card, she noticed, made of the same heavy stock as the cover of *La Révolution Surréaliste*. Instead of an address, the card bore an image of a triangle, with a number marked in each corner—eighteen at the top, seven in the lower left corner, and four in the lower right. Above the triangle hovered the small image of an eyeball, with lines radiating from it in all directions. Inside the triangle were letters: along the left side, near the top, a tiny *C. de P. B.* and, lower down, the initials *C. S.* On the lower right side a tiny *L infâme* was written. More important looking text was written outside the triangle, at each of the corners. *Les portes de l'enfer*, at the top, *La tour de fer* on the lower left, *La prison de maître* on the lower right. Tom and Marinetti leaned in to examine this cryptic icon.

"They are too fond of riddles, arcana, and conjurer's tricks, these Surrealists," said Marinetti, glowering.

"If this is a map," Tom looked up to Ida, "I confess it bewilders me."

Ida's mind raced. The three numbers added up to twenty-nine—a number of no significance to her. *L'infame*, though… hadn't she recently heard those words? And who were C. S. and C. de P. B.? The Comte de something or other, perhaps. But not the unfortunate comte whose skull she had recently carried like a gruesome bowling ball: that poor fellow had other initials.

"Let us spare our legs," said Marinetti, picking up the card and examining it closely. "Before we set off after the journal, perhaps we must consider the possibility that this card itself is the map—my dear *donna Americana*, how did you get it?"

"Gabriel gave it to me when I was leaving the police station," she said. "He was there to pay Marcel's fine." That was it! She pointed to the word *l'infâme* on the card. "Marcel was in custody because he'd been caught painting the words *écrasez l'infâme* on the wall of some church."

"Paris is full of churches," said Tom. "Bless it. Do you remember which one?"

Ida tried to recall. Saint…something. Definitely saint something. Which was no help at all.

"The phrase *écrasez l'infâme* is a noble one," Marinetti intoned solemnly, placing a hand over his heart and standing taller. "It dates to the Revolution, when the French were men and hated the putrid faith of their fathers. The words refer to no particular church. They refer to Catholicism itself, with its accretion of…of accretions." Marinetti paused and made a glass-tipping motion to the barman, who returned with a fresh glass and filled it with wine.

"*Les portes d'enfer* means 'the gates of hell,'" said Ida. "That's the closest thing on here to the entrance to a catacomb."

"Farfetched, farfetched," said Marinetti, draining his glass between the first and second iterations of the phrase. He turned on his heel, stared at the wall, and turned back, as if pivoting on an axis. He breathed in deeply once, then again—a weight lifter preparing for a mighty feat of strength. He looked at Ida, eyes keen. "We must have a map of Paris—barman!" Marinetti pivoted again, in the direction of their server. "Barman! A map of Paris!" The barman turned his palms up, in a gesture of helplessness.

"I have a map!" said Ida, suddenly realizing that the guidebook she'd toted daily to and from the Louvre had a city map of Paris. She pulled the book—almost comically small—from her bag, opened the front cover, and began unfolding what turned out to be a remarkably large, and deeply creased, map of Paris, printed in pinkish ink with the parks marked in green, and a pale blue river bisecting the city. When Ida tried to spread it over the bar, Marinetti grabbed the guidebook and ran off toward the back of the establishment. With Ida and Tom in pursuit, Marinetti suddenly halted at one of the two round tables in the back of the room, and set the map down next to the glass lantern that lit the space dimly.

"Gather!" Marinetti roared, poking the map with his finger as if impaling it, "and look!" Paris sprawled below them in miniature. It bore no resemblance to the card's triangle. "You see? You see!"

Ida did not see. Nor, to judge from his expression, did Tom.

"*L'infâme!*" Marinetti stood bolt upright, his right arm stretched out, the finger that had only seconds before stabbed at the map now pointing to the heavens. "*L'infâme!* If your imagination was as poor and rotten as that of the degenerates who conceived this…this puzzle"—he held the card up in his left hand, holding it close to Tom's face, then Ida's—"what church would you consider the primary church of Paris?"

A name popped into Ida's head—the church Marcel had desecrated with paint. "Saint-Joseph-des Carmes!" she called out in triumph. Marinetti looked at her blankly.

"Perhaps…" said Tom, trying to spare Ida's feelings, "perhaps, indeed—but many, I think, would envision the Cathedral of Notre Dame." He looked at Ida with soft eyes, as if about to pat her on the hand.

Marinetti had no patience for Ida's contribution. "Notre Dame! Yes! *L'infâme* itself." He reached into his jacket for his fountain pen, shook it to make the ink flow, and circled the cathedral on Ida's map. He could have asked before defacing it, she thought.

"Eleven," said Tom. "On the card it's near the corner with the eleven. Does that signify anything?"

"It's the number of the district," Ida chimed in, eager to redeem herself. "The cathedral is in the fourth arrondissement." Before she and Teddy had left Lake Forest, she'd gone to the library and looked at books about Paris. One had a brightly colored map of the different arrondissements of the city, arranged in a kind of spiral of ascending numbers. She'd thought it funny, that spiral—the French capital city was organized like a gigantic escargot. Marinetti looked at her in appreciative surprise. For a tiny moment Ida liked him a bit more. "Where on the map," Ida asked, "is the seventh arrondissement?"

Marinetti pointed with his pen to an area west of the cathedral. The most prominent words on that portion of the map were *la tour Eiffel.* "The iron tower," he said, in wonder, "*la tour de fer.*" Marinetti looked closely at the card, then at the map. He held his finger up to the bottom of the triangle, noting how far the side extended, then put his hand on the map, noting the distance between Notre Dame and the Eiffel Tower. He ran a quick calculation in his head, then reached into his jacket pocket again and pulled out a small leather case. Opening it on the table, he revealed the contents: a gleaming nickel-plated compass, protractor, ruler, and a tiny pair of calipers. In answer to Tom and Ida's unasked question, he said, simply, "We are Futurists—we work with machines, blueprints." He shrugged, then said, "It is the way forward for us all."

"The eighteenth arrondissement is up here," said Ida, pointing to an area north of the cathedral and the tower. "Montmartre, or thereabouts."

"And the prison—*la prison de maître,*" said Tom, "could it be the Bastille? It's in about the right spot."

Marinetti swiveled around twice, then clapped Tom on the back with a mighty blow. Tom winced as Marinetti boomed out, "Precisely, sir! Absolutely correct! The Surrealists celebrate the decadent imagination of de Sade, who was held for many years in that edifice!" Marinetti seemed ready to dance or break out with a marching song. Instead, he bent over the map with his ruler and calipers, referred back to the card, then to the map again. After a moment, he spoke once more. "If the proportions are correct," he said, "*les portes de l'enfer* must be here!" He pointed to a street in the eighteenth arrondissement.

"But what about these other initials?" asked Tom.

Ida peered around Marinetti's looming bulk to look more closely at the map. "C. S. is where the Bureau of Surrealist Research is…and the sign outside said *Centrale Surréaliste:* C. S."

"So...these aren't people, but places?" asked Tom. "Then what is C. de P. B.?"

"The festering center," cried Marinetti, striking the table with his fist, sending his calipers flying to the floor, and causing the flame in the table's lantern to sputter. "The Café de la Place Blanche—where Breton holds court with his lackeys and sycophants. It's not far from the Bureau. Not far at all!" He struck the table again, and this time the candle in the lantern went out. In the shadows at the back of the Bar Americain the phosphorescent words on the Surrealist's card glowed faintly: *invitation aux catacombes*. For a moment, the trio stared in silence.

"We still have some walking to do," said Ida, "but now in quite a different direction."

"To the gates of hell!" shouted Marinetti in triumph, rushing for the exit, then halting abruptly and returning to retrieve his calipers.

26

Marinetti, though older than his companions, proved to be a tireless trekker on what Ida soon came to view as a forced march onward to the gates of hell, a hike that often left her and Tom trailing some distance behind. Marinetti's limbs moved stiffly, like a wind-up automaton, but he made good time, despite an unfortunate habit of reaching an intersection ahead of his companions, abruptly turning a corner and disappearing from their view, then reappearing moments later, striding purposefully in the opposite direction. Finally, Marinetti came to the front of a nondescript gray building and stopped abruptly. A small brass plaque by the doors read *Compagnie D'Assurance Moreau.*

"We have arrived," announced Marinetti, as Ida and Tom pulled up beside him, puffing. Tom produced a small comb from his pocket and fussed with the part in his hair.

"Yes, but where?" asked Ida. The gray building and an unassuming tobacconist's shop were the only businesses on a block of featureless apartment buildings.

"Our destination," said Marinetti, but without a great deal of conviction. Even the arm he raised to indicate the gray building rose and fell without his usual panache.

"Then what should we do? Dig down to the catacombs?" asked Tom, a rare note of irritation in his voice. Ida noticed Tom had introduced a slight unevenness in the back of his part, thought of reaching out and fixing it for him, but thought better of it. Behind Tom, something at the next intersection caught her artist's eye. Color. A red every bit as bright and glossy as the one van Eyck had used for Mary's robes.

"The map, woman!" commanded Marinetti, extending an open palm toward Ida and dragging her attention back from the intersection and that intriguing flash of red. "That is…

if you please," he added, in what appeared to be an arduous attempt at conciliation. He radiated impatience as Ida fished the tiny guidebook out of her pocketbook and passed it into Marinetti's large waiting hand. He struggled with the fold-out map as it flapped in an unpredictable breeze, while Ida raced to the intersection, where she pulled up short, gasped, and turned to race back to where Tom was now assisting Marinetti in trying to hold together the now wind-torn map.

"Gentlemen," Ida announced, "I believe I have found—" But she did not finish her sentence. Marinetti had just ripped her folding map from the guidebook, crushed it into a ball, and hurled it down into the gutter.

"Bourgeois!" he cried, kicking the map. "Sentimentalist!" he continued, crushing it under his heel purposefully. "There"— he pointed to the Compagnie D'Assurance Moreau—"lies our destination." He strode to the door, gave the handle a mighty yank, and discovered that the door was locked.

Steady on, thought Ida. Paddle through the rapids. "Gentlemen," she announced again, louder, "you may wish to come with me."

"Now? When we are so close to our goal?" asked Marinetti, incredulously. "Tom, have you had occasion to learn the art of lock picking?"

Tom did not dignify the query with a reply and looked instead to Ida. "What have you found?"

"Only the gates of hell," she said. Marinetti, still bent over the lock, released the door handle from his grip and rose to stare at Ida. Tom looked impressed, and both men followed Ida to the intersection. There, just around the corner on the boulevard de Clichy was an astonishing sight. It was a building unlike any Ida, Tom, or Marinetti had ever seen. Three stories tall, it was topped with battlements like a castle, a small tower protruding from the top, the stone walls below painted a glossy red. On the second story an elaborate frieze depicted winged demons laughing maniacally while hurling a woman, nude but for scant drapery, into an inferno. The ground floor was stranger still: grated windows went almost unnoticed next to a pair of red doors surrounded by the huge, open mouth of a horrible goblin with a snub nose and enormous eyes, his fangs forming a grim archway over the entrance. Above the hell-mouth a sign in lurid letters read, simply, L'ENFER.

It presented quite a composition, thought Ida—stranger and more lurid than anything she'd seen at the Louvre. The van Eyck red of the glossy paint gave her a twinge, and something told her she must get back to her own painting. She had Mrs. Rawling's money in her pocketbook, enough for now if she was careful—yet she felt it was urgent that she return to painting. But why? And why now? The answer seemed to flutter in the air, like the birds van Eyck had painted in the Ghent altarpiece that Dora had told her about. Then it was gone.

"This…edifice," said Tom, quietly, "may well be what we seek." Marinetti grunted in assent and sped toward the doors, while the others hurried to catch up. Marinetti was just about to reach for the doorknob when Ida called for him to stop.

"Look," she said, pointing to a small placard near the door:

L'Enfer (Hell)

Cabaret Unique au Monde

Tous les Soirs de 8 h ½ à 2 h du matin

Fermé le dimanche

Attractions Diaboliques

Supplice des Damnés

Etc.

Liquers et Sirops

A. Alexander, Directeur-Administrateuer

"For tourists," scoffed Marinetti, pointing to the English word *Hell* in the first line, "shedding the inhibitions learned in church."

"And they won't open for three hours," added Ida. "What do you propose?" One look at Marinetti's expression prompted her to add, "Surely not breaking in…"

As it turned out, there was no need to batter down the

doors; one of them suddenly popped open and a man wearing red and black Renaissance hose and doublet emerged, grasping a plumed cap in his hand. A bent cigarette dangled, limp and unlit, from his lips. He squinted at Ida, Tom, and Marinetti and said, in a flat voice, "Show's tonight—you here for dress rehearsal?" Adding, when they hesitated, "Half price."

After Tom paid for the trio's admission, they discovered the scene inside exceeded the exterior in strangeness: a low, dim black corridor led to a vaulted room whose ceiling teemed with plaster demons in attitudes of gleeful sadism, tormenting the damned with pitchforks, whips, and wickedly curving scimitars. Small tables clustered around the room's perimeter, each with a black candle casting a wavering light. The room was unoccupied, except for a table where a pair of German businessmen quaffed glasses of lager. A sallow young man dressed as Mephistopheles pushed a broom across the floor. "Anglais?" he asked, looking at Tom's suit. "Sit anywhere," he continued in an Irish accent before they could respond. "Kitchen's closed, but we can do you a consommé."

"We are not here for soup," Marinetti announced, his hand cutting a line in the air. "We are here to enter the catacombs."

"Pity. Consommé's very good here," said the Irishman, pushing the broom before him as he left the room. With no other recourse apparent, Ida, Tom, and Marinetti took seats at a table.

A moment later they were approached by the man in Renaissance costume. "We have brimstone—that's whiskey—or we can make you a 'soul-of-the-damned' cocktail…a favorite of our American guests. It's mostly gin. Two drink minimum at night, but for the rehearsal it doesn't matter." Tom ordered damned souls all around. Ida was about to ask about the catacombs when Tom silenced her with a hand on her forearm.

"Look," he whispered, "the show's beginning!"

It was indeed: the Irishman had wheeled a coffin on a gurney into the middle of the room, and another man, dressed all in black, climbed in. The Irishman went off to a corner of the room to adjust a large horizontal mirror, and then gave a thumbs-up to the man who had taken their order, who nodded and disappeared into the back. He emerged moments later to distribute drinks, and then stood by the coffin.

"Ladies and Gentlemen...*mein herren*...lost souls in jeopardy," he called out, without much enthusiasm, "behold, as the deficient soul meets his most fitting fate!" The man in the coffin smiled broadly, then stifled his grin and tried to affect a look of terror. A puff of smoke poured in from somewhere, eerie music played on a tinny phonograph, and the man vanished, replaced by a skeleton. Tom turned to grin at Ida. Marinetti gripped the table with both hands either in fear or moral outrage.

"Enough!" roared Marinetti, leaping to his feet. "Where is the manager?" The Renaissance man with the bent cigarette approached them rapidly, motioning for quiet.

"Sir, please, we—" the manager began.

"Take me to the catacombs!" roared Marinetti, his hands twisting an imaginary pepper mill.

"But you are already in hell, as you see—"

"We're looking for catacombs, the real ones. The Surrealists, you see—" said Tom, in a conciliatory tone.

"Ah, I see. You want upstairs," said the manager. "The poet Desnos has a studio on the top floor."

"No, we want to go underground," insisted Ida, holding up the card Gabriel had given her and displaying its symbol. The manager's demeanor changed instantly.

"I see. Flynn!" called the manager. "See that they settle *l'addition*, then take these people to the catacombs. There's been a misunderstanding." He glared down at Tom, adding, "No refunds on admission, and you'll need candles—half a franc."

Moments later the Irishman led them down a flight of stairs to a room full of theatrical scenery, papier-mâché devil's horns, and a half-scale guillotine. He gave them each a black candle and waited while Marinetti fumbled with his matches to light them. "Through there." The Irishman pointed to a heavy oak door, on which someone had chalked the same triangular symbol they knew from Gabriel's card. "Mind you, don't go far. The Surrealists come in large groups—that helps drive away the rats and brigands. You might find both."

Marinetti pulled the door open and plunged into the darkness beyond. Tom and Ida followed. The heavy door swung shut behind them.

27

The engine gave a lusty lion's roar as the biplane swept down toward a runway on the desert sand. The sun shook its golden mane and smiled on the pilot and his companion—or so it seemed to them, elated as they were when the airplane came to a stop outside the Quonset hut that served as a hangar at this little airfield outside Tunis. The two men leapt down from the pair of open cockpits that sat one behind the other. On the ground they pulled goggles off to reveal pale patches on their otherwise sunburnt faces. The pilot, shorter than his passenger, pulled off the white silk scarf knotted round his neck. He shrugged off his heavy brown leather jacket with its sheepskin collar—perfect for the cold of elevation, stiflingly hot in the blast furnace of desert wind. The other man was taller and wore an overcoat more suitable to city life than the chill atmosphere above or the heat below. He fished in his deep pockets, produced a flask of whiskey, and nudged the pilot, who took a deep swig before passing it back with a smile. Teddy received his returned flask with a similar grin and drank deeply. Oh, he was writing now, he thought. Adventure like this, and the words will surely follow soon enough. His smile dimmed a bit at the thought of a typewriter on a desk in a dusty room somewhere. But he felt certain the words would come soon enough.

Jay, stiff after the long flight, walked slowly toward the corrugated metal Quonset hut and Teddy followed, removing his overcoat and draping it over a shoulder. There was nothing for him to do: Jay would arrange for his plane to be looked after. It was a gray Curtiss JN-4H, with curving exhaust pipes and the word *Frieda* painted below the cockpit in cursive script. Jay loved the aircraft as he loved no one and nothing else. He would recite its technical specifications in loving detail to anyone who would listen, and a man with his kind of money always found someone willing to listen, if only in exchange for the drinks Jay was happy to provide. He had paid a Frenchman in Algiers for the flask Teddy carried for him. He would pay, too, for whatever accommodations they found in Tunis. It was good to travel with someone, especially someone a bit younger, and dependent on him for all expenses—such conditions allowed Jay, whose older brother had flown in the war, to play the senior sibling for a change. He punched Teddy playfully on the arm and grinned. Footloose in Paris days ago, now dashing across north Africa with a detective from Chicago, of all people: this was freedom to Jay. His father and brother be damned.

"When we get to town, I'll check all the big hotels," said Teddy. "If Antheil's there, we'll find him."

"All right," said Jay. "And then we should hire one of the locals to take us into the desert on a couple of camels. When in Rome..."

Teddy nodded and rubbed his chin. It was a shame he'd managed to grow only a little stubble; with a full beard, he could have looked like a pirate or a sheik. Still, the thought of the photo of himself wearing a keffiyeh scarf while riding camelback pleased him immensely. It would look fantastic in all the papers when his book came out.

"After we've bathed and gotten up to whatever they get up to here with hookahs and harems, we'll move on to Tripoli!" said Jay. "Get my bags down from *Frieda* while I square things with the locals. Tripoli—then Cairo, what do you say?"

Teddy beamed, his heart pumping yes, yes, yes. The journey would take a little longer than he'd reckoned, but he'd wire Ida again from Tripoli. Or Cairo. Anyway, she'd appreciate more time to paint without him pestering her to come out and play. He must remember to have her send along some of old Mrs. Rawling's money—can't let Jay buy every round.

Alice watched a yellow smudge of light work its way slowly

across the stone floor, just as she had the day before. Except for the half hour or so when she observed two mice race around the perimeter of the room, then scuffle together—were they fighting or making love?—there was nothing else to watch. Her wrists were still bound, though at least they were in her lap rather than behind her back. And someone—she doubted it could have been Lewis—had left a thin mattress for her while she slept. The mattress helped sometimes with the pain in her spine, though it had come back now, a feeling something like fire and something like needles. Her ankles were bound as well, so her options were limited to sitting propped up against the wall or lying down. She'd tried lying on one side, then the other. She told herself the shifting helped a little, and sometimes it did.

Lewis came in twice a day to leave bowls of polenta and water. Seeing the wound that she'd left on his face was Alice's only true satisfaction in these degrading circumstances, where a grate in the floor served as the lavatory and any standard of hygiene was impossible. Nights were long, and not without terror: she thought she heard scurrying rats and wondered how she would defend herself if they grew bold. Days were long too.

Yesterday, when the sun-smudge had reached the biggest of the cracked, reddish flagstones, Lewis came in. And today here he was again, right on schedule.

"Fresh water," he said, slopping the contents of a clay pitcher into the bowl Alice had lapped up earlier. There was never enough water. Lewis loomed above and glared down at her. Part of her didn't want to look, but then there was the wound to consider. Yes—it wasn't healing very well, and that was something to lift her spirits.

"Look all you want," said Lewis, icily. "It doesn't mean a thing. You do understand we'll have to do something about you because you know who I am." He turned and left the room, slamming the door behind him.

In the next room, Lewis sat down at a wide, makeshift table—boards stretched over two step ladders. Technical diagrams were strewn over the surface, along with lengths of copper wire, pliers, carpenter's pencils, and an envelope bearing the logo of the Paris Ritz. Lewis picked up this last item, opened it, and read the note on a card within. He chuckled bitterly and returned the paper to its envelope. That bitch Alice may have had at him with a glass shard, but at least the other bitch, the American from the salon, was suffering for how she'd humiliated him. Humiliation was worse than pain, worse than disfigurement. She had to pay. Oh, she was paying even now—he was sure of it.

28

Rats and…brigands? Had the Irishman really said "brigands"? The word struck Ida as archaic, even comical—had the fellow been joking? It was impossible to tell. Rats were to be expected down here, but what other dangers might they face? Ida looked at her companions, holding their flickering candles aloft in the surrounding darkness. If set upon by bandits, murderers, or any other sort of criminal, their arsenal consisted of Marinetti's calipers, Tom's umbrella, and Ida's handbag. And did they even know where they were going? Gertrude had said only that Antheil was in the catacombs under Montmartre, near a Hungarian restaurant.

"Paprikás should be south of here," said Marinetti, turning a slow circle and assessing the surroundings. "That's the only Hungarian restaurant in Montmartre, as far as I know. Now, which way is south?" Ida pointed to her left. But the only way open was straight ahead, down a narrow, dark, downward-sloping corridor of damp stone. The trio resolved to turn left at the first opportunity, with Marinetti taking the lead, and Ida the middle. Tom—who passed his cheese to Ida apologetically so he could both hold his candle aloft and carry his umbrella—brought up the rear.

The corridor continued downward for what must have been two hundred featureless yards before opening onto a chamber so large the light of their candles failed to reach the far wall. The floor was even, covered in flagstones, with a mound of some kind rising before them about thirty feet away. Marinetti beckoned impatiently and led them toward it. Ida gasped as they approached: it was a tidily assembled pyramid, as tall as Tom, composed entirely of human skulls. On the floor before the pyramid sat a small stone plaque, like a modest tombstone into which a crude cross had been gouged. Painted in red beneath the cross was a triangle with an eye above its topmost point—the same as the symbol that appeared on the card Gabriel pressed into Ida's hand at the police station. The police station? Ida felt a chill. It was as if those gendarmes belonged to another world, along with the artists at Gertrude's salon, the bored staff of L'Enfer, the Alsatian Martin at his shop counter, and van Eyck's Chancellor Rolin. None of them seemed remotely real down here. Ida felt as though she were deep under water, or no: in an empire of the dead. The whole world of the living—the present itself—was the merest froth on the surface above.

"A monument to the dead," said Marinetti, walking slowly around the pyramid of skulls, his candle held high. "It is like Paris itself, with its centuries of churches, museums, triumphal arches, and tombs. Each of these skulls is like one of the city's palaces or museums, the past, the past, the past," he said, pointing to three skulls in turn, "all piled above us—dwarfing the present, eclipsing the future! I will allow the wretched Surrealists this much. When they come here, they see what their civilization really is—a pile of venerated bones, among which the living, denying their own strength, creep like timid mice." He stooped quickly, and held his candle low, perhaps hoping for mice to emerge on cue. When they failed to appear, he stood up so quickly his candle went out. Tom and Ida listened from the far side of the pyramid as Marinetti struck several matches and cursed eloquently in Italian before managing to relight the wick.

"I quite disagree," said Tom when Marinetti's profanities subsided.

"Disagree with whom?" asked Marinetti. "The macabre Surrealists?"

"On many matters, yes," said Tom, walking slowly around the pyramid. "But at present, I mean, I disagree with you."

"But the past is death," replied Marinetti. In the darkness Ida saw movement from his direction. When Marinetti's candle went out again, she concluded that the motion had been some sort of agitated arm-waving.

Tom went on talking while Marinetti struck even more matches. "The past is not death, nor is it dead," said Tom. "The past is very much alive." Looking at the skulls in the flickering candlelight, Ida could not say she found his statement comforting. She began pacing slowly around the chamber, noticing now what must be a wall to her right and approaching it cautiously.

"I think of this sort of thing often," said Tom. "We ourselves—what are we but a moment of the past, a moment containing everything that has gone before? Take the Surrealists—don't they grow out of a rich soil? Are they possible without Rimbaud, Baudelaire, the gothic novel, Goya's etchings of his nightmares? What would they be without having absorbed all that? Merely people who bore you with tedious accounts of last night's dreams. Even anachronistic relics like the tarot deck come alive when the imagination encounters them, and, in turn, they animate the imagination of the living and give it shape. The mind of the present grows strong when it takes old artifacts and makes them new. Our personal dreams become part of a larger story, a more resonant one."

"To repeat the past is to be a walking corpse," said Marinetti, finally relighting his candle.

"Plausibly, yes," said Tom, "but the Surrealists don't merely repeat the past. Take that ledger of theirs, and the whole idea of research—they bring something new to the past. They bring what you love, my dear Marinetti. They bring a scientific spirit, a genius for analysis. Baudelaire may have unleashed the monsters of the imagination, but the Surrealists anatomize and label them. They need the past, but know their own moment too, and make the two fit together. That's not repetition, is it? They know the past in a way the past did not know itself."

Sea changes, thought Ida, as she peered forward in the dark—he's talking about sea changes. The transformation of things lost in the deep. *Those are pearls that were his eyes...*

"They make a zoo—a circus for fools and children!" grumbled Marinetti. "Any ordinary machine is more beautiful than their...their..."

"Leg bones!" cried Ida. Marinetti and Tom fell silent, their heads turning in the direction of Ida's voice. Ida had reached a wall to the north of the pyramid, a wall lined with stacks and stacks of bones. Femurs to the left, tibia to the right, if she remembered the anatomy book that she'd studied in the Lake Forest library. She bent to pick one from the floor. It was as small as a child's. She let it drop.

Tom and Marinetti joined Ida by the far wall. By the light of their three candles, they could see a patch of deeper darkness—a wide, arched gateway in the wall of bones. They passed under it, and saw a corridor beyond, running both left and right.

"Which way?" asked Tom.

"We divide and explore," said Marinetti. "Tom to the left, I to the right. Count to two hundred while you walk, then come back and report. *Cara* Ida, you stay here with this heap of soup bones."

Ida wasn't keen on being left behind but was equally reluctant to set out down an unknown corridor. She nodded, watched the two men set off in opposite directions, and began to count. Ten, eleven, twelve... Her ears strained in the darkness. At first, she could hear footsteps, then she heard nothing. Fifty-one, fifty-two... She wondered if she should extinguish her candle: its little circle of light made her feel exposed. But then she remembered that she had no matches to relight it. One hundred twenty...one hundred twenty-one... Then Ida gasped as something small scurried over her foot. One hundred sixty... What was that, down the corridor to the right? It sounded like a load of coal clattering down the chute to her father's coal cellar. And now, a shout! Another—could it be Marinetti's voice? She couldn't tell.

"Tom?" called Ida, taking a few steps down the left-hand corridor. "Tom! Something's wrong!" Beasts or ruffians, maybe—there really were dangers in the catacombs. She pictured hooded men with curving knives.

Footsteps—she heard them, coming quickly. But from which direction? From both?

"Ida!" It was Tom's voice, coming from where a tiny light gleamed down the corridor. "Are you all right?" He emerged quickly from the darkness, his candle guttering in one hand, his umbrella brandished like a sword in the other.

"Brigands!" Ida whispered, pointing down the corridor where Marinetti had vanished. "I heard shouting, and something moving, something large." Just then a scraping noise emanated from the corridor to the right, and an uneven step could be heard. One man? More?

Tom pulled Ida back into the large chamber. "Shall we go to Marinetti's aid?" His words were rushed and low.

"But...they're coming here," said Ida. "We should hide." Tom nodded, and flattened himself against the wall of the chamber, crouching low next to the archway. Ida stood on the other side, pressing herself against the damp stone. Tom placed his candle on the flagstones behind him and held his umbrella upright with both hands. Taking one last look around the chamber to orient herself, Ida blew out her light. Better to hide in darkness than to become a target...or was it?

The strange metallic scraping sound grew closer. "We may have to fight," whispered Tom. Just then Ida heard heavy breathing and knew that whoever, or whatever, was approaching had arrived.

"Now!" Tom shouted, and Ida swung the wheel of cheese with all her might.

Tom tripped the intruder with his umbrella, and as the unfortunate man fell forward, he caught the force of Ida's energetically swung hard Alsatian cheese full in the face.

It took some time to survey the damage, but when Tom retrieved his candle and helped Ida light hers, they beheld the aftermath of the brief moment of shouts and flailing bodies, and saw Marinetti prone on the floor below them, thoroughly soaked, his nose bleeding, his right foot lodged in some kind of rusted kettle. The only sound in the deep silence of the catacombs was that of a wheel of cheese rolling off into the darkness. Tom looked to the imaginary portraits of his ancestors for guidance on the etiquette of the situation and received none. This was not the sort of thing that happened in Boston.

A moment later, Marinetti sat up on the floor, catching his breath and staunching the flow of blood with a handkerchief, while Tom eased the kettle from the poor man's foot. Ida, holding a candle above the two men, thought for the first time that Marinetti looked old. It was his animation that gave him the aspect of a younger man, but he was well on into middle age, and in the candlelight, his skin looked as creased and yellowed as the newsprint on which his Futurist manifesto—now decades old—had been printed. Perhaps this explained his loathing for the Surrealists, thought Ida: they were in vogue, now, while he, a partisan of the future, was becoming increasingly a figure of the past. The pyramid of skulls behind him did nothing to diminish this impression.

"I came to a place where the floor was loose gravel," said Marinetti, in a quiet voice. "It gave way. I lost my footing, and I slid down into a stream of some kind." He bent his head to sniff at his jacket. "Not sewage, anyway. But it was filled with rubbish, and this item"—he pointed to the kettle Tom had finally detached from his foot—"attached itself to me. I made my way back and was attacked." Marinetti looked around warily, asking, "And what became of the assailants?"

"They got away," said Ida.

"I regret that we are the culprits," confessed Tom at the same moment.

"Understandable, in the confusion," said Marinetti, shaking his head. Never had Ida been so glad to have her own statement ignored in favor of one made by a man. She took this moment to look for the errant wheel of cheese. As she glanced down the corridor that Tom had traveled, she saw a single bright spot of light.

"Gentlemen—look!" she whispered. Tom and Marinetti

joined Ida, and the three peered around the corner. The light was definitely approaching.

"What did you see down there?" Ida whispered to Tom.

"A door, a yellow wooden door. I tried it, but it was locked," he whispered back.

"Come!" Marinetti whispered harshly. He covered his candle with his hand and limped as quickly as he could down the corridor, as if a bold charge would restore his wounded pride. Ida and Tom shielded their candles and hurried after.

The light in the distance bobbed up and down, so bright it had to be electric. Suddenly it stopped, and they heard a noise—part scrape, part knock. "Is anybody home?" a woman's voice sang out. The door opened and light poured out into the corridor ahead of them, revealing a young woman with bobbed hair and a miner's headlamp. She wore overalls and carried a white tureen with both hands.

"Boski!" a man's voice boomed from the room beyond. "And better yet—goulash! Come in, come in!"

29

Boski!" the voice behind the door cried—a young voice, a man's voice, a voice filled with delight. Ida knew the name Boski—Sylvia had mentioned a Boski at Shakespeare and Company, and there couldn't be that many Boskis wandering around Paris. Boski, Ida remembered, was Antheil's wife. Perhaps their quest in the catacombs was nearing its conclusion.

Boski passed through the yellow door, and it swung shut behind her, taking the pool of light with it. Ida lost no time; motioning for Tom and Marinetti to follow, she strode boldly forward, looked over her shoulder for affirmation from her companions, and knocked on the door. It was somehow less intimidating than approaching the clerk at the Ritz. But when a moment of silence followed her knock, she heard own heartbeat and wondered if her confidence was at all justified.

"Who...who is it?" asked a man's voice from beyond the door.

How on earth to answer? Antheil didn't know her, thought Ida, and he clearly didn't want visitors. She had no idea how to begin to explain why they had come or what they wanted.

"Filippo Tommaso Emilio Marinetti, artist and leader of the Italian Futurists!" boomed Marinetti. "I and my companions"—he paused, as if not sure how to complete his sentence—"come in peace!" He stood behind Ida, so she couldn't see him waving his arms during this declaration, but the sudden reduction in wattage indicated that he had somehow managed to extinguish his candle yet again. Marinetti's angry, whispered, *"Figlio di puttana!"* confirmed Ida's suspicions. She didn't need to speak Italian to understand.

The door swung slowly open. A handsome, round-faced young man with a shock of light brown hair stood before them in shirtsleeves, his dungarees held up with suspenders, a broad smile spreading across his face. "George Antheil. Congratulations—you're the first to find me," he said. "Do come in." Ida, Tom, and Marinetti stepped into a surprisingly cozy room lit by an oil lantern with a table made from a crate, two chairs, a camp bed, and several wooden boxes. Tools and spools of wire littered the floor. Boski stood at the workbench, taking the lid off the tureen she had been carrying in the corridor. A drawing of a woman—more machine than human—was taped to the wall. Ida, who was famished and whose feet hurt from walking, breathed in the aroma of the goulash and nearly swooned.

George welcomed them in, apologizing for his humble furnishings in an accent Ida decided was Philadelphian, or possibly from New Jersey. After quick, friendly introductions Boski beckoned Ida to the workbench, while George offered the chairs to Tom and Marinetti, then turned a box on end as a seat for himself.

Ida must have been eyeing the goulash like a hungry wolf, for the first words out of Boski's mouth were, "They only gave me enough for two…but we'll get you a cup of it. Come on, pretend to help me make tea for the gentlemen." Boski lit a paraffin burner, used a cup to ladle water from a bucket into a kettle, then dipped another cup into the tureen, filled it with goulash, and offered it to Ida. "So," said Boski, in perfect, lilting English, "do you come here often?"

"First time." Ida smiled, after gulping hungrily from her cup. "And you?"

"Oh, I visit George every day, but it's important to his plan that I be seen around town—he wants everyone to think he's gone to Africa on his own—my bold explorer!" She batted her eyelashes in an exaggerated gesture of besotted femininity, then laughed. "But he's helpless on his own, so I bring him dinner from the restaurant. Today, it's goulash. The restaurant's nearby, and I sometimes work there," she explained. "The old wine cellar leads to the catacombs. But what brought you underground?"

Ida finished her cup of soup. She would gladly have gulped down the whole tureen if it weren't Boski and George's dinner; and there didn't seem to be any other food in the room. "We needed to find George—don't tell, but Gertrude tipped us off," Ida confessed. Boski's brow clouded at this last revelation, and Ida hastily explained the situation—how Alice had raved on about George's upcoming *Ballet Mécanique*, then gone missing, and how Ida and her friends hoped George could shed some light on things. The men, meanwhile, sat in intense conversation, Marinetti asking questions and George responding with reference to a chart he unfurled for their reference.

"I don't know that I can help," said Boski, frowning, "and I'm afraid George is boring those poor gentlemen with technical talk—it's all he thinks of nowadays, his mechanical miracle of music. Let's not join them; there aren't any more chairs, and I can't bear to hear George go through it all again." Her expression lightened. "Don't misunderstand; it is impressive, what he's contrived—synchronized music without musicians—but you wouldn't believe how often I've had to hear him talk it out. I think the real reason he's in hiding is that he knows he'd… what do you Americans say…'spill the beans' if he was in the cafés up there." Boski shot her eyes toward the city above.

The news was disappointing, but the stew was not, especially not with hunger as a sauce. "The goulash was wonderful," said Ida, half hoping Boski would offer her what remained in the tureen.

"I'll show you to the restaurant after dear George has sufficiently fatigued your friends," said Boski. "It's a humble place, but better than any of the other restaurants where I work."

"And where do you work?" asked Ida, making conversation while George drew some lines on his chart and Marinetti measured them with the calipers he drew from his case.

"Oh, most of the time I work at the restaurants in the expensive hotels on the Right Bank," replied Boski. "Right now it's the Ritz. We Hungarians—at least those of us from Budapest—speak so many languages we're always in demand to wait tables at the international places, and since George gave up playing piano concerts to write music, we're as poor as a pair of sparrows."

"I know the feeling!" Ida wondered for a moment if working in the grand hotel restaurants might be preferable to employment by Mrs. Rawling. "Do you like working there?"

"You do get to eavesdrop, but mostly it's dull—the businessmen talk business, except when they're with their mistresses, and then they don't talk about anything. But the other day one group was talking about George! Oh, Georgie has them fooled—they were convinced he was in Africa. One of them was a writer, too: Wyndham Lewis. Do you know him?"

Ida felt all of Paris crash down on her. Lewis at the Ritz? Was this the same night he was there with Teddy? "I do know Lewis," Ida replied. "Who was he with?"

"I was working late, and he was at the bar with two Americans. I think they'd dined there earlier, and they were deep in their cups. I thought of introducing myself—I've seen Lewis across the room at Miss Stein's salon."

He might not remember you, but he remembers me, thought Ida, recalling the violence in Lewis's eyes when he'd banished her to the wives' room with Alice.

"Those two Americans," Boski continued, "one was a guest I've seen there before—typical example of the 'American abroad,' loud, happy to drink, eager to throw his money around, and with that pleasant American tendency to leave big tips. An aviator—he was always sure to mention that. I didn't recognize the second American."

"What did the second American look like?" asked Ida. Realizing she'd sounded strangely urgent, she said, "I paint—I need to see a scene."

Boski, long accustomed to artists and their eccentricities, tried to remember. "He was tallish," she paused, seeing the bar before her, "and when I brought out the dinner rolls, he took three of them from the plate and juggled them, catching one in his mouth."

Teddy. That could only be Teddy.

"At first, I thought the juggler was flirting with me—he asked for some hotel stationery, and when I brought it, he wrote a note. Some men will put their room number down and pass it to you—*cochons!* But it wasn't for me. The juggler gave it to Lewis and told him to give it to someone, a wife or a girlfriend, perhaps. The two Americans—oh, it was hilarious, and I had to bite my tongue—they resolved to drink the night away and fly to Africa to look for George at dawn! The note must have been his farewell."

"And...and Lewis took it?" Ida heard her own voice quaver, but Boski seemed not to have noticed the change in tone.

"He did and left not long after. The Americans were still at the bar when I went home. For all I know, they're in the jungles of Africa now, shouting for George among the giraffes and chimpanzees!"

The kettle sang out, and soon Ida helped Boski bring tea to the men. Cups were in short supply, so they rinsed out the one Ida had used for soup and pressed it into service. As they approached the table with tea, Boski looked up at the picture of the mechanical woman on the wall and sang out a spiky, modern line of music: "In the beginning without any mother the girl was born a machine."

"Excuse me?" said Marinetti, harkening to Boski's voice.

"It's a line a poet friend wrote for a libretto that never came to anything," Boski replied, placing cups of tea on the table. "George's *Ballet Mécanique* was going to accompany a film by Fernand Léger, but it all fell apart, alas."

"Léger!" Marinetti stiffened in his chair. "He could have been one of us, once he tore himself away from Picasso's slavish band of Cubists. He understood the beauty of the machine!" Marinetti continued to pour praise and blame on Léger for several minutes while the others finished their tea.

"This has all been most interesting," said Tom, "and thank you for your kind hospitality—but it seems none of us knows anything about the fate of poor Alice Toklas. We must report back to Miss Stein—and we're keeping you from your dinner."

George cleared his throat. "But you must understand that now that you've seen me here, I can't let you go," said George. "Boski, quick—my pistol!" Marinetti's hand shot from his side to reach high inside his jacket, and George's eyes widened at the realization that his joke had gone awry. "A jest! A jest!" He laughed, shaking his head. "Forgive me—I've been down here too long and have the manners of a sewer rat." Marinetti let his hand drop and forced a smile.

"I'm so sorry we can't share dinner," said Boski. "You must all be very hungry—but I'll show you the way to Paprikás. They'll take good care of you."

Boski led the way, her miner's lamp beaming as she walked briskly through the catacombs on a winding route that led, some minutes later, to a round metal door left half an inch ajar and emitting a thin beam of light. Boski entered alone, emerging a minute later with a smile. "I told Andris you're our friends—he'll get you a table upstairs. Best hurry—the show's about to begin!"

30

F *ais gaffe à toi!"* exclaimed the shopkeeper, steadying the wobbly McAlmon, who had staggered into him outside his patisserie. McAlmon dropped back one unsteady step and paused to take one more puff on the clay pipe he'd been smoking as he walked. It wasn't the first time he'd stumbled that day—enough Pernod would do that to you.

A sallow man in his thirties with bristling dark, upright hair and close-set eyes that always looked like they'd pop out if opened any farther, McAlmon wore a wide, loosely knotted yellow bowtie, a pair of scuffed brown and white spectator shoes, and a rumpled black suit dappled with pipe ash. Something about him gave off the air of an itinerant Kansas preacher's son gone bad with drink and idleness—which was, in fact, precisely what he was. Despite appearances, though, there was always money in his pockets, thanks to his marriage to an English shipping heiress. She'd married him to placate her father on the sole condition that McAlmon get lost somewhere while she traveled the world in the arms of her girlfriend. So here he was, getting lost. And writing the greatest novel his generation would ever produce. Or he would write it someday soon. He almost believed it.

Why, McAlmon wondered, swaying a little as he furrowed his brow—why had that man used the informal *toi*? Holding a wavering index finger aloft to bid the shopkeeper to wait, McAlmon squinted in concentration, unaware that the man had returned to the counter in his shop. They weren't friends, at least not as far as McAlmon could remember, and the phrase the man had used...how would he put it in English if he were translating it for the literary magazine that he published sporadically on his wife's credit? "Watch it, buddy!" or "Look out, pal!" Something like that. He must know the man from somewhere, thought McAlmon. Must have stood him a drink. And speaking of drinks—he looked up, blinking in confusion at the sight of his own extended finger, and let it drop—now there's a sight. The Café du Dôme. Two rows of little round tables and cane chairs clustered on the terrace under a fluttering deep green awning. Always full of Englishmen and Americans, it was a spot that attracted them like moths to the flame with those bright schooners of lager, gleaming merrily and bright in the late afternoon light. Anyone here today with whom to start the evening early?

Well, there were a couple of painters' models—country girls with impassive expressions trying to pass as sophisticates. Eugénie, one of them was, wasn't she? And the other? Dunno. But they'd be good fun if it weren't for that bowler-hatted, wiry little artist Pascin, who sat between them with a proprietary air. McAlmon had worn out Pascin's patience too often, but… who else was here, among the chatty Americans grinning at the novelty of a legal drink? No one he knew at the next table, just a couple of tweedy Brits, but behind them? Yes, right there. He knew that man. Tall, good-looking, broad in shoulder, brown-eyed, strong-jawed, with a trim mustache, shirtsleeves rolled to the elbow, and enough buttons undone to show the dark hair on his chest. Wasn't he cold, seated there alone in the waning daylight?

A tatty, torn fisherman's sweater was draped over the other chair at his table, as if to indicate another person occupied the space, but McAlmon knew the sweater belonged to the young man who sat alone at the table, a notebook open in front of him, a freshly sharpened pencil in his hand. Though his first novel was getting Hemingway a lot of notice, it had not brought him a lot of money, at least not yet, and his limited wardrobe testified to that fact. Hem wore that sweater everywhere. McAlmon waved and smiled, but Hemingway's eyes, intent on the page before him, did not move. Nor did any other part of him, even though he radiated an intense energy, a force held—only just—in reserve.

"He has the look of a hunter alone in the jungle, does he not?" It was Monsieur LaVigne, proprietor of the Dôme, standing at McAlmon's side with a steadying hand on his elbow. "A hunter silently stalking his prey, and soon to strike," added LaVigne in a low murmur. The comment would have been ridiculous if directed at anyone else sitting at a café table with a notebook and a half-eaten plate of mashed potatoes, but McAlmon had to admit there was something in it where Hemingway was concerned. But this wouldn't get in the way of a good night's drinking; and broke writers, McAlmon knew from long experience, like nothing more than a fellow who picks up the tab. McAlmon nodded at LaVigne and lurched his way through the obstacle course of tables and chairs until he stood just behind his fellow writer.

Did Hem truly not see him here? McAlmon leaned in to have a look at the notebook on the table. There was just a single sentence. *A man*, it read, in clean, firm cursive, *can be defeated, but not destroyed*. McAlmon plonked himself down on the chair with the sweater, knocked his pipe twice on the table to clear it of ash, stowed the thing in his jacket pocket, and smiled ingratiatingly up at the taller man.

"Hey, Hem—trying to write?"

Nothing. Not so much as a blink. Hemingway's eyes burned—no, smoldered—and remained riveted to the notebook before him.

"They've got a whole new crate of Frascati at Dino's," McAlmon chirped. "It'll remind you of Italy and all the fun you had there with the ambulance corps." Still nothing. "Be a pal and tag along. On me." No reaction. Nada. Nothing at all.

McAlmon leaned back, inadvertently knocking Hemingway's sweater to the ground. "Lemme just get that for you, Hem," he said, springing to his feet only to discover that springing was not an action for which this afternoon's bottle of Pernod had prepared him. An inadvertent pirouette left him clinging to a seated Englishman's shoulder, apologizing, then pausing a moment, nauseated, when he dipped to grab the sweater off the flagstones. Upright again, though dizzy, he cracked a thin smile. Got it that time, eh? Nothing like savoir-faire.

"Monsieur!" It was a waiter, pointing from across the terrace at the pocket where McAlmon had stowed his pipe. *"Monsieur— vous êtes en feu!"* Now that was more like it, a little formality in that *vous*, not like the patisserie man's *toi*. Now how should he translate that? "Sir," yes, definitely "sir" and not "mister," to get the sense of French formality that English didn't allow in its pronouns. *"Monsieur—vous êtes en feu!"*—so that'd be "You, sir, are on fire." But with an exclamation point, the way he said it. Only now did McAlmon's head pivot down toward the pocket the waiter had indicated. Jesus wept! Smoke! He plunged his hand into his pocket only to jerk it back with a yelp—the pipe had set his suit alight.

"Gangway!" cried McAlmon, crashing through the clutter of chairs and tables, of English tweeds and startled American accents, on his way to the café interior and, he hoped, a pitcher of water. *"Fais gaffe à toi!"*

Monsieur LaVigne looked calmly from the edge of the terrace at McAlmon's retreating back, then glanced with concern at the immobile Hemingway, who remained as still and silent as a sphinx through the entire affair. The writer's eyes scalded the notebook with intensity, and his mustache gave a tiny, sneering twitch. LaVigne knew that tick—when it occurred, he sometimes thought, Hemingway seemed to inhabit a kingdom of ire beyond mere anger, beyond contempt. When that happened, LaVigne sometimes feared that the force coiled inside this man would burst out, and that he could—not with hatred, but with the calm majesty of a lion—annihilate them all.

Hemingway's hand moved over the sentence he had written in his notebook. He crossed out one word, *man*, and wrote above it: *fool*.

31

Tom, Ida, and Marinetti dipped their heads and passed through a low doorway and into the wine cellar of the Hungarian restaurant, where a tall but stooped man in a white apron and bristling mustache greeted them with a curt bow. He pointed to his chest, muttered, "Andris," and motioned for them to follow him up narrow winding stairs into the steamy clamor of the kitchen, where huge pots simmered, clouds of fragrant steam filled the air, and servers and line cooks barked and growled at each other over a steel counter piled with towers of earthenware dishes. Andris led them hastily through the kitchen, while Ida dodged first a dishwasher with a pile of bowls, then a tiny man hurrying by with an enormous, dangerous-looking skewer. Once in the dining area, Andris motioned toward one of the small round tables against the back wall. Tom and Ida sat on hard wooden stools, but Marinetti headed for the exit instead, muttering excuses about having had a long day and a blow on the head with a wheel of cheese. Even before Marinetti reached the door, servers arrived at the table with terracotta plates, each covered with a slice of thick, round fried bread topped with sour cream, bacon, and a pale cheese that Tom sniffed carefully, nose close to the plate. When he looked up, he was smiling broadly. "Made from curds," he said approvingly. "I believe they call it 'quark.'"

They can call it whatever they want, thought Ida, but it's not going to be around for long. She and Tom ate ravenously, drinking harsh red wine from clay goblets and observing the crowd—Hungarians, for the most part, with a smattering of talkative, shabbily dressed artist types. At one table a white-haired, formally dressed couple smiled at one another over a bottle of wine, the woman toying with her pearls, clearly delighted to find herself in such bohemian surroundings. Andris briefly stopped by Tom and Ida's table a few minutes later, and, observing the rate at which the food was disappearing, snapped his fingers, signaling a server bring them more. *"Pas besoin de payer,"* the server whispered to Tom, bending low. "Andris says no friend of Boski's is allowed to pay." Shortly afterward, the server returned with broad soup plates brimming with heavenly goulash.

While Tom and Ida ate, two men came in the front door carrying large, battered suitcases. They spoke briefly to Andris, who gave orders for the unoccupied tables in the center of the room to be taken away. The two men soon set to work unpacking their suitcases. The first man, short, with bushy black hair and a mustache to match, wore a tight, somewhat ratty black sweater—he seemed to be in charge. The other—Japanese, Ida guessed—had a mop of thick hair, and wore a checked flannel work shirt, much like a lumberjack's. The two worked quickly, together assembling a strange apparatus. First, they secured two posts, some three feet tall, into the floor. Next, they ran a kind of net beneath the posts, and strung wires between them at different heights. The Japanese man laid a thick hemp rope on the floor in the form of a circle surrounding the poles, while the man in the sweater retrieved an array of strange little puppets and other figures from the second suitcase. Ida and Tom glanced at one another, then leaned forward for a closer look at what appeared to be circus figures, some just a few inches high. There was a ringmaster ingeniously fashioned from twisted wire; a clown with a protruding bit of pipe for a nose; an elephant almost a foot high made from wire tubing and bits of a cleverly cut tin can for ears; a sword swallower with a silvery wire blade that went down his throat; and so many more. Tom sat back in his chair, clapped his hands together, and grinned from ear to ear

"Mesdames et messieurs!" called the Japanese man, when the miniature circus was assembled. *"Je vous présente—le petit Cirque Calder!"* He rushed to the side of the room where he had previ-

ously placed a wide-horned Victrola and turned the crank. Ida recognized the song. "It's Dolores del Rio," she said, leaning over to Tom.

"It is!" he whispered back. "Her hit, 'Ramona'!" Ida and Tom clunked their heavy goblets together in a toast. They watched, amazed, as the man in the sweater worked strings and manipulated the ringmaster puppet, waving his wire arms to introduce a series of acts. And what acts! A tin horse ran around the roped-in circle, a wire acrobat balanced on its back. Was it a wind-up toy? A puppet on a secret wire? Before they could decide, the acrobat was gone, replaced by the clown with a rubber tube running from the back of its head. The man in the sweater breathed in and out of the tube, first making the clown smoke a real cigarette, then inflating a balloon that projected from the clown like an ever-expanding nose before it burst. Next, wire trapeze artists were set in motion, their momentum carrying them through a series of shockingly realistic tricks before they dropped to the net below. Wild applause broke out among the restaurant's diners, and Tom pounded the table and shouted, "Bravo!" The circus came to an end with a chariot race around the ring, just as captivating as anything in ancient Rome. Some Hungarians at a nearby table cheered mightily, having wagered with one another on the winner.

As the two men began packing the equipment away, Ida wondered: was this the art that Marinetti wanted? Modern, made of metal, wire, rubber, and everyday odds and ends, without so much as a whiff of the must of museums; an art people cheered and made bets on, with none of the deadening reverence of the Louvre's long and silent corridors. No, no, it was not like what Marinetti described in his manifesto. There was nothing of destruction about it, only joy. And wasn't it taking an art as old as the Romans—the circus—and building on it to make something new? This was more like what Tom had talked about: a transformation, a sea change.

While Ida pondered, the Japanese man lugged the suitcases out to the street, and the man in the sweater took a seat at the table next to her and Tom, lit a cigarette, and began bending some bits of wire—coat hangers, perhaps?—into loops and swirls.

"That was astonishing," gushed Ida, leaning across the table and touching Tom on the hand.

"It reminds one why one comes to Paris," replied the beaming Tom. "Nothing like that in London, still less St. Louis. In Boston—well, I'm sure they'd find some reason for it to be banned."

"What about the other big show—Antheil's. I heard you talking about it in his room earlier." Ida regretted having missed out on this.

"A curious discussion," said Tom. "Marinetti was quite intrigued by the technical side of things—I suppose that's a Futurist for you."

"But did Antheil say anything at all that could shed light on Alice?" Ida persisted.

"I'm afraid not," said Tom. "Although he was very glad to talk mechanics with Marinetti. Synchronization was their great theme. Apparently, George has found a way to make all of his instruments play in precise coordination—a matter of wiring. And that's what Marinetti really wanted to understand. He kept asking about whether the wiring could be extended in some fashion. Could the cables from George's apparatus be attached to something much longer and run all over the city of Paris? I thought this was very strange—I don't suppose he wants to coordinate all the city's church organs."

Ida recalled Marinetti's admiration for Marcel's use of the phrase *écrasez l'infâme* and nodded in worried assent.

"Still," Tom continued, "Marinetti did ask about the location of a great many churches, and whether the catacombs ran beneath them. Notre Dame, Sacre Coeur, Sainte-Chapelle. George couldn't help with any except the last one—he drew a map for Marinetti showing how to reach the tunnels beneath Sainte-Chapelle."

"Whatever for?" asked Ida.

"No idea," said Tom. "But it wasn't just churches Marinetti was interested in—he wanted to know about underground routes from Antheil's concert hall to any number of other places: the Louvre, the Sorbonne, the Bibliothèque Mazarine— that's quite a library, the Mazarine, full of rare and ancient books. I should like to go back someday."

"He...he wanted to run wires from the concert hall to all these locations?" Ida furrowed her brow. She knew Marinetti was eccentric, but what could this mean?

"Yes, but George didn't seem to think it strange," said Tom. "I think he was just so carried away with the *how* that he didn't question the *why*. George is very American that way, don't you think?"

Her eyes closed, her voice strangely detached, Ida remembered the words: "'We want to demolish museums, libraries, academies of any sort,'" said Ida. "'We want to exalt movements of aggression... We want to free our world from the endless museums that cover her like graveyards.'"

"Blimey!" said Tom. "What?"

"That's Marinetti's manifesto," said Ida. "I read it to Teddy the day after Gertrude's salon. Teddy wanted to get...up-to-date."

"But that manifesto is from almost twenty years ago," Tom said skeptically. "I'm afraid Teddy's notion of the present is no longer up-to-date."

"But don't you see, Tom...don't you see?"

"I see that Marinetti worries that his movement is in eclipse. You notice how he reacts to the Surrealists, the one group everybody talks about nowadays."

"No." Ida shook her head. "I mean, yes, he does resent them. But there's something else—doesn't it sound like he..." Ida paused. It was madness. It couldn't be.

"Like he wants to make the manifesto come to pass?" Tom spoke quickly, his voice low and urgent.

"But that would mean the destruction of—" began Ida.

"Of everything we love most about Paris," said Tom, finishing her sentence. "Sorry," he added. "I didn't mean to cut you off. But surely…is Marinetti really a violent man?"

"You saw him reach in his jacket when George joked about getting a pistol," said Ida. "Do you suppose he was looking for his fountain pen?"

The two sat in silence for a moment. "It could work, you know," said an American voice beside them. Tom and Ida looked over at the man in the black sweater, the same man who had conducted the circus. On the table before him he had twisted some wires into a kind of web, connecting ingenious little steeples and columns. "Alexander Calder—folks call me Sandy," he said, introducing himself. "I studied engineering back in the States. The trick would be synchronizing everything, but if your friend George has figured that bit out, then theoretically everything could be wired up to go off at once."

"Go off?" asked Ida.

"Isn't that what you were talking about with the destruction of museums?" asked Sandy. "Sorry—I'm a shameless eavesdropper. But it wouldn't be hard, you know. Since the war, all of France is full of surplus ordinance and explosives."

"Time to go—if we're going to catch the next Metro." It was the Japanese man, suddenly tableside and addressing Sandy. He had finished packing away the circus.

"Sure thing, Sam," said Sandy, bending his wire model into a ball and passing it to Sam. He kept one short length of wire, twisted it deftly a half-dozen times, and passed it to Ida—a perfect hairpin in the form of an owl, two coils forming its eyes. "By way of apology for butting in," he said, and left without saying goodbye. She marveled at the simple, ingenious figure of the owl a moment, then slipped his gift into her hair, and called out a thank you to his departing back.

"Wasn't Alice going on about these technical matters at the salon, a couple of days before she disappeared?" asked Tom.

"She was. But…would it be mad of us to go to Gertrude with this? It sounds so implausible," said Ida.

"Yes, but it's all we've got to go on," said Tom, "after walking

half the city above ground and the other half below." Ida nodded as a waiter came and cleared their empty dishes away, while
Tom cast an assessing gaze over her. "You look completely
done in. Let me arrange for a taxi and I'll take you home," Tom
continued. "If I'm to stay in Paris to see this matter through,
then I'll need to send some telegrams tomorrow morning, and
stop by my bank… I do seem to have made some unexpected
expenditures. Let's meet at the restaurant across from your
building for a late lunch, and we'll go see Miss Stein."

On the one hand, it seemed to Ida as though she and Tom
were succumbing to a shared insanity. What did the French call
it when a pair of people did that—*folie à deux?* On the other
hand…Ida shuddered to think what could be at stake. She worried over it all the way to her building, with Tom next to her in
the taxi as it drove south from Montmartre, then passed the
Tuileries gardens, and crossed the Seine on the Pont Royal in
the evening's light rain. He walked her up the stairs to the door
of her rooms, stood next to her in the corridor and touched
the part in his hair. This is the moment when people who are
courting would kiss, thought Ida.

32

It took an extraordinary effort of will for Marinetti to leave the Hungarian restaurant without eating, or even resting his weary body on one of the wooden stools for a moment. He was ravenously hungry, and his calves and thighs burned from the day's walking. His shirt was stained with blood, he worried his face would bruise from the blow he'd received in the catacombs, and he felt a distinct twinge in his left side from the fall he'd taken. His ankle had been cut badly by that cursed kettle he'd stepped into, and he worried about tetanus or worse. He simmered with resentment at those two American fools, Tom and Ida—they'd attacked him, after all. And they'd done so out of pure, cowardly panic, without even knowing that they worked at cross-purposes with him. Well, he'd put one over on them to be sure. Even now they suspected nothing about the great work he was engaged in, or how that chatty boy Antheil— who was not without genius—had given him all he'd needed to bring it to fruition. Now, where to find a taxi stand? There would be no rest tonight, not if preparations were to be made properly.

Marinetti dragged himself to the nearest intersection and looked up and down the cobblestone street. There was no taxi stand in sight, but—the gods smiled on him! A cab pulled up, tall, black, and boxy, with yellow doors and a checkerboard stripe down the side, stopping right in front of Paprikás. Marinetti wheeled around and hailed it with both arms. Fortunately, the cab's previous riders—a man in a black sweater and a Japanese fellow without a jacket—were struggling to unload some heavy suitcases, and Marinetti was able to reach the taxi before it pulled away. To speed things along he helped remove the last suitcase from the cab, passing it to its owner, who nodded his thanks. Curious, he thought: there are no hotels nearby. He didn't notice the two men enter Paprikás.

"Saint-Ouen," barked Marinetti, settling into the back seat of the taxi. The driver hung his head, shaking it from side to side. A trip to that working-class suburb at this time of night would leave him far away, and he'd most likely have to make the long drive back to Paris without a paying fare. "I'll make it worth your while," Marinetti added, flashing a wad of francs. The driver glanced back over his shoulder, frowning, but put the car in gear and pulled away. The orderly streets of Paris slowly gave way to a landscape less densely populated, and to streets less well paved. As they neared the area of *les puces*—the great flea markets of Saint-Ouen—paving gave way to mud on the streets, while stone, brick and plaster buildings yielded to clapboard and the occasional vacant lot. Marinetti gave directions, and soon enough they arrived at a small yellow house wedged between a weed-choked plot of land and a crumbling viaduct. It sat on a long, narrow lot at the end of which two tumbledown sheds leaned on one another near some railway tracks. The cabbie, whom Marinetti tipped well, but not extravagantly, drove off with a face of stone.

Marinetti turned keys in the two locks that secured the doors and proceeded immediately down a pair of narrow stairs to a basement room where Wyndham Lewis sat in shirtsleeves, bent over the small pool of light a lamp cast on a cluttered, makeshift table. Though Marinetti had made no efforts at stealth, Lewis turned in surprise. Evidently, he had been so absorbed in dissecting a dead mouse with a paring knife he hadn't heard his companion enter. Marinetti chose not to comment on the mouse or on the cut—was it infected?—on Lewis's face. Lewis had his foibles, but they often proved useful in the work—the magnificent work—they had embarked on together.

"I have discovered Antheil's secrets," said Marinetti, "all of them. But we must act immediately—tonight." *Che diavolo!* What had Lewis done to that mouse?

"How many of our people shall I gather?" asked Lewis.

"All of them—all that you can find. There's fuel in your automobile?" asked Marinetti.

Lewis nodded.

"Bring them here, and we'll issue them what they need to start. But what," Marinetti gestured with his chin to an envelope sitting on the table just beyond the remains of the mouse, "is that letter?"

Lewis passed it to Marinetti with a grin. As Marinetti read it, Lewis explained how the American detective, Caine, had asked him to give it to his wife. "But I didn't!" he added, with a gleeful snicker that cut short at the sight of Marinetti's glare.

"That was foolish," muttered Marinetti, too exhausted to feel anger at Lewis's sadistic self-indulgence. "Now she's poking around where she should not be looking—hoping to find her husband, whom she should know is in Africa. You'll have to put a stop to this." He paused. "And do something about Eliot too, if he doesn't leave for England as he professes he will. Though I doubt he cares for Alice or the detective. He's merely struck by Mrs. Caine and her"—Marinetti's hands grasped the air—"her not inconsiderable charms. But he is of the Puritanical type. He'll go back to England, and his lunatic wife."

"It will be my pleasure to deal with Eliot," replied Lewis, his smile wide, his eyes without emotion. "We can dispose of Alice at the same time."

This gave Marinetti pause. But Lewis had, he reluctantly admitted, a point: Alice knew too much. Marinetti's lip curled at the sight of the flayed mouse, but he said nothing.

Lewis's car roared off into the night, headlamps gleaming like lidless eyes. He knew the hours—indeed, the days—ahead would leave him and his colleagues dead tired, but the result of their labors would be legendary, impossible to ignore. Anything Picasso had done, or could do, would look feeble beside it. They would talk of nothing else at Gertrude's salon. Indeed, they would talk of nothing else in all the great capitals of the world. Oh, he'd show them, all of them, the smug, complacent cretins.

The long, low car ran swiftly down the empty roads of night, Lewis's fingers twitching at the wheel. Soon he pulled off the road, stopping in front of a tumbledown warehouse that listed unsteadily to one side, not far from the Saint-Ouen flea market. With some effort, he opened the huge padlock, heaved the heavy wooden sliding door to the side, and turned on the lights. The small desk near the entrance held a candlestick telephone, and after some fumbling Lewis spoke into it and waited for the call to be connected.

"Wake up!" Lewis's voice rang shrilly in the vast and silent room. "Yes, I know what time it is—no, I have not 'lost my damned mind'—listen, listen, it's time. Yes, tonight. We have what we need, but we need to start now. Immediately. Round up your comrades and we'll begin. Hurry!" Lewis hung up the mouthpiece. If only more of the ragtag crew he wished to assemble had telephones, his night would be shorter, but there was nothing for it—he would have to drive into the city and bang on the doors of sleeping men.

Before he left, he turned and looked with satisfaction on what he and Marinetti had assembled: crate after army-green crate marked *Achtung Explosivstoffe*, *Matière Inflammable*, or *Danger—Explosives*. They had better use their biggest lorry, thought Lewis, and they'd better not smoke.

33

Bodies swarmed in the darkness, some in coveralls, some still wearing whatever they'd had on when Lewis had collected them for the great work. Lewis stood by his car outside the battered warehouse, watching figures carrying crates of dynamite out to a blue van with a rattling engine, and waiting for the man he sought to emerge from the open warehouse doorway. When he finally saw the man's squat silhouette outlined against the harsh warehouse light, he approached. The two shook hands and spoke briefly, then Lewis got into his car and coaxed the engine to life. When he drove off, the blue van followed his car down the rutted road, through the industrial district, and on into Paris. The little caravan came to a stop in front of the gaping devil-mouth of L'Enfer.

A quick knock, a long wait, and the door cracked open. A few hurried, whispered words, and the double doors opened wide. Men sprang from the back of the truck, receiving crate after crate from their companions within, then spool after spool of copper wire, all disappearing into L'Enfer's gaping goblin maw.

All night the men labored, splashing and clattering through the grimy damp of the catacombs. A short, solidly built figure in a dark suit held an electric lantern high in an underground chamber lined with human bones, nodding in approval as others strung cables down tunnels, fixing them to the walls with metal brackets.

"How long?" Lewis approached, recognizing the man with the lantern.

"For the first site? We can be done by noon, maybe sooner."

"And for the whole of the project?" asked Lewis.

"Days. Can't say how many. When we've laid all of your explosives in place, we'll arrange to bring in some of our own supplies. The locations are secure, but they are not convenient."

Lewis grunted. He did not like delays. "And you know the underground routes for the laying of cable?"

"We know. Marinetti is a mere tourist in these catacombs. We are the natives. We know all the routes."

"Yet you didn't know young Antheil had set up shop just around the corner?" Lewis sneered.

His companion, Marcel, smiled a thin smile that was no smile at all, and said nothing. Lewis was arrogant—a nasty boy who'd lucked into playing a role in what promised to be the greatest manifestation of the human imagination since the guillotine liberated the king of France's head from his quivering royal shoulders. Yes, thought Marcel, this work would be a great thing. And if it required consorting with swine like Lewis, so be it. Not all visionaries were Surrealists, he had to admit; Marinetti was no Surrealist, but his dream was grand, and truly Surreal in and of itself. And Marcel had to confess, disappointing as it was, that not all Surrealists were visionaries. Gabriel, for example, had grown soft—the only revolution he sought was the misty revolution of dreams; that hard-eyed Czech Toyen was right about him, and right to join in this endeavor. She can gloat when it's all over, to heal her bruised ego from that humiliating night at the Café du Place Blanche. But for now, she must be as quiet as the rest. If Gabriel caught so much as a whiff or whisper of the great work underway, he would run to the police like a shopkeeper's housewife. No, leave him to dote on his protégé Dora, and let him gape with wonder when the true Surrealists liberated Paris from the edifices that imprisoned the city's—no, the entire civilization's—mind.

Night turned to morning, morning wore on into afternoon, and the men still labored in the depths. They would rest but little in the days ahead. Marcel, who seemed to need no rest, sat in the passenger seat of the rattling blue van as the driver steered it out of the city and into the secluded countryside. After an hour they arrived at a stone cottage, where an old man in a peasant's blouson led Marcel and the driver to his barn and watched as they loaded three heavy crates into the back. As they were preparing to leave, the old man pried open a crate, fished out a stick of dynamite, and, with a lopsided, toothless smile, pulled a match from behind his ear, struck it on the van's fender, and lit the fuse. Marcel froze at this recklessness, until the old man hurled the dynamite into an empty field and dissolved into laughter at the panic the explosion wrought among the chickens wandering the farmyard. Marcel handed the man an envelope thick with banknotes and leapt into the van. Peasants. Sometimes they were more surreal than the Surrealists.

Half an hour later, on a muddy road many miles from Paris, the van sputtered to a halt. Out of fuel. Marcel smacked the driver on the back of the head and sent the fool off on foot, a rusted red metal gas can in his hand.

An hour later a gendarme on a bicycle pulled up beside the van, which he did not recognize as local. A lost city-dweller, perhaps? Or one of those smugglers bringing hashish down from Belgium? Well, he thought, I'll soon find out. Let's have a look in the back.

Marcel watched the officer approach and clenched his fists.

34

D azzling shafts of morning sunlight broke through the heavy clouds that had besieged Paris for days, the light refracting erratically through the glass goblet of sparkling water on Ida's café table. She watched as wiry tangles of light danced on the tabletop, bringing Sandy Calder's nimble, cable-twisting hands to her mind. Sandy handled wire the way Picasso handled perspective, thought Ida—it leapt under his guidance, eagerly performing every trick the master commanded. She took the owl hairpin he'd given her from her handbag, held it in the palm of her hand, and admired its perfection and simplicity: two simple loops made the body, two smaller ones the legs beneath, and an astonishingly clever pair of spirals made two vast, wise, uncannily hypnotic eyes. Such humble material—not silver, nor even copper. It may have started as a coat hanger. Yet here it was, an owl, the symbol of wisdom. Sea changes, thought Ida. Something simple becoming something new, rich, and strange.

A little stack of saucers in different colors—the French waiters' way to note a customer's growing charges—indicated she had finished her morning croissant, along with her tea and two cups of coffee. Ida rarely drank more than one cup, but she'd been out late with Tom the night before and had slept little, and what sleep she'd had was haunted by dreams of the catacombs with their walls of bones. Now she breathed the jittery air and found she couldn't keep her fingers still. She toyed with her new hairpin, then twisted her hair into a bun and secured it with the owl. That accomplished, Ida opened the sketchbook that sat on the table before her, pulled hard and soft pencils from her handbag, and stared at the blankness of the creamy page. It would be some time before Tom was due to arrive. She could set up, climb the stairs to her room, and work on her copy of van Eyck, but she hated to waste this rare and precious sunlight.

Ida took up her soft-leaded pencil and drew a long, curving line that ended in a small spiral. Sandy would approve, she thought, smiling at the ease and confidence of the line. Nothing fiddly or indecisive about it. A few more lines and she'd turned it into the profile of a boat, the spiral becoming an ornament on the prow. Yes, that was it. She would pass the time by drawing Waterhouse's *Lady of Shalott* from memory— the long-haired woman in white, full of luscious trepidation as the river took her away to she knew not where. Three candles in front of her, one burning, two extinguished, and a bit of blanket or tapestry trailing in the water—she must have drifted through the night. But, no, thought Ida, let the boat be more of a canoe. Let the riverbank forest be tall Wisconsin pines. And for God's sake, give the woman a paddle. And give her a wide mouth like Ida's own, not that precious little budding rose that Waterhouse painted. You can't have a prow ornament on a canoe, so let that spiral be…what? An owl, perched on the prow. Why not? It was no less likely than tapestry and candles.

How long had the waiter been standing beside her? Ida smiled at him and ordered another coffee, expense be damned. Flipping to a fresh page, she began to sketch again. Not a spiral this time—a big circle near the top of the page. Like a clock. Yes—like the clock from that di Chirico picture she saw in *La Révolution Surréaliste*. A cannon to the left, and…what else? Two artichokes in front. And sinister architecture all around. Use the soft pencil now, to get the shadows and bring a sense of menace. Were there figures in the background? Ida tried to remember, couldn't be sure. She could go upstairs, look in the journal, and make a better copy. But she had already drawn a figure under the clock in the background: a man in a dark robe standing behind a table, some small objects set on its surface. A vendor of some kind? No, more like a magician. *Le Bateleur*, from the tarot deck. What was he doing there? He did not look like a friend. Change the clock to a full moon, rub out those spiky artichokes and put hounds in their place, big ones, with baying mouths. This was her other tarot card, *La Lune*, the moon that spoke of secret conspirators. It made for an unnerving picture, but it felt…it felt right, somehow, thought Ida. It was no kind of copy, but it felt quite right. When Ida finally took a sip, she found her coffee was already cold.

She had just turned to a fresh page in her sketchbook when she saw Tom waving from across the street. As he strode up to her table in a light brown suit, Ida realized this was the first time she'd seen him without his umbrella. He sat, smiling, summoned the waiter, and ordered lunch for both of them: salad Niçoise with tuna, green beans, and firm red potatoes. When it arrived, Ida closed her sketchbook and tucked in.

"I was just at the Western Union office. Told them I was your cousin," said Tom, with a sly grin.

"Whatever for?" Ida was a bit surprised at Tom taking such a liberty.

"So they would tell me if there'd been any message from Teddy for you," he said. "Nothing—well, nothing yet. But who knows how he might have tried to communicate. Shall we stop in at Shakespeare and Company on the way to Miss Stein's? People leave messages there all the time."

It seemed unlikely that Teddy would have sent something by airmail, or reached out through the international bohemian grapevine, but there was that letter Teddy gave to Lewis. Maybe Lewis had left it for her with Sylvia Beach at the bookshop. And besides, Sylvia's shop was on the way to the rue de Fleurus. Ida acquiesced to the plan. Recalling the thinness of her sheaf of francs, Ida once again allowed Tom to settle the check, and they set off, in the dappled sunlight beneath the slender chestnut trees.

"Quiet," said Sylvia softly when Tom and Ida entered her bookshop. Sylvia motioned with her head toward one of the comfortable chairs in the center of the shop, where James Joyce sprawled, asleep, his eyeglasses dangling from a single ear, dirty smears on the knees of his trousers, and one shoe kicked loose from his foot resting beneath his chair. His big toe jutted defiantly through a hole in his sock. "Shame's Voice had a late night, and if we wake him, he'll start punning in three languages. Have you come to return…what was it? Djuna Barnes?"

"No," said Ida, "it was Miss Stein and a few other things, but I haven't brought them…I've come to see if there's been a message for me, perhaps from Wyndham Lewis?"

"Let's see, let's see," said Sylvia, her brown corduroy suit making a soft shushing sound as she searched behind the counter. "Ida Caine…two messages, but neither's from Lewis. One from Miss Maar, one from Miss Stein. Both came yesterday." She passed Ida an envelope and a folded square of blue paper.

"Miss Maar?" asked Ida.

"Dora Maar. A young Surrealist, and lately a friend of Picasso's. About your size." Sylvia's hands traced a graceful hourglass in the air.

"Oh!" said Ida, opening the envelope. The note inside read, simply, *Comrade Ida—you did not finish writing in the ledger. Please come back soon and we can complete your research. Dora.* Ida nodded. She'd like to comply, but there were more pressing matters. The other message, whose words were scrawled in a loose hand running from one corner of the page to another, gave an even simpler message: *Come at once, do, dear Ida do. Gertrude.* Ida passed it to Tom.

"Shall we oblige Miss Stein at once?" he asked. Ida thought that was a fine idea, and a few minutes later Hélène was ushering them into the salon room at the Stein residence. Gertrude sat in her chair at the far end of the room, holding her poodle on her lap and looking as if she hadn't slept in some time.

"Ida Caine, Ida Caine," said Gertrude by way of greeting, "and…Tom, still not gone to England's green and pleasant land, I see." She gave the couple a curious look. Tom gave a nod that was more of a bow, then looked to Ida to speak.

"I got your note at Sylvia's," said Ida, waving the square paper. "We wanted to stop by anyway but—is there news?"

"Only this," said Gertrude, lifting a sheet paper from the heavy oak table beside her. She held it disdainfully between her thumb and forefinger. "Come and see."

Tom and Ida crossed the room. Ida took the proffered sheet and read aloud: "If you want to see your Alice again, you will not go to the police, you will not pry into her location. You will wait until the fifteenth and all will be restored. Do nothing and speak to no one. We watch you."

Gertrude winced when she heard the words but continued before Ida could say anything to comfort her. "Hélène found this paper in an envelope outside the door not long after your last visit. Had your husband not gone missing, I may have suspected you of putting it there."

Marinetti, thought Ida, a realization dawning on her. Marinetti had been in the courtyard when she and Tom had arrived on their previous visit to Miss Stein. He had been leaving, turned awkwardly, and then come in with them. It could easily have been Marinetti who left the message. Is that why he had acted so strangely? She felt a sharp pain deep in her stomach. She hoped she'd been wrong to suspect him, but now…the thought of being in the catacombs with a criminal, possibly a violent one, made her tremble.

"Sit, please, dear Ida," said Gertrude, gesturing to a divan. "You look unwell." Ida sat, staring at the note. Tom put a hand on her shoulder, and a moment later Ida explained her mad theory about Marinetti, that he may be planning to destroy much of Paris using Antheil and his concert as the mechanism for setting off a series of explosions. Marinetti was working with Antheil or, more likely, setting Antheil up to take the blame. Ida's words came quickly and sounded both plausible and utterly crazed. Would Gertrude believe her, or call for a doctor to take this madwoman away?

Gertrude sat in stony silence for a moment. Never had she looked more like Picasso's portrait of her, thought Ida. Tom was right—Valloton's painting of Stein was a better likeness than Picasso's, but a worse painting. Then Gertrude's mask dropped, and she looked up, worried, vulnerable, not sure what to do.

"I dare not go to the police station," said Gertrude in a trembling voice. "Who knows—maybe I really am being watched, and I can't bear to think what they'd do to Alice."

"Then Tom and I must go for you," said Ida, standing. Gertrude raised a hand as if to bless her.

35

H ere," said Jay, "hold this." He passed a rickety typewriter up to Teddy, where he sat in the aft seat of
Jay's biplane. Teddy had been wondering why Jay
asked him to stay in the aircraft while the shorter man went
into the mud-brick, tin-roofed office at this small windswept
airfield outside Tripoli. He was even more bemused when Jay
emerged from the office with a bottle of wine in his hand and
a typewriter under his arm, a sheet of paper still flapping in
its cylinder. What exactly was Jay's game? Whatever it was, the
little clerk in the round red cap chasing after him didn't seem
to want to play.

"Put the typewriter up high, and pose like you're writing
something," Jay barked, turning to dismiss the clerk with a
wave of his hand. When the clerk objected in angry Arabic,
Teddy passed the wine bottle to Teddy, fished for his wallet,
and pressed a couple of French banknotes into the confused
clerk's hands. "There," he said. "Happy now? *Tout va bien?*" Jay
looked up at the bewildered Teddy. "Be a sport and pass me
down my camera. I'm going to explain to this excitable fellow
that he needs to take my picture. I'll climb up front in the plane
and hoist the bottle of wine, you just look like someone about
to finish the novel chronicling my adventures—serious, like."
Teddy tucked the wine bottle under his arm and reached down
beneath the seat, where Jay's camera and lenses were stowed in
a leather case with brass fittings. But by the time he'd hauled
it out, Jay's attention was elsewhere. The clerk's hat now sat
angled back on Jay's head, and he was shouting, "Where's the
tassel? The fez won't look right without a tassel!"

"No tassel," the confused clerk protested, searching for English words. "No fez—is *chechia* hat. No fez, no tassel."

Jay drew more banknotes from his wallet and, having tucked them into the pocket of the clerk's starched white shirt, turned back to take the camera from Teddy. "Careless little fellow lost his tassel." A few minutes later, Jay sat in the front cockpit, red hat askew on his head and bottle raised high while Teddy balanced the typewriter on the biplane's hull with his fingertips and pretended to type.

After several photos and some convoluted negotiations in French and broken English, Teddy sat in the passenger seat of a battered blue-gray French jeep, grinning almost as widely as Jay who kept one hand on the wheel and another on the wine bottle as they tore down a rough desert road. Their guide, a barefoot, radiantly charismatic teenager perched behind them, kept assuring them the ruins they sought were a few minutes away. "Those pics will wow them back in Greenwich!" Jay shouted through the silk aviator's scarf he pulled up his face to stop the choking sand.

The ruins, it turned out, were almost a half hour away. When they arrived, Jay ordered Teddy and the guide about, setting up for a photo in which he stood in front of a row of broken columns half-buried in the desert sand, Teddy seated cross-legged on the ground beside him. "Okay, Ali Baba," Jay shouted at the guide, whose name was Ibrahim, "show Ted here our surprise!"

The teenager loped back to the jeep, fumbled around in the back, and emerged with the typewriter from the airfield in his hands and the clerk's red hat on his head. At Jay's direction he placed the hat on Teddy's head and set the typewriter in front of him, its sheet of paper fluttering in the strengthening wind. "Now hold still while the boy takes the picture," Jay instructed, striking a heroic pose, reconsidering, then striking another slightly different one, hands on his hips like a lion-tamer in the circus ring.

"Did you…" Teddy began, his fingers stoking the typewriter keys, but his voice trailed off. He was about to say "steal this," but he thought better of it. He was a long, sandy way from anywhere, with hardly a franc to his name, and Jay was his only ride back to any place. "Did you buy this from the little man at the airfield?"

Jay looked down with an impish grin, plucking the hat from Teddy's head and putting it on his own. "Sure, Ted. Let's say I did. You know what? Let's bring it to Cairo! You can be typing while I lie back on some pillows like a Pasha with my arms around a dark-eyed belly dancer. Hey, hold up a minute!" The last comment was directed to Ibrahim, who was delightedly turning knobs on Jay's camera. "Hold up while I take a leak on some statuary. No pictures!" He tossed the hat back to Teddy.

Teddy watched Jay walk off behind a column and a wind-worn sandstone torso. Jay staggered a little, and Teddy noticed that the wine bottle in the sand beside him, which he'd uncorked for Jay on the jeep ride, was nearly empty. Jay had chugged it while driving, not thinking to share.

Teddy took the hat from his head and stared into it, as if an answer to his unasked question would emerge like a magician's rabbit. No answer came, but the question did—whose adventure am I on? Jay thinks it's his, an escapade to tell the boys back in Greenwich or at the Princeton Club. And he's right, isn't he? Teddy's other hand wrapped around the wine bottle's roundness. We're living in his story, not mine. He squinted to keep the sand from his eyes, looked at the stolen hat, the stolen typewriter. And I'm waiting here with all his other props, he concluded. Not quite knowing why, he thought of Ida's startled eyes the night he told her they'd go to Paris.

"Goddamn wind!" shouted Jay, from behind the broken statue. "Now I'm covered in piss! Ted!"

36

Ida had no pleasant memories of the sixth *arrondissement* police station, except perhaps for the iron railing outside, where she'd bumped into Tom after her last run-in with the gendarmes. Had it really been only days ago that Tom had looked up at her in smiling surprise? It felt like something that happened to another person, on another continent. Striding forward, Ida pulled the door open and passed in, glancing back to see Tom following behind her. The interior was much as she remembered. The benches ringing the walls were less populated this visit than on her last. Indeed, there was only a single dozing *clochard*—wasn't he one of the drunks she'd seen on her first visit? The clerk who glared down from the fortress of the tall oak kiosk was clearly of the same genus as the one who'd been so unhelpful before, but Ida now knew that his glare meant nothing. She adjusted the strap of her bag, squared her shoulders, and declared, "We are here to report a crime."

"Violent or nonviolent?" intoned the clerk, his voice echoing down from above, like that of a minor deity, much wearied by mortals and their sniveling prayers.

Ida looked at Tom, who nodded. "Violent," she said.

The clerk handed down an official-looking pink form. As Ida reached up the clerk looked past her and addressed Tom, saying, "You may complete it on behalf of your wife, or you may allow her to write it, but do ask her to be concise."

Tom opened his mouth to object, but Ida touched his arm. The remark was beneath response. She sat on a bench and fished in her bag for a pencil, pulling out her guidebook and sketchbook as she searched, and laying them on the bench beside her. "*Plaignante*," she read on the form. The word was not immediately familiar.

"Complainant, or plaintiff," said Tom, looking over her shoulder and noticing her hesitation. "That's us."

Ida thanked Tom in clipped tones. Seeing that the clerk's comment about wives had stung Ida and that his own attempt to help was a misstep, Tom quickly excused himself. He quietly asked a passing officer the way to the lavatory, and then disappeared down a flight of stairs. Ida continued to fill out the form, but with increasing consternation. "*Auteur présumé du crime*"—that's Marinetti, of course, though it felt strange to write his name down as a criminal. After all, it was Ida herself who had recently bashed his head with an Alsatian cheese, not the other way around. "F. T. Marinetti," she wrote, adding "*et alia.*" Among others. Somehow a bit of high school Latin seemed appropriate when identifying an *auteur's* collaborators. And she knew there would have to be accomplices for a crime of this scale, the destruction of an entire city's cultural heritage.

Ida's brow clouded as she continued to fill out the form. *Lieu du crime*—location of the crime—what could she say? The catacombs. That would have to do. And, since Marinetti's conversation with Antheil had involved so many details about Sainte-Chapelle, the ancient chapel of the French kings, she added its name as well. *Heure et date du crime*—when it had taken place. What could she say? "The crime lies in the future," she wrote, thinking the phrase perhaps too formal. The final question dismayed Ida the most, not least because there was only an inch or so of space to write amid the clutter of official seals and small print. *Description du crime.* What could she say that would not sound absurd? "The suspect plans to dynamite the most precious churches and museums in France simultaneously, and by means of an…"—here Ida was really at a loss—"automatic musical ensemble." Ida scratched her chin and looked over the words. It did look absurd written like that. Worse than absurd: unhinged, insane. But it would have to do. She could explain better in person.

Ida rose, passed the form up to the clerk in his tower, and was told to sit and wait to be called. Returning to the bench, she found Tom already seated there. "May I look inside?" he asked, tapping the cover of her sketchbook. Ida froze. It was… it was a little like being touched. But it was Tom, and… "Yes," she said. "Yes, do."

Ida watched as Tom paged through the sketchbook, looking carefully at each image, sometimes flipping back to look again. The early pages had been filled in Chicago: quick sketches of the Art Institute's copies of Greek and Roman statues; more detailed versions of Winslow Homer's seascapes; a charcoal sketch of a museum guard biting into an apple he tried to conceal in the cuff of his uniform jacket. Tom paused on that one for a while and smiled. Next came a sketch of Teddy holding an enormous piece of cake, looking as if he planned on downing it in a single bite. Then came sketches Ida had made on the train to New York and during the Atlantic crossing—Teddy in his new hat; Teddy rushing past a porter at the Cleveland station when he'd nearly missed the train after popping out for a drink; Teddy standing in the bow of the ship, gesturing vaguely in the direction of Europe. Teddy at the Café Dupont, laughing with a somber Lewis. Then three attempts to get the composition of van Eyck's *Madonna of Chancellor Rolin* right, and another few with architectural details from the background of van Eyck's painting. Following these was Ida's vague, unfinished self-portrait (she'd stared into the mirror all that morning, she remembers, waiting for Teddy to drag himself from bed). Then a smudged-out portrait of a man—Teddy, again, though she'd erased the face—juggling onions. Tom hesitated for just a moment, seemed about to speak, but said nothing. And finally, there were the two strange sketches from this morning—Waterhouse's *Lady of Shalott* transformed into a woman paddling a canoe, more grim-faced than Ida remembered, and the oddly menacing cityscape she'd remembered from di Chirico, with added hounds and *Le Bateleur* lurking in the background.

"Were you," Tom picked his words carefully, "*happy* when you drew these?" Their eyes met, and for reasons she could not understand, Ida felt tears welling up in her eyes. "I'm so sorry," said Tom, softly. "Thank you for showing me your work."

"The inspector will see you now," said a gendarme, standing on the staircase. "Room 203—to the left, and he asks that you be quick about it." Ida looked at the tall young policeman with his floppy blond hair and kind face. He seemed familiar—yes, it was Clement, the assistant who had accompanied Inspector LaMarck's to Gertrude's salon.

Tom and Ida made haste to the designated office. They knew even before they stepped inside that the interview was not destined to go well, noting that the frosted-glass door bearing the number 203 had another inscription as well, the name Ida had feared she might see: "Inspector LaMarck."

"Oh dear," said Tom. "I believe we know this man."

Paddle on, thought Ida, whatever rapids lie ahead. She pushed open the door. The little inspector that Ida had last seen at Gertrude Stein's place now sat behind a desk so large as to be almost comical—he looked like a child. An angry child.

"Sit," said LaMarck, without rising to greet his guests. Tom and Ida obeyed, settling on two low, uncomfortable wooden chairs. LaMarck held the pink form up in the air as if it were evidence against them. "Explain," he said, looking only at Tom.

"We have uncovered a plot to destroy some of Paris' most important buildings," said Ida. "The police must get involved."

It was as if she had said nothing. The inspector kept a steady gaze on Tom, saying again, "Explain."

"It's as Mrs. Caine says," replied Tom firmly. "We were seeking Miss Alice Toklas, who, as you well know, has gone missing. During our investigations—" LaMarck cut him off with a raised hand.

"You do not investigate," said LaMarck, his head shaking slightly, his trim little mustache twitching. "The police investigate. You meddle. Or blunder. You…concoct absurd fantasies about crimes that have not been committed."

"Now see here—" Tom began.

"No. You must see," said LaMarck, angrily. "You allege that one Mr. Marinetti will destroy much of Paris, using as his instrument"—here he looked to the form, and, quoting the words exactly, continued—"an 'automatic musical ensemble.' What evidence do you bring with you, and why should I not have Mr. Marinetti informed of your libel against him?"

Ida rose to her feet, put her hands on LaMarck's desk, and leaned forward. She drew a deep breath, fixed him with a level stare, and explained, step by step, how she and Tom had gone to the catacombs; how they had found Antheil; how Marinetti's questions had led them to believe that much of Paris was in danger; how Marinetti's manifesto had called for the destruction of museums and universities and churches; how he had asked for information about how to reach such places via the catacombs; how he had asked about Antheil's system for linking instruments electronically and synchronizing them; how he had expressed particular interest in the royal chapel of Sainte-Chapelle; and how a kidnapper's note left at twenty-seven rue de Fleurus was probably left by him as part of the plot. He likely held Alice prisoner even now, Ida concluded. She sat down, flushed but satisfied that she had said her piece.

LaMarck paused before speaking. "And do you have this note in your possession?"

"We do not," said Tom, "but we can certainly fetch it."

"Indeed," said LaMarck, "you could fetch it—or fabricate it. Now." He swiveled to look at Ida. "You have been to Miss Stein's residence, have you not? I never forget a face, you know."

"I have," said Ida.

"We have become aware that hashish is consumed at these salons. Answer me honestly: have you deranged yourself with hashish? Are you in fact deranged by the drug even now?"

Ida and Tom blurted their objections, and for a moment LaMarck sat silent. Then he shot out of his chair and smashed his palm down on the call bell that sat among the scattered papers on his desk. His lip curled in irate disdain as he rang the bell again, then again, until a weary-looking gendarme came to the door.

"This woman is hysterical," declared LaMarck. "See that she and her"—he looked at Tom icily—"her minder are escorted out of the station, and make sure that they do not return. And you may both consider yourselves fortunate if we do not contact Mr. F. T. Marinetti, who has been libeled. The French Republic takes such things very seriously," he added, shooting a glare at the departing Tom and Ida, "even when the maligned man is a foreigner."

☙

"Well," said Tom, "how would you say that went?"

Ida forced a wan smile. "Are all the French policemen like that?"

"I am pleased to say I have never before dealt with the French police," said Tom, "except for Inspector LaMarck. He will be of no use to us whatsoever."

Ida agreed. What, then, could be done? "Let's go to Sainte-Chapelle," she decided suddenly. "It's the one place to which Antheil knew an underground route. If Marinetti is really planning to dynamite the place, perhaps we could find some evidence, and bring it to a more sympathetic policeman."

Tom agreed, but reminded her that L'Enfer was closed on Sundays, as was Paprikás, so they would have to enter the chapel through the main entrance and hope to find their way to the crypt below. The two walked briskly south, then along the Seine, pausing to purchase a firm-crusted baguette from a street vendor to share. They crossed to the Île de la Cité in silence, eating as they walked. The great cathedral of Notre Dame rose to their left. But it was another church they sought—through the arched gates of the ancient palace of the kings of France and into the courtyard beyond. There they found Sainte-Chapelle, tall and gray, standing where it had stood since the thirteenth century. It had long served as the private chapel of French royalty, had been damaged badly during the Revolution, and was restored to its former glory in the days of Napoleon. They entered its hush through a tall, open doorway.

The sight before them stung with beauty. Up—up—up went their eyes, borne heavenward by walls more glass than stone, more glowing color than mere glass, more spirit than matter. The ceiling blazed with golden fleur-de-lis studding the radiant blue like miniature suns. At the end of the apse a high rose window burned with holy light, surrounded by windows depicting the Nativity and the Passion of Christ. Ida dipped her hand in the stoup of holy water and crossed herself. Tom hesitated for a moment, then followed suit. The two then walked silently to the center of the room, turning slowly to see the high pointed windows shimmer with blue and golden light. Neither of them could say how it happened, but when they turned to speak to one another they found they were holding hands.

"You see," said Tom, pulling away from Ida, and spreading his arms, his voice a hush of reverence. "You see…"

Ida nodded in silent assent. She saw. If there were any chance that this magnificence was in danger, they must persevere, mad as it may seem.

The pair walked slowly around the chapel, pausing in front of the large, decorative stone features on the walls. They were shaped like four-leaf clovers—Ida recalled from her art books that they were called quatrefoils—and inside each was a painted scene decorated with gilded glass. In one scene King Saul met with David, both dressed as medieval lords. In another, Joseph's brothers, wearing the cowls of European peasants, sold their unfortunate kinsman into bondage. The village behind them looked thoroughly French despite the camel. "I wish I could speak to Marinetti now," Tom said, "with all his talk of the past as a burden. Just look—look at how the people who made all this received the old stories and found ways to make something ancient into something very much their own. The past wasn't past to them, it was alive, and because it was alive it could change." Tom pointed to a nearby quatrefoil. "Their Noah built a galleon, not an ark." He turned to Ida, passion in his voice. "We have our past, and we can't forget it…but that doesn't mean we don't live."

We have our past…but that doesn't mean we don't live; Lake Forest flashed in Ida's mind, all oaks and verandas, then she saw her passage across the ocean with Teddy, and her nights spent alone in their rented rooms. For a moment Ida thought—but she didn't know what she thought. A docent strolled past, mentioned the time, and asked politely for them to leave. A guard nearby looked less likely to be polite if they tried to stay. They would have to find another way to seek whatever lay beneath Sainte-Chapelle.

37

To enter the Bristol hotel is to enter a world that speaks so quietly it almost whispers. The clerks at the desk do it, and the guests—mostly British—find themselves matching their tones to those of the dark-suited staff. Whether you stand on the checkerboard tiles of the lobby or sit comfortlessly in one of the pew-like benches beneath the small statue of Artemis, you might even hear the building itself whisper. What does it say? Nothing like "opulence," or "ostentation," but those of a more attentive disposition will swear they hear a word that might be "restraint." It's what Tom liked most about the place, apart from the bountiful English breakfasts laid out in the oak-paneled hush of the hotel restaurant. But now, striding as fast as he could through the lobby and up the stairs, he had no patience for whispers. Indeed, something inside him wanted to scream, or bawl, or yelp.

He flung open the door of his room and stepped through with purpose—or apparent purpose, for when he reached the center of the room he stopped and stood ramrod straight and utterly still, a storm-tossed ship suddenly becalmed. The door gaped open behind him. The corridor and tidy room were silent, forgetting even to whisper. He stood, and the thought that lurked in the depths swam up to meet him. Why had he held Ida's hand there, in Sainte-Chapelle? And why, why had he let go? Oh, he knew why. He knew exactly.

It had been three years since he last stood in the nave of Sainte-Chapelle with Vivienne, the sublime light dancing through the stained glass from the angelic heights above them. Maybe it had been the slanting light, the carvings, the heart-stopping beauty of the place that kept Viv from making one of her scenes. She respected beauty, after all, if she respected anything.

Not the sugary beauty of her father's paintings, in which

girls were either playing insipidly with round-faced dolls or, if a bit too old for such diversions, looking much like china dolls themselves. They whispered blandly by pianofortes or, perched limply on settees, combing one another's hair. No, she liked something more substantial, the crafted beauty of line and curvature, of gilt, glory, and shadow—not her father's pictures. She liked the gilded picture frames her grandfather made. He was a gently smiling little craftsman with his working-class accent and the spicy anecdotes to match. In Bloomsbury they never really forgave Viv for not being able to lose her grandfather's vowels, not completely. Of course, there was much more than that to forgive: her fits, always frequent, became more furious every year. Stout Clive Bell once had to carry her out of his flat over his shoulder as she bit, scratched, and howled. Tom had run after them, of course, but not fast enough to avoid hearing Virginia's plummy voice muttering that Viv was like a bag of ferrets poor Tom had to wear around his neck. By his reckoning, she'd ruined a thousand evenings for him, or more. He couldn't bear to count. And mornings, afternoons, and sleepless nights too. Her demons were ancient, atavistic colossi that knew nothing of clocks or calendars.

Whatever the reason, Viv hadn't ruined Sainte-Chapelle— not that day, anyway. But she'd ruined every other day on that stay in Paris, where he'd taken her on the threadbare hope that a change of scenery would bring a corresponding change in her internal weather. She'd tried her usual tricks at first, here in this very hotel: hiding his wallet and his keys, stealing the papers he needed to take round to writers for *The Criterion* and stuffing them beneath the mattress. Anything to keep him from leaving, if only for another minute. And then when she stood between him and the door, half-dressed and livid, her hair a Medusa's tangle, she'd insulted him, told him the most horrible lies, thrown ashtrays and coat hangers at him, screaming at him to go at once. And that was the truth of it, with Viv: Tom couldn't go, and he couldn't stay.

He couldn't even shelter in silence without setting her words loose to crawl over him like a knot of asps. "Why do you never speak? Why, why won't you talk to me?" she'd hiss, before shrieking "Speak! Speak!" He said nothing, enduring all in silence. On the last night she broke a window with his umbrella and threw it to the street below. "Speak," she screamed, "or get out!"

Get out, then, Tom muttered to himself. Get out of this room and go to Ida. He couldn't stay in this room, couldn't stay another day in his impossible marriage. He thought of Vivienne twisting in the arms of the hospital orderlies, biting her own tongue until she spat blood. Get out, and go to Ida, old Possum, he told himself. What holds you back? Not love, admit it. He looked at the gold band of his finger, thought of the altar at Sainte-Chapelle, the shafting light proclaiming the eternal glory and the eternal law. The elders in his gallery of ancestors remained silent, deep in shadow. They let the light above the altar speak for them.

Tom's whole body shook. He couldn't stay and he couldn't go. A bellhop pushing a cart laden with baggage down the corridor glanced through the open door, saw Tom's quaking back, and turned discreetly away. A weeping man is best undisturbed. When he passed again, his cart emptied, Tom had not moved.

38

The streets of Montparnasse buzzed with the to-and-fro of a late Monday morning, though perhaps less so here than in the city's more businesslike, less bohemian districts. Ida felt self-conscious about her clothing as she sat at an absurdly small marble-topped table outside the undistinguished café where she and Tom had arranged to meet. She wore her flat shoes, a long skirt of heavy chambray and a bulky, dull red shirt she normally only wore for painting. She hoped no one would notice the two streaks of brighter red on the sleeves where she'd brushed up against the still wet robes of the Virgin Mary in her copy of van Eyck. It was a good outfit for the catacombs, she thought, but for a Paris street? Well, this was bohemian Montparnasse, haunt of many artists. She couldn't be the only person with paint on her shirt.

When Tom arrived, Ida instantly became less anxious about her own clothing: Tom wore brand new hiking books, khaki trousers, a web belt, a long-sleeved camp shirt with epaulettes, and a shiny new canteen on a leather strap. The only thing missing was a pith helmet, thought Ida, stifling a giggle—but he did have a compass attached to his belt with a leather thong, and he held an electric lantern in his hand. She couldn't help but smile as he settled in the chair across from her and motioned to the waiter for coffee. "Just come from the Boy Scout jamboree?" she asked. Tom's eyebrows shot up in surprise, then a wide grin broke slowly across his face.

"I took the liberty of visiting an outfitter first thing this morning," said Tom. "I believe they equip gentlemen on their way to the French colonies. So, I was hoping I looked more like the governor of a remote province in Indochina than a scout leader." Ida looked Tom up and down and decided not to say she'd been picturing him more as a junior scout than a troop leader. "I got you this," he said, passing her the electric lantern—a rectangular battery with a wire handle and a bulb mounted on top. "Might help keep us oriented down below."

"But how will we even get to the catacombs?" asked Ida. "L'Enfer won't open for hours—not even for previews."

"I thought we'd try our luck at Paprikás," Tom suggested. Action was what was needed: it was that or try to tell Ida about all he'd thought and felt about her, and about Vivienne, as he'd stood shaking in the Bristol Hotel. And he couldn't face that now. "It won't be too long before they open. And from there I think I can figure the underground route to Sainte-Chapelle." He reached into one of the many pockets on his shirt, then another, and finally another, extracting a much folded, hand-drawn map. "See, here, I've drawn the route to Sainte-Chapelle—the one that Antheil described to me and Marinetti," he said, struggling to find space for the map on their small café table, "and then I worked out the route Boski took us on from Antheil's lair to the restaurant. The red lines are tunnels, the black lines are streets, and the letter X marks landmarks above ground."

Impressed, Ida peered at the map closely. "And what are these boxes, marked with different numbers of stars? Tombs? Points of entry?"

"Cheese shops." Tom looked slightly abashed, adding, "It's an old map."

Tom and Ida were the first guests to arrive at Paprikás, where the young, silent waiter who led them to a table suppressed all but the slightest sign of amusement at Tom's outfit. After they'd settled beneath the chalkboard with the day's menu, the waiter returned and stood, pencil in hand, ready to take their order.

"We'd like to see Andris," said Tom.

"We're really not here to eat," added Ida. She'd like to avoid having Tom pay for yet another meal and could hardly afford one herself. "We're just here to go through the wine cellar."

The waiter remained silent and looked perplexed.

"Wine cellar," said Tom, in French, then in English. The waiter shook his head and shrugged apologetically. "*Vinkäl-lare*," he tried. "*Cantina di vini.*" No progress.

Ida reached quickly into her bag for a pad and pencil, sketched a large wine bottle, then added an arrow pointing down. Tom joined in, pointing first to the sketch, then pointing vigorously at the floor. The waiter nodded and departed.

Tom and Ida looked at each other. "Do you suppose that worked?" asked Tom.

"I think he must only speak Hungarian," said Ida. "Surprising for a waiter."

A moment later, the waiter returned with an earthenware pitcher and goblets. He placed the goblets on the table and filled them with dark wine.

"Andris?" said Ida, gesturing vaguely with her hands in a failed attempt to indicate a tall, stooping man. "Monsieur Andris?" The waiter nodded again and departed.

"Sweet Lord!" said Tom, putting down the goblet from which he'd drunk, his mouth stained purple and distorted in a grimace. "I've…I've never had anything like it!"

Ida quickly sipped her wine. It managed to cloy with sweetness while simultaneously burning like red pepper. The aftertaste—what was the aftertaste? she wondered. She pictured an X at the exact midpoint of a line, at one end of which was the inside of a pencil box, at the other a wrinkled leather boot. Her eyes were still watering when Andris emerged from the kitchen in chef's whites and an apron, smiling as he approached the table.

When Tom explained why they'd come, Andris's smile grew wider. "Forgive young Mihály," he said, chuckling. "He thought you wanted our cheapest wine. It's awful," he admitted with a smile, "but it has a high alcohol content—many of the poets drink it."

"Doesn't Mihály speak French?" asked Ida, working her tongue in her mouth in an attempt to be rid of the wine's pungent aftertaste.

"Not yet," said Andris. "He's a sculptor, fresh from Szeged. He's come to Paris penniless, hoping to make his name. Here," he added, standing to pull a small framed photograph from the wall. "Before the war, I used to support many artists." The photo showed a younger Andris, splendidly dressed, standing with a group of people in front of a stately country house. "Yes, I am he, in the center. That is my wife in a dress she had made on our first journey to Paris. But these three young men? A composer, a painter, and a poet. I would bring such people to the house and let them stay for weeks, sometimes longer. Ladomér stayed almost a year. He was quiet, there was room. We didn't mind."

He offered the photo to Ida, who gazed at it in wonder. "Yes," said Andris, "in another life, before the war, I was an aristocrat—as I still am, at least in title. Though my fief," he gestured at the roomful of tables, "is now reduced to these premises, I still like to support artists. That's why you ate for free and will again. Tom is a poet of some name, yes? And you, you're a painter?"

Ida hesitated. "She is," said Tom. Ida shot him a look, its emotion located midway between gratitude and reproach. "I've seen her work," Tom added. "Influenced by the Surrealists."

"Ah," said Andris, smiling at Ida. "No wonder you liked young Calder's circus. All you Surrealists admire him!"

"Did the young men in the photograph go on to fame?" asked Ida, anxious to change the subject. Was she—could she be—a Surrealist?

Andris's brow darkened. "Unfortunately, the war that took our house, our fortune, and in the end our land, also took two of our little group. Ladomér lived but wrote no more.

"I'm so sorry," said Ida.

"As am I," Andris breathed deeply, "but we pick up what is left, and make what we can from it—I am still a patron of the arts. And doesn't a patron owe artists better wine than this?" He sniffed at the pitcher and smiled.

"We'd better not indulge," said Tom. "We have a different sort of favor to ask."

Soon Ida stood once again in the catacomb corridor outside the Paprikás wine cellar. She switched the electric lantern on and it cast a bright yellowish light on Tom's map. They confirmed their route, then were off down the corridor. As they passed the yellow door to Antheil's room, Tom asked, "Shall we knock?"

"Better not," Ida whispered. "Let's stay with our mission." They walked on, following corridor after corridor, passing through chambers empty or filled with bones, until they came to a square gap in the wall of the rough-hewn hallway that marked their turn for Sainte-Chapelle. Ida shone the light on the space beyond, revealing a different sort of corridor. Where the catacombs were stone, the hallway beyond was lined with cinderblock. Where the catacombs were atavistic, primal, this hallway seemed modern. Flat-floored and downward sloping, its ceiling was arched, and at long intervals held metal brackets for absent electric bulbs. Pipes, tubes, and wires with frayed cloth coverings lined the wall to their left. Tom indicated that this was their route, and he and Ida entered. The corridor sloped increasingly downward, the walls beading with moisture.

"Where does this take us?" asked Ida.

"Under the Seine, to the Île de la Cité," Tom replied. "The French built these tunnels during the war, to keep communications open if the Germans destroyed the bridges and made boat crossings dangerous. There were Zeppelin bombers in those days. They often darkened the sky over London too, and we hid underground when they dropped bombs."

"And these tubes and wires—could any of these have been laid by Marinetti?" Ida looked at the wall of cables, wires, and pipes, jumping back a little when one made a sudden whooshing sound.

"*Le pneumatique*, I think," explained Tom, "makes that sound—in Paris, pneumatic tubes deliver mail between local offices. I'm sure they used them in the war. As for the wires—I couldn't say what any of them do. And I've no desire to cut one. Who knows if they carry a live current?"

They continued on, the downward slope eventually coming to an end, an upward gradient beginning. After what seemed like a very long time, Tom motioned for them to stop. "We've arrived," he said, placing his map in the beam of Ida's lantern. "We should be beneath Sainte-Chapelle—but there's nothing here."

"Wait," said Ida, flashing her beam farther down the corridor, where a darker shadow seemed to indicate a door or opening. They walked on and saw an archway to their left, with a battered pine door, the wood split in two. "The wood is freshly splintered," said Ida, touching a shattered board. "No rot, no moisture." They pried it open and passed into a chamber beyond.

Tom and Ida stayed close to one another, walking slowly into a vast space that revealed itself piecemeal to Ida's darting lantern light. The chamber was square—no, rectangular, and of modern construction, with tiled walls and a concrete floor. As they moved inward from the edge, they saw that the low ceiling was supported by concrete pillars, around which clustered... what? They approached the nearest pillar and found two crates placed at its base. Ida held the lamp while Tom fished a folding knife from his shirt pocket. With a little effort, he pried the lid from the crate and pulled it aside with a scraping sound. Ida shone the light down on the contents: stick after stick of dynamite, along with a little metal apparatus from which a copper wire ran out of the box and across the floor. Ida followed the wire with her lantern light—it led to another set of crates beside the next pillar.

"Look!" Ida said, moving the circle of light over the floor. "The crates were moved here recently." The deep dust underfoot had been disturbed by dragged crates and several pairs of boots. The two walked slowly around the chamber, examining each corner, each pillar, each set of crates carefully.

"Are we—below the crypt?" wondered Tom when they had completed their circuit of the room.

"I don't know," said Ida. "But from the way these crates are positioned, I'd say whoever put them here wanted them close to the pillars for a specific reason."

"And I think I know the reason," said Tom. "To take down the pillars. And whatever's above us—Sainte-Chappelle, I fear—is to crash down with them. What are we to do?"

"Hush!" whispered Ida. A noise sounded out in the corridor—footsteps, more than one set of them, accompanied by a flashing of electric light. "I think the people who delivered these crates have returned."

Tom and Ida hid behind a stack of crates and Ida switched off the electric lantern. She could hear herself breathe and felt Tom's warm presence beside her in the dark. What had they gotten themselves into?

With a great bright flash of light, several figures entered the chamber. One held an electric lantern high, revealing himself and his two companions—policemen in uniform. Ida recognized one of them: Clement, the young gendarme Inspector LaMarck had treated with such contempt at Gertrude's salon. He had seemed kindly then, and, however skeptical Inspector LaMarck had been at the station yesterday, the police would have to believe them now. Ida stepped from her hiding place into the circle of light, and Tom followed.

"Officer Clement!" she cried. "We have much to tell you."

Clement started, staring in disbelief at Tom and Ida for a moment, then looked to his fellow officers. "I wouldn't have believed it, but the inspector was right." He turned to face Tom and Ida. "Monsieur, madame, you are under arrest."

39

Ida really couldn't complain about Officer Clement, who was nothing but courteous on the long journey out of the catacombs. He asked that she and Tom remain silent and gave instructions for officers to cuff Tom's hands. This done, Clement hesitated a moment, apologized, and then carefully cuffed Ida's hands himself. Thus bound, Ida found it difficult to balance as she walked the uneven surfaces of the catacomb floors. She kept her gaze down, but slipped once, landing in a filthy puddle and staining her skirt with black oil. Soon she had lost her way entirely: they were following an unfamiliar route, one that brought them through the ancient catacombs to a concrete bunker, and after that into a narrow corridor with tiled walls and electric lights. This, in turn, led to a heavy metal door beyond which, Ida was surprised to discover, lay the Cluny-Sorbonne Metro station, bright and bustling, where passing commuters stared at the handcuffed young woman and man being escorted by the police. When they reached street level, the police herded Tom and Ida into the back of a blue-gray police van. Clement sat between them.

"Ida, I—" Tom began.

"You must not speak, either of you," said Clement. "We will take statements from you at the station, and we cannot have you agreeing on any kind of deception." He looked at Ida sympathetically, adding, "My apologies, Madame Caine."

At the now familiar Montparnasse police station, Tom and Ida were taken to separate rooms. Ida was fingerprinted, then photographed, then a bored clerk asked her endless questions about her nationality, address, sources of income, marital status, religion, and on and on. She answered compliantly, her voice flat. Part of her felt certain she would soon be released; another more insistent part feared jail awaited her, perhaps years of it.

And what would become of Tom? Or Teddy—how would he ever find her? She realized suddenly how alone she was. Alone and adrift, with no far-off galleon's sail visible on the horizon.

After an interminable wait on an uncomfortable bench in a locked room, a policeman escorted Ida down to the basement level, past several barred cells where dangerous-looking men made lewd remarks as she passed. Around a corner and through a set of heavy double doors lay the women's wing, where the policeman removed her handcuffs and gestured for her to enter a cell. "This way, madame," the gendarme said, with mock courtesy. Ida entered, and the door slammed shut heavily behind her.

Ida's eyes adjusted slowly to the dimness of the room, which was lit by a single yellowish bulb imprisoned in a metal cage-like fixture hanging from the ceiling. The bare concrete room held two sets of bunk beds with thin, fraying mattresses, ratty gray blankets, and no pillows. A grate in the floor near the wall was to serve as the toilet, a snub-nosed tap knee-high on the wall was the only source of water. It appeared that Ida had two roommates. One of her two companions sat atop the iron radiator and grinned at her with a gap-toothed smile, the other perched on a bunk, face in her hands, sobbing softly.

"Welcome to L'Hotel des Flics," said the smiling woman, heavyset and middle-aged in a dirty blouse and a long skirt, each the same grayish-pink shade as her skin. "Forgive our room-mate—she is not used to such accommodations." The woman, correctly interpreting Ida's stunned silence, added, "And I see that you aren't either, *cherie*. So much the better for you to have lived a fine and sheltered life!"

When Ida still offered no reply, the woman continued, "I am called Marinade—not because it is the name my parents gave me, no, no, but because I am always soaking in wine." At this she gave a deep guffaw that seemed to come straight from her belly. Her laughter reminded Ida of Gertrude Stein that night in the salon.

Ida quietly introduced herself in her accented French. "*Amé-*

ricaine, eh? " said Marinade. "You are wise to come to France—I could never abide a nation like yours, one that bans alcohol. And this sad one over here," she pointed to the sobbing young woman, "is Claudile. She comes from Normandy, but let's not hold it against her." Claudile turned away to face the wall. "But tell me, Ida Caine"—in Marinade's mouth the surname sounded like *can*—"tell me, what brings you to our city of lights? The wine? Or has the roaring American stock market left you with too much money, so you've come here to throw some of it away?" Marinade continued smiling and seemed to find everything that came out of her own mouth amusing. It could be worse, thought Ida.

"I came to paint," she said, simply.

"Ah, *une artiste*! Well then, I won't ask what's landed you here. Vagrancy, failure to pay rent, indecent behavior, public drunkenness, assaulting an officer with a paintbrush, Cubism—one of those offences, to be sure."

"Something like that," said Ida. How could she even begin to explain the real reason she was here? She could barely believe it herself. Realizing her replies might seem curt, even antisocial, Ida decided to make conversation. Who could say how long these two would be her only companions? "And yourself, Marinade? Do you come here often?"

Marinade laughed as if this were the finest joke she'd heard in weeks. Perhaps, judging from the mood of her sobbing associate, it was. "It is my holiday retreat," she said, with a smile. "This time I'm here for forcibly introducing a pimp's face to a chair. But it wasn't for selfish reasons, you must understand. It was for this one." She indicated Claudile, who stole a quick glance in Marinade's direction. It was the first time Ida had a look at Claudile's face—it was as pale as her ash-blond hair, fine featured, and very young. Her eyes were remarkable, thought Ida, like something Renoir would paint, though they didn't show at their best just now, red and puffy from tears.

"Are you…" Ida trailed off.

"A prostitute? Me?" Marinade burst into another one of her

belly laughs. "A barfly, yes, and happy to drink what a man can buy me, but a prostitute? Never. Nor is this one, not really." Marinade extended a leg and poked Claudile in the ribs with a big, grubby bare toe. "You needn't be ashamed, lamb. Not your fault." Claudile looked up but was not comforted. "Her parents ran out of money trying to farm fields of stones," said Marinade, leaning forward and putting an arm around Claudile's narrow shoulders. "They sent her to an agency in Paris that claimed they'd find her a place as a maid, but these agencies, they aren't angels. And a bad one will sell a girl to a pimp. The little dove here was sold to a bad pimp. When I saw her on Place Pigalle, that little shit had already hit her more than once. Not in the face, which must be kept pretty, but here." Marinade held her belly with both hands. "And he said he'd cut her where she stood if she didn't start to behave."

"My God," said Ida. Robert McAlmon, the American writer who did not write, had talked about Place Pigalle the night she'd left him drinking with Teddy.

"Of course, I didn't like his threats," said Marinade, "and I was two bottles into the evening, so I let Henri speak for me."

"Henri?" asked Ida.

"Henri is the only reason pimps leave me alone, but they took Henri away when I came to this place."

"Was he arrested as well?"

"Ha! No, no. They'll bring Henri to me when I leave." Ida looked perplexed. "Henri," Marinade explained, "is a seven-inch knife, and the best bodyguard for a woman like me in this nasty old world."

"But I thought you hit the man with a chair?" said Ida, impressed, repelled, and confused.

"Only after Henri had a good look at his spleen from the inside. But I never blame Henri for my troubles. So now, you are an artist? Stop an old drunk from gabbing, and make some art. This can be your canvas"—Marinade gestured at the stained concrete wall, marked here and there with etched graffiti—"and here is your brush." She fished beneath the bunkbed, pulled up a shard of stone. Ida turned it over in her hand, looked at it. Yes. It would scratch well and leave a white mark like hard chalk.

Ida stood before the wall, and began to sketch in lines, working large, taking the whole surface for her canvas. A figure to the left, stout and strong, with clever eyes. A figure to the right, slim, beautiful, with almond eyes downcast, and flowing robes. Rough in the outline. Crosshatch the shading as best you can.

Claudile had stopped sobbing and looked on with wonder. Marinade, for once, sat silent. The shard scraped softly in the silence of the cell.

It was *The Madonna of Chancellor Rolin* that Ida drew, but now Marinade took the place of the chancellor, while Claudile stood in for Mary. The likenesses were good, thought Ida, as good as one could make in bad light and using a shard of chalky stone. Where van Eyck's chancellor held a book, Ida drew a knife, the word *Henri* etched on the blade. The weapon was held like an offering to the robed Mary with Claudile's face. But what to place on Mary's lap, where the infant Jesus was held in the original? Not a child—that would be cruel for a woman in Claudile's position. Let it be a lamb, then. An icon of Christ, of innocence. That felt right. And the angel holding a crown above Mary's head? Ida roughed in the wings and robes, paused a moment, and then looked at Claudile, who was flushed and breathing deeply, fascinated. Why not? thought Ida and drew her own face on the angel.

For a background, Ida turned van Eyck's colonnade into the bars of a prison cell, with a vaguely sketched city sprawled beyond it. Then, high in the air above the city, Ida drew a flight of birds. They weren't in the original at all.

Marinade, still silent, made the sign of the cross. Claudile stood, staring raptly at Ida's mural, then approached Ida hesitantly, searching for words. Ida took her in a silent embrace.

40

Tom stared into his tin bowl in despair. It held a soggy hunk of bread and a few swallows of watery white bean soup, in which the presence of beans seemed more theoretical than materially manifest. And there wasn't so much as a bite of cheese in evidence. Mustn't grumble, though; at least he had the cell to himself. And if he couldn't be by Ida's side at a time like this, he'd settle for solitude, at least while it lasted. The presence of four bunks in the cell made him suspect his solitude would not long prevail.

Indeed, in some sense, his isolation had already dissipated. Tom felt keenly the ominous presence of his ancestors glaring down from their portraits in the gallery of his mind. Row upon row of Eliots, Stearns, and Greenleafs glowered at him; the fallen fruit of the family tree, rotting in a prison cell—and a French prison cell, no less! How could it have come to this? Tom dared not meet the cold gray eyes of William Greenleaf Eliot, the patriarch who led his family west from Boston and brought the light of Unitarianism to the wilderness of Missouri. Rectitude nested like an eagle in the jutting crag of his beard; gravitas perched on his bare upper lip, his swooping white hair spread from a strong central part like the wings of a disapproving angel. William Greenleaf Eliot had borne the word of God to the godless, commanding that churches be built—and they were built, along with schools and a red brick library whose eaves caught the wind in a mighty "shush." William Greenleaf Eliot had denounced the golden calf of the saloon owners and brewers, had civilized the bankers and the riverboat owners. He considered all people of St. Louis, no matter their error-ridden denomination, his parishioners, and he was a man of such conspicuous modesty that he'd refused to allow the grateful flock to name their new university after him. He insisted they name it after Washington instead, geographic confusion be damned. As damned as his jailbird grandson, eating a bean soup no Bostonian would deign to grace with that name.

Tom held his head as a half-dozen great-aunts tut-tutted, great-uncles scowled, and the great patriarch himself quivered in outraged righteousness. "But I was trying to save a church!" he cried out, alone and underdressed in the gallery of ancestral portraits. His epaulettes and military-style web belt seemed more ridiculous than ever. "A church, yes," the portrait of William Greenleaf Eliot spoke, ice in his voice and pale fire in his eyes, "but what sort of church? Decked out in what gaudy half-pagan vanities? And did I not see you douse yourself in the water of superstition and make the papist sign of the cross?" Tom trembled, but the voice did not relent: it rose ever louder. "And who was the woman?" Now came the thunder. "She. Was. Not. Your. *Wife.*"

Tom rose and turned around in the gallery. Every eye of every dowager and minister, every endower of charitable institutions, every university trustee, bank president, and pilgrim, stared him down. "Say something for yourself," they said. "Explain." He brushed the sweat from his forehead, looked up, and opened his mouth to speak.

"In here," barked the policeman, yanking open the cell door and shoving a solid, short man into the room. Tom looked at him blankly, collected himself, and suddenly fell back on the ingrained etiquette of his people. "It's Marcel, isn't it?" he said, rising and extending a hand. "What an extraordinary surprise."

Marcel glowered and said nothing.

"So…" Tom faltered. "How—how are things at the bureau? Surrealist research going…as well as…" His voice trailed off.

Marcel threw himself on a bunk, rubbed his forehead, then sat and fixed Tom in a steady glare. "And how did you come to be here?" he asked.

"A bit of confusion," said Tom, regaining his composure. Tom's inborn reticence made a pact with his acute sense of the sheer implausibility of the truth of the matter, and he settled on a strategy of avoidance. "I'm sure it will all be sorted out soon."

"That all you're going to say?" asked Marcel, curtly.

Tom looked at Marcel's dirty black trousers and turtleneck, and the stains—oil? paint? tar?—on his hands.

"Yes," said Tom, suddenly wary. "And you?"

"Graffiti, once again," muttered Marcel, not meeting Tom's gaze. "I expect I'll be out soon enough too."

The silence that followed grew long and deep.

Inspector LaMarck leafed through the reports on his desk and grew increasingly agitated. He stood, paced around his office, picked up a sheet of paper and stared at it. Yes, it was Clement who had brought the Americans in. It was always Clement when you didn't want it to be. He should have given strict instructions for it to be Tetrault or Garneau, or any of a half-dozen others who would take a suitably flexible approach to evidence. But it had been Clement, that irksome embodiment of petit-bourgeois conscientiousness who would no sooner plant evidence than he'd steal a centime from the cashbox at his mother's poultry shop. To swap him out for another would violate procedure and could look bad later. It would look bad, too, if Clement put two and two together, which even he could manage now and then. LaMarck throttled an imaginary goose, only to look down and see he'd crumpled the document in his hands into a wrinkled ball.

"Clement!" he shouted out the open door. "Clement! You'll need to fill out the C-11 form again. You—you blotted a line." *Cochon. Roi des cons.*

"Yes, Inspector," said Clement, appearing at the doorway. LaMarck sneered and slammed the door shut, pacing once more around his desk. He sat, drew a cigarette from a silver case, then failed to light it with his shaking hands. *Con. Roi des cochons. Cul des culs.* LaMarck threw the cigarette on the desk and rifled through the day's other reports. Prostitutes, pickpockets, drunken *clochards*, and…what's this? Well, on top of the Clement affair, this needed attention. He reached for his telephone. On the second attempt, the switchboard operator connected him to the man he sought.

"We have Marcel."

There was a pause. "I heard he'd been pinched. It's good it was your boys and not someone else's. What have they got on him?" The voice was tired and accented. Marinetti had had a long, tense night.

"It wasn't my boys it was some clod out in the countryside. But a man I trust pulled some strings, and Marcel's here now, cooling his heels. Don't fret, we treat the guests in our cells like royalty."

"Treat him any way you want. But we need him back. His crew only answers to him, and only he knows where they've cached their best materials," Marinetti said.

"We'll have him out, don't worry yourself about that. But it'll take a day or two. The best I can do without arousing suspicion. Thank your saints he had the sense not to fight that bumpkin policeman who found him." LaMarck was prone to lecturing but restrained himself from going on. For all of Marinetti's erratic ways, he was serious about these matters, dead serious.

"We appreciate your cooperation. A great dream makes for unlikely allies, yes?"

"The enemy of my enemy is my friend," agreed LaMarck. "But there's something else here, bigger than Marcel. We arrested the American girl—the detective's wife. Along with another American, a Mr. Eliot, perhaps her lover."

All weariness vanished from Marinetti's voice. *"Meraviglioso! Fantastico!* But that's wonderful, Inspector. You have no idea how happy you've made me."

"And you have no idea how unhappy you've made me," said LaMarck. "They came in with allegations that you were going to…well, that you were doing what you are in fact doing. But they named Sainte-Chapelle as a target." The inspector paused, a feeling of betrayal growing within him. "Sainte-Chapelle, for

God's sake! We agreed—no churches. I would look the other way if you destroyed those treasonous bastards in the *Sénat* and the *Assemblée Nationale*. Go ahead, blow the Palais du Luxembourg and the Palais Bourbon to pieces, along with your libraries and museums. The political vermin are traitors to France. But—hear me—no churches."

Marinetti held his tongue.

"And?" said LaMarck, impatiently. "If you want us to turn a blind eye, you will abide by the agreement. Yes?"

"Yes," said Marinetti. "Yes, of course—these Surrealists, they can be overzealous in their anticlericalism. Set Marcel free and I'll see to it he understands."

"Sainte-Chapelle is the holy chapel of the kings of France!" LaMarck said, his voice rising as he touched the fleur-de-lis pendant that hung at his throat. "The past kings and, God willing, the future kings. As for archives and galleries—pfft. Let the intellectuals and artists whine. It's what they do best."

Marinetti tried not to take the comment personally. What was he himself, if not an artist—soon to be the maestro of the greatest performance in history? Mere politics was for little men like LaMarck, too small-minded to even comprehend that the *Sénat* and *Assemblée nationale* were unworthy of inclusion in the great work, which would liberate France from something much more important than a political regime. But let LaMarck find that out on the great day itself. Until then let the bourgeois bastard think he'd have his way. He was too useful to alienate. "And the Americans—you'll see to it that they stay locked away, yes?"

"I'll do what can be done. But the wrong officer has become involved." It wounded LaMarck to admit the limits of his power. "And if we make much of the explosives in the tribunal, we will draw a great deal of attention from my superiors, which will imperil the whole operation. I can hold them on a minor charge only, and a fool judge may let them go with a fine."

"Understood," said Marinetti, before placing the handset back on the column of the telephone. He rubbed his eyes. They would have to give up Sainte-Chapelle. A loss, a grievous loss, but not vital. But Notre Dame? No, you couldn't leave the cathedral of Notre Dame standing. As a formal element, it pulled together the whole of the performance. (Was "performance" the right word? No—the conflagration). He would simply have to tell Marcel to be more careful.

41

Panic and drowsiness made a strange combination, thought Ida as she perched on the narrow, pew-like bench outside the chamber where the Tribunal de Police would meet. She had spent a night, a day, and a second night in jail, and on both nights had slept as poorly as she expected once she settled into her narrow bunk—the mattress was thin, the bedframe squeaky, and one of her companions (she suspected Marinade) snorted and snored with the hardy vitality of a prairie buffalo. At least there hadn't been fleas; for this, she thanked her thin blanket and its chemical odor. Morning brought only a watery bean soup and hunk of hard, stale bread, the same fare that served for each jailhouse meal. And never any coffee—alas, not so much as a demitasse.

Now she sat, unkempt, drowsy, and worried in a locked, windowless room in the building adjacent to the station. Clement had taken her there after she had filled out endless police forms and signed reams of documents, some of which she'd been too broken down to read. The sound of Clement's rubber stamp was torment, each hollow *thunk* driving a rusted nail into her head. She was thirsty, dizzy, and numb. The policeman looked at her sympathetically, and almost patted her hand. "It won't be a real court," he said, "just the tribunal next door. It's where we take drunks and derelicts and other disreputable but harmless types." As soon as the words left his mouth he looked as though he wanted them back. "And others who have done no great harm," he added, embarrassed.

Ida had no way of telling how long she'd been sitting on the narrow bench—fifteen minutes? An hour? Time bent and folded—a Cubism, no, a Surrealism of the clock, she thought, and almost managed a thin smile. Finally, the door opened, and a policeman jerked his head, indicating she should rise and follow the man. The officer led her down a hallway and into a small semi-circular chamber, set up like a miniature auditorium, with a raised wooden desk at the front facing three tiers of seats. It had the look of a senate chamber shrunken to a petty scale. The desk dominating the front of the room was flanked by the flag of the French Republic on one side, and a bored-looking police clerk on the other, rifling through papers on a clipboard. A corpulent, balding man in robes, whom she took to be the judge, sat at the desk chewing on something and staring blankly into the middle distance.

"Comrade," rasped a voice from the first tier of chairs. Ida, startled, looked up and saw it was Marcel, seated between two police officers. "I trust you slept well," he called down, halfway grinning as the gendarmes pulled him roughly from his chair and led him toward the door.

"The next case," said the man with the clipboard, flipping to a new page, "is that of Mr. Thomas Eliot and a Mrs. Ida Caine. Here is Mr. Eliot now." There was a bit of confusion as Marcel and his captors tried to depart by maneuvering past Clement, who eventually managed to lead a bedraggled Tom, his hair part in ruins, into the room. A shout of "death to the pigs!" followed by a thump and a long, low groan, echoed in the corridor.

Tom looked at Ida, and mouthed words she could not quite make out.

"What is the charge?" said the judge, in a tone of profound ennui.

"Trespassing," said the clerk. "For both of them."

"Trespassing where?" asked the judge, sounding as if he truly wouldn't care if they'd been trespassing in his own bedroom.

"The catacombs," said the clerk.

The judge rubbed the back of his neck and stifled a yawn. "A fine, then. Fifty francs each, or a week in the cells. And bring another cup of coffee, hot this time."

With no further ceremony, Tom and Ida were escorted back

to the police station, where Tom's canteen, Ida's handbag, and the electric lantern were all returned to them. A clerk behind an iron-grated window demanded payment for their fine.

"It's terribly embarrassing," Tom said to the clerk, "but I haven't enough money with me—I simply didn't expect…"

Ida begged him to allow her to pay, and, when he didn't object, she did, opening her handbag and peeling banknotes from her ever-diminishing stockpile. A hundred francs—that left Ida with hardly anything. Even after Tom paid her back, she'd still be short of making the rent, which was now well past due. What could be done? Perhaps if Teddy returned, then he could wire his family. It would kill him, but what else was there? Her family was out of the question when it came to money, and she couldn't let Tom pay her rent, she simply couldn't, though she knew he would if she asked.

"Comrades!" came a voice from down the corridor. It was Marcel—no, it was Gabriel calling, with Marcel at his side. "I have just liberated Marcel at that very same cashier's window— the hungry maw of the police must be fed, no? Come with us, won't you? There's an automobile waiting outside." Ida and Tom followed the Surrealists out to the street, where a bright, late-model yellow roadster sat humming curbside, headlamps jutting out like frog's eyes. A wide rear compartment could seat three, while one passenger could join the driver in the narrow front compartment—a driver who, despite a low-pulled cloche hat and goggles, looked strangely familiar. She pulled off her goggles—it was Dora Maar. "Ida!" she cried. "You poor thing. Come sit by me." She patted the seat beside her. Ida obeyed, grateful for the plush comfort of the roadster. Everything about the vehicle—the robin's egg blue of the crushed velvet bench seat, the gleaming chrome implements, the walnut dashboard—sang of comfort and luxury.

"I have to meet some people nearby," said Marcel. "Tom, Gabriel, you go with Comrade Dora. No need to worry yourselves over me." With that, he turned and loped down the street at a fast clip, pausing to look back over his shoulder before ducking down an alleyway. Gabriel shrugged and climbed aboard Dora's car, Tom following suit.

"Now, where to?" asked Dora, looking back over her shoulder.

"I'm afraid I must go to my hotel, the Bristol," said Tom apologetically. "I hadn't expected to stay on, you see, and need to make arrangements."

"And you can drop me at the Bureau," said Gabriel. "Research calls!"

"And you?" said Dora, pulling her goggles on and putting her gloved hands on the steering wheel. "Where shall I drop you, Comrade Ida?"

Ida paused. She needed a change of clothes but feared going back to her rooms—it would mean passing Martin's shop and being asked for the rent she could not pay. But where else was there to go? "Let me think," she temporized, "while you drop off these gentlemen." With a soft rumble the car eased away from the curb.

The men were deposited at their destinations, first Gabriel, then Tom, who proposed meeting Ida for lunch tomorrow at the restaurant near her building. When the two women were alone, Dora lifted her goggles to her forehead, smiled at Ida, and asked where she would like to go. Dora's smile vanished when Ida's answer came in silent tears.

"I can't go to my place," Ida sighed, trying to regain her composure. *Mustn't let Waterhouse paint me helpless and adrift.* "The trespassing fine I paid—it was my rent. I can't go home, but there's nowhere else."

Dora's eyebrows furrowed briefly, then she placed her suede-gloved hand on Ida's forearm. "It's money, yes? Then come with me." The yellow car murmured confidently as Dora steered it away from the Bristol, heading west. They drove down tree-lined avenues of grand apartments, which gave way to stately embassies on leafy grounds. Then came rows of tall, elegant townhouses on quiet streets, and the occasional detached house surrounded by ancient trees. Dora's car came to rest in front of one of these—a gray stone house fronted by a portico set amid well-trimmed hedges. "Welcome to Neuilly," she announced. "Come with me—you look like you could make good use of a bit of pastry with plenty of strong coffee." Ida's spirits stirred at the thought.

Soon they strode through a long foyer, their shoes clattering on the marble floor. A bronze goddess on a table; a painting of a horse in a gilt frame—if Mrs. Rawling were here, thought Ida, she'd ask me to serve the cake. "Maxine!" Dora called out down the hall. "Bring coffee and something to eat for two. We'll be in my room."

A lilting *"Oui, madamoiselle"* followed them up the stairs, where they soon found themselves in a sun-drenched bedroom, conservatively furnished. Nothing but a table filled with cameras distinguished it from the bedroom of any Lake Forest debutante. Dora's father might have been the only architect not to get rich in Buenos Aires, thought Ida, but he'd certainly made a fortune somewhere.

"It's embarrassing to speak of money," said Dora, opening an ivory box on a bedside table. "Just say what you need, no apologies, no thanks." Ida hesitated. "Oh, Comrade," Dora said, with a shrug, "it's not like I earned it."

"A hundred—two hundred francs," blurted Ida. Once the rent was paid, she'd need to eat.

"There," said Dora, folding the money into Ida's hands. "And you'll—forgive me—you'll want to freshen up a bit and put on some different clothes. It looks like you may have fallen into something."

Ida saw, not without a touch of embarrassment, that Dora was right. Her skirt was stained, and she could only imagine how her hair looked after two nights of fitful jailhouse sleep.

A kindly looking older woman Ida assumed was Maxine arrived with a tray. "Just leave it on the table," said Dora, "and draw a bath for our guest." Ida nearly swooned at the smell of coffee and the thought of bathing, properly bathing, in a real bathtub.

An hour later, Ida stood in a gold and blue dress of modern, drop-waist cut, the collar and waistband adorned with a Greek key design. Dora had offered her shoes in matching gold, and Ida found with surprise that they fit, the heel lifting her so she stood an inch taller than her host. "Sit," said Dora, motioning to the bench in front of the vanity. "I'll brush out your hair."

It was all so strange, thought Ida, as the brush stroked her hair back. Dora, who'd seemed so advanced, so sophisticated; Dora, who ran with the Surrealists and was accepted by them; Dora, who'd met Picasso and sat at café tables with André Breton—here Dora seemed like the teenager she no doubt was, sheltered in the comfort of her family's nest. What must she think of me? Ida wondered. Come from America with nothing to my name, crawling through catacombs, in trouble with the law?

"You must take more money," said Dora. "A few hundred— it won't be missed."

"I can't," said Ida, her spine stiffening. She'd been raised by people who had escaped poverty through hard work, people who looked down on charity cases and sighed with relief that those were other people, not them. "I'm sorry, but I'm just not capable—"

"You don't know what you're capable of," whispered Dora, leaning close. Her mouth found Ida's, in a kiss.

"Oh," said Ida, almost silently. "Oh."

42

Sunlight held Ida and Dora in quiet suspension for a moment after Dora's kiss had released Ida's lips. Dora looked into Ida's eyes, and her lips parted, either to speak or to kiss again, when heavy steps approaching the open door made both women start. Suddenly, a man in a dark suit stood before them, the great dome of his forehead pale beneath slicked back salt-and-pepper hair.

"*Tatínek!*" cried Dora. "Papa!"

"Hello to you both—and will your friend stay for dinner?" asked the man, his French cultivated and slightly accented. Dora looked expectantly to Ida, who nodded hesitantly. "Good," said the man. "I'll have Maxine set another place at the table. *A bientot!*" He gave a perfunctory smile and left, after which Dora gave Ida a smile of her own.

"I'll apologize in advance for my parents," she said with a shrug. "Let me take your photo, and we'll go down." She selected a camera from the table cluttered with them, crouched on the floor near the vanity, and reached out to touch Ida's cheek with an index finger, turning her head to catch the light. "There—now don't change a thing," she said, staring hard for a few seconds. "Done. Now, off to our crucifixion."

Downstairs, the two joined Dora's father and her round-faced, soft-jawed mother in the long, narrow dining room. They sat at an oval table draped with a stark white tablecloth. Maxine served an olive tapenade, and after introductions and a brief exchange in Czech among the family members, the conversation, such as it was, switched to French.

"Has she given us pimento?" said Dora's father, poking at his tapenade.

Silence reigned. "Has she, do you think?"

"Has who given us what?" asked Dora's mother, absently.

"The cook, I suppose," he replied.

"The cook?" asked Mrs. Maar.

"Has she," said her husband, "has she given us pimento. In the tapenade?"

"Well," said Mrs. Maar, "I suppose you might ask."

A fork clicked on a plate. Someone chewed. Someone swallowed. Outside a bird, perhaps a starling, warbled for a moment, then gave up the effort.

Dora shot a side-eyed glance at Ida and raised her eyebrows apologetically.

"What, go to the kitchen and ask the cook?" said Mr. Maar, after this long interval. He sounded surprised.

"Ida dear," said Mrs. Maar, her husband's question bouncing off her like a little rubber ball, "aren't you one of Dora's classmates at the Académie Julian?"

"No," Ida began. "I—"

"Now does that," Mr. Maar interjected, extending his fork in Ida's direction, a morsel resting upon it, "look like pimento? I mean, does it, to your eye," he paused a moment, "appear to be pimento?"

"I couldn't say, exactly," said Ida, "but…"

"Maxine!" Mrs. Maar called out. "Maxine?" Maxine arrived at the doorway. "Maxine, ask the cook if she made the tapenade with pimento." With a quick nod Maxine disappeared.

By the time Maxine brought in grilled salmon and green beans on a shiny chrome cart, little had been determined about pimento in the tapenade, though all conceivable avenues of inquiry into the matter had been thoroughly exhausted. As Maxine served the fish, she reported that there was no pimento in the tapenade. For reasons Ida couldn't quite explain, one of the framed photos from the Bureau of Surrealist Research flashed in her mind: a cluster of bourgeois men and women, staring intently at a mantelpiece on which there was nothing whatsoever to see.

"Perhaps," said Mr. Maar, taking a great pause to consider his words, "perhaps it isn't pimento at all, then. Perhaps," his eyes brightened, and a wide smile crept slowly across his face, "perhaps it is red bell pepper—like in Buenos Aires!" He slapped his thighs. "Red pepper!" he chuckled to himself, his voice rising an octave. "In the tapenade!"

Dora buried her nose in a wine glass. By the time Maxine was ready to serve yogurt with slices of pears, conversation had long since given way to the sounds of cutlery scraping on fine china, punctuated only by the distant, occasional yipping of a small yet determinedly emphatic dog. At least the cool, crisp Sancerre was good, thought Ida, mirroring Dora's gesture. A clock chimed wearily in the corridor.

Released at last from this Babylonian captivity—for it had been that, thought Ida, nothing so dramatic as a crucifixion, but still exceedingly long—Ida sat with Dora in a small parlor stuffed with heavy mahogany furniture and Chinese vases. This was not the world Ida had left behind in America, she thought, but it was most certainly the world Teddy had fled, and was, perhaps, fleeing still.

"Here," said Dora, fetching a pen and note paper from an escritoire. "You never did get to write in the ledger back at the Bureau of Surrealist Research. Perhaps you could write something now. It would be a kind of antidote to all this, wouldn't it?"

Ida sat at the escritoire and tried to write. She tried to remember what she had thought when Dora had dealt the tarot cards. It seemed so long ago, and words would not come. The black pen felt luxurious in her hand, a snub, gold-nibbed thing. It sat complacently between Ida's finger and thumb, and without further thought, she began to draw with it. A line, let it be longer, let it curve. Let it be the outline of a face. A man's face—give him the aspect of a magus or mesmerist. A line or two on the forehead to show his age. Something in the eyes—boldness, but also desperation. Or was it determination? A man who would make his mark before fading from this world. Marinetti, then. A fair likeness, better than fair. *Le Bateleur*, she wrote, beneath it. The magician. A slope of shoulder just suggested. A shame she'd left no room for his hand to hold a wand.

"This was the man in the cards?" asked Dora. She'd hovered close and unnoticed over Ida's shoulder the whole time.

"It was," said Ida. "I know that now. If you put this in the ledger will others see it?"

"No one looks in the ledger," replied Dora. "The ledger exists so that people will write—or draw. It's not for reading so much as for writing."

"You'll place it there for me?"

"I will," said Dora, "for you."

The way Dora said that last word—playful, knowing—opened a great chasm, an echoing space Ida knew that she ought to fill with words. A pregnant moment passed.

"Forgive me," said Ida. "It's been a long couple of days, and I need to rest."

"I'll have Maxine make a room up for you," said Dora. "Come morning, we can talk."

The next morning, Dora and Ida took breakfast in the garden, at an iron table under a broad pergola. Ida wore the same gold and blue dress she'd donned the previous evening; Dora had chosen a similar one in rose and white. Café au lait steamed invitingly, and bread, jam, and sliced apples crowded their small plates. Dora had given Ida a sketch pad with thick, creamy paper, and now sat contentedly in the dappled shade while Ida blocked in her hostess's profile with broad strokes from a soft pencil. Try to get it right, Ida thought, that curious mix of sophistication and naiveté. Large eyes help with that—wise, but with a hint of the puppy dog. No. Better than that—add just a touch of a female, Parisian Huck Finn. Think adventure—that's Dora, that's her exactly. Rafting away from Neuilly and down the river to find Picasso and Breton. What did she say her dream had been? A woman's hand, reaching from a shell.

"There," said Ida, and Dora rose to stand behind her.

"It's me," exclaimed Dora, with a little clap. "You've captured me better than a photograph!"

"But I know so little about you, really," said Ida. Time to face the chasm that had yawned open between them since yesterday. "Tell me, when you brushed my hair, and then... Tell me, what did that mean?" The words did not come easily. For some reason Ida thought of churches, first communions, girls in white. "I don't know," said Dora. "I don't. But isn't all the fun in finding out?"

"I can't say," said Ida, adding, after a pause. "But I should get back home—the rent's past due. And I really must see if there's a message from my husband." Ida felt she should touch Dora's hand, and did.

"I'll take you," said Dora, no trace of disappointment in her voice. "If I may."

"You're very kind," Ida replied. Dora's hand felt cool to her touch.

Back in Paris, Ida stepped from Dora's car at an intersection, her clothes bundled under her arm. She offered her thanks and turned toward Martin's shop to pay the rent at last. She was about to open the door when she thought to look across the street—if Tom were early, he might already be at the restaurant where they had planned to meet. She spun around and squinted into the light. Her view of the outdoor tables was blocked, though, by a long automobile that held a man reading a newspaper. A familiar man—Lewis! Rage boiled in Ida's veins. Lewis, that bastard. Lewis, who never delivered Teddy's message. Lewis, who'd given her the worst hours of her life, worse even than jail—all that time not knowing if Teddy were alive or dead. Ida strode across the street, unthinking, an eagle swooping down on its prey. She reached in the open driver's side window and yanked the paper from Lewis's hands.

"You!" she sputtered. "You!"

Lewis's alarm faded when he recognized his assailant. "Now,

now." He placed his hand on her forearm. "You're upset, but I have something to show you."

"What could you possibly have to show me?" Ida pulled away and glowered.

"It's about Teddy. He needs you. Get in quick and I'll explain." Lewis made what must have been his best attempt at pleading eyes. The effect was ghastly. But still…Teddy, thought Ida, Teddy. She crossed to the other side of the car, got in, and glared as Lewis started to drive.

Moments later, on a quiet street, Lewis stopped the car. "Here," he said, reaching for something below the seat, "this will be explanation enough." He lunged at Ida, grabbing her head roughly from behind with one hand, while the other pressed a strange-smelling cloth to her face.

Ida struggled only briefly. Then the bright world went black.

43

A shard of blistering light tore through Ida's skull before shooting down her neck and spine. A light with crushing weight, a light that shrieked. On my back, thought Ida. I'm on my back on something cold, my arms behind me, and I cannot move. Move. She arched her back, tried to breathe, but found herself drowning, drowning slowly in a heavy darkness whose sister was sleep, whose mother was fear. Mother Fear spoke, ordered her not to sleep. She willed her eyes to open but they would not obey until, at last, they did.

Ida let her head loll sideways and tried to focus. Dust on a floor of stone. Dim light, and something a few feet away from her—a bowl on the floor, and movement: a mouse scurrying away from the bowl's rim. Breathe deeply and wake. Wake.

"I know you." The voice, less voice than a kind of croaking, came from behind Ida. With a mighty effort Ida turned her head, and saw a figure across the room, knees hunched up, arms bound. It was a woman's form leaning against a wall in the gloom. "I know you," the voice came again, a little clearer. Ida recognized the face—it was Alice.

Ida tried to speak. Nothing. A second attempt, and the words came raspingly. "Ida Caine," she said.

"Water in the bowl," said Alice, her voice throaty. "Saved you some." She gave a little shrug, adding, "Don't mind the mice."

Ida squirmed over to the chipped ceramic bowl, rolled onto her side, managed to lift her head to awkwardly drink a sip or two before knocking the bowl over and spilling what water remained.

"Alice," said Ida, struggling to sit, and finally managing it. "Alice, I've found you." She felt foolish even as the words left her mouth. She hadn't found anyone. She'd simply ended up here, wherever here may be. Ended up a captive—her theory about Alice confirmed, but her own fate at best uncertain, at worst, well…best not think of that.

"It's Wyndham Lewis out there," said Alice, clearing her throat and motioning toward the door with her head.

"I know," said Ida.

"But why?" asked Alice, her voice a whisper.

How to explain? And what did she even know? Ida thought back to the moment of her own abduction, when she so confidently walked right up to Lewis's car, so stupidly climbed inside. He had been waiting for her, and to judge by the chloroform under the seat, he'd planned to bring her here and imprison her with Alice. It could only mean one thing—Lewis was part of Marinetti's mad scheme. It made no sense otherwise, though it still made precious little sense at all. Why would Lewis want to be part of Marinetti's madness? Ida thought back to Lewis's behavior at Gertrude's salon, how furious he was that Alice had become the center of attention, how humiliated he'd been when Ida put him in his place. She saw Lewis burning with rage on the sidelines of the salon, on the sidelines of art and literature, and she thought yes, yes, she could almost understand. Almost. But how to explain all this to Alice?

"Something…" Alice worked the words from her dry throat, ore pried from a mine's rock face. "Something to do with Antheil?"

Ida nodded, and searched for words. From somewhere far above came a sudden thud, a yelp, a man's voice cursing, then a scuffle of some kind, coming closer. And now a crash from just outside the door.

"Bite again and I'll pull your goddamned teeth out." It was Lewis's voice, shrill with fury. The door flew open, and Ida flinched at the burst of light. Two figures in silhouette in the doorway, one large, one small. Ida recognized Lewis's face as he hurled a woman in a rose and white dress into the center of the room, where she fell on the floor with a sickening, heavy smack of flesh on stone. Lewis wheeled around and slammed the door shut. Dora. It was Dora Maar.

Tom sat at the café across from Ida's building on rue Victor Cousin. Ida was late, but of course he understood: these had been exhausting days, and most irregular. At least the staff at the Bristol had been understanding—as hotel people tend to be, when shown currency in sufficient quantity. He planned on spending a little currency here at the café as well—he'd asked for a bottle of good chardonnay with two glasses, and he had let the bottle sit. Cool from the cellar, the green glass beaded with sweat. "Always wait for your guest before pouring," said a dowager aunt, rail thin and eagle-beaked in her starched white dress as she leaned forward from one of the gilt frames in the gallery of his ancestors. "We're not savages."

Tom looked her in the eye, said nothing, lifted the bottle and, maintaining eye contact the whole while, poured himself a glass. The dowager gasped. Tom reached up with his long-fingered hands and turned her portrait to face the wall. "Anyone else?" he said, casting a defiant eye down the gallery of portraits.

"Monsieur?" It was the waiter, giving Tom a quizzical look.

"Nothing," said Tom, slightly abashed. "Sorry." He raised his glass in salutation.

He would wait for Ida. He'd wait as long as it took. Bohemians took their time, didn't they? Let them, let her. Let me. He would wait, outside a French café, sipping his wine. *Vive la vie bohème.*

A bruise on her thigh, that was all Dora had suffered, remarkably. And in his rage and haste, Lewis hadn't thought to bind her.

"I followed you," said Dora, struggling to untie Ida's hands without success.

"This," whispered Alice. "Here." She squirmed her shoulders, indicating as best she could the space between her back and the wall. Dora crossed the room, and Alice leaned to the side to reveal the treasure she'd hoarded since her first day of captivity—a shard of dark glass from a broken wine bottle. Aided by its sharp edges, Dora soon freed Alice and Ida from the ropes that bound them hand and foot.

Feeling the blood rush back into her limbs, Ida could only imagine the welcome release that Alice must be experiencing—a quick, tingling pain that signaled the end of greater pain. "You followed me?" Ida asked Dora with wonder.

"I saw you get into that car with Lewis and," Dora looked down, "I was curious…no. Jealous. Worried. I don't know. I followed you." Alice looked from Ida to Dora and back again. "I parked a block from here," Dora continued. "My car's not inconspicuous—I walked over, and watched for an hour. People have been coming and going—lots of them. Loading trucks with something. I waited until I thought everyone was gone and came in through a window." I was right to see the Huck Finn in her, thought Ida. Dora continued, "There was no one on the ground floor, so I went to look for you upstairs. That's where he was—and here I am now."

"Is he alone?" asked Ida.

Dora paused to think. "I believe so," she said. "For now."

Alice, who had been rubbing her legs, stood slowly with Dora's help, flexed, and began to pace around the room, her limbs loosening slowly. It had been many days since she had moved about freely. "I need to know what's going on," she said. She bent to pick up the water bowl, held it to her face, and licked what dampness remained from the bottom and sides. "But not now. First, can we get out of here?"

Ida put her ear to the door and listened. Nothing. She tested the knob gingerly, and found, as she'd expected, that the door was locked. "It's too heavy to force," she said. She looked to the bleary light of the small high window on the opposite wall, made from thick glass blocks. "And there's no getting through there."

Dora sidled up next to Ida and touched her hair. "I think I know what to do," she whispered. Ida stiffened. There was a sudden tug at the back of Ida's head. She felt her hair fall down her neck, and Dora stepped away, something shiny in her hand. It was the owl hairpin Sandy Calder had made for her.

"I can bend this," Dora whispered, working the wire pin in her hands, "just so. And now here's a little something Marcel taught me." She knelt by the door, doubled the wire over, slid it into the keyhole, wiggled it until something caught, then slowly worked it further in. One click, then two, and a third. The three women clustered by the keyhole, staring. In the silence, it came: a final, soft click. "There," breathed Dora. "There."

"Shall we open it?" whispered Ida, almost inaudibly.

"What if he's out there?" asked Alice.

Dora cupped her hand and listened, pressed up against the door. "No one's there," she said, softly, and pushed the door open. Lewis looked up from the crumpled newspaper he had been smoothing out on the table before him and mouthed a silent profanity.

"*Merde!*" screamed Alice.

"Shit!" shouted Dora.

"Now!" Ida yelped, but Alice had already shot through the door—a scrawny cannonball aimed at the center of Lewis's abdomen.

The laws of physics were not broken, though the tumble of limbs flying in their various trajectories put the limits of those laws into question. In an instant, Dora hung from Lewis's back, her thumb gouging at his right eye. Alice clung to his right leg with both of her arms, trying to bring him to the floor and hindering his movement. Ida, grabbing the hairpin that had dropped from Dora's hand, swung at the wound on Lewis's cheek. He screeched as she opened his old lesion. Swinging his bulk, Lewis cast Dora off, then stumbled and crashed to the floor. With stunning speed, Alice stood over him, a wooden stool raised high in her hands. She brought it down on his head with a crash, and the man lay still.

"Quick, before there are others!" cried Dora, bounding up the narrow stairway. Alice dropped the stool and limped after her, assisted by Ida, whose loosened hair now took on the aspect of a lion's mane. At the top of the stairs, she looked back on Lewis, writhing on the floor, and spitting curses.

A moment later, the yellow car sped away with Dora at the wheel and Ida and Alice in the seat behind.

44

É poisses de Bourgogne—remarkable! At last, he had found a wheel of it, and just across the street from the café where he sat drinking wine and waiting for Ida, who was now almost an hour late for their appointed lunch. But he wouldn't worry, not yet. Things had been, shall we say, irregular of late, and tardiness was certainly understandable. Tom smiled the lopsided grin of the slightly tipsy and held the wheel aloft over his head as he left the shop and returned to his café table. He hadn't wanted a whole wheel of cheese, really, just a little something to spread on the café's crusty bread, but Époisses de Bourgogne? It was almost impossible to find since the war, yet here it was. He'd carve out a thin wedge now and bring the rest back to England. Must have something to nibble on, and he wasn't going to order lunch until Ida arrived. Nor would he lower himself to the disappointing cheese standards of this terribly ordinary café. A few extra coins in the waiter's outstretched hand guaranteed the man wouldn't interfere with Tom's consumption of the contraband cheese; indeed, the fellow brought out a knife and a plate of bread. Another glass of wine, a little of the E. de B., and sunlight. He could wait as long as he needed to. Noticing his shirt was untucked and taking a long, quizzical, lip-puckered look at the laundry label sewn onto the left shirttail, Tom missed the sight of a tall sandy-haired man in a much-rumpled overcoat loping into the cheese shop, a man he'd met once before—Teddy Caine.

In the shop, Martin looked up languidly from his spot behind the counter, then rose with a start. "Monsieur Caine!" he exclaimed. "It has been some time."

"Just back from Africa, thought I'd stop in for a bit of—"

"Camembert, of course, as ever," said Martin, finishing Teddy's sentence for him.

"No," said Teddy, tapping his lip with an index finger and looking at the array of cheeses before him. "I think it'll be—"

"Langres, Martin!" came a woman's voice from the back of the shop. "He always has Langres!"

"That's it," said Teddy. "A wedge of Langres—just a thin one." He had only a few francs left in his pockets.

Martin turned sullenly to cut and wrap a wedge of Langres, a pale, soft cheese that miraculously combined creaminess with a tendency to crumble delightfully. He glowered over his shoulder at the young American. Teddy, for his part, had found the hurt in Martin's eyes incomprehensible. The look seemed like that of a man who'd been profoundly, bitterly betrayed.

"Take it," said Martin, shoving the cheese, somewhat haphazardly wrapped in butcher's paper, across the counter at Teddy. "And there's the matter of the rent, quite past due."

So that explains his dirty look, thought Teddy. "Ida didn't pay it, then?" he asked in genuine confusion. "I'll run up and ask her about it."

"You may run up, but when you come down, you must have the rent—or your possessions in a bundle. I am bound by honor to evict those who do not pay." But what would this Langres-eater know of honor, thought Martin. Still, though, one must stand on principle.

Teddy gave a carefree smile, paid for his cheese, and bade Martin farewell. Must have slipped Ida's mind, the goose. As Teddy stepped out to the street, a woman's voice called from the back of the shop, "Enjoy your wedge of Langres!" in a tone of victorious delight.

Upstairs, Teddy discovered that Ida was not in evidence, so he flung himself on the narrow bed, kicking off his right shoe and throwing a forearm over his eyes rather than reaching to lower the blinds. His journey with Jay had been truly remarkable—Algiers; Tunis; Tripoli; and endless, spectacular Cairo: Cairo of the dusty bazaars and stacked baskets; Cairo of the slow, wide river; Cairo of the sticky, tar-like hashish; Cairo of that strange, hidden casino. He wished he'd made it to the pyramids on foot or by camel, but at least he and Jay had seen them from the air, more or less. He couldn't wait to tell Ida about that.

Teddy shifted uncomfortably. Telling Ida about Jay buzzing the great pyramid in his airplane would be fine, and he imagined over time he'd grow better and better at telling the tale in bars from Paris to Chicago. He'd improve his narrative until, someday, it would all become rote, and people would start to sigh at old man Caine boring everyone with tired tales of his youthful hijinks. But Teddy had long carried within himself an uncomfortable and only recently acknowledged truth—he might tell tales, but he would never write. Had never written. Did not want to write and didn't know the first thing about it. Hell, he thought, shifting his arm, and looking from half-closed eyes at the stack of books on the floor, he didn't even like to read. He sat up, leaned forward, and reached out to where Ida's wooden panel leaned against the wall. He turned it around, saw that the picture of Chancellor Rolin and the Virgin Mary was nearly complete. The girl's been busy, he thought. She always liked to paint, and she was good at it. But what was he good at? What, even, did he like? He turned the painting back to the wall.

Watching Jay, Teddy reflected, had been the most compelling part of the entire journey. Not the most dazzling—there were many candidates for that. The sun rising over the wind-raked Mediterranean; the coast of Italy emerging suddenly from under a bank of clouds; the silver-coin bangles glittering on that woman's beckoning arm in the half-light of a Cairo alleyway. Seeing the pyramids from the air would have topped everything, if he hadn't been dizzyingly drunk when he saw them and trying hard not to vomit. But Jay—what exactly had it been about Jay's behavior that had gotten to him? Teddy furrowed his brow, tossed himself back on the bed, shook his head as if driving away flies.

Tom shook his head slowly. No, no, no. This would never do. He reached up into the gallery of ancestral portraits that hovered invisibly above him, touched the picture of the aunt that he had turned to face the wall, and turned it gingerly back the right way. The arctic blast of her gaze spoke more than words, and Tom suddenly saw himself now as she must see him—unkempt, tie loosened, drinking alone in the middle of the day, long after he should have been back at his desk in London; recently emerged from a French jail cell; besotted—yes, admit it, besotted—with a married woman, a bohemian *artiste*, who was most emphatically not his own wife. Tom straightened up and retightened his tie knot, leaving the silk marked with fingerprints of fine Époisses de Bourgogne cheese.

"*Service!*" he cried, holding up the empty wine bottle. "*Une autre bouteille*—another bottle, if you please." The subjects of several portraits exchanged grave looks of concern.

"It was the poetry that did it," drawled an ancient man painted against a dark background in a minister's frock coat. "Nothing good's come of poetry since Longfellow died."

Jay, laughing hollowly at the Ritz; Jay, beaming with pride at his aircraft; Jay, stealing a typewriter to use as a photo prop; Jay, tossing coins from the balcony to watch the beggars of Tunis fight for them; Jay, in the casino, losing aggressively at the roulette table, his forced laugh echoing; Jay, running from his older brother and his America—from an America that belonged to thick-fingered, grasping, smugly ordinary men, and always would; Jay, with the speed of airplane motors, the rush of drunkenness, the glow of feeling special in the foreign streets of the foreign poor; Jay, starring in a nonexistent motion picture about himself in which everyone else was merely an extra. What kind of man does all of that?

Jay ran from things, and ran to, well…to staged photos, to fantasy, to nothing. If you take away the writing, thought Teddy, I'm almost Jay. And there's not a word of writing to take away.

He kicked his left shoe to the floor.

❧

Tom did not love Vivienne, no more than Viv loved him. When she wasn't in a sanatorium for her nerves, she clung to him. She clung out of neediness and fear and madness, but she didn't love him. And he stood by her because, well, because...

"Because you should, because you must," said Tom's ancestors, speaking in terrifying unison.

"Because you must fight your inborn sin," added the dowager aunt, still bitter after her sojourn facing the wall. "Think of your mother, your father, and the memory of your blessed grandfather." Here William Greenleaf Eliot bowed from his picture frame, the wings of his white hair retaining their rectitude in defiance of gravity. "Think," added the aunt, "of your wife, and the vows of holy matrimony."

"Holy matrimony," said the ancestors, again in unison. "Renounce the scarlet woman, Ida Caine, and all your shameful desire."

Tom grabbed the bottle and quickly sloshed more wine into his glass. His thirst was terrible today, he thought, staring into the bottom of his glass. And where *is* Ida? He was starting to worry. Tom, his gaze still fixed on his glass, didn't see the yellow car pull up across the street, nor did he see Ida alight from the vehicle and slip into Martin's shop.

45

While Tom drank and began to worry about Ida's absence, Ida was preoccupied by worries of her own. Dora's driving, for instance. After the women's escape from Lewis, adrenaline coursed through Dora's body, and she drove accordingly, careening through the rutted streets of Saint-Ouen and into Paris as if pursued by packs of predators. She wove in and out of traffic, nearly clipping a milk truck on the rue de Rome and terrifying a pedestrian who'd strayed from the curb by the Louvre, his nose buried in a guidebook. When she pulled up outside twenty-seven rue de Fleurus she was flushed, wild-eyed, and smiling.

"Won't you come in to see Gertrude?" asked Alice, stepping gingerly from the car.

Ida and Dora followed Alice, entered the foyer, and were greeted by an emotionally overcome Gertrude and an equally impassioned Basket. Amid the embraces, tearful thanks, and hurried explanations, Ida looked for an opening to make her exit. Alice and Gertrude clearly wished for some time alone together. And Ida had to get home to her rooms and pay the past-due rent, or she'd risk finding her few possessions in the street, along with Mrs. Rawling's painting. She needed, too, to check for messages from Teddy, and there was something else she was meant to do but couldn't quite recall. Her mind buzzed and crackled with nervous energy, even as her body called out for rest. When Hélène placed a generous glass of plum brandy in her hand, she drained it in a single gulp.

"I must get home," Ida whispered to Dora, while Gertrude held Alice tightly in her arms.

"I have to go as well," Dora replied. "My parents thought I was dropping you off and coming straight back—they'll worry."

The two said their goodbyes to the hosts of Paris's most

renowned salon, promising to be in touch tomorrow. But what was to be done about Marinetti's plot? About the police? That would all have to wait. For now, Alice and Gertrude must be left to their tearful reunion.

After Dora's yellow car pulled up outside Ida's building, Ida crossed the street and headed directly into the cheese shop, determined to pay her rent at last. Once inside, Ida looked over her shoulder and through the window at Dora, waiting in her car outside, and waved for her to leave. After seeing Dora at home with her parents yesterday, Ida had unconsciously fallen into the role of older sister, and it seemed natural for her to direct Dora's actions. The girl was late getting home; her parents would be worried. As for how Dora would explain the state of her dress—well, that was going to be her problem. Unless such things weren't really problems for a rich girl. The thought of wealth reminded Ida of the rent—to be settled at last.

"Mrs. Caine," said Martin, perhaps a touch less warmly than he had in the past.

"Fear not—" Ida began. She meant to finish her sentence with "I've come to pay the rent at last," perhaps in a jaunty, courageous tone. But when she reached for the green handbag in which she kept Dora's two hundred francs and what remained of Mrs. Rawling's money, she found it was missing. Impossible! How could she possibly misplace her handbag? But the events of the morning had addled her, and she hadn't realized until now that it must be in Lewis's car.

"I...am not afraid," said Martin, in evident confusion, "and you should know..."

"The rent," said Ida. "I know, the rent. It's just that there's a slight complication."

"That is most unfortunate indeed." Martin shrugged. "If it is not paid immediately, you shall have to vacate. But you must know—"

"—that it's not your fault." Ida completed his sentence. "Yes. No. I mean to say, you've shown great patience, and I appreciate it, believe me I do. It's just that—"

"Your husband!" a woman's voice called out from the back of the shop. "It's your husband. Mr. Caine has returned. He is upstairs now." Ida stiffened and caught her breath. "With a wedge of Langres!" trilled the voice, with more than a hint of self-satisfaction.

Ida was up the stairs in a shot.

Ida stood in the corridor outside her rooms, only partially sure that she wanted to open the door. Teddy owed her an explanation, at the very least. But he was never a great one for explaining, and when it came to apologies, he was—Ida wrinkled her brow. Deft at sidestepping them, that's what he was. His charm let him get away with things: he could always make her smile or laugh. He could do something boyish or clever or hold her wordlessly in his embrace until she was distracted by something else. She mustn't let him, not after his disappearance. As tired as she was, she mustn't allow that. But she couldn't fight, not today. She'd had too much of that, too literally, too short a time ago. She opened the door with an uncertain hand.

Teddy sat on the edge of the bed, looking at her van Eyck copy where it leaned against the wall by the door. In a second, he was on his feet, his lean, lanky body pressed up against her, his arms reaching around to hold her. But before he could embrace her, Ida took a step backward into the corridor. "No," she gasped, but then she saw the sorrow in his eyes—a deep sorrow, a child's sorrow. She stepped forward, leaned into him, and let his kiss touch her neck.

"It's been such a long week since I left," he murmured, his head on Ida's shoulder. Had it only been a week? Ida marveled. Surely, she had aged—no, grown—more than was possible in a week's time. How could she even begin to tell this tall, boyish man what had happened to her?

"Lewis never gave me your letter," she said, gently pushing him back and looking past him, out the window. "I thought you were dead."

❧

You're not bad, you lot, thought Tom, his words slurred even there, in the imaginary gallery of his ancestors. He'd lost count of the number of times his glass had been refilled. "You're not such a bad lot at all, and you've stood me in good stead—even you, you old..." He paused before the portrait of an appalled William Greenleaf Eliot. "You old Bible-waver, you." He chucked the eminent minister on the chin. "But you must allow for the *appetites*."

"Something to eat, monsieur?" asked the waiter, barely showing his concern for the increasingly drunken mutterings of this strange American or Englishman, who was now the only guest on the terrace.

"Eh? Ah. Cheese," said Tom, sticking his thumb into the spent rind of what had indeed been an excellent Époisses de Bourgogne. God knows where Ida had gotten to. If she went looking for him at the Bristol, she was sure to leave a message. And at some point, she was bound to come back here. He'd be vigilant. He'd wait as long as it took, and not miss a thing. "Eagle eyes," he said, pointing to a portrait of his grandmother, known for her nearsightedness. "Shan't miss a thing."

"Saint Michel-Sang? I am not familiar with that cheese," said the waiter.

"Anything, then," slurred Tom, waving his hand in the air. "Even Port Salut. No, no, not that." Tom grimaced at a frowning William Greenleaf Eliot. "We'll have a nice English cheddar, won't we, Grandpapa?" The waiter, not quite understanding this strange foreigner, shrugged with Olympian indifference, and went to fetch the cheese.

❧

"It's just—I've changed," said Teddy. "Or maybe it's really that I haven't."

Ida sat on the bed while Teddy paced. She had too much to tell, and not nearly enough energy to tell it, let alone chide him for running off. Let him speak about himself, she thought. It'll give you plenty of time to rest, and there's clearly something on his mind he needs to shape into words.

"We got out of Lake Forest, you and I. We did it. And I'm proud of myself, or I want to be. We weren't like the others, right?" He looked at Ida, still with the eyes of a hurt, bewildered child. Was Teddy right? Was being different and getting away what had mattered to them? Well, it was surely what had always mattered to *him*, Ida knew that. And it was why she'd been drawn to him, wasn't it? When he talked of Paris, it came like a gust of cool wind from across the lake on a relentlessly muggy Midwestern summer night.

"But all I can think is—is, well, it'll sound strange." Teddy shook his head and leaned against the wall. "I'm Pinocchio," he said. "I'm a goddamned Pinocchio."

"Because you like to tell lies?" asked Ida. Teddy the detective, Teddy the bootlegger, was that what he meant?

"I'm Pinocchio because I want to be a real boy, but what am I?" Teddy held his head in his hands and started to pace the narrow room.

"You're my husband," said Ida.

Teddy appeared not to hear. "I came here to write, but…but I'm not a writer," he stammered. "No more than I'm a detective. And I'm no artist, either. Did you see those—those scribbles on the wall at the Stein place? I don't understand those. I never will. But you do, don't you?" Teddy fixed Ida in his gaze. She decided not to answer. "I won't become McAlmon, anyway." Teddy didn't really want a response from her, that was clear. "I won't be a joke of a writer who doesn't write. But what am I, then? I thought I was like Jay, but I'm not. He's just someone I thought would make me special if I joined him on his adventures. It's always like that; before Jay, it was Lewis who made me special—with him I was a real literary man at last. And before Lewis, there was…" Teddy trailed off. There was me, thought Ida; before Lewis, I was the one who made you unusual. Back in Lake Forest, when you married beneath your station, that made you stand out. But now that you're in bohemian Paris, a match like ours is nothing special, or even interesting. Ida's brow furrowed and her lower lip quivered, but she said nothing.

"Anyway," Teddy said, petulance in his voice, "I don't want to be a hollow rich boy like Jay. And I couldn't, even if I wanted to, not now, not here. Not without the money."

"Not without the money—meaning 'not while you're here with me,'" said Ida, more quietly than she'd intended. She knew what Teddy's parents thought of him marrying her in a courthouse, then running off to France. She knew why they'd cut him off. A poor girl, a Catholic no less, who'd seduced their son and made him throw his future away. They had definite names for her, she was sure of it, names she wouldn't let form in her mind.

Teddy was at her side instantly, sitting on the bed with a warm arm around her shoulders. "But it's not about money—that's not why we're going back," he said. "That's not it at all. Here, I'm nothing, just another American pretending to write. Back home maybe I can make something, or someone, of myself."

"How can you make your way back?" asked Ida. "We haven't a franc, and the rent's past due."

"Yes, they told me we have to leave today," said Teddy. "Jay will have the Ritz put us up for the night. Or, if you don't want to be in his debt, we can stay with Lewis. My father will wire money for our voyage home."

Home? Ida wondered where that was. A gulf opened between her and her husband. A week long, an ocean wide. The floor moved beneath her feet like the deck of a ship on rough and swelling seas. She tried to focus on the painting that sat across the room from them, but it swam and grew bleary to her tearful eyes. Mary seemed to stand, to walk out through the colonnade to the waiting city beyond.

"I'll stay," said Ida. "I'll stay in Paris." The words came out quickly and they surprised her. There was so much more to say, but no words would come.

"What?" Teddy looked at her as if shocked to find someone else in the room.

"You can go back to Chicago," Ida said, standing and starting to gather her few clothes and possessions. She placed them in her battered suitcase with her painting kit. "I belong here."

Teddy stood, unmoving. He opened his mouth and said nothing.

"And keep away from Lewis," added Ida, before slamming the door behind her.

A moment later, the door to Ida's building opened, and out she came, a suitcase in one hand, the painted van Eyck panel in the other. There was nothing here for her, there was no one. And she had no money. Where to go, where to stay? Perhaps Sylvia Beach would let her sleep at the shop for the night. And Gertrude Stein—surely Gertrude would feel she owed Ida something. And what for money? Could Boski get her work at a restaurant? She felt there was a great void before her, a nothingness. It was exhilarating. It was terrifying. She had nothing. But—there. There was Tom, slouched at a café table across the street, his jacket fallen to the ground behind him, his shirt untucked. He had evidently removed one shoe and placed it on a chair beside him. Only the part in his hair remained unmussed—the rest of him seemed as rumpled as the newspaper she'd torn from Lewis's hands mere hours ago on this very street.

Ida crossed rue Victor Cousin. "Tom." She touched his shoulder, standing beside him and suddenly remembering the important thing she'd forgotten—to meet Tom for a late lunch. It was half past four, but here he was, still waiting for her. He rose unsteadily from his chair.

"My Ida, my dear, dear Ida," Tom began. Every ancestor snapped to attention, and he wilted under the weight of their collective disapproval. "My Ida, how I wish, how I want…" Was he drunk? My God, was he! "How I wish, but you see, you see—" Tom waved his hand in the air, indicating the invisible gallery that surrounded them. "But I'm simply—they—I…"

He sagged at the knees. "It's loveless, you know, with Vivienne, but I'm simply not capable…"

"Oh," said Ida, reaching up and pulling Tom's head toward her own. "I don't think you know what you're capable of."

The waiter, having finally dug up some cheddar, left it on the table and walked discreetly away as the couple melted together in a kiss.

46

Ida woke early and spent the first hour of the morning pacing slowly around the room alone, taking in Picabia, Picasso, André Masson, and thinking about how the morning light really did show Miss Stein's paintings to great advantage. After coffee with Alice—Gertrude was sleeping in—Ida secured paper and pencil, and then had Alice pose for her in the salon, seated with Basket in a carved chair. Considering everything she'd endured, Alice looked quite well-restored by a night of comfortable sleep.

Ida considered her subject. "Try it with a knee up," she suggested, then, "No, back the other way, but turn your head a little away from me." That was it. The shadow made Alice look pensive. Resolute, even. Don't let the likeness be too literal. Let it express what was inside; let's see whatever it was that made Alice endure, night after night, in that horrible dungeon where Lewis had kept her. That's who Alice had always been. If this were a painting, perhaps she'd color those shadows, the way Matisse did. He'd use green and orange, wouldn't he? Yes, that's what he'd do. But what's needed is something a little different. Deep blue and red. Make the colors strong, like Alice. And remember what she said on your first visit here, when you told her Lewis sent you—"Come in anyway." Maybe something around the eyes could catch her wryness. Don't miss that.

"I think he's waking up," murmured Alice, trying not to break her pose but indicating the room across the foyer. She was referring to Tom, who had escorted Ida to twenty-seven rue de Fleurus the previous night—if staggering over uneven cobblestones and occasionally leaning on Ida's shoulder could be considered the actions of an escort. But the movements from beyond the door weren't Tom's.

"He's still on the sofa," yawned Gertrude, standing on the

threshold, a purple silk dressing gown draped over her body, giving her a distinctly imperial impression. "So far, sofa, so far." She walked over to Ida, patted her shoulder, and looked down at the sketch of Alice and Basket. Gertrude paused a little longer than Ida expected, then sat on a divan, patted the seat beside her, and summoned Alice. "Draw us together," Gertrude commanded—well, it felt like a command, albeit a gracious one, spoken the way a hostess might say, "Have some more wine." Ida turned to a fresh sheet in the sketchbook Alice had given her and set to work. She'd just begun blocking in their figures when a groan drifted across the foyer. "Now, that would be Tom Eliot," declared Gertrude. Ida hesitated with her pencil above the page. "Go to him, girl," Gertrude said with a smile, extending her arm with a sweeping motion and pointing to the doorway. "Go!"

Ida went. The last time she'd been across that foyer was the night of the salon, when she'd been expelled to what she still considered the wives' room. It was dark in the little room, so she pulled the curtains aside to let in a blast of morning light. A crumpled pile of clothing on the sofa groaned—it was Tom, as hungover as he'd ever been during any ill-conceived night on the town in his Harvard days. "Rise," commanded Ida, "and, while you're at it, shine." She stretched out her arm and poked him in the ribs.

Tom sat up, tousle-headed, then reached for his rumpled suit jacket on the floor and began searching the pockets with some urgency. He found his comb at last, exhaled deeply, and gathered strength as he reinstalled the part in his hair. This accomplished, he looked sheepishly up at Ida standing next to him. "I...ah. Last night, after you found me at the café..." he began, carefully, looking about as if not entirely sure of his surroundings. "That is...if you don't mind—where are we?"

Of course, he'd never been in the wives' room at Miss Stein's. Ida was tempted to tell him they were in Cairo, or New York. He'd catch on, but not right away, not in this state. "Gertrude took us in," she reminded him.

"Oh—very kind of her, very kind." Tom spoke as one might speak if one's head were made of exceptionally fragile glass. "I, ah, well…" He looked up at Ida again, adding, "Did we…did we…?"

"We kissed," said Ida, quickly. "I kissed you," she clarified, then added a decisive, "I'm not sorry."

Tom blinked and shook his head, much the way a horse shakes off flies. A slow smile broke across his face, then vanished, then broke again as he met her gaze expectantly.

"Breakfast," called Hélène from the doorway, "is served in the salon." She motioned them across the foyer.

Ida practically floated away on the aroma of fresh French coffee.

"Go to the police?" Gertrude sat at the head of an Italian Renaissance table, across from Ida and flanked by Tom and Alice. The ruins of a lavish and revitalizing breakfast lay all around them—baked toast with egg; fresh bread; pots of jam and honey; American-style strips of bacon; slices of a miraculous Bosc pear. Hélène hovered in the background, tending to an urn of coffee and, for Alice, a pot of Earl Grey tea. "The police have shown us two faces—one of bureaucratic ineptitude, and another of open scorn. Anything in this district will end up with Inspector LaMarck, and I will not speak to that…that person." She uttered the last word with a glacial iciness. "No, never again."

"But it's a matter of kidnapping—and also of saving who knows how many buildings in Paris," said Tom.

"What we saw under Sainte-Chapelle is undeniable," Ida affirmed. "And there are three of us—Alice, Dora, and me—who can speak against Lewis."

Alice shuddered and nodded at the comment.

"Of course," affirmed Gertrude, putting her hand on Alice's shoulder. "But what have they done so far about Sainte-Chapelle? Or anything at all?"

"We don't know," said Ida. "But nothing less than a public scandal will bring LaMarck to act," she conceded.

"Then," Gertrude nodded, "a public scandal it shall be. When is Antheil's concert?"

"Tonight! Eight o'clock, at the Villon," said Alice.

"It's not far." Gertrude spoke with slow deliberation. "And our salon guests will start arriving shortly after six. If we can't trust the police to act—certainly not in time to stop the concert—we'll have to do it ourselves, won't we?"

"Yes," said Tom. "If I understood Antheil correctly when we spoke in the catacombs, it's not until the finale of the concert that all the instruments play together—and if Marinetti's been successful, this is what will set off explosions across the city. It's incalculable what will be lost: Notre Dame, the Louvre, who knows what else?"

"Get word out that we want a big gathering tonight." Gertrude looked from Alice, to Tom, to Ida. "Tell Sylvia Beach to let on that there will be plenty of the good brandy tonight, and Alice's special baking. That'll pack them in. And tell them I'll unveil a new work of art. When they're a bit tipsy and pliable, we'll mobilize the troops."

"Do you have a new painting?" asked Ida.

"Just last night a particularly unusual piece of Surrealism made its way here—it looks uncannily like a van Eyck, but the bishop or saint or chancellor looks just like Mr. Eliot." Gertrude winked at Ida. "We'll have him pose beside it."

Tom looked at Ida in smiling incomprehension and was met with her sudden blush.

James Joyce, who never came to the salon, was among the first to arrive. Perhaps he'd been moved by something in the note Gertrude had left for him at Shakespeare and Company, or perhaps Sylvia had sold him on the idea of Miss Stein's best brandy—he certainly seemed to take to it with enthusiasm. He clutched a glass firmly in hand as he stepped sideways from painting to painting, eyes never more than a few inches from the canvas. At the far end of the room, he paused at the easel placed by Gertrude's favorite chair. He reached for the drop cloth that shielded Ida's van Eyck from view, but Alice was upon him in a trice and slapped his hand away.

The room filled quickly, and no attempt was made to guard the door or turn away the lesser lights of Modernism. Sylvia Beach was there in a purple corduroy suit with a large brown velvet bow tied about her neck, linking arms with a plump French blond she introduced as Adrienne Monnier, proprietress of a French bookshop just around the corner from Shakespeare and Company. Tom pointed out some of the regulars to Ida—broad-shouldered Francis Picabia, recently converted to Surrealism; the svelte young Jean Cocteau, a leather portfolio under his arm as he flirted with one of Sergei Diaghilev's male dancers from the Ballets Russes; the impossibly glamorous Leonor Fini, cradling a sleeping kitten in her hand; Gabriel, without his partner Marcel; and the little Lithuanian painter, Chaim Soutine, whose eyes focused with odd intensity on the sliced roast beef laid out on a credenza.

"There's Dora," said Ida, suddenly conscious that she still wore Dora's dress, though it had been cleaned and pressed that afternoon by an industrious Hélène. Dora waved from where she stood across the room, flanked by André Breton and Pablo Picasso, whose intensity was somehow reinforced by the compact nature of his frame. Breton's voice, rising in excitement above the din, could be heard proclaiming the inherent Surrealism of the Middle Ages and the monuments of the past. Behind Breton and his companions stood Claude McKay, rumored to be departing soon for Harlem. He looked wistfully around the room, waving to friends as he caught their gaze.

"Let me just fix that for you," came a voice from over Ida's shoulder. She felt a slight tug at the back of her head and turned to see Sandy Calder with his friend Sam. Sandy had deftly plucked Ida's owl hairpin from her bun with one hand, while using his other hand to hold the rest of her hair in place. He

gave the hairpin a twist with one hand—such nimble fingers—
and slipped it back in place. "Did I really give that pin to you
like that?" he asked, then looked to his companion. "What was
I thinking, Noguchi? Don't let me do that again!"

"Perhaps if you hadn't left all the packing up to me, I could
have corrected your mistakes..." Sam replied, smiling, while
the two made for the buffet as only hungry young artists can.

Poets jostled dancers and painters; lithographers and choreographers and photographers laughed and mingled as the
brandy flowed freely from decanters Hélène struggled mightily
to keep filled. Writers who did not write and sculptors who did
not sculpt proved that they did have some energies, reserved,
apparently, for the consumption of free food and drink, along
with the improvising of bawdy songs. Robert McAlmon,
church-bred beneath all his dissolution, sang harmony in a
sweet, high tenor.

"There are fewer Surrealists than usual," Gertrude remarked
as she sidled up to Tom and Ida, "and not a Futurist to be
found. I believe we are confirmed regarding just who our enemies are." Just then a cackle pierced the air, and over the heads
of the crowd Ida spied a tuft of red hair bouncing about in
considerable animation: Ezra Pound had arrived. And right behind him was that great painter of Parisian low life, Jules Pascin
with—no, it couldn't be—Marinade, whom Ida had last seen
in a jail cell. "Jules always shows up with a criminal or a prostitute—such great fun!" said Gertrude, rushing off to embrace
the painter. Marinade had already found a brandy decanter. She
was clutching it by the neck and looking like she had no plans
to let go, even though a great walrus of a man, whom Tom
recognized as the English writer Ford Madox Ford, was doing
his best to pry it loose from her grip.

"Now's the time," said Gertrude, returning to Ida's side,
"if we're to rouse this rabble into a proper mob." Hélène expelled a little Spanish art critic from his seat on an ottoman,
and Gertrude took up a position atop it with the dignity of
a Caesar about to declare that he most assuredly had come,

seen, and conquered. Cocteau, who had been pushing toward her through the crowd and drawing papers from his portfolio, seemed crestfallen, but remained silent.

"Citizens of Bohemia!" she cried. "Lend me your ears!" A hush fell over the room. "Citizens," Gertrude continued, "we face a grave threat." The silence intensified, only momentarily interrupted by the crashing sound of broken glass: Marinade and Ford had, apparently, failed to resolve their dispute over proprietorship of the brandy decanter. Gabriel looked around the room with bemusement: normally at a moment like this Marcel would shout, "Death to the pigs" from somewhere in the back of the room. "A grave threat indeed," Gertrude continued, her arms held up like those of a pagan priestess about to invoke the aid of a goddess. "A threat to what we hold most dear—a threat to art and beauty. Alice," she cried, "inform the people!"

All eyes turned to Alice, who cut her way through the crowd to where Ida stood. "Not I," she said, her voice loud and firm. "I will not speak, but this woman, this artist will—the artist whose work we will unveil tonight. Welcome, please—Ida Caine!"

Ida balked, but Alice nudged her forward. Gertrude stepped down from the ottoman and gestured for Ida to take her place. Ida drew her breath and looked with trepidation at the massed Modernists. Could she speak? If she could speak, could she ever explain what needed to be explained? Yes. She'd paddle through the rapids and come out the other side. She took a step up onto the ottoman. "Citizens!" she called out. It felt strange, but she would own this moment, speak her sentences confidently, the way she painted her lines on canvas. "Tonight, there will be a concert at the Villon theater—the premiere of George Antheil's *Ballet Mécanique*."

"Antheil!" someone cried, raising a glass of brandy. "Antheil!" roared the crowd in response. Only stone-faced Stravinsky, skulking at the back of the crowd, refrained. Those nearby heard him mutter, "That insolent puppy" under his breath.

"By means of a scheme too strange, too…Modernist to be

explained here," Ida began nervously, not entirely in control of the whirlwind around her, "the enemies of art have rigged Antheil's clever electric instruments so that"—here are the rapids, thought Ida—"so that the great museums and cathedrals and libraries of Paris will explode at once when the concluding notes are played." The crowd began to murmur. Ida held up a hand, and willed her voice to firmness. "This must be stopped!" The crowd fell silent. "They kidnapped Alice! They hate beauty!" Ida shouted. "They hate beauty and...and they stole my rent!"

The mass of bohemians erupted in a spasm of passion. "*Arrêter les philistins!*" "*A bas les criminels!*" "*A bas les rentiers!*" Stop the philistines! Down with criminals! Down with the landlords!

Suddenly Gertrude stood beside Ida on the ottoman. "Ida Caine is the creator of this—a new artwork, reviving the old and making it live anew!" Alice pulled the cloth from Ida's version of *The Madonna of Chancellor Rolin* and held the painting aloft. "Behold the angel of Bohemia crowning the holy Virgin of art! And the cold-eyed landlord looking on!" Tom, noticing anew the resemblance of Ida's Chancellor Rolin to himself, looked about uneasily. "Let us carry it before us," shouted Gertrude, her voice rising. "Let it be our standard as we storm the Villon, end the concert, and save the beauty of Paris!"

The crowd exploded with cheers. Berets were thrown in the air. Surrealists embraced Cubists; Russian dancers leapt onto tables and spun in pirouettes; Soutine grabbed the roast beef and held it over his head in triumph; Marinade grabbed an abandoned glass of brandy from a table and guzzled it. While the crowd roared, Ida noticed Ezra Pound fleeing out the door. Stepping down from the ottoman to the window, she watched him mount a rickety bicycle and speed away, elbows and shirttails flapping madly in all directions.

In mere minutes, the mob of massed, drunken Modernists had spilled out into the courtyard, where Gertrude's ancient automobile, Godiva, sputtered and roared. Alice took the wheel and Gertrude sat in back attended by Cocteau, while Sandy and Sam, along with Tom and Ida, stood on the running boards and clung tenaciously to the doors. Godiva made much noise and little headway as the throng of Modernists surrounded it and began a shouting, singing parade through the narrow streets of Paris to the Villon.

Dora marched in front, holding Ida's painting aloft like an icon inspiring holy crusaders on the road to Jerusalem.

47

Godiva rattled and thundered and shook its way over the cobblestone streets. Festooned with artists and writers and dancers perching on the running boards, clinging to the sides, and (in the case of two of the Ballets Russes ballerinas) sprawled on the hood, the old rattletrap of an automobile took on the aspect of a carnival float. Bystanders gawked at what must surely be some sort of parade, led by Dora bearing Ida's copy of *The Madonna of Chancellor Rolin*. Was it a religious procession? A breakout from a lunatic asylum? A hallucination? Whatever it was, it made a great deal of noise, with an insistent horn honking, accompanying chants of *"Vive la vie Bohème!" "Vive le Louvre!" "L'art pour tout! L'art pour l'art!"* and, inexplicably for those not familiar with Miss Stein's writing, "A rose is a rose is a rose!" Stravinsky frowned and clutched his head, but marched dutifully beside the leaping, shouting, twirling Modernists, many of whom had the foresight to grab a glass or decanter of plum brandy on the way out of Miss Stein's residence.

Ida and Tom, having been crowded from the running boards, now trotted alongside Godiva, holding hands like high school sweethearts. Ida hardly knew what she felt—the thrill of the throng; apprehension at what lay ahead at the Villon theater; a vague distrust of the whims of this artistic rabble; embarrassed pride at her painting held up to the eyes of all. The only thing she knew for certain was that she was afraid they wouldn't arrive in time.

"Where do you imagine Pound rushed off to?" Tom shouted to Ida over chants of *"Toklas toujours! Et vive Miss Stein!"*

"No idea," Ida replied. "Maybe the concert?"

"He and Lewis edited a magazine together," Tom bellowed. "A thing called *BLAST*. Makes me wonder…"

Ida nodded. It was worrisome—could Pound have gone to warn Lewis or Marinetti? Nothing to be done about it now. The crowd had morphed into a creature with two hundred arms, a roaring voice, and a will entirely its own. Ida doubted even Gertrude could take command now.

They turned the corner to a tiny cobblestone square, one side of which was dominated by the façade of the Théâtre Villon. A sign on the door announced that the concert was sold out, while a man paced back and forth in front of the entrance. As they neared, Ida saw that the man was Antheil, dressed in a starched white shirt and cheap suit. She rushed ahead to greet him, Tom by her side.

"Jesus," said Antheil, at the sight and sound of the approaching mob. Turning to Ida, he added, "No tickets left!"

Godiva lurched to a halt outside the theater, and, as Gertrude and Alice rose to stand on their seats, the crowd circled the vehicle. Led by the Ballets Russes dancers, they linked hands and began to dance and chant. Just outside the circumference, Tom and Ida huddled with Antheil, shouting to be heard by each other.

"What's going on?" Antheil yelled, half-smiling, but with wary eyes.

"I'm terribly sorry," Tom began, but the remainder of his statement was drowned out by the crowd.

"What?" shouted Antheil.

"We have to stop the show!" Tom tried again, a drop in an ocean of noise.

Antheil shook his head, unable to hear Tom above the roar. They were getting nowhere, Ida concluded, rising on tiptoe to look over Antheil's shoulder at the theater door, which had just cracked open to reveal Lewis, peering out at the chaos in the square.

"That's him!" came a voice, clear and powerful as a claxon—Gertrude, high above the crowd, pointed at Lewis in the doorway. "Avenge Alice! Save Paris! Find Ida's rent money! Rush. Him. Now!"

ALICE B. TOKLAS IS MISSING   259

What happened in the following moments has been told
in as many versions as there were participants, and, eventually
many more. Future historians of Modernism will struggle to
determine the exact nature of the truth of this great scrim-
mage, but the general contours of the event are known with
some certainty. As Miss Stein's Modernist throng rushed forth
with great strength, they were met by an opposing force that
poured from the theater doors: Lewis at the head, with Marcel
and a motley horde of Futurists close behind, accompanied
by a phalanx of radicalized Surrealists clutching concert pro-
grams. A great, mad donnybrook ensued, accompanied by the
equally cacophonous sound emanating from the now open
entrance to the theater, as sixteen pianolas, untold numbers of
kettledrums, a siren, and an airplane engine blared, plonked,
banged, thrummed, and rattled toward a thunderous, climactic
pandemonium of noise. James Joyce soon grabbed Marcel by
the lapels, shouting something about violins and violence as
he shook the Surrealist vigorously back and forth. Lewis, his
bandaged face giving him a thuggish look, waded through poets
and actors, searching to his left and right, evidently striving to
reach Gertrude and Alice in their automotive citadel. Stravinsky's deep-souled Slavic glare reduced one minor Surrealist to
a quivering mass of fear. Dora squared off with the red-sashed
Toyen and Tom grappled with a long-haired Italian Futurist,
while Ida craned her neck, searching for Marinetti and for a
path into the theater. How long until the finale? How long until
an electrical charge ran through the wired-up catacombs and set
off a conflagration? Lewis's crowd now seemed to be playing
for time, gradually falling back toward the theater as Gertrude's
Modernists pressed forward, chanting, in unison, "Alice! Paris!
Ida's rent!" There was an irregular popping of flashbulbs, as
photographers documented what appeared to be a Modernist
succès de scandale for *Paris Soir* and the *International Herald Tribune*.

All was impasse, siege, and foes evenly matched, when
suddenly a new sound cut through the chants and discordant
music—the incessant ringing of a bicycle bell accompanied by

a high-pitched cackle. It was Pound, crouching and mounted on the handlebars of his own bicycle as it cut through the crowd, powered by the mighty pedaling of an undershirt-clad Ernest Hemingway. Hemingway dismounted the bicycle in an instant, striding broad-shouldered through the crowd, his trim mustache twitching, a leaping, screeching Ezra Pound at his side. Lewis retreated in haste to the door and turned to bar Hemingway's path. "You!" Hemingway bellowed.

"No!" screeched Lewis, as Hemingway leaned back, cocked a well-toned arm, and, with the motion of a major league baseball pitcher, delivered a punch that landed squarely on Lewis's damaged face. The blow connected with a satisfying, manly thud, just as a flashbulb popped. Lewis lay supine on the threshold and was immediately trampled under of an onrush of painters and novelists, belletrists, and connoisseurs. Ida and Tom joined the stampede.

The theater they entered was eerily empty—evidently Marcel and Lewis had bought all the tickets, and their minions had rushed outside to join the melee. The musician-less instruments plinked, plonked, and thumped, rippling crescendos and rumbling bass beats. As the crowd of artists entered, dancing and shouting down the aisles, Ida ran to the stage. Antheil arrived first, accompanied by a dancing Boski, glowing with pride at her husband's triumph. "Success!" yelled Antheil, leaping up and down. "Success! Success at last!"

Ida grabbed Antheil by the shoulders. "Shut it off!" she cried. "How do you shut it off?"

"What? But it's almost finished!" cried Antheil. "Just as soon as that piano roll runs out!"

No! Ida followed Antheil's gaze to a wooden box with a crank on its side that was slowly devouring a perforated roll of player piano music. She dove for the trailing end of the diminishing scroll, as an aghast Antheil rushed after her shouting, "Hey-Hey-*Hey!*"

Ida stretched her arms out, caught the scroll with both hands and yanked it backward. For a moment, there was a tug-of-war, woman vs. machine. The music ran backward, then forward, and the airplane engine shuddered. The paper slipped in Ida's grasp, and she tore desperately, rending the final eighteen inches from the rapidly disappearing scroll. The machine devoured what it could; the mechanical instruments delivered a final crescendo, and the instruments fell silent. For a moment, the mob stood still, its collective breath held, the only sound the slap-slapping of the torn scroll in its reel. Ida's ears strained for the sounds of explosions from outside. None came. Her face flushed, she pirouetted to face the crowd that had rushed in from outside, a triumphant Hemingway, and a sweaty Tom, who wielded an umbrella he'd purloined from the cloakroom like a paladin's blade. "*Victoire!*" cried Ida. "*Victoire!*" waving the torn paper above her head like a glorious banner, to the tumultuous cheers of the multitude. Those with an eye for art history saw in the gesture a perfect replication of Delacroix's *Liberty Leading the People.*

Far, far above, in the evening sky, a biplane's engine thrummed. Behind the goggled and helmeted pilot, Marinetti tossed armload after armload of leaflets over the sides, each announcing the liberation of Paris from the burden of the past. He stared quizzically at the city below him, which stubbornly refused to erupt into flames, and wondered if he had miscalculated the timing. The pilot, at least, was sticking to their plan, and banked away toward the south, and the warm light of Italy.

48

Once again, the morning light dazzled Ida, pouring in from the window behind the settee where Gertrude held Alice in an attitude of peaceful repose. After the preceding night's storm of events, the soft breeze and birdsong seemed like emblems of the most perfect calm. Ida's canvas was spread before her on the easel like a sail bearing her off to a land that promised—what? Calm? Adventure? She didn't know. What she did know was that Gertrude needed to hold Alice just a little closer. She motioned with her hand, and Gertrude understood, shifting slightly and giving a contented sigh. Yes, that made for a better line—the volume of their bodies now formed part of a more harmonious composition, implying dynamism within the stillness. Ida made Gertrude and Alice hold their pose for upwards of an hour, but they didn't seem to mind at all. All the same, one shouldn't push.

"Perhaps we should break for a while?" Ida suggested.

"You're the boss," said Gertrude, releasing Alice from her embrace. The boss? Ida wondered. Gertrude, after all, was the one paying—she'd commissioned the portrait to hang in the salon. But perhaps in Bohemia the one who paid the money was merely paying tribute to… Ida hesitated. She'd intended to use the term "true art." Should she? She smiled silently.

"I'm off to the tub," said Gertrude, stretching and rising to her feet. "Nothing like a soak on a Sunday."

"And I'll take Basket for a short walk." Alice grinned at Ida. "It feels safe now, what with the police hauling Lewis off to jail." Ida remembered the late arrival of the gendarmes at the Villon last night, how they'd pulled the rioters and revelers apart and sent them on their way. Young officer Clement had stood like a nervous schoolboy as Miss Stein sat above him in her car, and summoned Dora, Ida, and Alice in turn to give statements against Lewis. Clement took extensive notes in a careful hand, nodding and serious all the while. At the end, he ordered two officers to scrape the groaning Lewis from the cobblestones and deposit him in the back of a waiting police van alongside a scowling Marcel and several of his minions.

"Shall I have this shipped to—where did you say? Lake Forest?" Alice asked, indicating Ida's van Eyck copy, leaning by the door. Ida considered for a moment. The painting was unscathed by its adventures the previous evening, but she still hadn't corrected the chancellor's face. But let it look a bit like Tom. Mrs. Rawling, yawning over lemonade, would never know the difference. And it pleased Ida to think of Tom in Mrs. Rawling's parlor—they were sure to have mutual friends to discuss.

"Yes, please. When it's convenient," Ida said. Alice smiled and left the house, Basket bouncing alongside her. Ida continued painting, working on the background—a wall of pictures she would put within her painting. All those years as a copyist were paying off at last, she thought, as she reproduced the exaggerated hand of an André Masson. By the time she'd gotten the beige right, and the whorl of curled fingers, Alice and Basket had returned.

"I'll check in on Gertrude," Alice said, tossing a bundle of papers on the small table beside Ida's easel. "I stopped in at Sylvia's. You might want to take a gander at those before we get back to business." She nodded at the bundle before heading upstairs.

Ida reached for the *International Herald Tribune*, which perched atop a small pile of envelopes. She leaned back and snapped the paper open, revealing a photograph of Hemingway delivering his great, thumping punch to Lewis, whose face had distorted into a mask out of Greek tragedy at the moment of impact. Above the photo in gigantic type was a headline: "HEMINGWAY SAVES PARIS!" Ida's eyes skipped lightly over the text of the article, catching only a few phrases here and there: "grace under pressure," "police removed many caches of explosives," "Hemingway says Paris is 'a moveable feast, and Lewis nothing but an ant at the picnic,'" and something quite shocking Hemingway said about Lewis's eyes. Of greater interest was the reproduction of a flier found littering the streets of Paris following the events at the Villon. Every other word or phrase came straight from the Futurist manifesto, and the list of buildings pronounced "demolished for the liberty of the imagination" was extensive—Notre Dame, the Louvre, the Académie des Beaux-Arts, and that great opera house, the Palais Garnier, were among them. Ida set the paper down and shook her head at the thought of what might have happened.

Three of the envelopes Alice brought home from Shakespeare and Company were addressed to Ida. The first was on thick, creamy paper so luxurious to the touch that Ida ran her hands over it slowly twice before opening it with her palette knife. It came from Dora Maar, who began by praising Ida for her magnificent struggle with the piano roll at Antheil's concert. Dora went on to invite Ida to a meeting with the Surrealists—the *good* Surrealists, she stressed—at the Café de la Place Blanche. André Breton wanted to introduce Ida to Giacometti, who'd expressed an interest in seeing Ida's little Calder piece. Ida touched her hairpin as she read that last sentence; had she accidentally become a collector, like Miss Stein? The note closed with a postscript about how Dora still wondered what Ida might be capable of.

The second envelope, gray and long, was addressed to Ida in Teddy's hand. She hesitated a moment, holding the drab-looking thing up in this room of brilliant colors and sunlight. She paused, then quickly slit it open. There it was, that boyish handwriting, telling how his parents had wired money for transport home, and how he'd taken the train to Le Havre, where he would board the SS *Île de France,* bound for New York tomorrow morning. Folded in with the note was a ticket for her own passage, two fifty-franc notes, and a list of train departures from Paris to Le Havre. If Ida rushed to the Gare du Nord and caught the afternoon express, she could still join him. She thought a moment, then decisively stuffed the banknotes into her red handbag—a gift from Alice's collection—and placed the ticket and Teddy's letter back in the envelope.

One more envelope, bearing the insignia of the Bristol hotel, was also addressed to Ida. She knew it came from Tom, his handwriting as straight and level as railway tracks on the prairie. He wrote apologetically about his need to depart at once for London. He invited her to visit for the Royal Academy art show at Burlington House next month, eagerly offering to help with arrangements. "I believe you'll like London," he wrote, "and may come to love it, if you choose to stay—as, for my selfish reasons, I most dearly hope you will." Ida noted the signature: *Your Tom.* Not *Yours,* but *Your.* What did he want with her in London? Ida wondered—and what would happen if she went? She smiled quietly. What was it Dora said? "All the fun's in finding out." Well, we'll see, we'll see. Two smaller pieces of paper were enclosed with the letter—a check to cover the fine she'd paid for him at the tribunal; and what appeared to be a hastily written note asking, if she came to London, would she kindly bring one of the cheeses mentioned on a rather long list.

Ida sat back in her chair. A bird—a kingfisher—perched on the windowsill and sang. Its feathers shone in the light. She would paint it, she mused, into the background of her new picture. She would paint, and she would stay.